Betsy Was a Junior
and
Betsy and Joe

The Betsy-Tacy Books

Book 1: *Betsy-Tacy*

Book 2: *Betsy-Tacy and Tib*

Book 3: *Betsy and Tacy Go Over the Big Hill*

Book 4: *Betsy and Tacy Go Downtown*

Book 5: *Heaven to Betsy*

Book 6: *Betsy in Spite of Herself*

Book 7: *Betsy Was a Junior*

Book 8: *Betsy and Joe*

Book 9: *Betsy and the Great World*

Book 10: *Betsy's Wedding*

The Deep Valley Books

Winona's Pony Cart

Carney's House Party

Emily of Deep Valley

Betsy Was a Junior
and
Betsy and Joe

Maud Hart Lovelace

Illustrated by Vera Neville

HARPER**PERENNIAL** MODERN**CLASSICS**

NEW YORK • LONDON • TORONTO • SYDNEY • NEW DELHI • AUCKLAND

HARPER**PERENNIAL** ● MODERN**CLASSICS**

HarperCollins books may be purchased for educational, business, or
sales promotional use. For information, please e-mail the Special Markets
Department at SPsales@harpercollins.com.

Betsy Was a Junior was first published in 1947 by Thomas Y. Crowell
Company. First Harper Trophy edition published 1995.

Betsy and Joe was first published in 1948 by Thomas Y. Crowell Company.
First Harper Trophy edition published 1995.

FIRST HARPER PERENNIAL MODERN CLASSICS EDITION PUBLISHED 2009.

Library of Congress Cataloging-in-Publication Data is available upon
request.

ISBN 978-0-06-179472-8

24 25 26 27 28 LBC 15 14 13 12 11

Foreword

I'm embarrassed to admit that, unlike many of her most ardent fans, I didn't meet Miss Betsy Warrington Ray until I was an adult . . . in my thirties!

I was introduced to her by my children's book editor at HarperCollins, Abby McAden, when I first started writing the Princess Diaries series. Abby (who, in addition to her work as an editor, also volunteered part-time as a children's librarian) felt the Betsy-Tacy books served as a superb example of a series that followed its heroine from occasionally flighty girlhood to mature young womanhood in a truly satisfying progressive arc.

And as can be observed by Betsy's legions of fans, who have kept the books about her in print for many decades, thousands of others have felt the same . . . and as soon as I read them, I became as devoted as any of them.

How could a series of novels in which the heroine has neither red hair, a tiara, magical powers, a boyfriend who is a vampire, or a cell phone be so bewitching? Well, Betsy won my heart not just because of the humor, vivacity, and realistic emotion with which her creator, Maud Hart Lovelace, imbued her, but also because of

her believable struggles to find her voice as an author
. . . not to mention true love (both of which echoed
my own struggles not just at Betsy's age but through my
twenties and even beyond).

How many of us can relate not only to Betsy's romantic (and authorial) travails but also to her friends—
like Tacy, refusing to give up her serviceable coronet of
braids just because "puffs" are popular, and pint-sized
Tib, always up for a party?

And how many of us have longed for a family like
the Rays (those of us who weren't lucky enough to have
such unconditionally doting parents, loving sisters, and
a loyal housekeeper like Anna, declaring us "puny" no
matter what kind of outlandish hat we're wearing)?

Slipping into a Betsy book is like slipping into a favorite pair of well-worn slippers. It's always a pleasure to live
in Betsy's world for a little while, to experience her simple
joys as well as her (thankfully short-lived) sorrows.

And Maud Hart Lovelace makes it easy for us to do so.
When, at the beginning of each "high school book," Betsy
reviews her old journals to remind herself of the triumphs
(but more often the tribulations) of the year before, it's
just like any of us glancing back at our old diaries:

> Her freshman year, and her joy in finding a
> crowd, her discovery about her writing, and her
> yearning for Tony.

"I've never been as in love with anyone as I was with Tony when I was fourteen," Betsy sighs to herself in *Betsy and Joe*, upon recalling ninth grade. Who can't identify with this? I know I still Google my freshman crush. And he never once came over to my house for onion sandwiches.

It is, of course, just before her freshman year (*Heaven to Betsy*) that Betsy first meets Joe Willard—he of the blond pompadour and recklessly protruding lower lip—at Butternut Center, when he waits on her at Willard's Emporium while she's buying gifts for her family (because the Rays always take presents home when they've been away on a visit).

Her life will never be the same, but Betsy doesn't know this, of course.

Her sophomore year, her trip to Milwaukee to visit Tib, the attempt to be Dramatic and Mysterious in order to captivate Phil Brandish, Phyllis' twin.

"After I got him, I didn't want him," Betsy morosely recalls.

Of course not. After all, Phil wanted to hold hands, and Betsy, we know, just wasn't ready to take that enormous step (as she famously informs the befuddled Phil in *Betsy in Spite of Herself*)—especially when she realizes her heart truly belongs to Joe Willard, upon whom

Betsy sets her sights her junior year, "when she had been all wound up in sororities."

But it was only "a small series of misunderstandings," Betsy tells herself, that kept her and Joe apart—not, as we all know, the fact that Betsy didn't, at that time, truly yet know herself. Surely she and Joe would end up together, as they were always meant to be.

Because in *Betsy Was a Junior*, just like every year, Betsy knows everything's going to be different! This time, Betsy's going to be the perfect friend and daughter, staying home and taking the place of her beloved older sister, Julia, who's leaving for her first year of college at the "U" to study music. Betsy's going to learn to play the piano, be elected a class officer, head up a committee for the junior-senior banquet, win the Essay Contest (as she attempts to do, every year) . . . and, of course, "go with Joe Willard."

It wouldn't be a Maud Hart Lovelace book if anything went according to Betsy's plans. But Betsy crashes and burns so spectacularly in *Betsy Was a Junior* that the novel quickly became one of my favorites of all time. Betsy tells herself so many times that she's going to buckle down and "be serious." She confesses to looking forward to a chance to finally getting to work "almost with longing." (This is something I say to myself ten times a day, only to be distracted not by a fudge party, like Betsy, but by a new episode of *Law & Order*. Speaking of which, mmmm, fudge.)

Later, Betsy's well-meaning decision to start a sorority at Deep Valley High School—the Okto Deltas, or Eight Devils—hampers her progress with her writing even more. Though the "progressive dinners," dances, sleigh rides, and theatricals the Oktos host boost Betsy's popularity immensely, especially with boys, her writing isn't the only thing that falls to the wayside, with disastrous but typically Betsy-esque results.

> She had prided herself on being a popular girl. But she had never been less popular. Of course, the "popularity" with boys had been nice. . . .

Friendships, Betsy's grades, and even poor sister Margaret's eyelashes—but worst of all, the competition against Joe Willard for the cup in the Essay Contest, which Betsy prizes more than anything—are all jeopardized, until Betsy finally realizes:

> Sisterhoods! . . . You couldn't make sisterhoods with rules and elections. If they meant anything, they had to grow naturally. . . . You ought not to go through life, even a small section of life like high school or college, with your friendships fenced in by snobbish artificial barriers.
> "It would be like living in a pasture when you could have the whole world to roam in," Betsy thought. "I

don't believe sororities would appeal very long to anyone with much sense of adventure."

(Though of course we know from Elle Woods of *Legally Blonde* that sororities can't be *all* bad.)

It's the whole world that Betsy's parents are determined to give to Betsy and her sisters, in spite of the fact that Mr. Ray voices a hope that his eldest daughter, Julia, will "meet someone she'll want to marry" after college and "settle down and use her voice for lullabies" instead of pursuing a career in the opera.

Don't worry: It's not that Mr. Ray has old-fashioned ideas on what a woman's place is. As Anna Quindlen wrote in her excellent 1993 speech to the Betsy-Tacy Society: "While the Rays have three daughters, early on two of them are already committed to having careers outside the home, Julia as an opera singer, Betsy as a writer. Betsy's parents are totally committed to this idea for them both . . . arguing vociferously that Betsy's work is as good as any that appears in popular magazines."

And "not once, in any book, does any individual, male or female, suggest to Betsy that she cannot, as she hopes to do, become a writer." It's just that "music is a very hard career," Mr. Ray worries, and Julia is "too young to make such an important decision." When events transpire in *Betsy Was a Junior* to make all of Julia's dreams a reality, however, Mr. Ray soon finds out where her true priorities lie and is satisfied about Julia's aspirations for her future. Because the Rays are always ready to support their daughters one hundred percent, as long as they aren't trying deceive anyone . . . most especially themselves.

But the art of self-deception is one at which Betsy Ray excels, one that again and again almost ends up costing her not only her career dreams—such as when "boys and parties" keep her from doing any "serious writing" in *Betsy Was a Junior* (and what aspiring writer of any age does not find this lament familiar?)—but also the love of her life, as when Betsy attempts to balance two beaus, Tony Markham and Joe Willard, in *Betsy and Joe*.

In fact, it isn't until Betsy buckles down in *Betsy and Joe*, actually managing to finish and send out her stories about "New York debutantes" (all of which are rejected—not that this bothers Betsy: she merely writes more and sends them out again, a perfect lesson for any aspiring writers out there . . . though in real life, Maud Hart Lovelace sold her first short story at age eighteen, for ten dollars, to the *Los Angeles Times*), stop using Magic Wavers in her hair, and be honest with herself and with Tony Markham, that she's able to achieve two of her longest held and most elusive goals, both of which involve Joe Willard.

It takes a trip back to Butternut Center and Willard's Emporium to seal the deal, however.

His blue eyes, under those heavy brows, were boring into her. His lower lip looked defiant, and so did the swinging walk with which he came toward her. She blushed.

"What are you doing here?" Joe asked. His tone was almost rough.

"Don't act as though you were going to put me out," she said. "I'm buying presents to take home to my family."

"Oh." He seemed nonplused.

"The Rays always take presents home when they've been away on a visit."

And so, with the expertise of a true artistic genius, Maud Hart Lovelace brings us neatly back to where we began with Betsy and Joe: exactly where the two of them met, so they could put aside their many misunderstandings and start over.

Because both of them have grown in the four years since the "high school books" began. They aren't awkward fourteen year olds anymore but adults. Things have changed . . . as they rightfully should have in a series that begins when the heroine is five years old and follows her from kindergarten to high school graduation. Suddenly Betsy Ray, senior, who didn't believe in holding hands her sophomore year, is rethinking some of her long held beliefs.

Then he kissed her. Betsy didn't believe in letting boys kiss you. She thought it was silly to be letting first this boy and then that one kiss you, when it didn't mean a thing. But it was wonderful when Joe Willard kiss her. And it did mean a thing.

Have truer words ever been written in any book? Because it most certainly would be silly to let first this boy and then that one kiss you, when it doesn't mean a thing (although it could be argued that you couldn't *know* it wouldn't mean a thing unless you tried it first with a variety of boys, just to be sure).

But when you are old enough—and when it is the *right* person—it most certainly *does* mean a thing, as Betsy finds out, the spring of her senior year.

By setting aside pretence (and Magic Wavers . . . though of course it is always nice to have curls now and again), and being fully herself, Betsy becomes at last who she's truly always wanted to be: a writer, the name on the calling cards she receives as an eighteenth birthday gift from her mother, the kind of heroine any author would be honored to have created, whether her books are about a charming turn-of-the-century Minnesotan aspiring authoress, or a reluctant princess:

Miss Betsy Warrington Ray.

—MEG CABOT, 2009

Betsy Was a Junior

For
BICK, TESS, MIDGE, MARION, EL,
CONNIE, MIL, PAT, *and* RUTH

Contents

"Haste thee nymph, and bring with thee Jest and Youthful Jollity . . ."

—John Milton

1

Taking Stock

BETSY RAY SAT IN a rowboat which was anchored in Babcock's Bay, two watery miles opposite Murmuring Lake Inn, where the Ray family had been spending the summer. The oars were folded across the boat and on the seat beside her lay a fat notebook which she used as a journal and several sharply pointed pencils. She sat with her arms bound about her knees, staring at a gauzy-winged dragon fly which had come to rest on the prow of the boat. Her expression was serious, not to say grim. She was taking stock.

Betsy was fond of this bay. It was strewn thickly with water lilies. Their flat green pads and creamy, richly scented blossoms floated on the water all around her. The shore was lined with trees—willows, cottonwoods, box elders. In other parts of the lake rows of summer cottages or low-lying farms came to the water's edge. This cove was remote; moored here, you might have thought that you were in a wilderness except for the fact that a green wooded point, jutting into the lake to the east, showed the rooftop of the Inn.

When Betsy wished to achieve the illusion of a wilderness she did not look in that direction.

Murmuring Lake Inn was a highly social place. Crowds of young people followed a careless routine —walks, boat rides, and leisurely games of croquet; bathing every afternoon at four. Mothers rocked, read and embroidered on the shady porches and vacationing fathers fished. Mr. Ray drove out from his shoe store in nearby Deep Valley every night, and in the evening there were launch rides and informal hops in the big parlor.

Betsy had had a gay summer. She was sorry it was ending tomorrow. She wondered now, staring at the dragon fly, and beyond him across the glassy lake, whether it had been too gay, but decided that it hadn't been.

"It's been wonderful," she thought. "It's just the sort of summer you ought to have at sixteen."

Betsy was sixteen and next month she would begin her third year of high school. She was exactly halfway through, which made this an excellent time for taking stock.

"I wish I was just beginning and had it all ahead of me," she said with a long romantic sigh. But she said it because she thought it was the proper thing to say. She was really pleased to be an upper classman.

She had certainly had fun. She belonged to a flexible Crowd of a dozen or so boys and girls who stirred up fun as briskly as the cook at the Inn stirred up hot cakes for breakfast. She had really been too frivolous, Betsy decided. Yet the two years had had their perplexities, too, their worries, and even their heartaches.

She had had heartaches over boys, over wanting to be popular. The Ray house, with its three daughters, was always full of boys but boys liked Betsy usually in a friendly sort of way. She had longed to be a siren like her older sister, Julia.

In particular, during her freshman year, she had had a heartache over Tony. Although a classmate, he was slightly older, more sophisticated than the rest. He had a bush of curly black hair, bold laughing eyes, a lazy drawling voice. Betsy had thought she was in love with him, but he had only liked her in a maddening, brotherly way. By the end of the year, however, her infatuation had ebbed away. She liked Tony still, almost better than any boy she knew, but now her feeling was as sisterly as his was brotherly.

"That's life for you," Betsy said aloud, and appropriately, the dragon fly flew away.

In her freshman year, too, she had had a heartache over losing the Essay Contest. Every year the two societies into which the school was divided competed for a cup in essay writing. Both years Betsy had been chosen to represent her class and both years she had lost to Joe Willard. He was an orphan who was working his way through school. Betsy liked him very much but she didn't like losing the Essay Contest.

She had minded it most the first year, for then she had felt guilty. She had not prepared for the Contest properly, she had not read the material she was supposed to have read. One of the great lessons she had learned in high school had come after that defeat. She had learned that her gift for writing was important to her and that she must never neglect it.

"I haven't really neglected it since," she thought. "I've kept up my journal, I'm writing a novel, I worked hard on my English assignments last year and I studied for the Essay Contest. I lost it again but this time it wasn't through any fault of mine."

She had not done her best because, by an ironical chance, the Contest had coincided with a quarrel she had had with Phil Brandish.

Phil Brandish had been the great outstanding triumph of Betsy's sophomore year. She had tried that year to acquire a new personality, to act Dramatic and Mysterious, and in this role she had captured Phil Brandish's interest. But she had not enjoyed pretending all the time to be something she wasn't. She had decided before the season ended that she preferred, usually, just to be herself.

"I learned a lot from that affair, though," she thought now, frowning. "I've had more poise with boys since then. Julia says I'm more charming. Of course, I didn't keep Phil, but then, I didn't want to."

He was a sulky, aloof boy whose chief charm had been a red automobile. He and his twin, Phyllis, were grandchildren of the rich Home Brandish, who lived in a mansion on the west side of Deep Valley. Phyllis went to boarding school—Browner Seminary in Milwaukee. By a coincidence this school was attended by a great friend of Betsy's, Thelma Muller, irrevocably nicknamed Tib.

Betsy's oldest and closest friend was red-haired

Tacy Kelly. They had been loyal, loving chums since Betsy's fifth birthday party. And they had been friends with Tib almost as long as they had been friends with each other. Tib was tiny, yellow-headed, as daring as she was pretty. Betsy and Tacy loved to think up adventurous things to do, but it had usually been Tib who did them. She had lived in a large chocolate-colored house. She could dance. She had exquisite clothes. Even when she was their daily companion, Tib had been a figure of romance to Betsy and Tacy.

And when they were all in the eighth grade, she had moved away to Milwaukee.

Last year Betsy had gone to spend Christmas with her. The visit to the big foreign-flavored city, the glimpse into Tib's life, with its sheltered private school, its encircling *Grosspapas* and *Grossmamas,* uncles, aunts and cousins, had been an illuminating experience. It was while visiting there that Betsy had decided to become Dramatic and Mysterious. The visit had had a thrilling ending for on New Year's Eve Tib had told her that the family might move back to Deep Valley.

"I wonder whether she really will come some day," Betsy thought. A breeze had sprung up, ruffling the water and bringing a faint, not unpleasantly fishy smell. The boat rocked dreamily.

Betsy roused herself, reached for her journal. Wetting

her pencil with the tip of her tongue she began to write.

"I'm going to make my junior year just perfect," she wrote. "In the first place I'm going to stay around home a lot. Julia is going off to the University and Papa and Mamma and Margaret will all miss her terribly—almost as much as I will."

It wasn't that Julia had ever helped much around the house, Betsy thought, lowering her pencil. Anna, the Rays' hired girl, was so efficient that there wasn't much need for any of the daughters to help. But Julia was so loving and vital. Her personality filled the house just as her music did. Julia planned to be an opera singer and was playing and singing all day long. She played popular music, too, for the Crowd to sing.

"I resolve next," Betsy continued writing, "to learn to play the piano. The family has always wanted me to take piano lessons and I've always dodged them. But with Julia going I'll just have to learn. I can't imagine our house without music. I'll start taking lessons and practise an hour every day if it kills me. (It probably will.)

"In school," she went on, "I want my year to be completely wonderful. I hope I'll be elected a class officer again. And I'd like to head up a committee for the junior-senior banquet. That's the most important event of the junior year. Above all I want another try at the Essay Contest. I want that terribly. I think I'll have it, too. And I'm really going to study. I'm going to try to get good marks. I've never done my best."

She read over what she had written, suffused by a warm virtuous glow.

"As for boys," Betsy concluded, and her writing grew very firm and black, *I think I'll go with Joe Willard!*"

She emphasized this declaration with an exclamation point and some heavy underlining, which was fitting. It was really the keystone of the structure she had built. Unconsciously, perhaps, she had figured out just what kind of a girl she thought Joe Willard would like, and that was the kind she was planning to be.

He didn't have money to spend on girls. He couldn't afford frivolity. When he started going around with a girl, she would surely be the kind Betsy had just described—one who was devoted to her home, who gave her spare time to some worth while thing like music, a leader in school.

But it would take planning to go with him, no matter how admirable she made herself. Unfortunately, Joe Willard didn't seem to want girls in his life. It was because of his shortage of money, Betsy felt sure.

"But I can make him see that money doesn't matter,"

she planned. "I'll just have to lure him up to the house." Once a boy came to the merry, hospitable Ray house he almost always came again.

It was pleasant to sit in a gently rocking boat, listening to killdees on the shore, and think about going with Joe Willard. Betsy had liked him for several years now. She had met him the summer before she entered high school, in the little hamlet of Butternut Center where he was clerking in his uncle's store. She was on her way home, after visiting on a farm, and he had sold her some presents to take to her family, and Tacy.

During the two years of high school a series of small misunderstandings had kept them apart, but he liked her, Betsy felt sure, just as she liked him.

"Not in a silly way," she thought. "We're just going to be wonderful, wonderful friends—for the present, that is," she added hastily. She was quite aware that it would be easy to be romantic about Joe Willard. He was so extremely good looking with light hair cut in a pompadour, and blue eyes under thick golden brows. His red lower lip protruded recklessly. He was not downed by the fact that he had no home, no parents and very little money.

"He'll have more money this year," Betsy thought. He had planned, she knew, to work with a threshing rig all summer, following the harvest northward. He had expected to earn three dollars a day and save it for his expenses during the coming school year.

"I suppose he'll work after school at the creamery again. That won't matter. He'll be able to come to see me sometimes, and we'll talk by the hour. How he'll love Papa's Sunday night lunches, and the way Mamma plays for us to dance!"

She sat still for a moment smiling at the distant chimney of the Inn as though it were Joe Willard.

When she smiled, Betsy's face lighted with a charm of which she was quite unaware. She didn't like her square white teeth which were, in her own phrase "parted in the middle." But her smile, quick and very bright, gave a hint of her response to life which was trusting and joyful.

She was a tall, slender girl with soft brown hair worn in a pompadour over a "jimmy." It was wavy now, but only because it had been wound the night before on Magic Wavers. She had dark-lashed hazel eyes, and a pink and white skin. This she prized mightily. It was, she considered, her only claim to beauty, and Betsy worshipped beauty.

If a fairy godmother had ever appeared in her vicinity waving a wand and offering favors, Betsy would have cried out unhesitatingly for beauty. Her favorite daydream was of suddenly becoming beautiful with "bright hair streaming down" like the Lily

Maid of Astolot's, or dark raven tresses.

The members of her Crowd sometimes exchanged "trade lasts"—T.L.s, they were called. A "trade last" was a compliment, heard about another person, repeated to him after he had first repeated a compliment heard about you. Betsy was always being told for a T.L. that she had been described as interesting, sweet or charming. It infuriated her.

"I want to be pretty!" she stormed to Tacy.

"You're better than pretty," Tacy answered sometimes and Betsy would respond inelegantly, "Pooh for that!"

After smiling for a long time at the chimney which was masquerading as Joe Willard, she slapped her notebook shut, put it back on the seat and took up the oars. Instinct told her it was almost four o'clock. Betsy often rowed over to Babcock's Bay in the early afternoon, which was "nap time" at the Inn. She liked to be alone sometimes to read, write on her novel, or just think. But she always got back for the bathing.

Slipping the oars into the water, she turned the boat about. She rowed unskillfully, her oars churned up showers of glittering drops, but she sent the heavy boat hurrying over the water.

2

Making Plans

THE LONG INN DOCK was lined with boats and draped with fishnets. Old Pete, smoking his pipe in the lee of the boathouse, hobbled forward with rheumatic slowness to pull Betsy in. She stepped out cautiously, the boat rocking beneath her feet, and lingered to talk with him. They were great friends. He sometimes told her stories about when her mother was a girl and lived at Pleasant Park across the lake.

"She was a handsome redhead. I used to see her out in her sailboat, 'The Queen of the Lake.' Her brother Keith would be with her, the one who ran away to be an actor. He was redheaded, too, and as handsome as they come."

"He's still an actor. He's with Mr. Otis Skinner this season in *The Honor of the Family*," Betsy had answered, glowing. Her mother's brother, Keith Warrington, was very close to Betsy although she had seen him only once.

She used his old theatrical trunk for a desk. She kept her manuscripts, notebooks and pencils in the tray, and wrote on the smooth top with pleasure, feeling that in some intangible way the storied background, the venturesome travels of the trunk added magic to her pencil. The trunk had come to represent her writing, her dearest plans for her life.

Old Pete said now only that there was going to be a change in the weather.

"This gloriously perfect summer can't last forever," answered Betsy. She ran up a steep flight of stairs, which spanned the high bank through a tangled growth of bushes and trees.

At the top she was greeted by a delicious smell from the Inn kitchens—baking cake, she thought. A clothes line hung full of bathing suits and stockings.

Betsy selected her own and paused at the pump which stood at one end of the porch just outside Mrs. Van Blarcum's office.

Mrs. Van Blarcum was small, spare, vivacious, always busy from morning until night. Mr. Van Blarcum was courtly, with drooping white mustaches, always leisurely. They had operated the Inn for many years and the same families returned summer after summer from Deep Valley and other Minnesota towns, as well as from Iowa, the Dakotas, Nebraska, Kansas and Missouri.

The Inn was old. It had received so many additions at different periods that it had quite lost its original shape and sprawled in strange directions, unified only by white paint and a narrow open porch across the front.

Guests overflowed the main building and slept in cottages. These ranged in an uneven semicircle among old apple trees around the smooth green lawn. The Rays had the cottage on the end of the point. It consisted only of two bedrooms with a porch in front. Unplastered, it smelled freshly of the lake which could be seen in a rippling silver sheet through the foliage outside the windows.

The three sisters occupied one bedroom. Julia and Margaret were there putting on their bathing suits, when Betsy dashed in. The bathing suits were all of heavy blue serge, trimmed with white braid around the sailor collars, the elbow-length sleeves, and the skirts which came to the knee over ample bloomers. With them the girls wore long black stockings and neatly laced canvas oxfords. Julia was tying a red bandana around her dark hair.

She was a beautiful girl with violet eyes, a classic nose, and white teeth which, unlike Betsy's, were conventionally spaced. She was shorter than Betsy, but made the most of every inch of height, longing to be tall because of her operatic ambitions.

"How's the novel going?" she asked Betsy, adjusting the ends of her kerchief artfully and looking in a hand mirror to see the effect.

"I wasn't working on that today; just writing in my journal. I'm making wonderful plans for next year. Gee, it seems funny to be an upper classman!"

"It doesn't seem a bit funny to me to be finished," Julia said. "In fact I feel as though I should have finished long ago. Eighteen years of my life gone and I haven't yet got down to music in a serious way! Come here, Margaret dear," she added to the younger sister, "and I'll tie your bandana."

"Yoo hoo, Betsy!" came voices from outside.

"No matter where we live or go," Julia said, laughing, "there's always someone yoo-hooing outside for you, Bettina."

This was true, and Betsy liked to hear it.

"There's been a grand crowd out here this summer," she replied, scrambling into her suit.

She had enjoyed getting acquainted with people from other places. There were two boys her own age from Deep Valley too. Betsy looked for them now as, tying her kerchief hurriedly, she rushed out the door.

Dave Hunt had already run down the stairs. He ignored girls and usually went fishing with the men. Yet his presence had added an extra fillip to the summer, for now and then Betsy found him staring at her out of deep-set dark blue eyes. He was over six feet tall and very thin, with a stern, spare face.

E. Lloyd Harrington was highly social. He, too, was tall, but fragile. He had beautiful manners and loved to dance. He usually wore glasses and was blinking now without them.

Julia was joined by Roger Tate, a University student. For a week he had been trailing her, talking about the U, as he called it, and making plans for the days following her arrival there. He was going to take her, Julia told Betsy, to a fraternity dance—whatever that was; riverbanking—that meant walking along the Mississippi, he explained; to lunch in Minneapolis tea rooms. He was teaching her to swim.

"Today I want you to go as far as the buoy," he said.

"I'll try." Julia lifted her violet eyes, smiled with intention. Roger blushed and began to talk hurriedly, almost senselessly, about side strokes and breast strokes. Betsy shook her head. She had seen plenty of Julia's conquests and they always amused and interested her. But she didn't like it at the end when Julia threw her victims over.

Dave went so far out into the lake that Old Pete blew a horn and summoned him back. Betsy could swim only a little, but she had fun with water wings and floated a long time, looking up into the blue world of the sky, thinking about next winter.

At five o'clock everyone went dripping back to his room to dress for supper.

A day at Murmuring Lake Inn did not have one climax; it had three: the three superb meals. Guests rose from the enormous breakfast swearing that they could never eat again. Yet they were waiting hungrily on the porches when the dinner bell rang. And although the noon meal was abundant beyond all reason, everyone was waiting shamelessly for the supper bell.

The Ray girls and their mother waited on the porch of their cottage. Julia and Betsy had changed into white dotted swiss dresses, Margaret into a yellow sailor suit. Mrs. Ray wore crisp pale green trimmed with bands of plaid.

"Papa's late tonight," she said. "He's almost always here by now."

An inadvertent tinkle sounded as one of the maids came out on the porch carrying a big brass bell. Before she had a chance to ring it guests started streaming toward the dining room. She swung it heartily and the loud metallic clangor caused those guests who were housed in cottages to start from their porches, except for the Rays.

"I'm starving," Betsy said.

"So am I," answered Mrs. Ray. "But it isn't civilized not to wait for Papa."

"At least three minutes," Julia said.

"There he is now," Margaret said.

Sure enough, a fringed surrey had stopped at the far side of the Inn, and Mr. Ray alighted.

"Why, he's helping somebody out," said Mrs. Ray. "I wonder who it can be."

Curiosity born of their quiet days sent them hurrying over the lawn.

They saw a small, golden-haired figure, very chic in a high-waisted, lilac-sprigged dress. Betsy stared. Then she shrieked. Then she began to run.

"Tib!" she cried. "Tib Muller!"

She and Tib flung their arms about each other.

"Where did you come from?"

"I rode out from Deep Valley with your father."

"But you belong in Milwaukee."

"No," said Tib. "We've moved back. I live in Deep Valley now. I'm going to go to the Deep Valley High School right along with you and Tacy."

They looked into each other's eyes, almost tearful with joy. Then Tib embraced Mrs. Ray, Julia and Margaret.

"Take her to Mrs. Van Blarcum and get her a room," said Mr. Ray, looking pleased with himself. He was a tall, dark-haired man, with hazel eyes like Betsy's.

Hand in hand, in a quiver of excitement, Betsy and Tib ran to Mrs. Van Blarcum. The room must be big enough for Betsy, too, they insisted, hugging each other; they refused to be separated. They reached the supper table late, but by this time they had quieted down enough to remember that they were sixteen, and they walked demurely across the dining room.

Mrs. Van Blarcum had put a chair for Tib at the Ray family table. Everyone was happily agitated by her arrival.

"When did you get back?" Mrs. Ray asked, as Betsy and Tib helped themselves liberally to crisply-fried lake fish, cottage-fried potatoes, stewed fresh tomatoes, green corn on the cob, cold slaw and muffins still warm to the touch.

"Just yesterday," said Tib. "Mamma and Matilda

are very busy settling, but they said I might come out when Mr. Ray invited me. I was so anxious to see Betsy." She spoke with a slight foreign inflection, a result of the years in Milwaukee with her German relatives.

"Have you seen Tacy?" asked Julia.

"Yes," said Tib. "I went up to her house last night. I could hardly believe it, how tall and grown-up she was. But after I had talked with her a minute I could see that she hadn't changed."

"Tacy is always the same."

"Margaret has changed, though," said Tib, smiling at Betsy's younger sister. "You're ten years old now, aren't you, Margaret?"

"Yes," said Margaret, looking up gravely out of large blue eyes, heavily lashed with black.

"Margaret has braids," said Betsy, lifting one.

They were short, but that didn't matter, for they were almost completely concealed by giant hair bows behind each ear, yellow tonight, to match the sailor suit.

"You're just Hobbie's age," said Tib, referring to her brother. She had two brothers, Frederick and Hobson. "You'll have to come up and play with him."

"Thank you," said Margaret politely, but the Rays knew that she was quite unlikely to accept the invitation. Margaret didn't play very much, even with girls.

She liked books, and Washington, her cat, and Abe Lincoln, her dog, and the company of grown-ups, especially a neighbor, Mrs. Wheat. She liked to be with her father and went with him on walks and rambles, always holding his hand and standing very straight as he did. The Persian Princess, her sisters called her.

Blaming the lake air, they emptied a plateful of muffins. It was filled again. For dessert stewed plums were served with Lady Baltimore cake. There were coffee and tea, both iced and hot, and big pitchers of milk.

Betsy stole a look around the crowded, clattering dining room. She was gratified to see that Dave Hunt was looking at her as usual. He looked away when she met his eyes. Lloyd was staring frankly at Tib, and as soon as supper was over he joined them to be introduced. All the boys and girls came except Dave.

Tib was gracious, a trifle flustered. She laughed all the time, a little tinkling laugh which sounded exactly as she looked. Betsy remembered having recommended such a laugh during her visit to Milwaukee.

It was on New Year's Eve. They had stayed awake all night planning new personalities, and Betsy had resolved to be Dramatic and Mysterious. Tib, they had decided, should be the silly type. She was really practical and exceptionally competent, but Betsy had declared that she must conceal it if she wanted to fascinate boys. Betsy had long since stopped acting Dramatic and Mysterious, but Tib was still acting adorably silly with very good effect.

Lloyd stared at her admiringly behind his glasses. He proposed getting Pete to take them all out in the launch. As they went chug-chugging into the lake, spreading ruffles of foam in the sunset-tinted water, he sat next to Tib.

When they returned he talked with Mrs. Van Blarcum and proudly announced a hop. Betsy was puzzled.

"But I thought there wasn't going to be one tonight. So many people are making an early start tomorrow."

"Plans have been changed. Guess why!" said Lloyd.

Tib laughed her little tinkling laugh and Betsy whispered, hugging her, "What you're going to do to the Deep Valley High School!"

Impromptu though it was, the hop was a success. Mrs. Ray and another mother alternated at the piano. Mrs. Ray knew only two dance tunes, a waltz and a two-step, but she played them over and over, and with such zest that they eclipsed in popularity the more extensive repertoire of the other mother.

Tib flashed from boy to boy. Betsy had plenty of partners, too. Julia danced most of the evening with

Roger, looking pensive, presumably because they must now be parted until the University opened its doors.

At last Mrs. Ray played "Good Night Ladies," Mrs. Van Blarcum served lemonade, and Betsy and Tib could get away.

Tib's room was on the second floor of the hotel. It was plainly furnished, as all the Inn rooms were, but with a drift of white towels on the wash stand and snowy linen on the bed. It smelled of the lake, and the girls were delighted to find that it had its own small balcony.

"We'll go out there and talk," Betsy cried, "as soon as we're ready for bed."

They put gaily patterned kimonos over their night-gowns. Tib tied her yellow curls with a ribbon and Betsy wound her hair on Magic Wavers. Then they went stealthily outside, sat down on the floor and looked upward.

Clouds had come into the sky; you could see the stars only through ragged holes. The tops of the apple trees stirred above the small dark cottages. Crickets were singing.

"How did you get along with your new personality after you got home?" Tib asked.

"Well, I took Phil Brandish's scalp," answered Betsy. "I got tired, though, of not being myself."

"I thought you didn't act very Dramatic and Mysterious tonight."

"I put it on when I want to. It's useful to know how. But as a regular thing I prefer to be myself. You were doing a grand job of acting silly, Tib."

"Yes. I laugh all the time when I'm around boys, just like you told me to."

"How does it work?"

"Fine. I didn't know many boys in Milwaukee, but I met some on the train and they seemed perfectly fascinated. It annoys Mamma. She keeps saying that I make such a false impression."

"Which is *just* what you're trying to do!"

They rocked with hushed laughter.

Betsy told Tib about the plans she had made in Babcock's Bay, how she was going to triumph in school that year and that she expected to go with Joe Willard. Tib listened raptly.

"You'll like Joe," Betsy said. "He's not only the handsomest boy I know, but he has so much character. Just think of him putting himself through school!"

"He sounds wonderful," said Tib. "I'm sure he's just the one for you, Betsy. Who shall I go with?"

"We'll pick out someone grand."

"It's going to be fun going to high school." Tib put her arm around Betsy. "I loved Browner and hated to leave it, but it will be thrilling to be in a school with you and Tacy—and boys."

The next morning the sky was overcast. Treetops were lost in mist. The chairs lining the Inn porches were too wet to sit down in, although there had been no rain.

The Rays and Tib packed grips and stowed them into the surrey. Good-byes flew over the green lawn, along the narrow porches. Mr. Van Blarcum, looking courtly, and Mrs. Van Blarcum, looking harried, followed them out to the carriage.

Roger looked melancholy. "I'll meet your train if you'll let me know when you expect to arrive at Minneapolis," he said to Julia.

Lloyd smiled at Tib. "We've just bought a new auto. How about a ride when I get back to Deep Valley?"

Tib gave an enchanting little giggle. "Maybe. I'm afraid of autos," said Tib, who was afraid of nothing.

Lloyd gave Betsy only an absent handclasp but she didn't mind, for from the outskirts of the crowd Dave was looking at her out of his deep-set eyes.

"If I weren't going to go with Joe this year, I'd try to make that Dave Hunt talk. I really would," thought Betsy.

3
Introducing the Crowd

THE RAY HOME STOOD AT the corner of High Street and Plum, facing on High which ran horizontally along one of Deep Valley's many hills. High was a broad leafy street full of comfortable homes. Two blocks from the Rays the red brick high school lifted its turreted roofs, and on top of the Hill stood the German Catholic College, a grey pile with a look of the old world about it. The nuns offered classes in English as well as in German, and Tacy's sister Katie was enrolled there for the fall term.

The Ray house was painted green, and although obviously new, it had a homelike look. Vines climbed the walls. There were bridal wreath and hydrangea bushes on the lawn, and hanging baskets filled with flowers festooned the small square porch.

This porch didn't look natural in the summer time without boys and girls perched on the steps and railings. Inside, too, the house seemed most like itself with a gay young crowd around. The piano, the center of everything, stood in a square entrance hall from which the golden oak staircase ascended. Julia always called this hall the music room.

The day the family returned from the lake Betsy's Crowd arrived in force. Tony Markham lounged in first. He tried to act nonchalant about their return but the affection he felt for them all shone in his big black eyes. He sat down on the couch and Betsy and Julia sat on either side of him, with Margaret crosslegged on the floor in front.

"Hi!" he called to Mrs. Ray. "Call off your daughters, can't you?"

"But we're glad to see you, Tony," the girls protested.

"Heck, I'll bet you never thought of me all summer!"

He gave Margaret a souvenir he had brought back

for her from his own vacation to Chicago, a metal teddy bear holding a red pin cushion in its arms.

"I'll keep it on my bureau," Margaret said, her small face crinkling in delight. Tony was her special favorite.

He strolled out to the kitchen to see Anna, who turned from the oven, smiling. She wore a clean coverall apron; her hair was twisted into a tight knot above her broad face. She too had been away on a vacation, to the Twin Cities.

"I saw your Charlie. He looked lonesome," Tony said.

"Ja, he was lonesome. He wants me to get married, Charlie does."

"Oh, Anna!" cried Betsy. "Are you going to?"

"Na, I'm not much on the marrying. Mrs. McCloskey used to say to me, 'Anna, why don't you marry Charlie? He's got such a good job as barkeep down at the Corner Café. He'd be a good provider.' But I'd say, 'Na, Mrs. McCloskey, I'd rather cook for you.'"

"And now you'd rather cook for us, wouldn't you, Anna?" asked Betsy, squeezing her arm. "Aren't we nicer than the McCloskeys?"

"Don't bother me now," said Anna, who wouldn't be disloyal either to the Rays or to the distant, perhaps fictional McCloskeys. "Go away and I'll have hot cookies for you in a minute."

❀ 36 ❀

Before the cookies were ready more visitors had come—Tom Slade, who hadn't yet left for the military school which he attended; Dennis Farisy, who had curly hair and a dimple in his chin; Cab Edwards, his boon companion. Cab lived just behind the Rays, a spruce smiling boy with shiny black hair. His father owned a furniture store, in which Cab had been working during vacation.

Tacy only telephoned from Tib's house but Alice Morrison, Winona Root and Irma Biscay came together. Irma had large soft eyes and a rounded figure, and although she made no effort, seemingly, to attract boys, she drew them as clover does bees. Other girls might lack a beau for long periods or short, but never, never Irma.

Winona was tall and dashing. There was an irrepressible gleam in her eyes, mischief in the white flash of her smile. Alice, as blonde as Winona was dark, was more sedate. She had to be; her parents were strict.

"Kids! Kids!" Carney Sibley rushed in, showing her dimple. She had a dimple in her left cheek only and the effect was piquant. Carney wore glasses but her prettiness triumphed over glasses. She was a senior, a frank, forthright girl, enormously popular with both boys and girls.

"What is it? What's the matter?" The Crowd started up.

"Come on out and look! Papa's bought an automobile!"

They rushed out the front door and a Buick was, indeed, standing at the hitching post where Phil Brandish's machine was wont to stand last year. Mr. Sibley, smiling broadly, sat behind the wheel.

Mr. Ray and Margaret hurried out, too.

"Where's Dandy?" Margaret wanted to know. Dandy was the Sibley's horse.

"He's gone to the country to live with my uncle," Carney said. She glanced slyly at her father. "We can't forget him though. Papa says 'Giddap!' when he wants the auto to go faster and 'Whoa!' when he wants it to stop."

Margaret slipped her hand into her father's, and Betsy knew she felt lonesome for Dandy. Her own heart yearned briefly toward the old bay horse who had driven the Crowd all over the county on endless high jinks. But the new automobile with its brass lamps, the high seats padded and upholstered in leather, was fetching indeed.

"I'm going to learn to drive it and then I'll take you all out riding," Carney said.

Her father drove away, but Carney remained to eat cookies and hear about Tib. Betsy had told the great news that Tib was back for keeps in Deep Valley. Alice, Winona and Tom remembered her. The others knew her only from Betsy's rhapsodic descriptions.

"Is she really as nifty as you say?" demanded Cab.

"Niftier," Betsy declared. "She came out to the lake with Papa last night, and you should have seen her bowl Lloyd Harrington over."

"When is Lord Byron Edwards going to meet her?"

"What about Casanova Farisy?"

"Neither of you has a chance," drawled Tony, sticking his thumbs in his vest. "Get out of the way, boys!"

Irma's laughter was appreciative of this wit.

"Maybe she'll come to my party. It's for girls only, though. I'm giving a party for Phyllis Brandish, Betsy." Irma had gone out with Phil frequently since he and Betsy had quarreled the previous spring.

"Do you know, Betsy," Winona asked, "that Phyllis is coming here to school?"

"How nice! Maybe she'll go with our Crowd." But Betsy said that only to sound casual. Personally, she thought Phyllis Brandish was too worldly for their Crowd. She didn't really like Phil's sister.

Julia came in just then and sat down at the piano. She began to play, and the Crowd, as though at a signal, hooked arms and formed a semicircle behind her. There were some good voices, Tony's deep bass, Dennie's tenor, Betsy's soft alto, Irma's sweet soprano. They missed Tacy, whose voice had a vibrant heart-stirring quality. Tacy had temperament, Julia always said.

"School days, school days,
Dear old golden rule days. . . ."

They sang ardently, and

"San Antoni . . . Antonio,
She hopped upon a pony,
And ran away with Tony. . . ."

Tony seized Betsy and galloped madly around the music room to show how it was done.

It was a typical gathering of the Crowd, but there wasn't another for several days. Until school began Betsy spent every waking moment at the Mullers'.

They had moved back into their chocolate-colored house, near Tacy's in the Hill Street neighborhood. It was large, with a tower in one corner and a pane of colored glass over the front door. In their childhood Betsy and Tacy had thought it the most beautiful house in the world.

It gave Betsy a queer feeling, such as you get from hearing a strain of old music or from smelling a perfume associated with bygone days to see the blue velvet furniture back in the Mullers' round front parlor, to smell coffee cake baking in Matilda's shining kitchen, and to watch Mr. Muller sipping beer.

Tacy, too, was happy and excited over Tib's return. She was a tall girl who wore her auburn hair in coronet braids. There was a peachy bloom on her cheeks; her Irish blue eyes looked both laughing and afraid. Tacy had been shy as a child and she was still diffident with teachers, some parents, most boys. But with Betsy and Tib she bubbled over with fun.

"I didn't laugh so much all the time I was in Milwaukee," said Tib, the day the three of them took a picnic up on the Big Hill.

They built a fire and made cocoa, smoky but delicious. Looking down the long slope, pied with goldenrod, asters and sumac, they told stories of their childhood, recalling how they had splashed themselves with mud and gone begging and how Tib had offered to marry the King of Spain. They planned triumphs for Tib in high school, paired her off hilariously with this boy and that one. Betsy repeated all the comments she had heard about Tib's coming.

"Heavens, Betsy!" cried Tib. "What have you been saying about me? I can never live up to it all."

"You can." Betsy was serenely sure.

"They'll be expecting a Billie Burke."

"You're prettier than Billie Burke."

"I admit I'm kind of cute," said Tib, prancing about. "I can fasten my father's collar around my waist."

"Tib! Not really!"

"Yes, I can. Of course," she added with characteristic honesty, "my father has a very thick neck. And I have a dark secret, a skeleton in my closet."

"What is it? What?"

"*Gott sei Dank,* skirts are long."

Betsy reached back to her Milwaukee visit for a shred of German. "*Was ist los? Was ist los?*"

"*Erin go braugh!*" shouted Tacy. "If you two are going to throw foreign phrases around, so will I. What is your dark secret?"

"Look!" Tib lifted her skirts dramatically, halfway to her knees. "I'm bowlegged! My dancing teacher broke the news to me. She doesn't think I can be another Adeline Genée."

"Do you mind awfully? About your dancing, I mean," Betsy asked.

"No. If I can't be a dancer, I'll be an actress."

Tacy was consoling.

"Well, the Deep Valley High School will never find out about your shame. Skirts are getting longer."

"And tighter," added Tib.

She began to tell them about the new styles, the long tight sleeves, the high directoire waistlines, the princesse dresses, the enormous hats. After the picnic they trooped down to her house and inspected her clothes.

She was very fond of purple in all shades. There were touches of purple, lavender and lilac on almost all the dresses which hung neatly on hangers in her closet, smelling of lavender water.

Tib now wore a pompadour like Betsy's. They tried

to tease Tacy into wearing one.

"No," said Tacy. "I want to go down in history as the only female of my generation who didn't wear a pompadour."

"But Tacy, you'll be a junior this year! An upper classman, just think!"

"I'll be an upper classman in coronet braids."

"Next Tuesday," said Tib, with a long expectant sigh, "is the first day of school."

On the first day of school, according to custom, Anna made muffins for breakfast. Betsy had a new sailor suit, navy trimmed with red and white, and Margaret had a brown one with brown and white checked ribbons. Nevertheless, it didn't seem like the first day of school.

In the first place, Julia wasn't going back. She didn't even get up for breakfast. By special permission from her father, who usually liked the family all present at meals, Julia celebrated her independence by sleeping through the breakfast gong.

And although Tacy came to call for Betsy and ate a muffin for luck, things still didn't seem natural, for Tib was with her, dancing along in a high-waisted lilac silk skirt and a thin white open-work waist.

Tib didn't flush easily as Betsy and Tacy did, but she was so excited today that color burned in her cheeks, making her look even prettier than usual.

"Meet my friend Tib Muller." "Meet my friend Tib

Muller," Betsy kept saying with elaborate carelessness along the crowded, clamorous highway which was High Street on the first day of school.

Tony sauntered up; Cab and Dennie came together, to give each other courage; Carney came, welcoming, with Irma, Alice and Winona.

In the Social Room the crowd around them was so deep that Betsy had no chance to look for Joe. She hadn't forgotten her plans, however. They were written in her mind as well as in her journal.

She caught a glimpse of Phyllis Brandish and waved. Phyllis waved negligently in return. Tib's triumph clouded Phyllis' arrival in high school and Betsy wondered whether Phyllis minded. But she didn't look envious.

The second bell, clanging loudly, drove them from the Social Room. They crowded through the upper hall past the case containing the cups for which the two societies, Philomathian and Zetamathian, competed annually: one for athletics, one for debating and one—as Betsy knew all too well—for essay writing.

They pushed on to the big assembly room with its alcove overlooking the rooftops of Deep Valley. Betsy, Tacy and Tib found seats together at the back of the junior rows. Miss Bangeter rapped for order and their junior year began.

4
Aft Agley

AFTER A HYMN, sung so lustily that it swam up to the ceiling and out the open windows into the treetops, Miss Bangeter read as usual from the Scriptures. The faculty sat on the platform, and Betsy observed that there were several new teachers. Some of the old ones were gone, and she was thankful that Miss Bangeter was not among the missing.

There was something noble about this high school principal. She was commandingly tall. A knot of black hair topped a dark hawk-like face which was usually grave, but knew how to flash into humor. Speaking with a Boston accent, she read rapidly but with intense conviction the parable of the sower and the seed.

After the Lord's Prayer, said in unison, the students made a quick round of their classrooms for registration.

Flanked by Tacy and Tib, Betsy went first to her English class. Foundations of English Literature, it was called this year. Mr. Gaston, a sardonic young man who had shepherded Betsy's class through composition and rhetoric, wasn't the teacher. He had been removed—rejoicing, it was said—to the science department. Betsy would have him for botany, she saw by a glance at her card.

She flourished the card toward Tacy.

"What do you think of this? They changed Gaston to science just in time to give him to us!"

"We're fated!" Tacy groaned. Mr. Gaston was an old enemy of Betsy's.

The new English teacher was named Gwendolyn Fowler. She had come from Miss Bangeter's Boston and looked not unlike her, having heavy black hair and white teeth. But she was short, shorter than

Betsy. Although young, she was completely poised and looked over the room with penetrating eyes, as though trying to pick out those pupils who would be hungry for what she had to give.

Joe Willard came into the room and Betsy's heart gyrated slightly. She poked Tib.

"There he is."

Tib whirled about to stare.

"No wonder you want to go with him! Who wouldn't?"

"Let's take him away from her, Tib," whispered Tacy.

"How can you? I haven't got him yet," Betsy whispered back.

But she would, she resolved.

He had grown over the summer, and he had changed. It wasn't only that he was better dressed—although he was. Last year he had been almost shabby. Today he wore a new brown suit and a brown striped shirt with a brown tie.

He seemed older; perhaps that was it. He had been traveling, of course, working with men. The summer in the harvest fields had hardened his muscles and had tanned him so deeply that his smooth pompadour and heavy eyebrows looked almost white. He had very blue eyes and a strong, well molded face. He walked with a slight, proud swing.

"He walks as though he knew he was somebody. Well, he is!" thought Betsy.

Although she liked English and was drawn to Miss Fowler, her attention wandered. She had resolved to speak to Joe and it agitated her, but she wouldn't let herself off. When the class was dismissed she strolled across the room.

She acted calm, like Julia, but her color deepened.

"Hello," she said.

His eyes warmed into friendliness. "Hello."

"How were the harvest fields?"

"Remunerative."

"Do you know that you've changed?" Julia had told her that it was good policy with boys to talk about the boys themselves. But that wasn't why she asked her question. It burst from her spontaneously.

"Sure," said Joe. "I've got calluses." He extended his palms.

Betsy spread out her own hands, glad that they were listed among her good points.

"Me, too," she said. "From rowing on Murmuring Lake."

"I don't see any. Softy!"

Betsy's color grew deeper still. She put her hands behind her.

"Isn't it a joke that we're having Gaston for botany? He's going to have his revenge about those apple blossoms." One of her quarrels with Mr. Gaston last year had pertained to the color of apple blossoms. Joe had taken her side.

"I'm sorry I won't be there to watch it. I'm taking physics."

"Grind!"

"Only softies take botany." He was laughing teasingly but all at once he stopped and said, "Well, I'll look for you when we start work on the Essay Contest."

"I probably shan't be chosen this year," Betsy replied plaintively. "There's a villainous Philomathian who always beats me. They'll put a better Zetamathian in. Anyway," she plunged boldly and smiled, "spring is a long way off."

He didn't rise to this bait; in fact he looked embarrassed, which for Joe Willard, famous for his poise, was most unusual.

"Oh, they'll give you another try at it," he answered lamely and looked so willing to terminate the conversation that Betsy said, "I hope so," smiled again and left him. He did not find a bantering parting word and this, too, was strange.

Betsy was puzzled at her failure.

"How did I look?" she whispered to Tacy as they moved on to the botany classroom.

"Cute," said Tacy.

Tib hooked her arm into Betsy's on the other side.

"How did you come out?"

"Oh, I made a beginning."

Betsy wasn't, however, satisfied with this beginning, and she didn't know where the trouble lay. If he had acted bored she would have feared that he just didn't like her any more. But he hadn't acted bored, he had acted embarrassed.

"What the dickens?" she wondered, feeling depressed.

Mr. Gaston looked at her more kindly than of yore. He had a weakness for Julia. Passing mimeographed instructions for herbariums, he asked Betsy softly, "Has your sister left for the University?"

"Not yet," said Betsy. She tried to throw into her tone the implication that Julia couldn't bear to leave Deep Valley because it held Mr. Gaston.

He nodded gravely, and passed on.

Betsy and Tacy parted from Tib, who was taking German instead of Latin, and went into the Cicero class. There was another new teacher here, a young Swedish woman named Miss Erickson. Betsy didn't admire her, although she recognized that Miss Erickson was pretty, with a pompadour like the rising sun. Her light blue eyes were like marbles and her shirt waist suit was forbiddingly neat.

There was a peculiarity in her speech. She never

used a contraction. She said, "can not, do not, shall not," never, "can't, don't, shan't."

"She'll be hard," Tacy whispered to Betsy.

"She's probably a pill," Betsy said. Tib had brought the word "pill" from Milwaukee. It was the very newest slang.

It was good to pass from the chilly air of Miss Erickson's room to the warm, familiar quarters of Miss Clarke, who had taught them Ancient History and Modern History and this year would teach them the history of the United States. She was a gentle, trusting teacher. She and Betsy and Tacy were good friends, for she was Zetamathian faculty advisor and they were enthusiastic Zetamathians.

Last of all came Domestic Science. One great advantage to being a junior girl was that you were eligible to take Domestic Science. You went down the broad creaking stairs past the statue of Mercury, and the Domestic Science room was a fascinating place, provided with rows of little stoves, small shining pots and pans. They must each buy three white aprons, Miss Benbow said.

Miss Benbow wore an immaculate, stiffly starched white uniform, but her face, unlike Miss Erickson's, was not stiffly starched. It was a little worried, kind, and eager to please.

"I think I'm going to love Domestic Science," Betsy

said. "I hate housework at home, but it's different with other kids around."

"And we can eat up everything we cook!" Tacy replied.

"We'll give handouts to Tib."

Tib didn't take Domestic Science. Her mother thought it would be ridiculous, since Tib had known how to cook for many years.

They returned to the assembly room for dismissal and to the cloakroom to retrieve their hats. The noon whistles had not yet blown but school was over for the day. The first afternoon was traditionally spent by the Crowd buying books and going to the motion pictures, perhaps with a soda at Heinz's Restaurant afterwards. Betsy was expecting to follow this routine, but as the school filed out to the stirring strains of the march from *Aida* played by Carney on the piano she had a sudden thought.

Joe Willard had always worked at the creamery after school. But "after school" meant four o'clock. Since school ended at noon today, he might have the afternoon free.

She wouldn't seek him out. She had gone far enough already. But he might just possibly seek her out. He might regret having turned her off and want to make amends.

"I'll just make myself available," she thought, and

suggested casually, "Let's wait for Carney."

Tacy, Tib and Winona agreed.

They loitered at the wide limestone entrance. It was a warm day. Up and down High Street lawns were still green, gardens were still gaudy. It would have seemed like summer except for

"... *that nameless splendor everywhere*
That wild exhilaration in the air."

Betsy knew her Longfellow, but she only thought the lines. She didn't say them out loud.

Winona must have had the same feeling.

"Gee, it's a swell day!" she said. "We ought to go riding. Maybe Carney will take us all out in her auto."

"Why, there's an auto now!" Tib cried.

But it wasn't Carney's, and it wasn't Phil's. It was empty, although surrounded by an interested group.

Almost immediately, its owner came through the door. She was easily identified, for her hat was tied down by an automobile veil, in a smart bow under one ear. It was Phyllis Brandish, but for a moment Betsy hardly recognized her.

Phyllis, who was small, with olive skin and heavily fringed yellow-brown eyes like Phil's, usually had Phil's sullen expression. But she didn't look sullen now. Her face was lighted by a glowing smile as it turned up toward the face of the boy who accompanied her.

He, too, was smiling. And he was so taken up with the laughter between them that he didn't even see the group of girls. Poised, assured, Joe Willard touched Phyllis Brandish's arm as he walked with her out to the waiting automobile.

She climbed into the driver's seat. He cranked while she pulled down the throttle. And when that was done she moved over. He climbed in and took the wheel.

The roar and racket of an automobile in the throes of starting blasted against the ears of the waiting students. The fumes of gasoline poisoned the air. Then Joe and Phyllis, in Phyllis' machine, moved off down High Street, and the group of girls found their voices.

"Why, Betsy," Tib began, "I thought . . ." but Betsy nudged her.

"Joe Willard and Phyllis Brandish! That's a new one!" Winona said.

"It won't last long, I imagine," said Tacy, glancing at Betsy.

But Betsy remembered the glow on Phyllis' face, the smile in Joe's eyes. The reason Joe had seemed embarrassed after English class was because he already had a girl. He was going with Phyllis Brandish!

Betsy felt as though she had had the breath

knocked out of her. Maybe she could take him away from Phyllis if she tried, but she wasn't sure she wanted to. That look on Phyllis' face . . . ! And Phyllis had always seemed so bored and hateful. For all that she had traveled around the world, and had gone to exclusive schools, and had beautiful clothes, this was probably the most wonderful thing that had ever happened to her.

"Besides," thought Betsy, stiffening stubbornly, "if Joe Willard can afford to go with a girl and he wants it to be Phyllis Brandish, let it be Phyllis Brandish!"

The other girls were laughing and joking as they walked along High Street. Betsy was silent and she and Tacy dropped behind the others.

"What's that," she asked Tacy, "about plans ganging aft a-gley. Just where is a-gley? I'd like to know. It's where my plans have gone to."

She was joking but she felt hurt inside. She had always thought that when Joe Willard got around to girls, he would start going with her.

5
The Party for Phyllis

BETSY WAS PROUD BEFORE everyone in the world except Tacy. She could hardly wait to persuade Tib she didn't care at all that Joe Willard had driven off with Phyllis Brandish.

"Really," she said, as soon as she and Tib had parted from the others, with plans to meet on the Sibley lawn after dinner. "Really, I'm rather relieved. I don't believe I want to settle down to one boy in my junior year. I think it would be a mistake."

Tib accepted this readily, as she accepted all Betsy's statements. She firmly believed that Betsy was the most wonderful creature in the world.

"Perhaps I'd better not start going with one boy, either," she answered anxiously. "What do you think, Betsy? Would it be a mistake for me, too?"

Betsy pondered. "Lloyd Harrington would like to go with you, I'm sure. And he's a great catch. I don't know, Tib. It just depends on what you want to do."

"I want to do whatever you do," Tib said. "If you don't want to go with just one boy, neither do I."

Betsy was glad to have her own attitude established before Irma's party for Phyllis, which took place on Friday afternoon. By Friday it was plain to the high school that Joe and Phyllis had a real case. She drove to school in her own auto as Phil did, in his. And every afternoon after classes she drove Joe down to the office of the *Deep Valley Sun*.

For it developed that Joe was no longer working at the creamery. After his return from the harvest fields he had been hired by Mr. Root, Winona's father, as a cub reporter and general handyman. Winona was bitter about it.

"I've been talking Joe Willard up to Papa for years," she said. "I told him Joe deserved something better than the job at the creamery. I told him Joe was the best writer in high school—excuse me, Betsy—and that he would make a swell reporter. And now he goes and gets himself a job on the paper and a girl, too."

"Take him away from her, Winona," teased Carney. "You have a wonderful chance. You can go down to your father's paper after school and hang around all you want to."

"That's a good idea," said Alice. "Especially since Pin has graduated." Pin had been Winona's beau last year.

"But there's Squirrelly, you know," said Winona, looking impish. "He kind of likes me, and I kind of like him."

Squirrelly was a senior with a headful of tight curls, high color and a deceptively bashful air. He was one of the stars of the football team. The supreme star was Al Larson, a brawny good-natured Dane who had been Carney's chief escort since Larry Humphreys and his brother, Herbert, had moved away to California. The Humphreys had gone with the Crowd in Betsy's freshman year. Larry and Carney had been really fond of each other. They still corresponded faithfully, a letter every week.

The day of Irma's party Betsy called for Carney. They joined Tacy and Tib at Lincoln Park and all walked together to Irma's house. It was a very warm day. They wore light summer dresses, held parasols, and all of them, except Betsy, carried little silk sewing bags on their wrists.

"Betsy," scolded Carney, "you ought to learn to sew."

"I despise sewing. I'm going to buy my dresses in Paris."

"But you ought to know how to embroider at least. There's so much sentiment in a gift you embroider. I embroidered Larry a laundry bag, and he was awfully pleased."

"Nobody would be glad to get anything I embroidered."

"I would," said Carney. "I'd love a hand-embroidered gift from you, Betsy."

"If I embroidered you a jabot, would you wear it?"

"Certainly I would."

"Is that a promise?"

"Certainly it's a promise."

"Girls, girls!" Betsy cried. "Be witnesses to this! If I embroider a jabot Carney promises to wear it. I'm going to call her bluff and embroider one."

"I'll help you," offered Tacy. "Me and my trusty needle."

"You'll help me! There's only one person in the world who would embroider a jabot worse than I would and that's you. You only carry that sewing bag because it matches your dress."

Tacy tried to hit her with it, but the ensuing chase was brief. Betsy stopped and patted her hair.

"We mustn't get hot and messy," she cried, "going to a party for the great Phyllis Brandish. My—almost—ex-sister-in-law."

Irma lived in a large substantial house, with porches and bay windows, set in a large lawn which had diamond-shaped flowerbeds on either side of the walk. Mrs. Biscay was soft-eyed and smiling like her daughter.

It was quite a large party because, since Phyllis was a senior, Irma had included a number of senior girls. Phyllis arrived late, wearing a dress of green Rajah silk cut in the new princesse effect and a large hat laden with plumes. She didn't try very hard to be friendly. She discussed Browner Seminary with Tib and seemed to take no interest in the things the girls told her about high school.

She didn't know whether she would be a Philomathian or a Zetamathian; she didn't expect to try out for the chorus; she smiled at the idea of going in for debating, and yawned when they discussed the football team.

"I doubt that I'll bother to go to the games," she said, "unless Joe has to cover them." She brought Joe into her conversation all the time. It was Joe this and Joe that.

"I think it's wonderful that Joe's a reporter," said Betsy.

"Is he doing just school news?" Alice asked.

"No," said Phyllis. "Lots of other things. He covers meetings in the evenings. It's a nuisance for me, but it's good experience for him. He wants to be a foreign correspondent, you know."

Betsy despised hearing Joe Willard's plans from Phyllis. She was the one he should have told about wanting to be a newspaper man!

"I think," she couldn't resist saying, "he's planning to go to college."

"Oh, of course," said Phyllis. "Naturally!"

But there was nothing natural, Betsy thought, about a boy without father or mother, who supported himself, going away to college. It was quite remarkable, in fact. She didn't say anything, however. She was careful to make sure that nothing in her manner gave a hint of her deep interest in Joe.

Irrationally, for she could take no credit, she felt proud of his new job. It was wonderful, she thought, for a sixteen-year-old boy to be even a part-time reporter. But it wasn't surprising that Joe had been able to do it. He had always been different from the general run of boys.

It was the reporter's job, of course, which made it possible for him to be friends with Phyllis. The Brandishes were rich. Their big rambling house across the slough was removed socially as well as physically from the rest of Deep Valley. Phyllis Brandish was snobbish. Betsy didn't think that Joe, wonderful as he was, would be acceptable to her if he were still working in the creamery.

As a reporter he was acceptable socially and he had always had an air. It wasn't only his striking blonde good looks; it was the way he carried himself. His life had made him more independent, more mature than the other boys. Compared to them he seemed like a man of the world. And the fact that he wasn't one of the high school crowd made him more desirable to Phyllis.

In a curious way Joe and Phyllis were alike. Neither one "belonged." They were different, Phyllis because she was rich and Joe because circumstances had always set him apart. He was accustomed to being different and had come to like it. Yes, Betsy thought, looking searchingly at Phyllis, who was chatting over an embroidery frame, in that way they were well matched.

"Always assuming," she thought, "that Joe brought plenty of money back from the harvest fields."

On second thought, she decided, he wouldn't need very much. He would need clothes, and he had evidently bought them. He was probably tired of dressing shabbily as he had been forced to do in his first two years of high school. As a reporter he would get passes to the shows that came to town, and since Phyllis had an auto and a big house to entertain in, he really wouldn't need more money than he earned.

Unconsciously Betsy kept watching Phyllis, trying to see something in the small-featured little face which could attract Joe Willard. To her Phyllis looked waspish, sharp, unlovable. But she conceded that the girl was pretty with her smooth olive skin and those strange eyes like her brother's, the great fluff of dark hair and her exquisite clothes.

"Probably," Betsy thought, "Joe doesn't realize how much those clothes do for her. He thinks that what they do for her is part of her. It almost is, for she has been rich all her life. She has an air, too."

She knew that Joe had not been influenced in his choice by the Brandish money or prestige. The fact that Phyllis was so cosmopolitan, that she had traveled abroad and had lived in New York—those things would fascinate him. But most of all, Betsy felt, their "differentness" drew them together.

She wondered how they had met and was glad when Carney asked the question.

"How did you and Joe get together, anyway?"

Phyllis laughed.

"I went to the *Sun* office to put in an ad for Grandmother; she was trying to find a new second maid. When I went back to my auto I couldn't get it started, and Joe came out and helped me."

"How did Joe Willard happen to know how to run a machine?"

"He learned this summer while he was working on a farm. The farmer had a Buick, too. Some farmers have a great deal of money, Joe says," Phyllis remarked, and seemed pleased to be able to offer information about such a strange species of human beings as farmers. Since almost all the girls had grandparents, uncles or aunts on farms they were both amused and plagued.

Irma's party was very elegant, with flowers all around the parlor and back parlor where the girls sewed and talked. At the dining room table there were more flowers, pink candles, little pink baskets filled with candy and nuts, even place cards. The refreshments were delicious—fruit salad, rolls, sherbet and two kinds of cake, devil's food cake with white frosting and angel food cake iced in pink. There were two dishes of sherbet apiece for those who wanted it, Irma announced. Most of the girls acclaimed this with enthusiasm, but Phyllis looked supercilious as she refused the second saucer.

"I simply can't like her," Betsy thought, and was relieved to observe that there was no real danger of Phyllis going with their Crowd. She thanked Irma graciously for their party but she didn't ask the girls to come to see her, and to Carney's impulsive, hospitable suggestion that she drop in on the Sibley lawn as most people did after school, Phyllis responded with a noncommittal smile.

After the party Betsy and Carney went down to the Lion Department Store and bought a jabot for Betsy to embroider. They were even more hilarious than usual in their reaction from Phyllis Brandish and from having acted so ladylike all afternoon. Carney asked Betsy to come home with her to supper and since they were still talking hard and fast at nine o'clock she invited her to stay all night. Permission was secured and Carney loaned a night gown.

Well-supplied with crackers, plums, layer cake, cheese and dill pickles, they looked over old snapshots and party programs, postal cards and souvenirs Larry had sent from California. They discussed the Humphreys.

Herbert and Betsy still corresponded too, but they weren't sentimental. They were what they had always called each other, "Confidential Friends."

Carney, in a sudden rush of words, grew confidential now.

"I wish I could see Larry," she said. "I'm afraid

that until I see him again, no one else is going to interest me."

She looked very serious, sitting in her long-sleeved night gown. Her hair, braided for the night, swung in neat pigtails.

"He'll come back to see you sometime," Betsy prophesied.

When Carney spoke again, she changed the subject.

"Do you know, Betsy, I was surprised when I heard that Joe Willard was going with Phyllis Brandish."

"Why?" Betsy asked.

"I always thought," said Carney bluntly, "that he would be a good one for you."

"Joe Willard?" Betsy asked. "Joe Willard?" She lay on her back and looked thoughtfully up at the ceiling. "He's a very nice boy. But to me he only means the Essay Contest."

Then it was Betsy's turn to change the subject.

"Doesn't it seem funny, Carney, to be a senior? Have you decided what you're going to do next year?"

"Yes," said Carney. "I'm going to go to Vassar if I can pass the exams."

6
Julia Leaves for the U

THE NEXT NIGHT BETSY and Julia hitched up Old Mag and went riding. It was almost unheard-of for Betsy not to be with a crowd of boys and girls on Saturday night. But for once she didn't want to be. Julia was leaving the following Tuesday.

Betsy had seen very little of her sister since returning

from Murmuring Lake. Miss Mix, the dressmaker, was in the house. Julia and Mrs. Ray were shopping all day long for materials and trimmings, as well as for hats, night gowns, underwear, shoes and all the other things Julia must take to the U.

"Anyone would think there wasn't a store in Minneapolis," Mr. Ray grumbled. "Why don't you just fill a trunk with her duds and let her buy what else she needs in the cities?"

But this was unthinkable. Mrs. Ray loved to shop. Every purchase must be discussed from all angles, colors matched, accessories pondered over. The two had been lost in a maze of clothes.

Betsy was glad tonight to have Julia to herself. It was a fine chance to talk, jogging along behind Old Mag, the reins held loosely, the whip in the right hand, but as a gesture merely. Old Mag always took her own gait.

Riding was a favorite evening diversion in Deep Valley, especially since Front Street and Broad Street had been paved. The Rays usually went as a family, Mr. and Mrs. Ray in the front seat, the three girls behind. They would drive down High Street past the high school and court house to the end, turn and drive up Broad past the library, the Catholic, Presbyterian, Baptist and Episcopal churches, and Carney's house. At Lincoln Park they would turn and angle down Second where there were more homes and more churches, livery stables, the post office, the fire house, the Opera House. Then, turning again, they would drive up Front past the Big Mill and the Melborn Hotel and Mr. Ray's shoe store. Sometimes they stopped for ice cream.

Out riding you continually passed and hailed friends who were likewise out riding, going up one street and down another while sunset died out of the sky. Occasionally an automobile whizzed past and then you had to hang on to the reins. Old Mag still detested automobiles.

Betsy held the reins tonight. Julia looked pensively over the pleasant streets, dimmed by the cool September twilight. She looked as though she were bidding them good-by, as indeed she was.

"I both hate it and love it," Julia said.

"Deep Valley? How could you possibly hate it?"

"Because it has held me for so long," Julia said. "And it isn't my native heath. Never was."

Julia was taking the music course at the U. She began talking about how hard she planned to work, not only at singing lessons but at piano, history and theory of music, languages.

"Of course," she explained, "the U wasn't my choice. What I would really like to do is go to New York or Berlin to study. But Papa thinks I'm too young for that, and I'm willing to go to the U first if he wants me to."

She drew her finely arched brows together.

"It's not so good, though," she said. "You ought to begin young in music. I'd like to start work with some great teacher. Geraldine Farrar made her debut when she wasn't much older than I am."

Betsy wanted to tell Julia how much she would miss her, but it didn't come easy to Betsy to say things like that.

"When you're gone, I'm going to go into your room every day and muss it up. I'm going to pull open your bureau drawers and throw your clothes on the floor. You know, make the place look natural."

"I'm not that bad, Bettina," Julia said, slipping her arm through her sister's.

"Worse! Gee, we're going to miss you!"

Old Mag's hoofs rang on the asphalt of Broad Street. Betsy and Julia bowed to the Brandishes, waved to the Roots, gazed thoughtfully at the first timid star.

"Yes, Papa and Mamma will miss me," said Julia at last.

"I'm going to stay around home more," Betsy said, awkwardly. "Go places with Mamma. Do the best I can."

"I'm very thankful that they have you, Bettina. I

don't see how 'only' children ever manage to leave home."

"Julia, I think I'll start taking piano lessons."

"What?" Julia received this declaration with such a cry of pleasure that it sent Old Mag into a trot. "Oh, Betsy, I'm so glad! How grand to have another musician in the family!" It was just like Julia to assume that Betsy's success at the instrument was already assured.

"I'll never be a musician," said Betsy. "But there has to be a piano being played around the Ray house."

"You'll study with Miss Cobb?"

"Of course."

Everyone in Deep Valley began piano study with Miss Cobb, a large, mild, blonde woman who was a Deep Valley institution, and one of its most widely admired heroines. Students of the piano who had any large talent ultimately went on to other teachers but their parents would have felt guilty about starting them with anybody but Miss Cobb. The fact that she had a particular gift with very small children was the least part of the explanation.

The town felt that Miss Cobb deserved its support. Years before, on the death of a sister, she had broken her own engagement to marry and had taken the sister's four children to raise. The little girl had followed her mother and the youngest boy had followed his sister. One of the two remaining boys was delicate. Miss Cobb kept on staunchly, year in and year out, teaching the young of Deep Valley to play.

"I remember," Julia said dreamily, "sitting down before the key-board and having Miss Cobb show me where middle C was. It's one of those memories that stand out like a photograph. There it is . . . me, aged six or so, all swelled up with importance, sitting on the piano stool with Miss Cobb's face quite close to me, and her gentle, kind voice saying, 'Now we always begin with middle C.'"

Julia stared at the star which was brighter now in the lofty leafy lane made by the treetops.

"If I were told today that I was beholding the Garden of Eden it couldn't possibly rate in importance with the way middle C seemed to me that day. It's queer, Bettina, to be thinking of that just as I'm leaving Deep Valley."

"Julia," said Betsy, "you talk as though you weren't ever coming back."

"I'm not," said Julia. She stared upward again and her violet gaze reached beyond the brightening star to wherever opera singers of the future were singing gloriously to hushed enraptured audiences. "Not to stay," she added. "Not in the way I'm here now."

Sunday morning Julia and Betsy went to the little

Episcopal church. They sang in the choir, and today, putting on their black robes and black four-cornered hats, both of them were aware that it might be a long time before Julia did it again.

The choir girls marched down the aisle, two abreast, singing. Julia looked rapt and far away, as always when she sang. But she loved the little brown stone church. Once during the prayers Betsy saw her lift her head and look around tenderly, then drop her face into her hands again.

Sunday night was always a special occasion at the Ray house. Friends of all members of the family dropped in for supper, which was called Sunday night lunch. Mr. Ray took charge, making the sandwiches for which he was renowned. There was talk and music. But tonight the shadow of Julia's departure hung over it all.

Everything was supposed to be just the same as usual, but it wasn't. Anna had baked a towering five-layer banana cake instead of the common uncomplicated kind. Mrs. Ray had provided roast chicken and other sandwich materials. Usually Mr. Ray made his sandwiches of anything which came handy— Bermuda onions, for example.

Most upsetting of all, Mrs. Ray had made a salad, a gelatin salad with fruit molded in.

"Why the salad?" Mr. Ray demanded, indignant.

"What's the matter with my sandwiches? Aren't they good enough?"

"Of course, darling!" Mrs. Ray cried. "Your sandwiches are marvelous. But I thought that just tonight, since Julia was going away . . ."

"What's that got to do with it? Anyone would think that Julia was going to the North Pole!"

But he felt as upset as anyone.

There was more company than usual, so many came to say good-by to Julia. Tony, unobtrusively helpful as always, passed sandwiches, poured coffee and made jokes with Mr. Ray about it being a wake.

"Bob Ray! You keep still! You stop that!" Mrs. Ray said.

When it was time for singing, Julia skipped the hymns and the old songs like "Annie Laurie" and "Juanita" . . . the kind which make people homesick. They sang "San Antonio" and "O'Reilly" and "Waiting at the Church" and that new song to which you danced the barn dance—

> "*Morning, Cy,*
> *Howdy, Cy,*
> *Gosh darn, Cyrus, but you're*
> *Looking spry. . . .*"

Everyone was noisier and gayer than usual, yet it wasn't a very successful Sunday night lunch.

The next day started off oddly: Julia was up so early. Her trunk was filled, closed and locked. It went off on the dray.

That night Mr. Ray took the family down to the Moorish Café. This was in the Melborn Hotel, which was run by the husband of Julia's singing teacher. Mr. and Mrs. Poppy, both stout, cosmopolitan and merry, joined the family at the table and it was a gayer occasion than the Sunday night lunch had been.

"New things are easier to do than old familiar things when there's going to be a change," Betsy decided profoundly.

It was hard for her to imagine what the house would be like without Julia, who had always been the buoyant center of it all.

On Tuesday, although Julia's train didn't leave until four forty-five, Betsy was excused from school at noon. Margaret had been excused, too, and Mr. Ray came home early from the store. These extravagant gestures were a mistake. The family sat around feeling strange, making conversation.

Mr. Ray asked Julia several times to let him know if her allowance wasn't big enough. He acted too cheerful. Mrs. Ray reminded Julia to buy some new jabots, and a pair of long kid gloves. Betsy made jokes that didn't come off and Margaret acted cross, which was always her defense against emotion. Anna kept coming in from the kitchen.

"Oh, my poor lovey! Going all the way to Minneapolis! Your bedroom will look like a tomb."

"No, it won't, Anna. I'm going to go in and muss it up, throw her clothes on the floor."

But the joke failed miserably.

"Her clothes have gone away already," Anna wailed. "The closet is as empty as though she had never been born. Charlie asked me last night, 'Did that McCloskey girl go away to the State University?' and I said, 'Na, Mr. and Mrs. McCloskey kept her right at home where she belonged.'"

At last, although Julia was going to eat supper on the diner, Mr. Ray went to the kitchen and put the coffee pot on. The Ray family always put the coffee pot on in moments of crisis. Anna brought out butternut cookies and everyone cheered up. They even got to laughing.

But just before she left for the train, when Old Mag was standing at the hitching post, Julia went to the piano and began to play. She played an operatic aria she had sung all last winter.

"Mi chiamano Mimi. . . ."

She sang a few bars and then broke off, and Mrs. Ray, waiting for her on the porch, wiped her eyes. And when Julia came out, very briskly, her eyes were red.

At the station things were exciting. School was over and Betsy's Crowd was there along with all of Julia's friends. Katie, rosy and smiling, had come down from the German Catholic College. Julia was a credit to Miss Mix in a new brown suit with a long fitted jacket cut in points, two in front and two in back. Her hat was enormous and she wore a corsage bouquet of little yellow roses.

Her face looked white and strained but she didn't cry again. Nobody cried. The Rays didn't believe in crying at trains. Margaret stood straight and smiled brightly at everyone who looked at her. When the train arrived the family trouped into the parlor car with Julia. Then they came out, and she appeared on the observation platform.

She smiled as the train pulled away and showed her white teeth set so close together. She leaned over the railing, blew kisses with both hands. She didn't look like Julia as Julia looked at home. She looked like Julia acting in a play.

Somehow that made everything easier. Mr. Ray took the family, Tacy, Tib and Katie up to Heinz's for ice cream. Everybody laughed and joked and felt better than they had felt for a week.

But when they got back to High Street the house seemed funny without Julia.

7
Howdy, Cy!

SCHOOL RUSHED IN TO try to fill the vacuum left by
Julia's departure. School had a new flavor this year
because of Tib. She was so small that when she sat at
her desk in the assembly room her feet did not touch
the floor. Miss Bangeter, to the general amusement,
provided her with a footstool. Yet she made her presence felt. Half the boys in school were smitten with
her, especially Lloyd and Dennie.

In September, as usual, the Zetamathians and Philomathians began a drive for members. Betsy was assigned to the membership committee and on Wednesday preceding the Monday on which the freshmen would choose their societies, the committee met in Miss Clarke's room.

Betsy went in with Carney, and was pleased to find Dave Hunt in the group.

"How that Dave Hunt has changed!" Carney whispered, and Betsy agreed. He had been in high school all along but he hadn't seemed important until this year. Over the summer he had been unaccountably transformed.

His extreme height—he was six foot three—was now impressive. Impressive, too, was his stoic calm. Dave Hunt seldom spoke but you knew it was because he did not wish to speak. He seldom smiled. But when a smile flickered over his stern, clean-cut face, it changed him from a deacon into a daredevil.

He was characteristically silent while Miss Clarke proposed brightly that money be appropriated to buy turquoise blue baby ribbon. The girls on the committee, Betsy and Carney, could make bows to pin on the new members. This was routine procedure.

"Maybe," suggested Betsy, "we might do something flashy this year. How about buying blue cambric and making arm bands for the Zets? Carney can sew."

"So can you," said Carney. "You're making me a jabot."

"Really?" asked Miss Clarke. "How nice! Sewing is such a valuable accomplishment."

Dave Hunt surprised everyone by speaking.

"Make a pennant, too," he said.

"A pennant?" "A big one?" Betsy and Carney waited radiantly.

Dave did not answer. His silence made it clear that when he said pennant he meant pennant, and that he couldn't possibly want a small one.

"Would we have any use for a pennant?" Miss Clarke asked, but her question was obviously rhetorical. "I don't suppose we'd be permitted to hang one on the stage unless the Philomathians did, too. Maybe it might work into the decorating, though. Certainly it would! That's a good idea, Dave," she added kindly.

Dave did not seem to hear her; she might have been a mouse squeaking. But the expression in his deep-set, dark blue eyes told Betsy and Carney that he expected a pennant. Two dollars were entrusted to the girls and they went down to purchase turquoise blue ribbon and cambric.

Thursday after school Carney hemmed arm bands while Betsy read aloud from "The Shuttle." They had saved a large piece of blue cambric and when the arm bands were finished they cut this into a triangle and Carney hemmed it.

"I hope it's big enough to suit him," Carney said. "He scares me. Doesn't he you?"

"He makes me feel about as big as a pin."

"Al says he's wonderful at football. He's sure to be a track star, too."

"He ought to be. Those long legs!"

Carney made her sewing very neat and Betsy inspected it with critically pursed lips.

Friday morning in the Social Room they approached Dave with an innocent looking package.

"Thanks," he said thrusting it into his pocket.

"Is it a secret what you're going to do with it?" Betsy asked, smiling.

But Dave didn't answer except with his calm gaze. That said, "Don't be silly. Of course it's a secret."

Monday morning Tacy and Tib called for Betsy as usual. Many Philomathians had been wooing Tib, but in vain. She already wore a blue rosette in her hair. Betsy and Tacy, of course, wore blue arm bands. These had been distributed to all Zetamathians secretly over the week-end. High Street was dotted with them, to the annoyance of passing Philos.

Cab, wearing an arm band, joined the girls. He was smiling broadly and several times, for no apparent reason, burst into a loud guffaw.

"Cab! What ails you?"

"You'll see."

Dennie, with arm band also, met them and the boys started ostentatiously to yawn.

"It's really too bad," said Tacy, "that you had to get up to go to school."

"We're going to school, but we didn't get up, did we, Dennie?"

"What do you mean?" asked Tib. "You must have gotten up. You went to bed."

"Oh, did we? That's what our mothers think."

"Well, you didn't stay up all night, did you?"

"All I've got to say," said Dennie, "is that it gets darned chilly along about three A.M."

This mystifying dialogue was interrupted by a cry from Tacy.

"Gee, is the school burning down? Look at that crowd!"

A churning mass of boys and girls extended from the big front doors out into the street. Cab and Dennie began to hurry and the girls kept pace. They saw that everyone was looking up at the cupola which rose high above the main building. They, too, stared up and saw something floating from the top of the peaked cap of roof. It was a turquoise blue pennant, the pennant Carney had hemmed.

Betsy, Tacy and Tib grabbed each other and began

to yell. After a moment Betsy paused to ask, "How did it get up there? That's a very steep roof."

"Search me," said Cab. "But it gets cold up in that cupola."

"Swell view of the sunrise, though," said Dennie, "and somebody had to stay on guard. . . ."

"Not that any Philo would dare—"

A Philomathian boy fell upon him from behind. As he thumped to the ground, Dennie grabbed the Philo. Boys were wrestling all over the school lawn. Dave Hunt, sober as always, was looking on and Betsy saw Joe Willard, grinning, take a swing at him. They locked in mock battle.

The gong, unusually loud and angry, broke through the uproar. Reluctantly holds were loosed, clothes straightened and boys and girls began to stream indoors. Everyone was talking at once.

"Who put it up?"

"He might have broken his neck."

"Squirrelly tried to get it down. He climbed as far as the cupola but Miss Bangeter stopped him. She's mad as a wet hen."

Carney pulled Betsy aside. "I feel like Barbara Fritchie or whoever it was made the flag."

"It was Betsy Ross, idiot." She lowered her voice and whispered, "Dave must have done it!"

Carney nodded. Her dimple pierced her cheek.

Miss Bangeter did indeed emit sparks of fury as she rapped the assembly to a semblance of order. She did not mention the pennant, however, and a noisy rendition of "The Men of Harlech" cleared the atmosphere somewhat. There wasn't much studying done that morning. A long ladder blocking the windows on the turret side of the building showed that the janitor was hauling down the pennant. But the query, "Who put it up?" still buzzed through classrooms and along the halls.

In the Social Room, after a tumultuous noon recess, the query was being answered. Nobody knew how the secret had slipped out. But it had.

"Dave Hunt put it up."

"Cab and Dennie and a bunch of other Zets stayed up in the cupola all night guarding it."

"Dave Hunt put it up."

"Dave Hunt."

"Dave Hunt."

Everyone was looking in Dave's direction, but his face was imperturbable.

When, at the end of the afternoon, the freshmen chose their societies, turquoise blue bows blossomed everywhere. The pennant, it was clear, had tipped the scales.

"You wait till next year. Just wait!" Philos were muttering. Winona hissed to the other girls after school, "Wait till next year. We'll get even."

Carney laughed. "Maybe you're going to get even now. Dave has been asked to stay and see Miss Bangeter."

"Gee, he's cute," said Winona forgivingly. "I wonder when he'll start taking out girls."

"He'll have to learn to talk first."

"Oh, I don't know. You could look at him."

No one ever heard what Miss Bangeter said to Dave, but no one had any doubt about what he said to her. Nothing, it was agreed. Nothing at all.

After the boiling excitement of this day the current of school ran smoothly. Junior class elections were held. Betsy was re-elected secretary. The junior girls were enchanted with Domestic Science. They began their study with canning, made grape jelly and peach jam. It was fun, as Tacy had thought it would be, to eat what they cooked.

Next to Domestic Science, Betsy liked Foundations of English Literature under little Miss Fowler. United States History as Miss Clarke taught it was supremely restful. In Cicero they struggled through the First Oration against Cataline under Miss Erickson's hard, marble-blue eyes.

They were supposed to be making herbariums for botany but not Betsy nor Tacy nor Tib had yet begun. The fall flowers were still abundant. It seemed such an easy thing to do to pick and press just one of each kind, that they forgot to do it.

Yet September was passing. Chauncey Olcott, as much a part of the season as the goldenrod, came to the Opera House. *Ragged Robin*, said the Rays, who went in a body as usual, was the best play he had had in years. It teemed with "good little people," banshees, will-o'-the-wisps, and tenderly wistful songs.

"Don't You Love the Eyes that Come from Ireland?"—Betsy thought of Tacy when she heard that one. "Sweet Girl of My Dreams" was almost as appealing as "My Wild Irish Rose," which Chauncey Olcott, wearing a plumed hat, sang as always after the second act.

Tony brought the songs up to the Ray house next day, but there was no one to play them! Betsy, who always found it easier to make plans than to carry them out, had not yet started her piano lessons. Not that she didn't miss Julia's music. It was unbelievably strange to have the piano silent. Mrs. Ray knew how to play but she had stopped practising since Julia had become so proficient. She never touched the instrument now except when Betsy had company and asked for her famous waltz and two-step. Fortunately, Carney could play and so could Winona. So the Crowd still sang sometimes around the Ray piano.

But having Tony bring the Olcott songs reminded

Betsy sharply of her resolution. At supper that night she said, "I believe I'll start taking piano lessons, if you still want me to."

"We certainly do," her mother said. And Mr. Ray added, "I could stand a few scales myself."

Betsy telephoned Miss Cobb and the next Saturday morning she walked down to Miss Cobb's house on a steep hillside street below the high school.

Betsy knew the little house from the days when Julia had studied there. The rooms were small, low-ceilinged, always comfortably warm and smelling of the potted geraniums Miss Cobb kept in the windows. There were a grand piano and an upright piano in the front parlor. In the back parlor was Leonard, the nephew who was ill. A slender fifteen-year-old boy with sandy hair and vivid cheeks, he often lay on a couch listening to the music. Bobby, the younger boy, was like his aunt, large and robust.

Miss Cobb's red-gold hair was dimmer than it had been when Julia studied with her. She wore glasses on a chain and snowy shirt waists belted neatly above black flowing skirts. Miss Cobb gave a feeling of largeness, and not only because of her Junoesque figure. It was the expression in her face, calm and courageous.

She was a gentle teacher. Under her tutelage you didn't have to worry too much about practising scales. Soon you were playing "The Merry Farmer" and "The Sailor Boy's Dream." She herself had studied abroad under a very fine master.

"She's a better musician than she is a teacher," Julia had remarked one time.

"And a finer human being than either," Mr. Ray had added.

Miss Cobb whirled the piano stool now until it was the proper height and Betsy sat down. Miss Cobb struck a note and said, as she had said to Julia, "This is middle C." Betsy liked that. It gave her a warm feeling of the continuity of life. Though she knew that she could never learn to play the piano as Julia did, she was glad she had begun.

Betsy missed Julia. Close as she was to Tacy, wonderful as it was to have Tib back, she missed the confidential talks in her sister's once brightly cluttered room. Now the room looked so unnaturally neat that she could not bear to go inside it.

The whole family missed Julia. Anna kept forgetting and would set five places at the table.

"That's a sign Julia wishes she was home, the poor lovey," Anna said darkly.

Mrs. Ray would never leave the house until the mail came and when there was a letter she telephoned Mr. Ray. They read them over and over and Betsy often read them aloud in the evening, Margaret sitting on her father's knee.

They were good letters. Just as Julia had always shared everything—bon bons, handkerchiefs, her excitement over a new opera or book—she was trying lovingly now to share this new experience. She described the campus, her classrooms and teachers, the dormitory where she lived. Roger had taken her to lunch in Minneapolis. She had found a bewildering number of friends.

She sounded happy. Nevertheless, there was that in her letters which told that Anna's divination might be correct. The pages were so full of longing and remembering. She asked about everything and everyone at home. The family wrote to her often. Betsy weighed the postman down with fat and supposedly funny letters. Yet Julia kept asking for more and more.

One evening toward the end of September Betsy wrote a long letter to Julia. She finished her homework and her telephone conversations, wound her hair on Magic Wavers and went to bed. Margaret was already asleep and Anna had gone up to her lofty room. Mr. Ray wound the clock and Mrs. Ray put Washington and Lincoln in the basement. Nobody locked doors in Deep Valley. Soon the lights were out and the house was still.

Betsy had barely fallen asleep when she was awakened by the sound of music. The air was shattered by great crashing chords. It was the new song everyone was barn-dancing to.

> "Morning Cy,
> Howdy Cy,
> Gosh darn, Cyrus, but you're
> Looking spry. . . ."

Betsy started up, but her room was dark. She ran to the door. The whole house was dark. In the upper hall she bumped into her mother and father. Mr. Ray was striking matches. From downstairs the music continued jubilantly.

> "Right in line,
> All the time,
> Jiminy crickets, but you're
> Looking fine . . ."

Nobody could play like that but Julia.

Betsy, Wavers and all, rushed down stairs, followed by Margaret, rubbing her eyes, and her mother, in a nightdress, and Anna, who came down from the third floor holding a lighted candle and shouting "Stars in the sky!" Just as they reached the landing Mr. Ray succeeded in lighting the gas.

Julia sat at the piano, playing, with tears streaming down her face.

"Julia!" The music broke off. Everyone fell upon her with hugs and kisses.

"What's the matter?" asked Mr. Ray. "Get fired?"

"No," said Julia. "I just got homesick and so I came home. Mr. Thumbler brought me up in the hack."

She wept and everybody wept.

"I never knew, until I went away from home, how nice we all are!" Julia sobbed.

"Oh, we are, are we?" asked Mr. Ray. He went up stairs and put a bathrobe over his nightshirt. When he came back he said, "Well, I'll go put the coffee pot on."

"Bring it up to our room," said Mrs. Ray. "We'll all get in bed there."

Betsy and Margaret went upstairs and piled into bed beside their mother. Julia sat down joyfully, taking off her hat and coat. She was going to stay until Sunday night, she said, pulling pins out of her hair. She hadn't needed to ask permission to come. At the U you were allowed a certain number of cuts.

"I just don't want to use all of mine in case I get homesick again."

Mr. Ray came up, a broad smile on his face, bearing a tray with a pot of steaming coffee, cream, sugar and cups. Anna brought cookies, apples, cold pie, a glass of milk for Margaret.

"Stars in the sky!" she kept saying, shaking her head. "Wait 'til I tell Charlie."

She went to bed then, but the rest stayed awake a long time, listening while Julia told about life at the University.

8

Those Things Called Sororities

JULIA HAD EXTRAORDINARY things to tell. Immediately upon her arrival at the University various strange girls had begun to deluge her with attentions. They had sent her flowers. They had offered to show her around the campus, to help her register, and to guide her to her classrooms. "Why, how kind of them!" Mrs. Ray cried. She sat upright in bed, the tray on her knees, looking at Julia with alert blue eyes. Her curly red hair fell around her shoulders over her lace-trimmed white night gown.

Betsy and Margaret wore outing flannel night gowns. Betsy, bristling with Magic Wavers, and Margaret, with little braids bereft of ribbons sticking out on either side of her small solemn face, leaned against their mother's shoulders, right and left.

Betsy cradled a cup of well-creamed and sugared coffee. She liked the warmth of the cup and the coziness of being three in bed; for the room was cool, although Mr. Ray had closed the window and opened the drafts in the furnace. Julia was wrapped in her mother's bathrobe. Mr. Ray, beaming with pleasure, sat cross-legged in the other easy chair.

"I didn't realize," he said, "that our State University was such a friendly place."

"It isn't," Julia answered. "I thought it was at first. Then it dawned on me that not all the new girls were being treated the way I was. Just a few of us were getting all this attention."

"I'm not surprised that you were one of them," Mrs. Ray put in. The members of the Ray family never made a secret of their admiration for each other.

"But how did it happen? What was up?" asked Mr. Ray.

"Those girls," Julia continued, her deep tone emphasizing the gravity of her words, "belonged to sororities. They were rushing me—that's the word they use. They want me to join, but I can't do it yet. Freshmen aren't allowed to join sororities—they can't even be asked—until spring."

"What is a sorority?"

"The word means 'sisterhood.' Isn't that nice, Bettina? And men have fraternities, 'brotherhoods.' Fraternities and sororities are terribly important. They are absolutely the most important things on the campus."

"Does everybody belong to one?" asked Mr. Ray.

"Oh, no. Just a fraction of the students."

"I don't see how they can be so important then." Mr. Ray selected an apple and started to peel it neatly with a little pearl-handled penknife.

"Each sorority has its own house," Julia went on eagerly, shaking back her loose dark hair. "The girls who belong to a sorority live in their house instead of in the dormitory. They have a chaperone and a cook and other servants. They give marvelous parties and invite the fraternity men. And the fraternity men give marvelous parties and invite the sorority girls."

"How do the people who don't belong manage to have some fun?" asked Mr. Ray, taking care that the peeling did not break.

"I have no idea," said Julia. "You simply have to belong to a fraternity or sorority if you want to have any fun."

"Seems kind of tough on those who don't." Mr. Ray laid the peeling carefully in an ash tray and quartered his apple, removing the seeds. He gave a quarter to Margaret who had been watching him expectantly, and he offered one to Betsy, but she shook her head. She was listening in rapt fascination.

"Have you been inside one of those houses?" she demanded.

"Yes," answered Julia. "To teas at the Epsilon Iota house, and the Alpha Beta house and the Pi Pi Gamma house. They aren't allowed to entertain freshman at anything but teas until spring. In April there's a week of rushing. Dinners, luncheons, parties of all kinds are crowded in. Girls who are being rushed by two or three sororities have a simply frantic time."

"I trust it doesn't come at examination week," said Mr. Ray. But nobody listened to him.

"What did they do at the teas?" Betsy wanted to know.

"Oh, the food was yummy! The tables were decorated with the sorority colors and the girls stood around the piano and sang their sorority songs. They wear pins and have a grip and a password. Of course, you don't find out what the grip and the password are until you are initiated."

"Sounds like a lodge," said Mr. Ray. "But lodges are open to anyone. It must be the same with those sorority things. It has to be. The University is supported by the taxpayers' money. Any boy or girl ought to be allowed to join—"

"Oh, but they aren't!" cried Julia. "The sororities are very, very exclusive. I'm lucky, I can tell you, that three of them are rushing me."

"Have you any idea which one you want to join?" her mother asked.

"Yes. I knew right away. The Epsilon Iotas. They're just my kind. I'm going to be an Epsilon Iota. And if I am, Bettina, you will be too, and so will Margaret. Sisters always join their sister's sorority."

"Gee!" Betsy cried. "I'd love to be an Epsilon Iota." The tray made bouncing impractical, but she reached behind her mother's back to tweak one of Margaret's braids. "How about being an Epsilon Iota, Margaret?"

"I'm a Baptist," said Margaret, blinking rapidly to prove that she was wide-awake. Everybody laughed.

"Well, I'd like to find out a little more about these sororities before you join one," Mrs. Ray said. "I'll go down to the library tomorrow and look them up. What I can't make out is how they knew they wanted to rush you. Did they pick you out just because you were attractive?"

"Oh, someone must have recommended me. Someone here in Deep Valley. Perhaps one of the teachers."

"What about that little Parrott girl who went up to the University last year?" asked Mr. Ray.

"She's a barb."

"What's that?"

"It stands for barbarian. It's what they call all non-fraternity and non-sorority people. It's sort of a joke, of course."

"Not a very funny one," said Mr. Ray. "The little Parrott girl is a very fine girl. I've sold her shoes all her life. She waits and buys them from me now when she's home for vacation instead of buying them in the Twin Cities."

Julia jumped up and hugged him, laughing. "She may buy her shoes from you but she isn't a sorority girl. Probably she doesn't want to be. I've seen her around the campus. She's awfully wrapped up in her studies."

"After all, that's what she's there for," grumbled Mr. Ray. He, too, got up and took the tray from Mrs. Ray's knees. "You all hustle off to bed now. Margaret's asleep already."

"No, I'm not." Margaret opened her eyes wide but she closed them again when her father picked her up and carried her away.

"I'm not sleepy at all," said Betsy. She was enthralled with Julia's romantic sisterhoods.

"Don't you go into Julia's room and talk," Mrs. Ray warned. "It's cold and you both need your sleep. Besides, I don't want to miss anything."

"She hasn't begun on Roger yet."

"We'll save him till morning," Julia said. "I'll unpack my dream robe and get right in bed."

"Your dream robe?" asked Betsy. "What's that?"

"It's what we call night gowns up at the U," Julia said. She kissed everybody and went into her room, tossing her shoes ahead of her and flinging her clothes on a chair. She was singing as she went:

> "Howdy Cy,
> Morning Cy,
> Gosh darn, Cyrus, but I'm
> Feeling spry. . . ."

"Gee," cried Betsy. "It's grand to have you home!"

True to her word Mrs. Ray went to the library next day. It was hard to tear herself away from Julia but she did. Julia visited school, looking very citified in her brown suit and hat. She went to see Miss O'Rourke, who had always been her favorite teacher and Miss Clarke, whom she called "dear old Clarke!" and Miss Bangeter, who was like everybody's conscience. Julia had dropped the student-teacher attitude. She treated the teachers as though they were her age or she theirs. She actually joked with them.

"I wonder whether I'll be like that my first year out of high school," Betsy thought.

After school the house was crowded. The Kellys dropped in, and Tib and Tony and a host of Julia's friends. At supper Mrs. Ray told the family about her research.

"I explained to Miss Sparrow that Julia was going

to join a sorority," she said, "and that I wanted to make sure she joined a good one. Miss Sparrow brought out the encyclopedia and the University catalogue and some other books, and I copied down the dates and places where the different sororities were founded. But I couldn't find out what the names meant."

"They're Greek letters, of course."

"I know, and they all stand for something, but the books don't say what. Do you know, Julia? It would help to get a line on them if we knew what their names meant. It would show us their ideals—"

"Mamma," said Julia, "you don't need to bother looking up anything more about sororities. I know which one I want to join. I want to join the Epsilon Iotas. I don't give a hoot what the name means. The girls just suit me. My idea of heaven is to be an Epsilon Iota and live at the Epsilon Iota house."

"Well," said Mr. Ray, "That settles that!"

Julia's visit was almost swallowed up by talk of sororities. There was a stream of company, of course; there were Julia's favorite things to eat; and there was music. Sisterhoods or no, Julia must show her mother and Betsy how her voice had improved, how the high tones were coming out and about the new idea in breath control. Her teacher was German, Fraulein Hertha von Blatz. She was very fine, Mrs. Poppy said. Julia talked about Roger, too, and other college men. She never said "college boys" any more; it was always "college men."

But they talked sororities at every spare moment, especially when Tacy and Tib were around. Julia was given to enthusiasms and she knew how to communicate them. The Epsilon Iota house became in her description an enchanted domicile. The various Epsilon Iotas—the dark, queenly one, the red-headed one, the twins, the stunning blonde—moved through Betsy's head like characters in a romance.

In Julia's window seat at night, Betsy plied her sister with questions. She learned that a sorority had a ritual which members went through at every meeting. She learned that initiations were mystical secret affairs. Secrecy, in fact, was the core of the fruit. The girls were bound together by secret vows.

"How can they be sure they like each other?"

"No girl can get in unless everyone wants her. There has to be a unanimous vote," Julia explained.

"But don't they ever have fights?"

"Probably not. It's all on a pretty high plane."

Sunday evening Julia went back to the University, and Betsy slept that night with sororities rolling about in her head like billiard balls.

She woke early, suddenly, as she often did when she had great ideas. The sky was stained dark red and gold, as though the trees on Deep Valley's circling hills had pushed their autumn colors up into the sky, but all were dull yet, unburnished by the sun.

Why not start a sorority, Betsy thought? She and Tacy and Tib. They had been friends so long. What could be more fitting than that they should be founders of a sorority?

A sorority was just what she needed to fill her winter. That had seemed empty somehow, since Joe Willard upset her plans by starting to go with Phyllis. She did not admit it often, but she felt hollow inside whenever she thought of that. None of her resolutions seemed important any more, except for the piano study, which gave her a healthy satisfaction. Her morale needed bolstering, and a sorority was so new, so dramatic.

"Of course," she thought, a smile playing around her lips as she lay in bed looking at the sunrise, "we couldn't have ours quite so serious as the real ones. Winona would never take any highfalutin' vows, and Irma and Tib are such gigglers. But we could have pins. We could have grips and passwords and a ritual—I could write it myself."

She jumped out of bed smiling, and going to the bathroom she took the cold bath she reserved for moments of decision. She took her curls down, with even more care than usual, and put on her most becoming dress.

At school she wrote notes to Tacy and Tib.

"I have something terribly secret and important to talk over. Can't we shake the others after school?"

9
Okto Delta

ON A GOLDEN HILLTOP overlooking Deep Valley,
Betsy, Tacy and Tib founded their sorority. They sat
in a grove of small maples, all the same color and
ridiculously bright. Below them autumn flowed like
spilled wine. Not only the trees, but the bushes, the
vines, even the grasses were ruddy. Descending rows
of rooftops glittered in the sun.

The girls had escaped from the Crowd by a series of manoeuvres. They left school by a side door, walked to the street below High Street, walked along that for two blocks, and entered the Ray house at the back. Anna was up in her room, and they foraged for food with muffled laughter which brought Margaret into the kitchen.

"We're going for a ride," Betsy explained. "A very mysterious, important ride."

A sympathetic smile quivered across Margaret's little face.

"Can I go, too? I'm all alone. Mamma's gone out."

"I'm sorry," Betsy said, "but this is something secret, Margaret." She felt a little wrench of guilt as Margaret's smile died away. "Will you help us, dear? We don't want anyone to know where we are, so if the doorbell rings don't answer until we're gone."

"All right," Margaret agreed. She went slowly back to the parlor, with her erect, dignified tread.

The girls found grapes and crackers. The front doorbell started to ring and they slipped out the back door. They dashed across lots to the barn, hitched up Old Mag and climbed into the surrey.

"Let's go up Agency Hill," Tacy suggested. "There's such a beautiful view."

This steep road had led to an Indian Agency back in pioneer days. Tom's Grandmother Slade told stories about it. Old Mag dragged the surrey patiently to the summit, where the girls turned off on a shoulder of the hill. At the maple grove they loosened Old Mag's checkrein and left her under a pink-gold tree.

"Now, what's it all about?" asked Tib, throwing off her hat. Tacy tossed off her hat, too. The yellow head and the auburn one looked like bright leaves drifting down as the girls sank to the ground.

Betsy added her hat to the pile. But she didn't sit down. Hazel eyes glowing, she swayed on her toes.

"Let's us—the three of us—start a sorority."

Tacy and Tib were stunned for a moment by the magnificence of the concept.

"Do you mean a real one?" Tacy asked.

"Just like they have at the U. Greek letters and all."

"What would they stand for, the letters?"

"Gosh, I don't know! We'd have to make something up." Betsy sat down in front of them, looking earnestly into their faces. "We're good ones to start a sorority. You know what the word means—sisterhood—and we've been friends so long. A thing like this would hold us together always."

"We'd hold together anyway, I imagine," said Tib. "We held together all the time I was in Milwaukee."

"But Tib! If we made vows of friendship. . . ."

"We don't really need any."

"Well, it certainly couldn't hurt to make them," replied Tacy. "I can't think of anyone I'd feel safer about promising to like." This struck her so funny that she burst out laughing. "Wilt thou, Betsy Ray, take me, Tacy Kelly, in holy bonds of friendship?"

"I wilt," chanted Betsy.

"Me, too!" shouted Tib, and began to fling leaves with such vigor that presently Tacy was gasping in the grass and Betsy's hair had fallen down.

She twisted it up determinedly.

"Stop acting like five-year-olds! Seriously, isn't it a grand idea?"

"It's a marvelous idea."

"It's a swell idea. Especially," added Tib, reaching for a grape, "if we give lots of parties."

"Oh, yes, we'll give parties and invite the fraternity men."

"What fraternity men?"

"Why, the boys." Betsy opened the box of crackers and they all began to munch. "We three will write the constitution and the ritual. And then we'll send invitations to the girls and ask them to join, and we'll have a meeting and initiate them."

"Who shall we ask?"

"Just the Crowd. Sororities are terribly exclusive. Let's see, there are three of us. Carney, Alice, Winona and Irma make seven. It would be nice to have eight, to make two tables of cards."

"Katie is pretty lonesome now that Julia's gone away. If you don't think she's too old . . ." Tacy hesitated.

"I'd love to have Katie. She's such a good sport."

"And we wouldn't always have to have a chaperone if she was along," Tib pointed out.

"That's right. Now we have to think of a name."

Betsy stretched out on her back. Tib sat with her face in her hands. Tacy dropped her head into crossed arms. There was silence in the grove, except for the rustling made by an exploring squirrel.

"These aren't oak trees, if you're looking for nuts," Betsy murmured. "Go away and let us concentrate."

She sat up suddenly.

"Do you think the name ought to be serious? We three feel serious about it, of course. But you know Winona. We'll have to make it sort of devilish to appeal to her."

"How about Eight Devils?" Tib inquired.

Betsy and Tacy stared in admiring unbelief.

"Eight Devils!" "Why, that's perfect!" "Tib Muller, I didn't think you had it in you!"

Surprised but elated at this triumph, Tib preened herself. "I think it's pretty good, too."

"Eight Devils!" Betsy repeated. "Now we have to put it into Greek. Who do we know who speaks Greek?"

"Probably Miss Erickson does, but I wouldn't ask her, the old pill!"

"Miss Bangeter knows everything, but she might not . . . she might not . . ." Betsy didn't finish the sentence. The others understood.

"Miss Sparrow would know." Miss Sparrow was Deep Valley's popular librarian.

"Of course. We'll ask Miss Sparrow. It's only the word eight we need to bother about. Devil begins with D and I know the Greek letter. It's shaped like a triangle. It's Delta."

"We're the Eight Deltas," shouted Tib. She jumped to her feet and started shwushing through the leaves. "I'll make the invitations, Betsy. I'll draw horns in all the corners and maybe a devil's pitchfork."

"Swell. We'll make them tomorrow after school."

"When will we write the constitution and stuff?"

"The day after that." Betsy rocked with joy. "Let's have the initiation Saturday night. We can have it at my house."

"Let's have a mock initiation before the real one. Put ice down their backs—that sort of thing."

"Oh, let's!"

"I feel as though we were kids again, making up a club," said Tib.

Betsy turned on her indignantly. "This isn't any kiddish club, Tib Muller! It's a sorority. You're going to take a vow never to get mad at us."

"I never get mad at you anyway."

"She's hopeless," Betsy said to Tacy. "Let's go ask Miss Sparrow."

They went back to Old Mag, who whinnied a

welcome. Betsy fixed the checkrein, and they climbed into the surrey. They drove down Agency Hill to the library, talking all the way about pins, grips, pass-words, whistles and salutes. With windblown hair and pink cheeks they burst in on Miss Sparrow.

"Miss Sparrow, what's the Greek word for eight?"

"Eight? Let me see! Why, it's o k t Ω," she replied.

"How do you spell it?"

"O-K-T-O."

"That's all!"

"Thank you!"

They rushed back outside. "We're the Okto Deltas!" "The Okto Deltas!"

"It sounds wonderful!" Betsy exclaimed, blissfully uncritical of the fact that it was a hybrid name, that Okto was a Greek word while Delta was only the Greek initial of an English word. It sounded just as good as Epsilon Iota.

Next day, all three were wool-gathering in classes. They deluged one another with notes and dodged their mystified friends. After school they went down-town and purchased cardboard, orange and black crayons, orange and black crepe paper. Orange and black, they had decided, were to be the Okto Delta colors.

They went to Tib's house, and locked in her room, they made the invitations. Tib cut the cardboard into diamond shaped pieces, which she folded into double triangles. The outer flap was colored orange and outlined in black to make a Delta. Superimposed was the black letter O with a devil curled inside. On the inner flap, the recipient was invited to come to Betsy's house on Saturday night to join the mystic order of Okto Delta.

Tib mailed the invitations next morning on her way to school, and when the three girls gathered that afternoon at Tacy's house, Katie's invitation, postmarked and looking very official, lay on the hall table.

They locked themselves in Tacy's room and began the constitution, Tib writing, Betsy dictating, Tacy adding witty bits. Before they had finished, the telephone began to ring. The other girls had come from school and found their invitations.

Excitement seethed over the wire and through the Crowd next day. When the boys found every girl engaged for Saturday night, they were curious and annoyed.

On Saturday it started to rain, a steady downpour.

"It's perfect, just perfect for an initiation," Betsy rejoiced.

Tacy and Tib came for supper, and after supper, in spite of the rain, Mr. and Mrs. Ray obligingly went to the Majestic, taking Margaret with them.

The first thing the girls did was lock all the doors and pull the shades. They tacked blankets over the parlor windows. There were orange and black candles in readiness but they didn't light them. Instead, when they had finished their work, they extinguished all lights everywhere.

The initiates found a dead black house veiled with sheets of rain. Early arrivals were forced to stand on the porch until all five had come. When the door was opened, Irma entered first.

"Shake the hand of friendship," said a deep sepulchral voice. Irma clasped a shadowy hand. Then her terrified scream rang out. Carney followed and she screamed. So did Alice. Winona and Katie were made of sterner stuff. Katie grasped the hand without a word, and Winona cried scornfully, "Calm yourselves, children! It's just a glove filled with cracked ice."

In the jet black parlor they were told to kneel in a circle. Again each girl screamed in turn as a small piece of ice slithered down her back. They were told by the sepulchral voice, sounding now more like Tacy's, and shaky with laughter, that they must eat worms.

"Sure. I like worms," said Winona. "Can I have a second helping? It's spaghetti, kids."

"It isn't! It's worms! It's horrible!"

The pandemonium became so great that it seemed best to light the candles. The founders were revealed dressed in sheets trimmed with black and orange crepe paper.

"Now sit down in a row. Make quick!" commanded Tib.

Betsy unfolded a sheet of foolscap paper and began to read.

"Respectfully submitted, the Constitution of the Okto Delta sorority. . . ." A sorority, she paused to explain, was a sisterhood. They were banding themselves together into a sisterhood.

"Hi, Sister Biscay," Winona hailed Irma.

"Howdy, Sister Root," cried Katie.

Tib rushed to silence them and Betsy continued:

"'Okto,' be it understood, is a Greek word meaning eight. 'Delta' is the Greek equivalent of the English letter D, which in this case stands for Devils, leaving the translated name of the sorority—"

"Eight Devils!" Winona interrupted. "Whoopee!"

Betsy frowned severely.

"The purpose of the sorority," she went on, "is to have a good time. The only theory it has to expound is, 'Laugh and the world laughs with you.' Requirements are being jolly, sticking by the bunch, and treating everybody square."

She proceeded to the rules and by-laws.

The officers, elected by ballot once a year, would be president, secretary-treasurer and sergeant-at-arms. The initiation fee would be two cents, the monthly dues ten cents. Money thus accumulated was to be used at the discretion of a social committee.

This committee, composed of two girls, would make arrangements for at least one festivity every two weeks.

"For example," Betsy interjected, "dances, picnics, cross-country tramps, mock weddings and stag parties."

Each member was to entertain the sorority every eighth Saturday evening in alphabetical order. Refreshments would be served.

"And they'd better be good!" someone shouted.

"We must now take the sacred vow of friendship," Betsy said, and Tib went around with an ink pot and a pen and everyone was asked to sign.

Winona took the pen doubtfully. "Do you mean that I have to stay friends with all of you forever?"

"That's right," Betsy replied.

"What if Irma takes Squirrelly away from me?"

"She can't. She's your sister in Okto Delta. She has to leave all our beaux alone."

"Heck!" said Winona, signing. "That alone is worth the dues."

Irma threw a sofa cushion.

"Sister Biscay! Sister Root!" cried Tib, dashing about.

Order was restored and elections were held.

Carney was elected president.

"I don't mind mentioning to the Sistren," Betsy said, "that I expect to be secretary-treasurer. I want the fun of writing up the minutes. I've even bought a notebook. See?"

"And I don't mind mentioning," said Tib, "that I expect to be sergeant-at-arms. You notice how well I've been keeping order. I'm little, but oh my!"

Obligingly, the Sistren made Betsy secretary-treasurer and Tib sergeant-at-arms. Betsy whipped out a pencil and began to write the minutes, reading them aloud when she thought they were exceptionally brilliant.

"The first thing to do," said Carney, taking charge, "is to decide on a whistle. We simply have to have a whistle. Otherwise how would we know whether it was an Okto Delta trying to call us away from our supper or just some dumb boy?"

"Yes, how?" asked Winona. "That's what I'd like to know."

"I will now listen," said Carney, "to any whistles the Sistren care to propose."

The response was a blast of whistles, loud, soft and breathy, in all combinations of notes.

"Wait!" cried Betsy. "Don't decide yet! I've got a wonderful one, but I can't seem to make it come."

She struggled but in vain. The Sistren waited loyally. They clapped her on the back. The sergeant-at-arms brought a glass of water. Still no whistle, and Alice grew tired of waiting.

"How's this?" she asked. Her whistle came clear

and firm: "Dee *Dee* Dee Dee Dee Dee Dee Dee!"

"Oh, that's cute!"

"That's grand."

"Let's take that one."

"Sister Morrison," scribbled Betsy, "proposed a whistle which was whistled and approved as whistled. Sister Root offered a handshake which was shook and approved as shook. Sister K. Kelly offered a salute which was saluted and approved as saluted.

"The Sistren Biscay, T. Kelly and Ray were appointed by the president to look up the matter of pins. A more suitable committee couldn't have been appointed. Sister Ray is especially competent. Long live our wise president!"

The pins, it was decided, when Betsy stopped reading aloud, would be engraved with the Okto Delta symbol, the triangle with a circle inside, such as Tib had drawn on the invitations.

"Gee, I'm important!" Tib said. "I thought up the name and I drew the first Okto Delta sign. What would you all have done if I'd stayed in Milwaukee?"

"I think we ought to entertain the boys," Winona broke in. "After all, there are other girls in school. If we're busy every Saturday night our boys will find someone to take out."

"Freshmen, probably."

"Yes. They certainly fall for the freshmen."

"Maybe they'll get up a fraternity," Betsy suggested.

"Eight boys, to match our sorority."

There was a chorus of approving cheers.

Nobody wanted to play cards that night. Making plans was much more entertaining. They had refreshments—sandwiches, cocoa and whipped-cream cake—and Winona played the piano.

> *"Morning Cy,*
> *Howdy Cy,*
> *Gosh darn, Cyrus, but you're*
> *Looking spry. . . ."*

They barn-danced. They cake-walked. They practised high kicking. Mr. and Mrs. Ray and Margaret came in before it was over, but secret affairs had all been disposed of so their presence didn't matter. They finished the whipped-cream cake, while the fun went on.

Tib stayed all night with Betsy and they talked the evening over jubilantly as they undressed and put on what Betsy, copying Julia, called their "dream robes."

"I never had so much fun in my life," Tib declared. "I'm so glad you thought of making up a sorority."

"It did go over with a bang," Betsy replied.

And it did. It was as great a success as she had hoped it would be.

"Now," she thought with satisfaction, waiting for sleep to come, "I'm going to begin to do things."

10
The Old Pill

SHE DID BEGIN to do things. But they weren't, or at least the first one wasn't, the sort of things that she had in mind. The first effect of Okto Delta in Betsy's life was catastrophic.

The excitement of the girls did not exhaust itself over the weekend, which was filled with feverish telephoning and rushing from house to house to discuss the new organization. The boys beseiged them with questions.

"What does Okto Delta stand for?"

"Don't you wish you knew!"

"Show me the grip. Come on, I won't tell."

"Tony Markham! Don't you know that sororities are secret?"

"Aw, it's only a club!"

"It's nothing whatever like a club," responded the indignant Okto Deltas.

The high school, when it convened on Monday, was as obtuse as Tony. It was accustomed to clubs which sprang up all the time like eager mushrooms, and it didn't know the difference that Greek letters made. It didn't realize at first how exclusive and important sororities were.

The girls enjoyed mystifying everyone.

"Sister Ray!"

"Sister Kelly!"

"Hi there, Sister in Okto Delta!"

"What is this Okto Delta?" fellow students inquired in complete good humor.

"Just wait! You'll find out!"

Betsy, in a line of marchers heading for the Latin class, passed Winona heading for the physics lab. These lines were fairly rigid. Students were not supposed to break away nor pause for conversation. But passing Betsy, the irrepressible Winona gave the Okto Delta whistle, "Dee *Dee* Dee Dee Dee Dee Dee Dee." She leaned out to take Betsy's hand in the Okto Delta grip. She gave the Okto Delta salute, four fingers lifted on either side of her head, and then on a sudden inspiration, crooked the fingers to make horns. Betsy burst out laughing and Miss Erickson, standing at the door of the classroom, regarded her disapprovingly.

Betsy and Tacy, who usually sat side by side, happened to be separated by a desk or two in Latin class. Bursting to tell Tacy about Winona's antics, Betsy raised her hand. Miss Erickson responded coldly, "Yes?"

"May I please speak to Tacy?"

"Certainly not," replied Miss Erickson. "Anything you have to say to Tacy can wait until the end of the period."

Betsy was annoyed. She was not accustomed to being snubbed in the Deep Valley High School. While Miss Erickson was explaining a difficult passage she wrote a note to Tacy.

"Erickson won't let me speak to you, the old pill. But after class I have a joke to tell you. Thy faithful Sister in Okto Delta, Betsy."

Folding this and marking it with Tacy's name, she passed it along the row to Tacy. Miss Erickson slapped her book shut.

"Betsy Ray! You may bring that note to me."

Betsy blushed. She remembered "the old pill" and blushed more deeply still. Of course, Miss Erickson might throw the note in the waste basket without reading it. That, thought Betsy virtuously, would be the honorable thing to do. But she might conceivably read it.

"If she does," thought Betsy defiantly, "it's just too bad."

She took the note, walked to the front of the room and held it out.

To her surprise Miss Erickson didn't take it. Instead she said, "We would all like to know what business you and Tacy have that is important enough to interrupt Cataline's orations. You may read the note to the class."

"Not . . . aloud!" Betsy cried.

"That is what I said," Miss Erickson answered.

"I . . . I'd rather not."

"You should have thought of that before you wrote it."

Betsy turned a still deeper crimson. After a brief, desperate hesitation, she threw off her accustomed droop, stood erect and read: "Erickson won't let me speak to you, the old pill. But after class I have a joke to tell you. Thy faithful Sister in Okto Delta, Betsy."

There was an aghast silence in the Cicero classroom.

Joe Willard, who never reacted like other people, looked amused, but everyone else looked frightened. Tacy was so pale that her freckles stood out.

Betsy glanced furtively toward Miss Erickson. She, too, was blushing. Angry color ran from the edge of her bright yellow hair down to her stiff white collar.

"Betsy," said Miss Erickson, "take that note to Miss Bangeter. Tell her the circumstances under which you read it to the class."

"Yes, ma'am," Betsy replied. She folded the note and went out.

Years seemed to fall away as she stood in the empty hall. She felt as though she were a little girl again in grade school, sent by the teacher to another room with a note. She had been proud then, but she had always felt a little frightened, too.

The hall was surrounded by classrooms from which came the murmur of monotonous voices. There was a water fountain, and she took a drink. She went to the cloakroom mirror and fluffed her hair aimlessly without really looking at her burning face.

Miss Bangeter's office was behind the assembly room. Miss Clarke, in charge of the study period there, smiled brightly as Betsy walked through. Betsy forced a sickly smile in return.

Being sent to Miss Bangeter was a strangely powerful chastisement. She was not unduly severe; she was known to be just and even generous. But she was such an awesome personage, she lived on such Olympian heights that there was a profound humiliation merely in bringing wrongdoing into her presence.

Knocking at the door Betsy reflected that it was the first time she had been sent to the principal's office for a reprimand. She had seen it happen dozens of times to boys and girls she knew. It was always happening to Winona. But Betsy Ray was supposed to be a different kind of person. She was the kind who is elected to class office, who has conferences with the teachers on school affairs, not her own misdemeanors. This was plain in the expression which crossed Miss Bangeter's face when she saw who had entered.

"Yes, Betsy," she said pleasantly. "What is it?"

Betsy's face was still suffused with crimson. She walked slowly and her throat was so dry that she could hardly speak.

"Miss Erickson asked me to give you this note."

"Miss Erickson wrote me a note?" Miss Bangeter sounded puzzled. Obviously she could not understand why Betsy was so perturbed.

"She didn't write it," Betsy said. "I did. I wrote it to Tacy or rather . . ." she paused. "Miss Erickson asked me to tell you the full circumstances, so I'll have to go a little farther back. I asked to speak to Tacy during class and Miss Erickson wouldn't let me."

"Was it about a personal matter?" Miss Bangeter asked judicially.

"Yes," said Betsy. "I couldn't speak to Tacy so I wrote her a note, and Miss Erickson saw me passing it and asked me to bring it to the front and read it out loud. So I did." Betsy gulped. "She told me to bring it to you."

Miss Bangeter accepted the folded paper and laid it aside. She leaned forward, crossing her arms on the desk, looking into Betsy's face with keen, grave eyes. She spoke in a tone of dignified intimacy.

"Just what do you think of all this, Betsy?"

"I think I acted very foolishly, but I think, too—" Betsy's tone grew resentful, and she paused.

"I know," said Miss Bangeter, "you think that Miss Erickson shouldn't have read your note. But you must take into consideration that she is a young, inexperienced teacher. She's just out of college, you know.

"Before you judge Miss Erickson, I suggest that you judge yourself. Wasn't it impudent to write a note after you had been refused permission to speak? Shouldn't you have accepted Miss Erickson's ruling not to discuss this matter with Tacy during class? Couldn't it have waited anyway? Was it really important?"

Betsy felt tears come into her eyes. She cried easily,

disgustingly so, she always thought. She was resolved not to cry now so she dared not speak. She clamped her jaws so firmly that she looked like a squirrel stuffed with nuts. Reaching out she opened the note and spread it in front of Miss Bangeter.

Miss Bangeter read it. A lightning flicker of amusement was gone so quickly that Betsy was not positive she had seen it, although she thought she had and it cheered her up a little.

"What do you think you ought to do?" Miss Bangeter asked.

"Go back and apologize, I suppose," muttered Betsy.

"Right," returned the principal crisply. "And I should say that it ought to be in front of the class. Don't you think so? Since the whole class heard the note?"

Betsy nodded. She got up. "Thank you, Miss Bangeter," she said and slipped miserably out the door.

Back in the cloakroom she looked into the mirror, with purpose this time. She ran her back comb through her hair, rubbed a chamois skin over her nose. She returned to the drinking fountain and took another drink. She reached the door of Miss Erickson's room, but she stood so long without opening it that it seemed to her she had been standing there for years and would be there forever. At last, with false briskness, she turned the knob.

Silence fell as she entered. Cicero's finest oratorical flights could not compete with this.

"Miss Erickson," said Betsy. But she looked at Tacy who was staring down, suffering. She turned determinedly and faced Miss Erickson. "I'm very sorry that I was impudent," she said in a firm voice.

"Did Miss Bangeter tell you to apologize to me?"

"No, ma'am," said Betsy. "But I told her I was going to."

"Very well," said Miss Erickson. "Your apology is accepted. But I will not let you be tempted to write more notes. You may move down to this front seat. Hazel will change with you. She can be trusted in the back row."

Hazel Smith was a friendly, freckle-faced girl whom Betsy liked. She looked sheepish as she carried her books back to Betsy's old seat. Betsy took her own load of books and moved to the front seat, another common indignity which she now received for the first time in her life.

It was a minor sensation around school, Betsy Ray calling Miss Erickson a pill, being sent to the principal, being moved to a front seat. Betsy acted jaunty about it, especially with the girls after school.

"After all," she said, "I was just living up to Okto

Delta. You know that fatal D!"

She told the story at the supper table, and Mrs. Ray was indignant with Miss Erickson.

"I never heard of such a thing," she said. "You learn in kindergarten that you don't read other people's mail."

"It's kindergarten stuff," said Mr. Ray, "that school isn't for writing notes, passing notes, receiving notes, reading notes, or anything else of that nature."

"You're right," Betsy admitted glumly. She felt extremely foolish. Okto Delta had started out wrong. It was different than she had thought it would be. It didn't seem to tie up with those plans she had made for the winter.

Those fine lofty plans came to vivid life a few days later when the family drove out to Murmuring Lake. Mr. and Mrs. Ray had been married there, at Pleasant Park across the lake from the Inn, and weather permitting they made this romantic pilgrimage every October fifteenth.

This year the day was red-gold and crisp. The Inn was festive under scarlet vines but a big stove crackled in the almost empty dining room. Mrs. Van Blarcum hurried in and out, and Mr. Van Blarcum, with plenty of time to spare as usual, chatted with them while they ate the traditionally magnificent dinner.

Afterwards, while Mr. Ray smoked his cigar, Betsy ran down to say hello to Pete. She couldn't find him, but standing on the dock she looked across the cool, twinkling water to Babcock's Bay and thought about the day she had sat in a rowboat there and mapped out her winter.

She had resolved, first of all, to try to take Julia's place. She hadn't, she admitted, done very well at that. She was almost never at home, and she remembered, with a twinge, rebuffing Margaret on the day she and Tacy and Tib planned Okto Delta.

She had resolved to excel in school, to become a leader, and instead she had had a quarrel with Miss Erickson. Joe Willard had dropped out of her plans, too, but that wasn't her fault.

"Anyhow, what's Joe Willard to me? I'm getting plenty of attention from boys this year," Betsy said aloud. She went on in her thoughts, "The only thing I've stuck to is my music. And I don't think I have a shred of talent for it. Of course—I invented Okto Delta. . . ."

That hadn't helped so far, though. It had even hindered.

She frowned at the distant blur of yellow cottonwood trees rimming Babcock's Bay and with intense concentration re-established in her mind the pattern she had set for her winter: thoughtfulness at home, good work at school, piano lessons. . . .

"And now," she added, "making something out of Okto Delta . . . something good."

She held Margaret's hand cozily during the afternoon ramble around Pleasant Park. As usual, with her father smiling in calm content and her mother vivaciously explaining, they visited the oak tree under which the two had become engaged. They stood in the bay window where the marriage had taken place, and had tea with the wife of the farmer who now owned the house.

Although they all missed Julia, they had a happy, satisfying time. And driving home Betsy told Margaret stories. At last, lulled by the beat of Old Mag's hoofs and the rhythmic creaking of the wheels, they sank into drowsy silence.

Betsy's thoughts went back to her plans for the winter. If a sorority was going to be any help, it must be a little more serious. Epsilon Iota, which Julia hoped so much to join, sounded very serious. But Okto Delta hadn't turned out that way.

"I must, I must, bring out the serious side," thought Betsy, rolling through the dark.

11

"Hence, Loathed Melancholy!"

MAKING OKTO DELTA SERIOUS was certainly uphill work.

The juniors in the sorority, who were studying Foundations of English Literature under Miss Fowler, had made the acquaintance of Milton's poems, "L'Allegro" and "Il Penseroso." Winona stalked into every Okto Delta meeting flinging up a long arm and crying,

"Hence, loathed Melancholy!" And the Sistren would chant in uproarious sing-song:

"Haste-thee-nymph-and-bring-with-thee-
Jest-and-youth-ful-Joll-i-tee-
Quips-and-cranks-and-wan-ton-Wiles-
Nods-and-Becks-and-Wreath-ed-Smiles . . ."

If Betsy ever shouted, "Hence, vain deluding joyes!" her voice was certainly drowned out in the racket.

But it is doubtful that she ever shouted, in spite of the good resolutions she had made riding home from Murmuring Lake. She relished the flattering laughter that arose when she read the minutes of the meetings.

"The second meeting of the Okto Delta sorority was held on October seventeenth at the home of Sister Root. The meeting was called to order by the president, and the Sistren showed undue mirth and hilarity during the reading of the minutes. (The secretary-treasurer is very witty, as well as pretty and good.)

"The appointed committee reported on the subject of pins. Sistren Biscay, T. Kelly and Ray had conducted this matter with their usual efficiency, and a local jewelry store is now engraving eight gold pins with the mystic Okto Delta symbols. The price of the pins should not cause fathers undue suffering for they are a mere one dollar per. They will be delivered shortly and will doubtless cause a sensation in the Deep Valley High.

"Sister Morrison moved that the meetings always be held in the afternoon. She was hooted down and didn't mind at all; it had been her mother's idea, anyway. Sister K. Kelly suggested a cross-country tramp for the following Thursday. This was agreed upon, one of her chocolate cakes being part of the bargain.

"Sister Root proposed opening the sorority to boys. This also was hooted down. Sister T. Kelly, who doesn't like boys, grew as red as her own locks with rage. Sister Root would have been abashed if she had been anyone but Sister Root. 'Let them get up a fraternity of their own,' said the wise secretary-treasurer.

"After this business meeting, conducted with skill and dispatch by our honored president, the Sistren brought out sewing bags, and their lily-white fingers flashed as they crocheted, tatted, embroidered, or just plain sewed. Sister Ray worked on the world's most famous jabot, destined for Sister Sibley's swan-like neck. They also toasted marshmallows and discussed important matters: to wit, boys.

"Sistren T. Kelly, Muller, Root and Ray gave a drama in one act entitled, *Woman versus Woman*, or *She Loved but Killed Him*. The actors were superb. The audience watched the brilliant portrayal of love and hatred with tense faces, swayed from tears to laughter.

"The Sistren were then served with a delicious lunch. They are noted for their delicate appetites, but on this occasion they unbent and really ate. The meeting then adjourned."

This meeting was described, a trifle more formally, in Winona's father's paper, the *Deep Valley Sun*. There was a good deal of talk about Okto Delta around school next day.

On the following week the sorority met with Carney.

"The Sistren didn't have a very successful business meeting for they were disturbed by the male element, including Dave Hunt. (The secretary-treasurer writes this name with a delicate blush; she thinks he's cute.) After an unladylike chase over the Sibley premises and the capture of several trophies, including Cab Edward's cap, the Sistren returned to the house and henceforth the male element inspected proceedings from the windows.

"The minutes of the previous meeting were read and objected to, although it has slipped my mind entirely why. I am sure it was a silly objection as Sister Ray always writes up the minutes in a concise, dignified manner, and no legitimate objection could possibly be found. Sister Biscay handed out the new pins and with difficulty collected a dollar from each member.

"After the business meeting the Sistren played cards. To find their partners they drew sticks of licorice tied with orange bows. For a head prize Sister Sibley gave an orange and black pincushion and for a consolation prize a lemon.

"When the delectable refreshments were served, Sister Root again brought up the matter of inviting boys into the order and seemed to receive some support from Sister Muller, who is too small to have any weight in such discussions. Both of them were sternly rebuked. Sister Sibley, our noble president, announced that she has learned to drive her father's auto and will take the Sistren in a body to the St. John game."

This meeting likewise was written up, in a slightly different vein, by the *Deep Valley Sun*, and the high school looked with interest at the gold pins, engraved with a triangle having a circle inside, which appeared on eight shirt waists the following Monday.

"Sister Biscay entertained the Okto Deltas at a particularly skippy luncheon. Places at the table were marked by clothes pin dolls dressed in orange and black. Five hundred was played, with only a few interruptions in the form of fist fights, ragtime, Sister Muller's 'Baby Dance,' and the 'Cat Duet' sung with feeling and some masterly caterwauls by Sistren T. Kelly and Ray. The head prize was won by Sister

Morrison. It was a peachy little doll dressed in an orange and black princesse dress. The booby prize, won by Sister Muller, consisted of a soap teddy bear. A gentle hint, Sister Muller!

"Sister Root insisted at the top of her voice that if we won't let the boys join, we simply must entertain them. Sister Muller seconded the motion, although anyone as small as she is should be seen and not heard. Then Sister K. Kelly, a genius of the first order, quieted everyone with a terrific announcement.

"She said that it was the Sistren Kellys' turn to entertain next time and that, since there were two of them, it would be only fair for them to entertain twice as many people. Therefore, each girl might invite a boy.

"Great was the rush for Sister Biscay's telephone, and the Sistren, who are well known for their beauty, charm and initiative, especially initiative, had no difficulty in ensnaring eight hapless males. This party will occur on the night of the St. John game to which Sister Sibley will take us in her auto. It should be quite a day."

It was. The St. John game was always the climax of the football season in Deep Valley. Excitement would have mounted in all breasts even though there had been no Okto Delta plans afoot. But these grew more sensational all the time.

Tib danced up to Betsy, Tacy and Carney in the Social Room.

"I have some of that cardboard left over from the invitations, and those orange and black crayons. Wouldn't you like to have me make an Okto Delta poster to put on the front of Carney's auto?"

The response was enthusiastic:

"Marvelous."

"Let's make an Okto Delta pennant, too."

"How about some orange and black arm bands?"

"Maybe," Carney suggested, "we ought to wear the school colors?"

"Oh, sure! But we could combine them with the Okto Delta colors."

"Let's all dress alike."

"What shall it be? Sweaters and tams? Gee, I wish we had black sweaters and orange tams!"

"Maybe next year. . . ." Betsy began, but Carney interrupted.

"Don't make me feel bad. Next year I'll be at Vassar."

"Just think!" cried Betsy. "You'll be an alumnus, the very first Okto Delta alumnus!"

"Betsy!" said Carney. "We're females, and the word is alumna."

"It's alumnae, I think," Tib interrupted earnestly. "I've never studied Latin but I used to hear them use that word at Browner."

"Oh, let's just say alum," said Betsy. "It sounds more casual, anyway. You will be the first Okto Delta alum."

On the day of the game the eight girls met at the

Sibleys', all wearing sweaters and tams with orange and black arm bands and carrying an Okto Delta pennant. Tib had made a huge Okto Delta poster which they fastened to the front of the automobile. Mr. and Mrs. Sibley laughed at these arrangements but their main interest was in Carney's manipulation of the steering wheel. She had been practising driving for two months now and was almost as proficient as her father, who still relapsed occasionally into "Giddap!" and "Whoa!"

It was an overcast day in November. The trees had been stripped of their last withered leaves. Winter was sharpening its knives, but Okto Delta made its own warmth as the girls, flushed and laughing, crowded into the automobile.

Carney's brother cranked the machine, which began to quiver and make explosive noises. Shortly it was rolling down Front Street, where the gaudy sign on the front, the pennant, waved by Tib sitting on Winona's lap, all the bright colors and frenzied cheering caused the most insensitive passers-by to stop, look and listen.

Waving and cheering, the Okto Deltas rode on to the football field at the edge of town. There were no stands. Spectators usually stood or walked up and down the side lines. Occasionally someone watched from a buggy or an automobile, but this wasn't considered sporting.

The Okto Deltas were full of school spirit, and after their spectacular arrival had been fully appreciated they piled out of the car.

Hazel Smith caught sight of Betsy, waved and started toward her. Then she noticed the display of sweaters and tams, the orange and black colors, the new pins gleaming. Trying to act as though she had been heading somewhere else, she angled away.

"Hi, Hazel!" Betsy cried. "Come on over!"

Hazel came, but diffidently.

"Stay and watch the game with us," Betsy said. She shouldn't have said it. It had been agreed that the Okto Deltas were going to remain as a unit throughout the whole game. But she thought Hazel looked odd.

"No," said Hazel, "I'm with somebody else. Is this your new club? Pretty skippy, aren't you?" She said it good naturedly, but Betsy was troubled by the speed with which she ducked away.

The Okto Deltas had no difficulty watching the game as a unit, at least so far as girls were concerned. No other girls approached them. Most of the boys they knew were either on the football team or among the scrubs who were also in uniform, hoping to be called as replacements. Lloyd Harrington wasn't on the team and he joined Tib at once, remaining beside her to instruct and explain. Tib was an excellent vacant-lot football player herself, but she asked naive questions and listened round-eyed.

Another boy on the side lines was Joe Willard.

Joe had never been able to go out for football because he worked after school. Heretofore, he had not been able even to come to the games. But he was here today as representative of the *Deep Valley Sun*. Bareheaded, wearing a heavy blue turtle-neck sweater, a swatch of yellow copy paper stuck in his hip pocket, he dashed up and down the side lines abreast of the battling teams. His face was glowing with excitement and Betsy remembered Cab telling her last year that Joe was good at football. He could have been an outstanding athlete, Stewie, the coach, had said. Joe had never seemed to mind not having time for athletics. He had said offhandedly that he would play in college. But watching him now, Betsy realized that it must have been a real deprivation.

Just as the first half ended without a score, Joe's peregrinations brought him upon the Okto Deltas. They were standing in front of their decorated auto.

"Hey, what's all this?" he asked, looking at Betsy.

"Haven't you heard about the new sorority? I thought you were expected to keep up with the news." Betsy smiled saucily, glad that there were plenty of curls pulled out beneath her tam.

"Only important news. What's the name of the thing?"

"Okto Delta. Greek letters, you know."

"Greek letters?" Joe looked puzzled. "I got ambitious and tried to learn some Greek one time. Okto isn't a letter; it's a word."

"Oh, don't be like Gaston," said Betsy. "The effect is Greek letters."

"The effect," said Joe, his blue eyes roving over the group, "is kind of cute," with which remark he sauntered off. The disgustingly general compliment gave Betsy no pleasure. He was freer with compliments these days, which meant, in her opinion, that they were meaningless. She would have preferred the pretended insults she was sure he heaped on Phyllis.

The Okto Deltas, eight strong, began to shout:

> "We'll whoop her up for D. V.
> We've got 'em on the run,
> We're going to beat St. John's boys,
> And the fun is just begun.
> There's Larson, Hunt and Edwards,
> They'll hit that line a few,
> With such an aggregation,
> We won't do much to you."

Betsy shouted along with the rest, but her eyes followed Joe's retreating figure.

Phyllis Brandish was sitting in her auto. He joined her and sat there until the second half. When he got out, she followed, a chic, distinctive figure in a russet red suit, fur boa and muff. Furs were the rage that year. For a while she accompanied him in his rovings up and down the field. At last, with a small intimate wave of her hand which seemed to say that she couldn't keep up with him, she retired to her auto again.

In the second half each team made a touchdown. Then Dave Hunt, providentially long-legged, kicked a goal and Deep Valley won the game. The clamor was terrific. Joe Willard was bellowing like a madman. The Okto Deltas were screaming and jumping and hugging one another, and Betsy acted as frantic as everyone else. Yet she didn't feel particularly happy.

She looked beyond the joy-crazed crowd to the naked brown trees on the horizon. She noticed the long, grave bands of cloud in the west. She was aware that Joe had dashed to Phyllis' auto, cranked it and climbed in. It lumbered across the field, then flew down the road, taking the story of Deep Valley's triumph to the waiting presses. She felt depressed as she swayed lightly with her arms on the shoulders of the other girls, singing, "Cheer, cheer, the gang's all here."

"Wasn't Dave Hunt wonderful?"

"Marvelous!"

"I've yelled until I'm hoarse."

Not only the Okto Deltas but almost the entire student body returned up Front Street blowing horns, ringing bells, cheering, singing and yelling. The team went into the Y.M.C.A. for showers and rub downs but the hullabaloo continued in the street outside. Nearby delicatessens were raided for nourishment. The Okto Deltas secured jelly doughnuts and cream puffs.

"I dare you to give a cream puff to that policeman," Tacy challenged Winona.

"Sure. Why not?" Black eyes shining and white teeth gleaming, Winona loped over to Patrolman Reardon who accepted the squashy pastry with a grin.

The uproar continued, but Katie said, "Tacy and I have to go home if we're going to give a party tonight."

"Well, you're giving a party all right. A pretty important one, the first Okto Delta party with boys."

"We must all go home and start dressing."

"But I want to wait and see the team!" Tib cried, protesting.

Carney laughed. "Almost the whole team is coming to our party: Al, Squirrelly, Cab, Dennie. It's too bad Dave Hunt isn't in the Crowd."

But Dave Hunt hadn't yet started taking out girls. He looked at them with his serious dark blue eyes, but he didn't talk to them. Nobody even suggested that he was afraid. Dave Hunt was afraid of nothing. He would start taking girls out when he was good and ready, everyone agreed.

12

Agley-er and Agley-er

TIB WENT HOME WITH Betsy. She had brought her
"dream robe" to the Rays before the game and would
return to stay all night after the party. She and Betsy
burst in late for supper, windblown, ruddy, hoarse,
but ecstatic.

"What did you think of the game, Mr. Ray?—
Wasn't it wonderful?—Wasn't it divine?"

He forgave them for being late and Anna reheated their supper. Mrs. Ray and Margaret sat with them while they ate, listening to extravagant accounts of the Deep Valley football team's prowess.

It was almost like having Julia home again to have Tib dressing with Betsy for the party. Returning from the bathroom, freshly bathed and fragrant with talc, they laced up one another's corsets. Betsy had just started wearing a corset. Her mother had brought it to her after a trip to the cities to visit Julia. Tib's waist measured only eighteen inches but she urged Betsy to pull on the laces to make it smaller still.

Margaret brought Washington in to watch and Mrs. Ray darted in and out, as Betsy and Tib made elaborate toilets, talking, laughing, borrowing, lending, squinting into hand mirrors, revolving before the long glass.

Tib had made black and orange bows for them to wear in their hair.

"I'll do your hairs for you, Betsy," she offered. One of Tib's small Germanisms was saying "hairs" for "hair."

"All of them? Which ones?" Betsy teased her.

"Hair! Hair! Ach, will I never remember?"

She fluffed Betsy's hair over the wire "jimmy" into an airy pompadour.

Betsy was taking Tony to the party. She liked him

better than any other boy, although they were definitely on a brother-sister basis. He wasn't going with the Crowd so much this year. He had always seemed more mature than the others, and his new friends were older boys, who were out of school and considered a little wild. With the Rays, however, he was the same loyal, teasing, affectionate Tony. And he seldom failed to appear for Sunday night lunch.

Earlier in the season Betsy had thought it would be perfect if Tony would start going with Tib. She had hinted this to Tony but without success.

"Aw, she's still playing with doll clothes!" he would say, indulgently scornful. He patted Tib on her yellow head, swung her off the floor like a child. He was definitely not impressed.

But E. Lloyd Harrington was impressed. He had showered her with attentions and Tib had reciprocated by inviting him to the party tonight.

He called for them in his father's auto. Tony cranked, then climbed into the back seat beside Betsy, while Lloyd, with Tib at his side, proudly grasped the wheel. The cold wind blew past their faces and Betsy was glad that her carefully constructed coiffure was tied in place with a party scarf.

The Kellys lived in a sprawling old white house at the end of Hill Street. Betsy had lived in a yellow cottage opposite for the first fourteen years of her life.

Beyond these two houses, which ended the street, hills spread in a half open fan. They were brown and bleak tonight under the cold bright stars.

Betsy was pleased to be arriving in Lloyd's auto when she saw Irma alighting from Phil's machine. Inside the house there were black and orange decorations, and Winona was pounding on the piano.

Betsy was soon encircled. She was joyfully aware that she attracted boys more easily this year. Even Phil was looking at her with interest and when someone started to play "The Merry Widow Waltz," which had woven itself through their romance last spring, he came over to her.

She looked up at him, widening her eyes into what she hoped was a soulful gaze.

"I wondered whether you would come."

"Did you, really?"

"As long as I live I'll never hear 'The Merry Widow Waltz' without thinking of you."

They danced, and Betsy's dancing was one of her strong points. He was so fascinated that Irma was obliged to make an effort to recall him. True, it wasn't much of an effort. It was hardly more than lifting her finger. But to force Irma to any sort of effort was a triumph. She attracted simply by existing, a fact which continued to exasperate her Sistren in Okto Delta.

The success of the party was surpassed only by the terrific success of the refreshments. Everyone always looked forward to refreshments at the Kelly house. Tactfully seizing a moment when Katie's chocolate cake, smothered with thick fudge frosting, was being cut, the girls said what fun it would be if the boys got up a fraternity.

Lloyd seemed to like the idea. "We could have a fraternity house like the boys have up at the U. My Dad's made our barn into a garage, and there are a couple of rooms above it. I have a phonograph up there and some books. It would make a swell club-house."

Tony scoffed. "I don't like fraternities. Too many fellows left out. Besides, I wouldn't tie myself down about what I'm going to do every Saturday night."

But for a number of Saturday nights following the Kellys' party, boys, as well as girls, were busy with Okto Delta. Okto Delta meetings were practically parties, parents complained. Tib didn't complain. Just out of a girl's school, away from the strict influence of *Grosspapas* and *Grossmamas*, she was intoxicated with the freedom of life in Deep Valley. Tib, who could cook and sew, who had always been famous for her practicality and common sense, now thought of nothing but fun.

She and Betsy pursued it together. Tacy would have

been a welcome third but she wasn't interested in boys. She enjoyed hearing Betsy and Tib talk about their adventures, the plots and counterplots by which they proposed to snare this boy or that, but she took no share in such enterprises. She was studying singing with Mrs. Poppy; that was romance enough for her.

This was in November, when waves of ducks were passing through Minnesota on their way to the north country. Mr. Muller and Fred went hunting every Saturday, and Betsy took to going home with Tib after church for Sunday dinner: duck with apple dressing, dumplings, brown gravy, served with butter-drenched sweet potatoes and often topped off by apple pie which came to the table under a crown of whipped cream.

After these succulent feasts they sat in Tib's room and talked.

They talked about clothes, about the new princesse style party dresses they were having made for the holidays, about the furs—like Phyllis Brandish's—they hoped they would get for Christmas. They talked about face powders and finger nail polishes. They talked about perfumes. But especially they talked about boys.

Betsy, having seen so much of boys during the past two years, didn't think they were quite so wonderful as Tib did, but she considered them important. Like most high school girls, she wanted more than almost anything else to be popular with boys. And this year she could call herself that. Of course, she didn't have Irma's magic appeal nor Julia's devastating effect, but she had a little more than her share of attention.

She was gratified to discover that she could hold her own with Tib. Tib was so pretty, so enchanting, so beautifully dressed, Betsy wouldn't have been surprised nor even very resentful if Tib had put her in the shade. But she didn't. It was true that the boys who liked Tib thought of Betsy only as Tib's best friend, but it was equally true that the boys who liked Betsy found Tib merely "cute." Like Tony, they patted her on the head and forgot her. Just as Betsy had foreseen long ago in Milwaukee, she and Tib made an excellent team.

They often spoke of Dave Hunt, the most desirable unattached boy in school. Last summer at the lake, Betsy had thought he was drawn to her, but she was beginning to doubt it. She wasn't the only girl he gazed at, and because his blue eyes were so deep-set and serious the gaze seemed to hold more significance than, perhaps, it had.

As for Tib, although she valued the prestige created by Lloyd's admiration, her affections leaned toward Dennie. He was an ingratiating Irish boy with a curly tangle of hair, fuzzy eyebrows and a dimple in his chin. He liked to sing and act the clown. Dennie and Cab, Tib and Betsy made a rollicking foursome.

They planned little parties for four which they called "soirees." Betsy and Tib secretly nicknamed each other Madame DuBarry and Madame Pompadour. They addressed each other as "M.P." and "M.D.," to the boys' mystification. Tib loved to cook dainty little suppers, which she served by candlelight. Betsy enjoyed trying out dishes she had learned in Domestic Science, especially English Monkey, made in a chafing-dish.

They undeniably had fun. School, of course, suffered.

Betsy, Tacy and Tib had let autumn slip into winter without starting their herbariums for botany. The fall flowers were gone, withered and dead beneath the first delicate fall of snow.

"What will we do about it?" Tib asked anxiously.

"We'll just have to find more flowers in the spring. That's when they bloom, tra la."

Dennie gave a hint which retarded their progress in United States History.

"Know what I do when I haven't got my lesson? I yawn. Clarke always has to yawn back and when she gets started she can't stop. It slows things up a lot."

Betsy tried it and was fascinated by her success. Miss Clarke yawned so prettily, too, tapping her lips with white, almond-tipped fingers.

Miss Erickson couldn't be persuaded to yawn, and Betsy was cold to the eloquence of Cicero.

She worked for Miss Fowler in Foundations of English Literature but so far Miss Fowler hadn't given her exceptionally high marks. Her stories and essays were returned critically marked up with red pencil.

One day Miss Fowler asked her to stay after class. The little Bostonian looked up at Betsy with her very bright dark eyes.

"Betsy," she said in that odd accent like Miss Bangeter's, "I want to tell you a secret. Can you keep a secret?"

"Why, yes."

"You may have noticed that I am harder on you than on the others. I'm harder on you and Joe Willard. And I want you to know the reason why. It's because you have more talent than the others." She paused, then added earnestly, "I think you have a real gift for writing, and I'd like to help you develop it."

Betsy was so taken aback that she could hardly speak.

"I'd like to have you do that, Miss Fowler," she faltered. She blushed like a freshman. "I'll work hard."

Miss Fowler smiled. "I said the same thing to Joe. You two are going to be picked on."

After this Betsy worked even harder on Foundations

of English Literature. And she enjoyed the Girls Debating Club which argued in November that "Immigration should be further restricted." She and Hazel Smith were given the affirmative side. The more Betsy saw of Hazel the better she liked her. It would be fun, she thought, to have her at a party. But this was not immediately possible for she gave so many Okto Delta parties that she couldn't very well have the ordinary kind.

She continued to work hard on her music. She practised daily and looked forward to her lessons, although she felt increasingly sure that, in this field, she had no talent. But she liked Miss Cobb and her visits to the small, warm, geranium-scented house.

Always sociable, Betsy fell into the habit of going into the back parlor after her lessons and talking with Leonard. He liked to hear about Okto Delta, and leaning his bright head on a frail hand, his eyes smiling and his cheeks flushed, he listened to Betsy's stories about the meetings.

Last year at this time he had been out on the football field. This year his illness was so pronounced that his aunt talked of sending him to Colorado. Betsy remembered that his older brother and sister had already died of this disease, and she tried to make the Okto Delta meetings sound even funnier than they were.

"I wish you came for a lesson every day," Leonard told her, weak from laughter.

"You'd be practically an Okto Delta if I did. You're getting to know all the secrets of our order."

Leonard approved of Okto Delta, one of the few outside the membership who did.

Julia came home for Thanksgiving. The train swept down the track with a special brilliance because it carried Julia. She alighted looking citified, and soon filled the Ray house with color and excitement.

She had joined the Dramatic Club. She had been singing solos everywhere. Roger Tate was coming for the weekend.

She brought all the newest songs.

"You are my Rose of Mexico,
The one I loved so long ago. . . ."

The Crowd harmonized richly, standing around the piano. Tom Slade's violin accompanied them, for he had arrived from Cox Military, bringing, as usual, the latest slang. "Ain't it awful, Mabel!" reverberated through the Crowd.

The Rays and the Slades always had Thanksgiving dinner together. It was at the Ray house this year and was followed about twilight by Mr. Ray's turkey sandwiches and coffee, and Grandma Slade's stories.

Listening to these from a pillow in front of the fire, Betsy saw canoes on the river, the raw log cabins of the earliest settlers straggling along the river bank, the Indian Agency at the top of Agency Hill and the Indians coming to take possession of it. They had come in canoes and in dog carts, riding ponies and on foot; a picturesque invasion; not terrifying like the one some years later, when red men came down the Valley pillaging, burning and killing. Deep Valley, now so peaceful, had been a perilous frontier.

The day after Thanksgiving Roger arrived. With his padded shoulders and condescending air, he cut a swath in Deep Valley. Betsy didn't like him very well, although he brought her a fraternity pennant. Julia still gazed at him with the soulful look her sister tried to imitate, yet Betsy felt sure his time was running out.

He and Julia talked about Greek letter organizations. Four sororities were rushing Julia now, but she still preferred Epsilon Iota.

"You're an Epsilon Iota type," Roger assured her profoundly.

Of course, she couldn't be asked to join until spring, but the girls were still showering her with subtle attentions—sweet notes, wee bouquets, affectionate strolls on the campus.

Roger had asked her to wear his fraternity pin.

Julia explained this college custom to Betsy.

"It's almost like being engaged to wear a man's fraternity pin. I won't wear Roger's—I don't like him well enough. But pins certainly change hands fast up at the U."

Betsy rushed to Tib, "Let's let Cab and Dennie wear our Okto Delta pins. Just for a few days, to cause a sensation."

It caused a sensation indeed. Hurt and indignant, Lloyd wrote Tib a scathing note; she countered with a cold one; he wrote back terminating their romance.

"Ain't it awful, Mabel!" Tib said pertly.

They made up, and Lloyd started wearing her pin. Squirrelly had acquired Winona's and Tony was wearing Betsy's now.

The winter grew increasingly chaotic; it wasn't at all what Betsy had planned.

"My plans," she told Tacy, without perceptible regret, "are going agley-er and agley-er."

13
The Curling Iron

IN DECEMBER THE SNOW deepened, the ice on the river thickened, trees snapped with cold and sleigh bells were heard in the streets. As always when winter set in, the tempo of life quickened. Just as people walked faster to stir up their blood against the cold, so they threw themselves, with a sort of defiance, into a host of activities—lodge dances, church bazaars and suppers, club affairs, thimble bees.

Betsy and her mother went Christmas shopping. Betsy bought stickpin holders for the Okto Deltas, and her mother bought fine handkerchiefs on which she would sew lace for the High Fly Whist Club ladies.

Betsy, Tacy and Tib too went on their traditional Christmas shopping trip. It was glorious to have Tib back for that. Three abreast they swung along a crowded, festive Front Street. Their laughter froze above their lips into white clouds.

As when they were children, they shopped for everything: jewels, perfumes, toys, furs—especially furs this year. Yet they broke with the past. They made some purchases besides the Christmas tree ornaments which had once been the sole glittering purpose of the trip.

"We're growing up and I don't like it," said Tacy, as they sat in Heinz's later, drinking coffee.

"We *are!*" Betsy leaned forward suddenly, tense. "*Look* at us sitting here drinking coffee! Just look!"

Tib and Tacy, moved by earnestness, looked into the mirror which ran along the wall.

They saw three girls wearing big, stylish, top-heavy hats. Betsy's was covered with green wings. They had laid off their coats and their shirt waists were trim and snowy. Their finger nails were polished.

"I don't see anything so special," Tib remarked.

"Why, we're sitting here drinking coffee," Betsy repeated somewhat lamely. "And not just for a lark."

Tacy's thoughts followed hers.

"We're actually juniors," she said, "stopping in for coffee after shopping, not freshmen or sophomores pretending to be juniors stopping in for coffee after shopping."

Tib looked confused. "You usually take chocolate," she said. "I've just got you in the habit of coffee because I come from Milwaukee."

"But Tib!" Betsy cried. "That isn't the point. The point is that we're so frightfully old."

"We might have husbands waiting at home," said Tacy.

"Wanting their suppers," added Betsy.

"Oh, it's not that bad!" answered Tib and they all began to laugh.

"Anyway, we have packages to carry," said Tacy, reaching for her coat.

Packages began to pile up in drawers and closets at the Ray house. Carols were being practised by the choir. Betsy wondered what gave these songs their magic. One strain could call up the quivering expectancy of Christmas Eve, childhood, joy and sadness, the lonely wonder of a star.

Tacy sang at Rhetoricals, too full of Christmas

spirit even to be very frightened. She looked beautiful, Betsy thought, her head, with its heavy auburn braids, thrown back, her blue eyes luminous.

> *"I heard the bells on Christmas day,*
> *Their old familiar carols play,*
> *And wild and sweet the words repeat,*
> *Of Peace on Earth, Good Will to men."*

Betsy and Tib were very proud of her.

The Domestic Science class roasted a chicken. The girls gathered around Miss Benbow while she made the dressing, singed and washed the bird, stuffed it and sewed it up. She slid the pan expertly into the oven.

"Now, while it's roasting, I'll dictate general directions for roasting poultry."

Her voice was monotonous, her treatment of the subject less persuasive than the savory odors emanating from the oven. Betsy's thoughts drifted away.

"Betsy Ray."

"Yes, Ma'am." She roused herself quickly.

"Will you baste the chicken, please?"

Betsy rose slowly. "Baste the chicken!" What did that mean? She knew little about cooking. She walked to the stove slowly and pulled open the oven door.

"Baste the chicken!" But baste was something you did with a needle and thread. Miss Benbow had used a needle and thread when she sewed up the chicken. She wouldn't want it sewn up again though. Anyway, it would be too hot to touch.

Betsy looked around frantically, and Winona mouthed instructions. Tacy lifted an imaginary object, dipped it down and raised it up, over and over again.

"She must mean sewing," Betsy thought desperately.

Her immobility and all the gesturing attracted Miss Benbow's attention.

"What is it, Betsy? Why aren't you basting the chicken?"

"How can I?" Betsy blurted. "I haven't a needle and thread!"

Laughter broke over the classroom. Betsy turned scarlet but she laughed, too, and so did Miss Benbow.

"Tacy," she said. "Show her!"

So Tacy came forward and the gesture which Betsy had interpreted as sewing proved to be spooning delicious juices over the crisply browned bird. Later this provided chicken sandwiches for the first of the Christmas parties.

A bigger one, a dance in Schiller Hall, was planned for the last night of school. Boys were maddeningly slow with their invitations as usual, and the Social Room buzzed with speculation when the last week began.

Betsy revolved her chances. They were fairly good, she thought. But she must look pretty tomorrow. She would wear her new Dutch collar. She was so absorbed in plans when the bell rang and they all marched into the assembly room that she gave only a careless glance to the note lying on her desk.

It was written in pencil on a sheet of notebook paper; it looked ordinary enough. But it should have been illuminated on parchment:

> *"Dear Betsy: How about the dance next*
> *Thursday night? Yrs, Dave."*

Betsy read it through and immediately read it through again. She read it once more to savor the heavenly sensation of triumph which filled her. This was nice; it was very nice; it was grand; it was swell.

Fortunately Miss Clarke was in charge of the assembly room. Betsy sped a note of acceptance on its way. She asked permission to speak to Tacy, who hugged her, and to Tib, who smothered a squeal.

All the girls were congratulatory but more than one reminded Betsy that Dave Hunt never spoke.

"I know. I know," she told them blithely. "I'm

memorizing *David Copperfield*. I'm going to recite it to him all the way down to the hall and all the way back."

Tib was going with Lloyd, and Tom, home from Cox Military for vacation, invited Tacy. She didn't accept immediately.

"I'm not sure I want to go," she told Betsy and Tib who leaped upon her indignantly.

"You do too want to go!"

"What's the matter with Tom? He looks stunning in his uniform."

"Oh, I like Tom all right. I just don't like dances."

"You like them when you get there. You accept!"

Tacy was indifferent about the whole affair, but Tib was almost as jubilant as Betsy. This was her first high school dance. Again she came to the Rays for supper, bringing a suitcase. They refused dessert and hurried upstairs, followed, of course, by Margaret and the cat, to dress in a giddy whirl.

They pinned starched ruffles under their corset covers and put on their prettiest petticoats. Petticoats this year were sheath-fitting to the knees, then foamed out into lace. Tib wore peach-colored stockings and Betsy wore red ones. The coveted new princesse dresses, peach-colored and red, were laid out on the bed.

"Now," said Tib. "I'm ready to do your hairs."

"Just a moment," said Betsy. "The bathroom was

so steamy that my curls are coming out. I'll freshen them up a bit."

Slipping into a kimono she raced downstairs.

She chattered gaily to Anna while she heated her curling iron over the gas flame. Still chattering, she wound the front middle strand of hair firmly over the iron.

"Lovey!" Anna interrupted. "What's that I smell?"

"Nothing. There's always a little smell when I curl. . . ." But Betsy lowered the iron quickly and Anna cried "Stars in the sky!" For the front middle strand of hair came along with the iron. It was tightly and beautifully curled around the smoking tongs. On her forehead there was only a charred fringe.

With a scream Betsy ran out of the kitchen. Her father rushed in from the parlor holding his newspaper and Margaret, Mrs. Ray and Tib clattered down the stairs.

"My hair! My hair! I can't go to the party!" Betsy burst into tears.

Her mother embraced her. "Of course, you can go."

"No, I can't. I know I can't."

"Let me look, *Liebchen,*" Tib commanded.

Mrs. Ray stepped back and Tib smoothed the singed ends with small, artistic fingers.

"I know what we can do. We'll part your hair in the middle and make the pompadour on either side and in back. That's the very newest fashion. The burned part will make sort of a bang."

"This reminds me of *Little Women*," said Margaret. "Remember how Jo burned Meg's hair?"

Betsy blew her nose and wiped her eyes, and they all went back to the kitchen where Tib, standing on tiptoe, took personal charge of the curling. Anna kept saying consolingly that Betsy was going to look puny—her own baffling word for pretty—and Mrs. Ray declared that it wouldn't surprise her at all to see Betsy start a fashion for bangs.

Betsy was laughing now.

"I doubt that," she said, "but at least it will give me something to talk about to Dave."

She was glad to have an anecdote in reserve when Dave strode in at eight o'clock. There wasn't a trace of a smile on his sober, hollow-eyed face.

"He must admit I look nice," Betsy thought, stealing glances in the music room mirror at a vivid, slender, dark-haired girl in a new red princesse dress.

He shook hands with her parents, held her coat and took her party bag, all in silence. Lloyd arrived but the weather was too cold for an automobile, so the two couples started off, walking. Lloyd and Tib soon dropped behind leaving Betsy to her fate.

There wasn't a word from the towering figure that moved in the darkness beside her. She mentioned

Murmuring Lake. No response. She tried to draw him out about the night he put the pennant on the roof. No success. Direct questions received laconic monosyllables.

"All right," thought Betsy, "if he wants me to do all the talking I'll do it." And she started talking about how she had burned her hair. She made it sound as funny as she could, but he didn't laugh. He was as mute as a post. She spun the subject out vivaciously with comparisons of girls' hair and boys' hair, girls' clothes and boys' clothes, and they found themselves at Schiller Hall.

"How did you get along?" Tacy and Tib whispered in the dressing room.

"Why it's unbelievable!" Betsy gasped. "He never said one word! Not a syllable!"

"But you can always talk, Betsy. You're an awful talker and he's *so* good-looking."

He was. When the girls came out into the shining ballroom, Dave was waiting, and Betsy's heart leaped up when she saw him, so tall, so straight, so dramatically stern. Without speaking, of course, he wrote his name three times on Betsy's program.

Mamie Dodd, who always played the piano for high school dances, was warming up her fingers with preliminary chords. These intensified the excitement as boys scurried about, seizing girls' programs and scribbling down their names.

Mamie Dodd swung into the opening waltz.

"You are my Rose of Mexico,
The one I loved so long ago. . . ."

Everyone began to dance and Betsy discovered that Dave was a very good dancer. Floating across the floor in his strong, masterful arms, she forgave him for his silence.

Was there anything in the world, she wondered, so much fun as a dance? She two-stepped happily with Cab to "School Days, School Days, Dear Old Golden Rule Days." Tony had asked her for the barn dance. They ran, kicked and sang:

"Morning Cy,
Howdy Cy,
Gosh darn, Cyrus, but you're
Looking spry. . . ."

She and Dennie sang too:

"O'Reilly, O'Reilly,
It's a name that is spoken of highly. . . ."

Betsy often sang as she danced, which helped out now with Dave.

When Mamie Dodd started to play "The Merry Widow Waltz" Phil glanced across the room. Betsy smiled at him sadly. Later they had a schottische together and talked of the old days.

Betsy hardly saw Tib. They were both far too busy for feminine society.

Joe and Phyllis dropped in late, as though at a casual afterthought. Phyllis wasn't dressed for a dance; she was wearing a suit and hat. The other girls' programs had all been filled, of course, so they had to dance exclusively with each other, but they didn't seem to mind.

Betsy watched them over her partner's shoulder. Joe danced springily, as though he were enjoying himself. Phyllis was languid; her upturned smile was teasing.

Betsy rejoiced fiercely that she had come with Dave Hunt . . . "an outstanding boy, a star athlete. Every girl in school has been hoping he would take her out, and for his first date he chose *me*."

But she saw no indication that Joe Willard knew or cared with whom she had come. He smiled at her. He even waved in high good humor. Betsy waved back radiantly.

After the dance everyone went to Heinz's. The Okto Deltas and their escorts pulled four tables together. They made a joyful racket. Dave Hunt's silence was drowned out, but parting from Tib, Betsy whispered, "Now for *David Copperfield*."

She wasn't quite reduced to *David Copperfield*. By discussing every person at the party, every single boy, girl, and chaperone, dancing in general and barn dancing in particular, Schiller Hall as a place in which to dance and Mamie Dodd as a musician, she managed to talk steadily to the steps of her own porch.

When they parted there, she was rewarded. She gave Dave her hand and said, "I had a very nice time." He didn't answer but he held her hand firmly, and his fascinating, unexpected smile flickered across his face.

"So did I. I'll take you to the next dance," he announced.

"Oh—will you?" Betsy cried joyfully. The absurdity of her response didn't dawn on her until she was telling Tib after the boys had left. Then they went off into peals of laughter.

"Oh—will you?" Betsy mimicked, dropping to her knees, lifting her arms beseechingly.

"Betsy! You *dumm kopf*! You are very lucky that he wants to take you again."

School next day was given over to skylarking. Boys were waving mistletoe; the blackboards were decorated with cartoons, slams and jokes. Assembly included a Christmas tree, with Mr. Gaston acting as Santa Claus. One after another various students were called to the platform to receive joke presents.

Suddenly Betsy heard her name. "Will Miss Betsy Warrington Ray Humphreys Markham Edwards Brandish Hunt and so forth please come forward?" She had started down the aisle with the first name. A new one thundered out with every step she took. She reached the platform covered with blushes while the assembly room roared with laughter.

Mr. Gaston, grinning broadly, held a curling iron.

"This," he read loudly, "is to curl the bang now growing on your lily-white, intellectual brow."

Betsy accepted it to hilarious applause.

She acted plagued, of course, and ran down from the platform, ducking her head. But she was really thoroughly pleased. She must be that most desirable object, a "popular" girl. "Popular" with boys, of course.

Before she dropped off to sleep that night, she relived the whole scene, smiling in the darkness.

"It was awfully silly," she thought. "But I'm glad Joe Willard heard that rigamarole of names. It showed him that I wasn't just sitting around home thinking about him."

14
The Strong Silent Type

THE CURLING IRON WASN'T the only joke present Betsy received that year. There were always joke presents in the Rays' Christmas stockings. Every year Mrs. Ray received an onion, tastefully wrapped, with a card from one Henry Tucker, who had once been her beau. The writing always looked like Mr. Ray's. Julia's old beaus sent onions, too, and Mr. Ray was often presented with a worn-out boot or shoe from Helmus Hanson, who ran the rival shoe store. Anna got chunks of coal from Charlie. Empty salmon cans from Washington, old bones from Abie bulged in Margaret's black-ribbed stockings.

This gave a flavor to Christmas morning quite different from Christmas Eve which was solemn and beautiful. By firelight and Christmas-tree light the family sang the old familiar carols. Betsy read from Dickens' *A Christmas Carol*, Margaret recited "'Twas the Night before Christmas," and Julia, grave and reverent, read the story of Jesus' birth out of the book of Luke.

When this was over, they turned out the lights and filled one another's stockings with smothered giggles which anticipated next morning's fun. "Now you all stay in bed until the house is warm," Mr. Ray always said.

In the morning he shook down the furnace, and heat came up through the registers along with the smell of sausages and coffee. After he had kindled a fire in the grate and Anna had set breakfast on the table to be consumed at will, the gong summoned the rest of the family. Each one rushed to the chair which held his stocking.

Theoretically each one unwrapped a gift in turn but it didn't work out that way. Mr. Ray always forgot to open his; he cared more about watching other people open theirs and sat with crossed legs, smiling benevolently, or moved about, gathering up the discarded paper and ribbons, folding what was usable and burning what wasn't. He handed out the larger boxes which were piled under the Christmas tree and kept going to the table to replenish breakfast plates.

"Have another cup of coffee, Jule. Eat another sausage, Betsy. It won't hurt you."

Everyone else snatched at his own gifts, exclaiming and squealing. Julia and Betsy received combing jackets, the latest fad. Lacy and beribboned, they hung on one's bedpost when not in use. Julia raved over a new blue bathrobe. Margaret clasped a teddy bear and *Mary Ware, the Little Colonel's Chum.* Betsy had her eyes on a big oblong box, wrapped in red and green tissue, which lay under the Christmas tree. It was just the right size to hold furs.

Sure enough, when her father reached that box, he brought it to Betsy. She tried to restrain her smile as she untied the ribbons.

"Now what can this be?" she kept saying, never doubting that it was her longed-for set of furs.

She lifted off the cover and found another box inside.

"This is a joke present!" she cried, but she didn't really think so. The second box, she noted hopefully, was plenty big enough for furs.

The second box, however, yielded a third one and the third, a fourth. The boxes were getting too small for furs now, except for a muff, perhaps. This one might hold a muff. . . .

But it didn't. It held a tissue-wrapped package, and that held another, and another.

"Stars in the sky!" Anna kept shouting, throwing her arms up and down.

Betsy, tearing off papers, hid her disappointment under laughter. The family watched her, laughing, too. Margaret watched from her father's knee, one arm around his neck. At the very end Betsy found a ring box.

"You're going to find an elegant ring, lovey," Anna interjected breathlessly. But the box held only a paper. Betsy unfolded it and read, in her father's printing, "HUNT."

"Hunt? Hunt? Dave Hunt?"

"We knew you'd think that," shrieked Margaret, her little freckled face blazing with excitement.

Her father was chuckling so hard that his stomach shook. "I don't see any 'Dave' on that paper. You've got Dave Hunt on the brain."

"But it says 'Hunt.'"

"Yes, 'Hunt.' Need a dictionary?"

Betsy jumped up, scattering the multitude of boxes. She was off like a flash, running upstairs and down, flinging open drawers and closets. Down in the vegetable bin she found a big box, the size of the first one.

Clutching it joyfully, she raced back to the fire and while the family crowded about, she lifted out a set of furs. They were fluffy blue fox, a neck piece, a muff, even a fur hat with a *chou* of green velvet on the side.

"Papa! Mamma!" She rushed about kissing, then ran to the music-room mirror.

She wore them to church later. She went with Julia, who was singing in the choir during Christmas vacation, and with Tony who had unexpectedly expressed a wish to go. The sidewalks were covered with a thin powdering of frost and the snowbanks seemed to have been sprinkled with diamonds.

Tony held an elbow of either girl. He was wearing a new overcoat, and his red Christmas tie looked well with his black eyes.

Betsy smoothed down her boa, reached up to stroke her hat, snuggled her face into the muff.

"Now, now, Miss Ray! Forget those furs and think about church."

"I am thinking about church. I'm thinking how nice I look in my new furs going to church. I just love Christmas!" Betsy added, sliding along the frosty walk.

"So do I," said Julia, "especially at our house. It's shocking how some people manage Christmas—tell each other ahead of time about their presents—no surprises, no suspense, no drama. Papa and Mamma put such a thrill in it."

"Why, I never thought it was Papa and Mamma," said Betsy, sounding puzzled.

"I appreciate our home more since I've been away," said Julia.

"I appreciate the Ray house myself," Tony remarked. "You may notice that I honor it with my presence now and then."

"In spite of the fact," said Betsy, "that you're quite indifferent to the daughters."

"Oh, quite! Quite!"

She grabbed him. "You'll go into that snowdrift. You and your Christmas tie!"

Laughing his deep laugh Tony struggled with her.

"Children, behave!" Julia said.

The church was filled with a spicy fragrance; the altar was luminously white. From her place in the choir Betsy watched Tony fumbling at the pages of the prayer book, hesitantly kneeling and rising. She heard his rich, deep voice in the hymns.

"I just love Tony," she thought to herself.

The text of the sermon came from that chapter in the book of Luke which Julia had read aloud last night— "*. . . because there was no room for them in the Inn.*"

Rev. Mr. Lewis said that the text was symbolical of Jesus' short life on earth and of the attitude of

Christians. He was ever asking for admission into their lives—their business, social and private lives—but he could not remain where there was graft in business, envy and hatred in society or sin in people's hearts. These things crowded him out.

"I'll never forget that sermon," remarked Julia, walking home.

"I liked it, too," Betsy said.

"Our lives can hold just so much. If they're filled with one thing, they can't be filled with another. We ought to do a lot of thinking about what we want to fill them with."

"See here!" said Tony, "I've heard one sermon today." But he didn't mind Julia's preaching; his black eyes were soft.

Betsy thought about it again after dinner, walking down to Miss Cobb's with a present for Leonard. Okto Delta had crowded a good many things out of her winter—reading, friends like Hazel Smith, telling stories to Margaret, even the early service at church she had always loved so much.

"It hasn't hurt my music lessons, nor my work for Miss Fowler. I wrote the best essay in class on The Elizabethan Age."

But she felt dissatisfied, and resolved to make a long list of resolutions when the new year arrived.

By New Year's, however, she had forgotten her

resolution to make resolutions. The holidays struck Deep Valley like a snowball, exploding with soft glitter in all directions. There were family dinners, visits to country relatives, parties for young and old.

Mr. and Mrs. Ray were always on the go, and Julia had a new "college man" down from the cities. He, too, brought Betsy a fraternity pennant. His fraternity was a different one from Roger Tate's.

Roger's successor was one Pat McFadden, a tall, resplendent Irishman with thick black hair, blue-grey eyes and a flattering tongue.

"He used to go with Norma—you know, that stunning blonde Epsilon Iota. And with lots of other girls. I took him away from half the co-eds on the campus," Julia told Betsy.

Betsy could well believe it. She and Tib were so infatuated that Julia was almost obliged to plot to get rid of them as she had when they were children. Even Tacy liked him—perhaps because he was Irish.

"Top of the morning," she would greet him, her blue eyes sparkling. They talked to each other in brogue.

One reason Tacy liked him was that he was a singer. He had a fine baritone voice. The Rays asked him to sing for everyone who dropped in, and the more people who dropped in the better he liked it. He usually sang the Toreador song from *Carmen*.

Carmen had been given in Minneapolis, and Pat and Julia had heard it together. They were enthralled by it but Mr. Ray grew tired of the Toreador song.

"I'll take your beau anytime, Betsy. Silent Dave is good enough for me."

The Okto Deltas had a whirl of parties, all written up in the *Deep Valley Sun*. There was an Okto Delta tree at Alice's, and Betsy acquired a fine supply of neckbows, back combs, pin cushions, hair receivers.

The Okto Deltas and eight boys drove to St. John in the Blue Jay, a big bob sleigh with hay in the bottom. The night was cold, the snowy landscape ghostly, but the stars had a living brightness in the rich purple sky. Betsy sat next to Dave, tucked under a buffalo robe. Sticks of lemon candy, each stuck into half a lemon, were distributed among the riders. They blew horns, sang in harmony, hopped out of the sleigh and ran alongside, throwing snowballs and even washing faces. Sleighbells jingled and the horses' hoofs rang, and there was an oyster stew at the end of their journey.

Next came the Okto Delta progressive dinner. This was for girls only and each course was served in a different home. It was exhilarating to troop from house to house in the biting cold.

They went to Winona's for the appetizer. With the fruit cup each one received a favor. They went to the Rays' for the fish course; to the Kellys' for turkey; to the Mullers' for salad.

For place cards Tib made cartoons of the girls; Betsy was shown in the new red princesse dress and out of her mouth in a balloon came "David Copperfield." At Irma's, where there was black and orange icing on the cakes, the place cards were slams again. "Silence is golden," Betsy's said. After dinner coffee was served at Carney's, along with apples, nuts and candy. Nut meats had been removed from the walnuts and mottoes were sealed inside. Betsy's said:

"Silence is more eloquent than words."

"The boys were almost crazy," Betsy wrote to Herbert, her Confidential Friend, "because they couldn't make out what kind of a party it was, nor whose house it was at, nor anything. Their royal highnesses were offended to think we could have any fun without them."

Perhaps the progressive dinner turned the trick. At any rate the boys decided to get up a fraternity.

They decided at a spirited party attended by the Okto Deltas in the clubhouse above Lloyd's garage. The eight couples played five hundred and the boys cooked supper in chafing-dishes. They became the Omega Deltas. (The girls thought they knew what the name meant.) There was only one fly in the ointment of general rejoicing. Tony refused to join.

"I tell you I don't like the things. They leave too many people out. I know a fellow who was left out at the U, a swell guy, too, and he was cut up about it. Do you know what they call the ones who don't join? 'Barbs,' 'barbarians.'"

Betsy was indignant. "We don't call the girls who aren't Okto Deltas 'barbs,'" she said. But she had a brief unpleasant memory of Hazel Smith at the St. John game. Okto Delta *wasn't* popular in high school, although so many of its members were.

Betsy did not like to recall this conversation, and she didn't like the fact that the fraternity-sorority business would probably force Tony out of the Crowd. Parties from now on would be for the Okto and Omega Deltas, of course. It was too bad of Tony, she thought.

On the last night of vacation Julia's crowd had a dance. Pat had brought along a dress suit and Julia wore black with a bright red rose at the V of the neck. Mr. Ray didn't like it very well; black was considered daring for girls. But Julia looked lovely, her skin transparently white against the dark silk.

They didn't go to Heinz's after the dance but came home, where Betsy's Crowd had just come in from coasting. They all raided the ice box, and Pat sang the Toreador song. (Fortunately Mr. Ray could sleep through anything.) When the gathering broke up the girls went to Betsy's room, which Julia was sharing during Pat's visit.

"Wasn't Pat in glorious voice?" asked Julia, striking a Carmenlike pose before the mirror.

"Glorious! I'm crazy about Pat."

"He wants me to wear his fraternity pin."

"Are you going to?"

"Maybe. It would certainly impress the Epsilon Iotas. Not that they need impressing!" She took her hand off her hip and dropped down on the bed. "What I'd really like," she said earnestly, "is to go to Germany next year with Fraulein von Blatz. She's going back to Berlin and taking a few pupils with her. Wouldn't it be wonderful if I could go?"

"Perhaps Papa would let you."

"I'm not going to ask him. He's said he wants me to go through college and I've agreed to do it. He's even promised to stake me to some study abroad later on, although he doesn't really want me to be an opera singer. Papa's so good to us, Bettina! No, I'll stick to my part of the bargain, but it's hard."

"Don't you like the U?"

"I'd love it except that I want to be a singer and singers ought to start young. As it is, I'm only interested in Epsilon Iota and my lessons from Fraulein."

"And Pat," teased Betsy.

"Patrick McFadden, certainly," answered Julia,

and started to take down her hair.

"What do you think of Dave?" Betsy asked.

"Oh, I adore that strong silent type. I could be crazy about him, Bettina, if he weren't yours and so awfully young."

Betsy was rapturous. "Really? Maybe I like him better than think I do. He *is* sort of fascinating. You don't know what goes on behind that sober face."

"I'd find out," said Julia, and began to hum an aria from *Carmen*, the one Carmen sings when she comes down from the bridge. Julia sang it under her breath and took the red rose off her dress and threw it at Betsy, just as Carmen tossed it at the hapless Don Jose.

"Oh, Bettina!" she broke off. "You ought to hear *Carmen*. And I ought to be singing it. Of course I'd probably have to be Micaela. That role is better for my voice. She's the girl Carmen takes Don Jose away from, a perfect namby pamby, not at all like me."

Betsy paid no attention.

"The strong silent type," she murmured thoughtfully.

15
O Tempora! O Mores!

THE STRONG SILENT TYPE, Betsy soon discovered, had drawbacks as well as charms. Dave Hunt was handsome, he was fascinating, and she was proud to be his girl. But he could be exasperating! She realized it as the date approached for the Inter-Society debate.

This was late in January, for after vacation came mid-year exams. All activities were suspended during their grim reign.

"*O tempora! O mores!*" groaned Betsy and Tacy, taking Cicero's classic cry for their own. Tib, although German was her language, seized upon it too. She even added to it: "*O tempora! O mores! O Himmel!*"

Alone, in groups, at school, at home, everyone studied. They chanted dates and botanical terms. They heard one another recite poetry which must be memorized.

"'Whan that Aprille with his shoures soote. . . .'"

"I wish that April with his shoures soote was here right now," Cab exclaimed. "Gosh, I hate this English stuff! Do you suppose they have it at the U?"

"Four years of it."

"Not in the engineering course, I'll bet. That's what I'm going to take. Engineers don't give a darn if the Ides of March are percèd to the roote. . . ."

"Not 'ides,' Cab! That's Shakespeare. This is Chaucer."

"Cheer up!" Tacy always said. "Maybe the school will burn down."

It didn't, and they passed in everything, although Betsy's grades weren't what she had planned on Murmuring Lake: Botany, 83; Domestic Science, 84, Cicero, 87, U. S. History, 90, Foundations of English Literature, 93. She rejoiced, nevertheless, and was in a mood for relaxation when word spread that there was to be a party after the Inter-Society Debate, refreshments and games in the Domestic Science room. Boys were asking girls.

Betsy waited, confident of an invitation. Was she not, this year, a "popular" girl? The other Okto Deltas were invited one by one, but nobody invited Betsy. Her confidence waned and her fears grew. She confided in Tib. Tib confided in Dennie who said in a tone of surprise, "Why, Dave is taking Betsy."

Betsy didn't believe it, and steeled herself to go alone. As a loyal Zet, she couldn't stay away. Besides, Hazel Smith was on the team and Betsy wanted to hear her. She was said to be the best girl debater in the state. When the night came Betsy dressed with palpitating care, and Dave arrived on time, serene and silent. The evening was saved for Betsy, although the Philos won the cup.

Soon after this an Okto-Omega party was planned, to be held in the "frat house" above Lloyd's garage. Lloyd promptly invited Tib and Al invited Carney. When Cab invited Irma, Betsy began to grow nervous. Again Tib made inquiries, from Lloyd this time.

She and Betsy planned out beforehand just what she was to say.

"You can call for me at Betsy's. We'll be going together, I suppose. By the way, who's taking Betsy?"

"Dave, of course," Lloyd replied.

Tib hastened to deliver this reassuring news, and during the next few days Betsy flung herself at Dave. She stopped him in the hall and after classes. She manoeuvred to stand beside him in the Social Room. He didn't speak, and she was in a desperate state when Tib arrived to dress with her for the party.

"I'll do your hair in puffs," Tib offered as a gesture of comfort. Puffs were new, and Betsy had not learned to make them. Tib covered Betsy's head with an airy regiment of puffs but Betsy stared in the mirror glumly.

"If he doesn't come I'll stay home."

"You'll do no such thing. You'll go with Lloyd and me."

"I won't. I'll stay home."

"And waste these magnificent puffs?"

Mrs. Ray poked her head in. "He'll show up."

"He'll show up," Margaret echoed gleefully.

Promptly at eight the doorbell rang. Anna shouted with a note of triumph, "Bet-see!" Betsy ran downstairs and there was Dave, with his hair brushed to a shine, a new bow tie and a pleased glow on his face.

"The strong silent type!" Betsy raged. She wished she could hurl it reproachfully at Julia, but Julia had gone back to the U where she had been asked to sing the role of Yum Yum in *The Mikado*. She was rehearsing daily and wrote of little else.

"I won't put up with it!" Betsy stormed later to Tib. "I just won't stand it!"

But she did.

The new term brought basketball contests with all the neighboring towns. Who could resist a proprietary stake in the star of the team? Dave could not take her to the games, of course; she went with Tib and her escort, but everybody knew that Dave would join them afterwards. She watched his long legs scissoring and leaping and heard the adoring roar:

"What's the matter with Hunt?
He's all right!"

Betsy thought basketball more thrilling even than football and talked knowingly of "those rough Spaulding rules."

Honeymoon Trail came to the Opera House, and she heard from Tib that Lloyd and Dave were taking them. It proved to be true. They sat in the parquet, and Betsy had the same uncanny feeling of being grown-up she had when she and Tacy and Tib drank their coffee at Heinz's. It couldn't be, she thought unbelievingly, that they were sitting in the Opera House at night, downstairs, with boys who had paid for their tickets! But they were.

"Old, old is honeymoon trail. . . ."

That was the hit song of the show. Betsy bought it and picked out the chords on the piano when she was alone. She found she could almost play it, which gave a tremendous impetus to her piano lessons and to the hour of practise she split into two parts and found time for every day.

January had been mild, but February came in cold and snowy. The air was filled continually with a white descending haze. Drifts climbed to the window ledges. The thermometer dropped to twenty, thirty, thirty-five below. Tacy and Tib, stopping to call for Betsy in the morning, wore scarves over their faces.

Tib came early so that she could do Betsy's hair. Mr. and Mrs. Ray both protested the practise.

"Betsy doesn't need puffs for school."

"But I'm coming right past the house, Mrs. Ray. I always stop anyway; and I love to do them."

She continued to come, and although Betsy felt a little silly she delighted in the puffs. Sustained by them she joined Tacy in singing the "Cat Duet" at Zetamathian Rhetoricals. It was definitely childish but it had to be sung; it had become a tradition in the Deep Valley High. Betsy read an original poem for rhetoricals. It was named "Those Eyes" and sounded a little like Poe. She wrote more poems than stories on Uncle Keith's trunk this year—when she found time to write at all. This was usually late at night, when she had finished her homework or come in from a party. The house would be quiet; cold, too, sometimes, but she put on a warm bathrobe. She curled up beside the trunk and read poetry and wrote it, and she had an uncanny feeling then, too. This wasn't Betsy Ray, the "popular" girl. This wasn't Betsy Ray, the Okto Delta.

The Sistren still met regularly, sometimes with boys, sometimes alone. The girls brought their sewing to the afternoon parties, and Betsy always brought the jabot. She offered to read aloud if someone would work on it for her and the famous piece of neckwear passed from hand to hand.

"What a souvenir for college!" Carney said. "Samples of everybody's sewing, as well as all these choice knots and spots."

"Those spots you refer to so lightly," said Betsy, "are where I was pricked by a needle. You're taking my heart's blood to Vassar."

Carney was looking ahead to the Vassar entrance exams and working harder all the time. Tacy was sobered by a growing interest in music, but Betsy and Tib continued irrepressible.

Madame DuBarry and Madame Pompadour revived their soirees. These were hilarious affairs, for Cab and Dennie were irrepressible, too. Fast friends, the same age and about the same height, they were a carefree pair. They were, Betsy admitted, more fun than Dave.

But he was fun, too, on outdoor excursions. Groups of four, six, eight Okto and Omega Deltas often braved the cold for moonlight strolls. One night for a lark boys and girls exchanged wraps. Dave was as comical as Dennie, parading in Betsy's furs. He was always the first to sight a pan of fudge set to cool on a doorstep—lawful booty, whether the doorstep belonged to friend or stranger.

In recompense for stolen fudge, perhaps, the groups went serenading. They sang in parts underneath lighted windows, their breath congealing into silver notes.

> *"Old, old is honeymoon trail. . . ."*
> *"You are my rose of Mexico. . . ."*
> *"My wild Irish rose. . . ."*

The Crowd, Julia often said, sang like a trained chorus. But the Okto and Omega Deltas were not quite the Crowd. They missed Tony's rolling bass.

As Betsy had feared, they saw Tony less and less. He still came to the Rays' now and then but he had dropped the Crowd and what he had put in its place was not good. He skipped school, hung around a pool hall which had a bad reputation in Deep Valley. He went with that fast clique of older boys he had been drifting toward early in the winter. Tony had always had a zest for new experiences whether good or bad. But he had been restrained before by his scornful, indulgent, deeply loyal fondness for the Crowd.

Betsy felt pricked all the time by worry about Tony. She wouldn't give in to it; she was having too much fun. But she looked for a chance to say a restraining word and one Sunday night she thought she saw it.

Sometime before she had revived her last year's successful experiment in "reforming." Phil's pipe still hung beside her dressing table. She discovered that Dave had a pipe and secured it to hang beside Phil's. Dennie gave her a sack of tobacco and some cigarette papers. Cab contributed a cigar.

Betsy had protested that. "You don't smoke! You're giving me one of your father's cigars."

"Well, gosh, Betsy!" Cab grinned. "If everyone else is going to be reformed, I want to be reformed, too."

Her father teased her about this enterprise and he brought up the subject as Tony and Betsy stood out in the kitchen watching him make his inimitable sandwiches. He always sat down to make them for he was growing heavier and his feet tired easily. There was often an admiring circle around his chair.

"Have you heard about Betsy turning Carrie Nation?" he asked, spreading slices of bread with butter which he had set out to soften earlier. A cold loin of pork and a jar of mustard stood alongside. "I can't make out why she doesn't object to my cigars."

"You're too old to reform," said Betsy, smoothing his silky dark hair.

Tony searched through his pockets and found a piece of billiard chalk.

"Here," he said. "Add this to your collection. You ought to try to keep boys away from the pool hall, Betsy. It's a den of iniquity, Miss Bangeter says."

Betsy said she would tie the chalk on a ribbon and hang it over her mirror. She laughed into Tony's black eyes which looked hurt, although he was smiling. A new group of guests came to watch Mr. Ray and Betsy went back to the fire. Tony followed with his lazy saunter.

They sat down and looked into the flames, and Betsy said, imitating a grave tone of Julia's, "There was truth in what Miss Bangeter said about that pool hall, Tony. I wish you'd spend less time there and more time—well, at the Rays', or out serenading with the Crowd."

"What Crowd?" asked Tony. His face looked a little bitter. "There isn't any Crowd any more, just a couple of frats. I'm a barb. You don't want me around."

"Tony!" said Betsy. "Don't be ridiculous!"

"Ridiculous, am I?"

"Everybody misses you. The Crowd, Papa, Mamma, Margaret."

"You said one true thing. Margaret does." Tony called out to Margaret, who was reading the funny papers in her father's big chair. "Margaret, I'll beat you a game of parchesi."

Margaret's face lighted and she ran to get the board. Betsy felt snubbed.

Dave came in just then, followed shortly by Squirrelly, and Tib, and Winona. Winona went to the piano and when the parchesi game ended Tony lifted his voice in song. But after the sandwiches were eaten he quickly said good-by.

He shrugged into his overcoat, set his cap at a rakish angle on his bushy curly hair.

"I'll see you when I need some more reforming," he said to Betsy and went out.

16
Margaret's Party

M RS. R AY GAVE A SERIES of three parties on three successive days. It was a common practice to give parties by threes, and practical as well. The same flowers could be used; the chicken salad could be made in bulk; above all the house needed to be disturbed only once. It was certainly disturbed. For three days the Rays ate in the kitchen. Anna was cross, Mr. Ray was moody, Mrs. Ray was glowing and abstracted, and the girls bursting with excitement.

Margaret, excused from school early, ushered the guests upstairs and showed them where to lay their wraps. She wore her party dress, a soft blue silk with invisible stripes, piped in pink. Stiff pink hair ribbons stood out on either side of her small, intent face.

Betsy, Tacy and Tib hurried in after school to put on their party dresses and serve. Balancing plates full of chicken salad, hot rolls, World's Fair pickles and coffee, and second plates with ice cream and angel food cake, they nevertheless found time to smile at the mothers of their friends. Boys' mothers were particularly fascinating.

On the first day Mrs. Ray entertained the church ladies and the wives of her husband's business friends. On the second day Deep Valley's fashionable and wealthy drove to her door. For these two parties her closest friends assisted merely, "assisted throughout the rooms," according to the *Deep Valley Sun*. Such intimates—the High Fly Whist Club crowd, the neighbors—came to the third party which was a more relaxed affair than the two preceding. It simmered down to a chosen few who 'phoned for their husbands and stayed to supper, eating up the last of the food and thoroughly discussing all three events.

They were still busy with this when Betsy went

up to do homework. Margaret had already gone to bed but she called out, "Come here, Betsy," and Betsy went into her room.

It was a small room at the end of the hall. It didn't look like a child's room somehow, in spite of a doll bed with a doll tucked in for the night. It looked like Margaret, neat, grave, full of quiet resources.

The bureau was very precisely arranged, with the pincushion Tony had brought her from Chicago in the center. There was a low rocker where Washington loved to sleep, a low well-ordered bookcase, a sewing basket Mrs. Wheat had given her for Christmas. Framed photographs of members of her family, a Perry print of the Stuart Baby and a colored picture of a collie dog were symmetrically spaced on the walls. Everything was so fastidiously neat that Betsy was surprised to see a doll dress hanging on the bedpost.

She started to remove it but Margaret said, "No. Leave it there."

"Does it belong here?"

"You and Julia keep something hanging on your beds," said Margaret, referring, of course, to the combing jackets.

Betsy, sitting down beside her, took care not to smile. Margaret didn't like being smiled at.

She was sitting up in bed wearing a warm flannel night gown. Without hair ribbons, her braids betrayed their brevity but they were glossy and her face was freshly scrubbed. As always when looking at her younger sister, Betsy admired the long dark lashes. They emphasized the beauty of her wide shining eyes.

"I've been thinking," Margaret said, "that I'd like to give a party."

"Why, that's fine!" Betsy replied. "Mamma is always trying to make you give a party." Which was true. Margaret did not care much for juvenile festivities, nor for children her own age. Urged by Mrs. Ray, they came to play now and then, and Margaret treated them with scrupulous politeness, but she greatly preferred the company of a book, or Washington and Abie.

"Mamma will be delighted," Betsy said. "Who shall we ask?"

"That's just it," Margaret cried. "I don't want to invite a lot of children. I've been lying here thinking about it, Betsy."

She sat up very straight and her eyes glowed.

"You see, Washington and Abie are named for George Washington and Abraham Lincoln, and they have their birthdays this month. So I'd like to give a party for Washington and Abie. I don't want a lot of people. I'd like to have just you and me give a party for Washington and Abie."

Betsy was touched and complimented.

"Why, that's a fine plan! When shall we have it?"

"Lincoln's birthday or Washington's birthday?"

❧ 195 ❧

"Maybe it would be safer to pick a day in between. Then neither one's feelings would be hurt."

"That's right. We'll pick a day right in the middle."

"Say, the eighteenth. I think that's Thursday. It's just as well to have it on a Thursday. Anna won't be around to mind our messing up the kitchen."

Betsy leaned back and began to plan. And Margaret hugged her knees in delight, for Betsy knew how to make beautiful plans. She always had and she told them as though she were telling a story.

"We'll have place cards," she said, "like we have at the Okto Delta parties. You and I will make them. We'll draw pictures of cats and dogs or we can cut them out of magazines and paste them on cards."

"I like to paste," said Margaret.

"We mustn't let Abie and Washington see us making them, though."

"Mustn't we?"

"No. We want them for a surprise. And when the day comes we'll brush Washington and Abie and tie ribbons into their collars."

"Washington looks best in pink and Abie in blue. . . ."

"What shall we give them to eat?"

"Something you've learned to make in your Domestic Science class."

"Creamed salmon on toast," said Betsy. She got up and kissed Margaret goodnight. "Go to sleep now, baby. We'll talk about it in the morning."

Margaret snuggled down with an ecstatic sigh.

"Oh, Betsy! It's going to be such fun."

They talked about it the next day and the next, but then came a diversion. Julia's letters about *The Mikado* had grown more and more feverishly excited, and Mr. Ray decided to send Mrs. Ray up to the Cities for the event.

"Julia would probably like her Mamma around to tie her sash and paint her face," he said. "It's a pretty big thing for a freshman girl to have the leading part in an opera."

Mrs. Ray thought so, too, and was very glad to go. In fact, she couldn't imagine Julia getting through it without her. Anna said she could run the house alone and the girls urged their mother to go.

"Now watch out for Margaret!" Mrs. Ray said to Betsy and went off on the four-forty-five. Her letters were even more feverish than Julia's, raving not only about *The Mikado* but also about sorority affairs.

Sororities were still not allowed to rush the freshmen much. Parties were reserved for the now impending Rush Week, which would lead up to Pledge Day and the Great Decision. There was no rule, however, against rushing mothers and the Epsilon Iotas, the Alpha Betas, the Pi Pi Gammas and the rest were certainly rushing Mrs. Ray. They were taking her to matinees, to teas, to luncheons, and Mrs. Ray knew, she wrote, why they were so nice to her. It was because Julia, a freshman, had been chosen to sing Yum Yum. And she was the most adorable Yum Yum!

Mr. Ray chuckled when he read the letters.

"Jule thinks we have a wonderful child."

"You think so yourself," Betsy retorted.

"We know darn well we have three of them," said Mr. Ray. "I'm certainly glad I made Jule go. She's having a big time."

Betsy enjoyed being lady of the house, planning meals, tying Margaret's hair ribbons. She brought friends in every day after school and she and Margaret didn't get around to making place cards. Betsy wasn't too troubled by this. She was accustomed to making extravagant plans which she didn't carry out. Margaret mentioned the party just once, as Betsy was hurrying off to school one morning.

"Shall I tell Washington and Abie about—you know what?"

"Oh, yes. Invite them."

"Will it be on Thursday?"

"Probably. After school."

Thursday noon Anna said, "I'll be gone when you get home from school, lovey. I'll have everything ready for supper, though."

"You don't need to," said Betsy. "I'll make a Domestic Science supper."

"Well, I hope it turns out," said Anna who didn't think too highly of Domestic Science since a recent day when cream puffs, tried at home, had failed lamentably to live up to their name.

"Be a good girl if you get in ahead of me," Betsy said to Margaret. Margaret smiled; she didn't speak. The party for Washington and Abie was still a secret between them.

Betsy fully intended to come home promptly but a succession of things interfered. Tib had to stay after school for make-up work and persuaded Betsy to wait for her.

"I won't be two minutes."

Cab and Dennie, as it happened, waited too, and when Tib came out of German class after not two minutes but ten, they proposed going to Heinz's for peach pecan sundaes.

"I have to go home," Betsy objected.

"Fine," said Cab. "Go home by way of Heinz's."

"We'll hurry," Tib promised.

And they hurried going down but coming home they loitered, acting silly, trying to walk on snow drifts which capsized under their weight. Tib and Dennie left them at the corner of Plum Street and Broad and climbing the hill with Cab Betsy realized suddenly how late it had grown. The sun was so low that the glow had gone off the snow. It went off her spirits, too.

"Oh, we can have a party for the animals anytime! It doesn't need to be this particular day," she thought, but she quickened her steps, and after she had parted from Cab she went still faster. Feeling guilty she sang and made a lively racket as she ran up the porch steps.

It seemed odd that no lights shone through the windows. Margaret knew how to light the gas. Going quickly into the dim hall, Betsy saw that preparations had been made for the party in the parlor. Four sofa cushions had been laid around a luncheon cloth spread on the floor. A magazine lay open with a paste pot and a pair of scissors near. Margaret must have started to make the place cards. But where were they? Where was Margaret?

Betsy went into the shadowy kitchen. She saw an empty salmon can, and the door of the oven stood open. Had Margaret been making toast to go with the salmon? Then where was it? Where was Margaret?

"She's gone over to see Mrs. Wheat," thought Betsy. But she knew she didn't believe it. If she believed that Margaret was cozily drinking cambric tea next door, she wouldn't have this queer feeling in her stomach.

Washington didn't look up from the couch where he was sleeping, but Abie had come to meet her and now brushed against her ankles.

"Where's Margaret?" Betsy asked him.

Abie barked, a sharp bark and was silent.

Betsy went to the foot of the stairs and called, "Margaret, where are you?"

She was relieved beyond all reason when Margaret's voice answered, "Here I am. Oh, Betsy, I'm so glad you've come!"

Margaret came running down the stairs. She was wearing her party dress, the blue silk piped with pink she had worn for her mother's parties. Her pink party hair ribbons were tied into awkward bows. One had a small loop and a long end; the other had a big loop and a short end. Betsy felt a pang at her heart when she saw those bows.

"I'm so sorry," she began. "I was slow getting home but we'll have the party tomorrow—"

Margaret interrupted.

"Betsy," she said. "Look at my eye lashes. Aren't they curly?"

"Why, baby, your eye lashes are always curly." But Betsy looked closely at Margaret's beautiful eyes. She drew her to a window and stared intently in the fading light. Margaret's eye lashes had been unusually long. They were short now and the ends were frizzled.

"Margaret!" cried Betsy. "What have you done?"

"I was trying to have the party," Margaret said. "You see, Betsy, Washington and Abie had been invited. I couldn't not have a party after they were invited. I started to make the place cards, but they kept looking and you'd said they weren't supposed to see and I was lonesome if I kept them shut up in my room. So I thought I'd let the place cards go and start the lunch.

"I thought I didn't really need to cream the salmon. They like it just as well the way it comes out of the can. But I wanted to put it on toast to make it a party. So I lighted the oven and it exploded."

"Exploded!" Betsy cried. "What do you mean?"

"It just exploded. There was a big bang. And it made my eye lashes curly."

"What did you do?"

"I turned it off," said Margaret. "Oh, Betsy, I was scared, though! I was awfully scared!" and throwing her arms around her sister Margaret began to cry. She cried in big wrenching sobs which tore at Betsy's heart. Margaret didn't cry often. She was the reserved one, the Persian Princess, she was very different from most girls' little sisters and brothers who were always crying.

Betsy felt a wave of awfulness. She hugged Margaret tight.

"Margaret," she said, forcing her voice to be steady. "Do your eyes hurt? Do they feel funny?"

It seemed to her that a century passed before Margaret answered.

"My eyes are all right. It's just that the lashes are curly. I'd like them that way if I hadn't been so scared . . ." and Margaret began to cry again.

Betsy knew that Margaret wasn't crying only because of her fright. It was her disappointment about the party, the long hours of watching for Betsy who didn't come. Betsy started to cry, too, from relief that Margaret's eyes were safe and because she was sorry and ashamed. But she cried for only a minute. It came to her suddenly that she was sixteen years old, too old to cry in a situation like this where there was something else to do.

She pushed the loose hair back from Margaret's wet cheeks and kissed her.

"We must light the gas and get busy," she said briskly. "Papa will be coming in and I've promised him a Dom. Sci. supper. It was horrid of me to forget the party, but I'm going to try to make it up to Washington and Abie. I'm going to let them sit at the table tonight, right beside us, on chairs. We'll have creamed salmon, of course. And Margaret, I'll tell you what we'll do."

"What?" asked Margaret, drying her eyes and blowing her nose.

"I'm going to bake them a joint birthday cake."

"What does 'joint' mean?"

"It means it will belong to them together. Half will be for Washington and half for Abie. I'll frost half in vanilla and half in chocolate. Come on now."

"We'll give Washington the chocolate side because he's the oldest," Margaret said.

Betsy had learned how to bake cake in her Domestic Science class. She baked a pretty good one. Supper was late but Mr. Ray didn't mind when he heard it was a birthday party. Betsy told him about the oven and he looked at Margaret's eyes keenly but he didn't ask how Margaret had happened to be lighting the oven alone. Perhaps he noticed that Betsy's eyes were red.

When Betsy said her prayers that night she started to cry again.

"Dear God!" she said. "It was good of you not to let anything happen to Margaret's eyes. And this is the year I made the resolution to be better around home. I was going to try to take Julia's place. . . ."

She hadn't, she thought, her conscience aching, done very well at that.

Julia had always been such a wonderful older sister. "Even if I tried, I couldn't be to Margaret what Julia has been to me. There's too much difference in our ages. Six whole years."

It must be lonely, she thought, not to have a sister nearer your age than that.

"I'm going to do the best I can," she promised God, "to keep close to Margaret. I'll never, never, never neglect her again."

She stayed on her knees a long time, her head buried in her arm, thinking about Margaret's frizzled lashes.

What if her mother had come home from the Twin Cities to find that something had happened to Margaret's beautiful eyes?

17

A Bolt from the Blue

MRS. RAY CAME home wearing a new spring hat, bearing gifts and radiant with pride. *The Mikado* had been a glorious success and Julia, an enchanting Yum Yum.

"Even the Twin City papers raved, Bob. Oh, I wish you could have been there! Five sororities sent her flowers. She carried those from the Epsilon Iotas."

"Is that the bunch she's going to join?"

"Yes. She's practically an Epsilon Iota now. They

can't bid her until Pledge Day, though." Mrs. Ray outlined briefly what they all knew already. Pledge Day came at the end of Rush Week. On the evening preceding, all the sororities gave formal dinners to which they invited only the freshmen they definitely planned to bid.

"And the freshman goes to the dinner of the group she plans to accept. Julia will go to the Epsilon Iota dinner. We bought her gown while I was in the cities, Betsy. Yellow satin with a train. It's stunning."

"What do you think of sororities anyway?" Mr. Ray asked in a grumpy tone.

Mrs. Ray hesitated. "Why, the Epsilon Iotas are charming girls. They were lovely to me. But I don't know. . . ."

"What is it?" Mr. Ray wanted to know.

"Well, they're so terribly important to Julia. I don't think it would be that way if she cared more about her University work. But she doesn't, Bob. She really doesn't give a snap about any of her studies except singing. What makes it so bad is that Fraulein von Blatz is going away next year."

Mr. Ray sat silent, troubled.

"I wish she could go to Germany with Fraulein," Mrs. Ray said.

Mr. Ray was silent a long time, and Mrs. Ray, Betsy and Margaret watched him while he puffed on his cigar, blowing thoughtful rings.

"No, Jule," he said at last. "I think I'm doing the right thing in asking her to go through the U. Music is a very hard career. She's too young to make such an important decision.

"I've told her she can do as she pleases after she's through college. I'll even scrape up the money to help her. But I'm hoping that she'll meet someone she wants to marry, settle down and use her voice for lullabies," said Mr. Ray looking pleased.

Betsy thought that he didn't entirely understand Julia. No matter whether she went through the University or not, Julia would give her life to music. But Betsy didn't speak, for like all the family she had a profound respect for her father's wisdom. She was even willing to concede that the experiment of college was a wise one. He wanted Julia to be sure, just as he had wanted Julia and Betsy to be sure before they joined the Episcopal Church.

Lent had begun and Betsy, Tacy and Tib had all given up dancing. Betsy was glad to make a sacrifice, for worry about Tony and repentance about Margaret weighed her down a little.

"Now," she wrote to Herbert, "will I show an unparalleled exhibition of courage, steadfastness, self-denial, etc.!!!!!!"

She did shortly, for she refused to go with Dave to

the basketball dance. (Not that he asked her; she refused him in advance, via Tib and Lloyd.)

Mrs. Ray had brought her the *Soul Kiss* music from the cities. Betsy found, to her delight, that she could play the waltz. Tony, Cab, Tacy and Tib sang it to her stumbling accompaniment—when Winona wasn't around, and they couldn't do better.

Miss Mix was making Betsy a new dress for Easter. Shadow rose, with a high waistline, long tight satin sleeves and a directoire sash, also of satin, knotted low on the left side. She and her mother bought her a black chopping-bowl hat trimmed with the same shade of rose.

The snow was melting and it was fun to walk after school with the sun on one's head and slush under foot. Robins and bluebirds sang in the bare trees and there were pussy willows and red-winged blackbirds in the slough.

Cars which had been put away through February were appearing in the muddy streets. Phyllis Brandish again drove Joe Willard down to the *Sun* after school. The Okto Deltas would have enjoyed rattling about in Carney's auto but Carney was working too hard for that. She was buckling down to study on those college entrance exams.

The juniors, too, were looking ahead. Every year they entertained the seniors at a banquet, which was the outstanding social event of the spring. One of

Betsy's wishes, when she made her plans on Murmuring Lake, had been to head up a committee for the junior-senior banquet.

"Do you know what committee I'd like to have?" she asked Tacy, walking to school on the day of the class meeting to discuss the banquet. "The decorating committee. That sounds queer, I know, because I'm not a bit artistic, but I have an idea I'd like to carry out."

"What is it?" Tacy asked.

"Turn the school into a park for banquet night. Move in potted palms, and some porch swings. Make the tables in the Dom. Sci. room look like picnic tables. Have a fish pond—we could fish for packages in it. And maybe a Lovers' Lane."

"Why, Betsy!" Tacy cried. "That's a wonderful idea."

"Oh, I hope I can do it!" Betsy cried. "I'm apt to be head of some committee, so why can't it be the decorating committee?"

The meeting took place after school and the Okto Delta juniors sat together. They had become more and more clannish since resentment at the sorority had begun to seep through the school. Betsy would have been with them but she sat on the platform with the other class officers. Stan Moore was president as he had been the year before. He and Betsy had both kept their offices and Betsy, secretly, hoped to be re-elected for the senior year.

Stan, a tall relaxed boy, usually conducted a meeting admirably but today he acted nervous. After rambling on about the banquet, stressing its importance, of which everybody was aware, and announcing the date in May which had already been fixed, he said that he was ready to name the committee heads.

"Oh, dear!" thought Betsy. "I hope I get the decorating committee."

Stan cleared his throat and started to read. He stopped and cleared it again but then he continued in a bold voice. It was a surprising list. The six Okto Delta juniors were all prominent in school, especially Betsy, Alice and Winona. But not one was named for any committee. The decorating committee went to Hazel Smith.

The Okto Deltas sat very still when Stan had finished. Betsy, on the platform, swallowed hard. When the discussion passed to other matters, they stole furtive looks at one another, but even Winona was silent.

At the end of the meeting Hazel hurried over to Betsy.

"I want to get you before somebody else does," she said. "Will you serve on my committee? Where's Tacy? I want her, too."

"There she is," said Betsy. "And thank you, Hazel! I'd love to be on your committee."

The class filed out of the assembly room. Carney, waiting in the hall, was puzzled by the dazed expression on the faces of her Okto Delta sisters.

"What's the matter?" she asked.

"We don't know," said Winona. "Maybe we all have poison ivy."

"Why do you say that?"

"Not one of us was given a committee."

"That's funny," Carney said. "I wasn't given a senior committee either. I thought perhaps it was because I was studying so hard." But that, everyone knew, was unlikely. Carney had always been outstanding in her class. "It looks as though they had something against us as a group," she added, looking sober.

"Can it be dear old Okto Delta?" asked Winona.

"I've heard," Alice said, "that we're called a bunch of snobs."

"That isn't fair," cried Betsy. "We're not the least bit snobbish."

"And we can live without their old committees," said Tib, tossing a yellow head.

But Betsy's mind flashed ahead to next year, her senior year, her last in Deep Valley High. She wouldn't, she admitted, like it at all not to have a share in next year's thrilling climactic activities.

The Okto Deltas ignored the whole matter at their next meeting, a particularly silly one.

"The Sistren," Secretary Ray wrote in the minutes,

"played statues, leadman, and other kid games. They acted dippy."

The girls tried to gloss over their unfortunate position in school, but they felt a little subdued and most of them applied themselves energetically to school work.

Betsy had had a good year in English. Her work had been merely acceptable in other classes; she and Tacy and Tib had not yet made their herbariums for Botany. But ever since Miss Fowler had praised her work last November Betsy had worked hard on Foundations of English Literature.

She always looked forward to English class, both because she liked the subject and because she enjoyed the competition of Joe Willard. They never saw each other outside of school but in English class there was a bond between them. They talked for each other's benefit sometimes; they sought each other's eyes when a good point was made; they smiled across the room when something funny happened. This intimacy always stopped at the door of the classroom and Betsy was surprised one March day to find him waiting for her.

His hands were in his pockets and he was smiling, his eyes very bright under the light crest of hair.

"Hey!" he said. "What do you think of the topic for the Essay Contest?"

"Why . . ." said Betsy. "I haven't heard what it is."

"You haven't? Well, it's a queer one: 'The History of the Deep Valley Region.'"

"'The History. . . .'" Betsy's face lighted with a smile of utter joy. She rose on her toes. "Joe Willard!" she cried, shaking her finger in his face. "You haven't a chance!"

"Oh, is that so!"

"Yes, it's so! Were you even born in Deep Valley?"

"I was born in Brainerd. But you didn't start taking notes on local history in the cradle, did you?"

"Practically," said Betsy. "You see, my father loves it. His people came to Iowa in a covered wagon and he was only nineteen when he struck out for himself and came up here. Besides, there's Grandma Slade."

"Grandma Slade?"

"Tom's Grandmother. We always have Thanksgiving dinner with the Slades, and you ought to hear her stories. Why, she was here when the Sioux went on the warpath, blankets, feathers, tomahawks and all."

"Look here!" Joe said, looking at her smilingly. "You mustn't be spilling all your material. I'm your rival, you know. I'm agin you. I'm the fellow the Philomathians picked just on purpose to outwit you."

Betsy's expression changed. She stopped smiling and a quick line of worry appeared between her brows.

"Come to think of it, the Zets haven't picked me. When did you find out that you were chosen?"

"O'Rourke told me this morning."

Her face smoothed out. "Then it's probably all right; Clarke will speak to me after History class."

"You haven't any doubt about being picked, have you?"

"N . . . n . . . no," Betsy answered. "Still . . . I've lost two years running."

"They couldn't put up anybody half as good as you are and you know it," Joe replied.

Betsy smiled at him. "Why, thank you," she said. "I didn't know you had it in you. I never expect bouquets from you, somehow—only brickbats. I'm not really worried about being chosen. Just the same, you can keep your fingers crossed."

He crossed his fingers, holding them high above his head as Betsy went away.

In History class Betsy looked at Miss Clarke with a certain urgency. It seemed to her, however, that Miss Clarke was avoiding her eyes. She was greatly relieved when, at the end of the period, Miss Clarke said, "Betsy, will you stop in to see me after school?"

Again relief flowed into Betsy's face. Her mouth swept upward in a smile.

"Yes, Miss Clarke. I'd be glad to."

She went out walking on air.

"What are you so happy about?" Tib asked.

"Clarke wants to see me after school. And I think it's the Essay Contest."

"Why, of course, you'll be chosen for that. You

always are," said Tacy. And Tib added, "You know you write better than anyone in school."

"Except Joe," said Betsy, laughing. "And I'm going to give him a run for his money this year. The subject is perfect for me, just perfect. Oh, I'm so happy!"

She was, she realized suddenly, eager to start work on a serious project. She found herself looking ahead to it, almost with longing. She would enjoy it all after her gay winter: the quiet of the library, her friend Miss Sparrow, the long hours of hard work, Joe's stimulating company.

He liked her. She knew he did, Phyllis or no Phyllis. If they were working together again at a little table in back of the stalls, they would get acquainted as she had often wished they could.

"I really want him for a friend," Betsy thought. "Not just that I'm sweet on him. We have so much in common. We were intended to be friends."

At noon she told her family the subject for the Essay Contest.

"Isn't that nifty? Can you imagine anything more perfect?"

"Have you been asked to compete yet?" her father inquired.

"Not yet. But I'm sure I will be."

"Of course, she will," Mrs. Ray said. "Even if the judges went out of their minds last year and the year before."

"They didn't," Betsy said. "Joe Willard can write. But I think I can beat him on Deep Valley history. At least I'll have fun trying."

She went back to school smiling.

But her heart sank, the smile left her face, when she entered the history room after school. For the smile on Miss Clarke's sweet, artless face was forced. She looked unhappy.

"Sit down, Betsy," she said. "I have some bad news for you."

"Bad news?"

"Stan Moore has been chosen to represent the junior Zetamathians on the Essay Contest."

Before she could stop them, tears sprang to Betsy's eyes.

"Oh, no, Miss Clarke!" she cried. "Not this year, when the subject is Deep Valley! I love Deep Valley! I could write about it! I could win!"

She stopped and rubbed the tears savagely out of her eyes.

"What am I saying?" she asked. "You must excuse me, Miss Clarke. Of course, you and Miss Fowler are quite right to try someone else. I've lost two years running."

"Betsy," said Miss Clarke, taking off her glasses and wiping her eyes, "Miss Fowler and I think you could write a better essay than any Zetamathian in the school. Maybe I shouldn't tell you that. But it's true."

"Then why. . . ?" Betsy asked.

"There's a lot of feeling around school," Miss Clarke answered, "that your crowd has everything. You are pretty outstanding, you know. Until recently there wasn't much jealousy. You were all democratic and popular. But this year . . . people don't like the sorority-fraternity business! They just don't like it.

"Zetamathian and Philomathian are school societies. They shouldn't be monopolized by any one crowd. If we gave you a third chance to compete in the Essay Contest, after you lost the first two years, it might add to the hard feeling which has already been built up against your group. You wouldn't like that, would you?" Betsy shook her head, unable to speak.

"If it was anything but Deep Valley history I wouldn't feel so bad," she said at last in a choked voice, and Miss Clarke, who had just replaced her glasses took them off and started rubbing them again.

"Never mind!" said Betsy, rising. "Stan will write a good essay. Good-by, Miss Clarke"—and she darted out.

She went to the cloak room where Tacy was waiting and buried her face in her coat.

Tacy put her arms around her. "You didn't get it?"

Betsy shook her head.

"But how could you help but get it?"

Betsy shook her head even more frantically.

"I don't know what Clarke and Fowler can be

thinking of," said Tacy, hugging her harder. "They must be crazy. It's just throwing the Essay cup away."

Betsy took her face out of the coat. She blew her nose and wiped her eyes and put some face powder on her nose. Hooking on to Tacy's arm, she started talking about something else and they went down the stairs and out of the school.

When she saw Joe Willard next day she was lightly regretful.

"They've given you real competition this year. No one less than the president of the junior class."

His face was swept with amazement and, Betsy realized with doleful satisfaction, disappointment.

"Stan Moore? Why, they must be crazy. Stan's a swell guy but you can write circles around him."

"You shouldn't have written circles around me last year and the year before," she said.

Joe scowled. He stood with his hands in his pockets, his thick light brows drawn together.

"I'll be thinking of you," Betsy said, "slaving down there in the library when the snow melts and the violets come out and the picnicking season begins."

Joe didn't answer. He strode off in the direction of Miss Clarke's room. But Philomathians were allowed no voice in Zetamathian affairs. After a moment Joe came out of Miss Clarke's room still scowling, and Stan Moore began work on the Essay Contest.

18

Two More Bolts from the Blue

ONE APRIL EVENING the Rays sat at supper talking
about Julia. Beyond the windows, winter still lingered
in a sad, opalescent sky. But the day had been spring-
like. Melted snow had been rushing down the gutters
in foaming rivers on which Margaret had sailed
boats. Betsy had walked to the slough for marigolds.
Mr. Ray wore a pansy in his buttonhole, and there

was rhubarb short-cake for dessert.

The Rays were talking about Julia because the week ahead was the supreme one to which she had been looking forward. It was nothing less than Rush Week. Luncheons, teas, and masquerades would lead in gay procession up to that formal dinner at the Epsilon Iota house for which she had bought the yellow satin dress.

"How do the freshmen get their bids?" asked Betsy, eating with good appetite.

"Through the mail on Pledge Day morning. Special delivery," Mrs. Ray replied. "In the afternoon they go to the house of their choice to be welcomed and cried over and given a pledge pin. It's very thrilling, the girls say."

"It's tough on the ones who don't get those special delivery letters," Mr. Ray remarked.

"Yes, it is." Mrs. Ray looked distressed. "I'm certainly thankful that Julia is one of the lucky ones."

"Week after next she'll be home for Easter and tell us all about it," Betsy said.

Anna, who was clearing the table, looked out the window. "Why, there's Mr. Thumbler's hack!"

Everyone jumped up and Mr. Ray observed, "It must be Aunt Lucinda."

Aunt Lucinda sometimes came to make a visit uninvited.

"Are there any creamed potatoes left?" Mrs. Ray asked anxiously. "And if you haven't cut the short-cake, Anna, cut it to serve one more."

"The McCloskeys," remarked Anna, "didn't have relatives who came just at mealtime."

Betsy and Margaret couldn't understand her grumpiness. They ran to the window to see Aunt Lucinda getting out of the hack. But to everyone's amazement it was Julia who alighted.

She was wearing her winter hat and coat and the effect was bleak. She looked very small, standing beside the hack in the twilight. Mr. Ray rushed out to pay Mr. Thumbler and Mrs. Ray, Betsy and Margaret followed. With their arms about Julia they ascended the steps, exclaiming joyfully.

Julia smiled and returned their kisses but her face was pale.

"You look sick, darling," Mrs. Ray cried. "Is that why you came home?"

"I'm not sick," answered Julia.

"We thought you were Aunt Lucinda," Margaret said.

"We were awfully surprised to see you, on account of next week being Rush Week."

"And the week after that, your vacation . . ."

"Never mind about all that until she's had some supper," Mr. Ray put in.

"I don't want any supper. I couldn't eat anything, really. I . . . I ate on the train." Julia took off her hat and coat and Margaret ran to hang them up. Julia sat down in the parlor and the Rays gathered about her, anxious now to know what lay behind her white strained face.

She told them at once. "The Epsilon Iotas have dropped me!"

"What?"

"How could they 'drop' you?" Margaret asked, bewildered.

"They're not rushing me any more. I'm not invited to any of the Epsilon Iota parties."

"Why . . . why . . . that's impossible!" Mrs. Ray gasped. "Not even to the formal dinner?"

"Especially not to that."

Everyone thought of the yellow satin dress, but no one mentioned it.

"I've been dropped," Julia repeated, her lips trembling. "I've been tried and found wanting."

"What perfect nonsense!" Mr. Ray interjected, but he, too, looked pale.

"Are the others still rushing you?" Mrs. Ray demanded.

"Yes," said Julia. "But that doesn't interest me. I'm going to be an Epsilon Iota or I won't be anything. I'll be a barb." She shut her lips tight.

The Rays were silent for a moment, stunned. It was incomprehensible. Julia, the beautiful, the talented, their darling . . . dropped! A barb!

"But why? Why? What do they think you've done?" Mrs. Ray cried at last.

"I don't know."

"Can't you ask them?"

"Certainly not! I have to act as though I didn't even notice they had dropped me. Of course, I can't help but notice it. All year the girls have been so lovely to me, and now they treat me almost like a stranger. They speak when we meet, of course. But that's all.

"One of them told me—she wasn't supposed to but she did—that they haven't stopped liking me. They act this way because they know they can't bid me, and it would hurt me more if they rushed me to the very end."

"But why can't they bid you?"

"The vote has to be unanimous, and someone doesn't want me."

"Well, the very idea!" Mrs. Ray cried. "I'd like to burn the University down!"

"I'd like to murder the whole bunch," Betsy exclaimed.

Mr. Ray put his arm around Margaret. "Julia isn't the only little girl whose feelings have been hurt, I imagine," he said. "It's a mighty funny thing that the State University, supported by the public, can have private clubs which are so important."

But Mrs. Ray couldn't think now about the ethics of Greek letter organizations. She was astounded and dismayed.

Julia was treated as though she were sick. She was put to bed and Anna brought up a hot lemonade. Mrs. Ray, Betsy and Margaret sat in her room talking in hushed voices while Mr. Ray tramped the house looking sober and distracted.

"Are you sure, are you sure, you don't want to join one of the others?" Mrs. Ray asked. "The Alpha Betas were very nice, I thought, and so were the Pi Pi Gammas."

"I'm positive," Julia said.

Mrs. Ray kept naming the Epsilon Iotas she had met on her visit. Ann, the dark queenly one; Patty and Joan, the twins; blonde Norma.

"I can't imagine them not being friendly."

"They barely speak to me. But don't you see? That's the kind thing to do. If I've been dropped there's no sense being nice and giving me false hopes."

"Have you any idea which one doesn't want you?"

"None in the world."

Mr. Ray paused in the doorway. "Are you staying home a while?"

"Oh, no!" said Julia. "I'm going back tomorrow night."

"Darling!" cried Mrs. Ray. "I don't think you'd better go back! Why don't you have a sore throat and stay home a little while?" But Julia shook her head.

"No," she said. "I'm going back. But just for today I'll have a sore throat. Oh, it's so good to be home!" She put her arms around Margaret who was sitting on the bed beside her, and buried her face in Margaret's lap.

"It was awful this last week!" she sobbed. "You can't imagine! Those girls I've grown to like so much, hurrying past me, looking the other way. Everyone asking me what sorority I think I'll join and me not joining any unless I can have the one I want."

"Whatever one you joined," said Betsy, choking, "you'd make it the best on the campus just by joining it."

But Julia, without speaking, shook her head.

The next morning early Betsy heard her stirring and went into her room. Julia was dressing.

"I'm going down to early church," she said.

"Mind if I go along?"

"I never mind having you along, Bettina."

They stole out of the house. Yesterday's puddles were frozen but robins were singing and flying about in a dim light. A Persian rug had been unrolled in the sky above the German Catholic College.

Julia and Betsy did not talk much on their way. They went inside the church and dropped to their knees.

The Rev. Mr. Lewis did not seem to notice them. He was always like that at early church.

"Lift up your hearts," he said.

"We lift them up unto the Lord."

"Let us give thanks unto our Lord God."

"It is meet and right so to do."

The altar was snowy and fresh, with candles gleaming, and the service passed like a dream. The Rev. Mr. Lewis said, "The peace of God which passeth all understanding keep your hearts and minds . . ."

Julia stayed on her knees a long time and when she and Betsy emerged at last into the cold and the daylight, peace shone in her face.

She squeezed Betsy's arm. "I'm all right now," she said. "Going to church is a wonderful help. It makes"—she laughed ruefully—"even sororities seem pretty small."

She went on thoughtfully, "I was weak to come home. It's a temptation to come running back to the warmth and tenderness of home when the world is cruel. But I won't be a coward any more. I'll go back to the U and go through Rush Week with my head up, and then I'm going to get down to work. I only wish Fraulein wasn't going away."

"When is she going?" Betsy asked.

"Not till the end of the term. I'm thankful for that. I have so much to be thankful for, Bettina! My family, my music, my glorious plans for my life. . . ."

Her face looked exalted, as it looked when she sang.

The rest were at breakfast when they came in, and Betsy had the feeling that the topic of conversation was abruptly changed. She saw her father look keenly at Julia's face, and later she heard him say to her mother, "We won't interfere. She has the thing licked."

During the rest of the day Julia was quite like herself. She praised the Perfection Salad Anna had made especially for her; she bathed white woolly Abie because Margaret delighted to assist at this function; and she sang for all the friends and neighbors who dropped in.

At Sunday night lunch Katie asked innocently, "You'll be having fun next week, won't you? Isn't it Rush Week?"

Betsy's heart melted with pity, but Julia was serene. "Rush Week doesn't mean anything to me. The Epsilon Iotas have dropped me. And since they're the only crowd I care for, I don't think I'll join a sorority."

"I wouldn't either in that case," Katie said in her sensible way.

A little later Julia drew Betsy aside. "It's surprising how much better I feel since I've said out loud in public that the Epsilon Iotas have dropped me. I dreaded that so, and it wasn't half bad."

She returned to Minneapolis that night, and when the family got back from the train Betsy started upstairs with her school books but her father asked her to wait.

"Your mother and I would like to let you in on something we've been discussing."

Betsy went into the parlor and sat down. He told her the news and it was another bolt from the blue.

Pacing the floor yesterday, he had decided that Julia should go to Germany next year. He had been thinking for some time, he said, that Mrs. Ray was right, that Julia was never going to want anything but opera. Well, if that was the case, she didn't need to stay on at the U and be made unhappy by this sorority business.

He had informed Mrs. Ray who had promptly wept for joy and pleaded with him to tell Julia.

"I was tempted to myself," Mr. Ray admitted, "although I knew it would be wrong. She has to learn to take hard knocks. We can't always take them for her, nor for you and Margaret either, Betsy. I was wavering, and then she came back from church and I could see that she was going to be all right. So we're going to let her go through this darn fool week on her own steam."

"It seems cruel," Mrs. Ray said anxiously. "But Papa thinks it's right."

"I think so, too," said Betsy. "Julia had sort of a . . . triumph . . . today. She would feel cheated if it was all for nothing."

"But, oh, what a week she has ahead of her!" Mrs. Ray cried pityingly. "Those parties! The gossip! Pledge Day morning and not being bid! How can she stand it?"

"She'll stand it like hundreds of other little girls are standing it," said Mr. Ray.

But he looked unhappy, too.

19
Still Another Bolt
from the Blue

THAT WEEK WAS ONE of the longest and hardest the
Ray family had ever known. All of them were suffering with Julia. Betsy and her mother talked of little
else. Margaret made her sister a penwiper. Anna
cleaned Julia's room, shaking the curtains fiercely as
though they were the Epsilon Iotas.

"Whatever *they* are!" Anna muttered.

Mr. Ray tried to cheer himself by planning Julia's

trip to Germany. He said over and over again how sensible they were not to tell her the good news this week, and Mrs. Ray agreed. But on the night of the formal dinners, Mrs. Ray weakened.

"Let's call her up and tell her, Bob. She won't need to tell anyone else."

"All right," said Mr. Ray, yielding suddenly. "She's gone through a tough week. There's no need to make her wear a hair shirt, after all."

Mrs. Ray flew to the telephone and called the dormitory, but Julia was out. She left word for Julia to call back. Julia didn't call, and the morning of Pledge Day Mrs. Ray 'phoned again. Again Julia was out. But she had received the message last night, the matron said.

"She doesn't want to talk to us," Mrs. Ray exclaimed. "She can't bear to. Oh, Bob, we should have told her before she went back!"

"See here!" said Mr. Ray. "All the other little girls who have been dropped by sororities or were never rushed at all haven't got families who are going to send them to Europe. If they can take it, Julia can. If she doesn't want to talk to us, it's because she knows we're a bunch of sissies who would only weaken her courage."

But Mr. Ray went down to the shoe store looking grim.

Julia came home next day, and according to family tradition Mr. Ray should have met her at the train alone, bringing her home to dinner under pledge of not letting her say a word. Today, however, the whole family went to meet her.

"No telling what kind of shape she'll be in. She may want to go right to bed."

"I'll have a hot water bottle ready," said Anna, who was a little vague as to just what kind of calamity overhung Julia.

"I wonder, I wonder whether she'll blame us for not telling her," Mrs. Ray kept saying.

Mr. Ray hitched up Old Mag, and, filled with mingled sympathy and dread, the family drove to the station. The train rushed down the track beside the river to a panting steaming halt and Julia stepped off wearing a radiant smile, a gigantic new spring hat and a corsage bouquet almost as big. She flew at her family kissing and hugging.

"Be careful!" Mrs. Ray cried. "Don't crush your flowers! They're so beautiful."

"Not so beautiful as what's underneath them," said Julia, and right on the station platform she slipped off her coat. On her shirt waist a gold pin was gleaming.

"Look! I'm pledged Epsilon Iota."

"Julia!"

"Were you at the dinner?"

"Was that why you weren't at home when we 'phoned?"

"No," said Julia. "I was walking all that evening. I

walked all the way to downtown Minneapolis and back. I had to keep walking to keep going. I was so unhappy. It was the worst night of my life."

"But then—how do you happen to be wearing the pin?"

"See here!" said Mr. Ray. "We can't go into all this standing up. Pile into the surrey and I'll drive you home."

"I won't stir one foot until we've heard it all," Mrs. Ray replied.

"Then come on in the station and have some coffee," said Mr. Ray, who hated standing on his feet. So over a ring of coffee mugs, with milk for Margaret, Julia told her story.

"Well, I've known all along that one girl was keeping me out." She began to laugh. "Now I know the reason why. I've promised not to tell, so all of you must promise not to tell. It's because of Pat. Norma—the blonde, Bettina—is one of the girls I took Pat away from. *She* was blackballing me.

"The rest of the girls were just crazy to have me, and the more things I did around school—singing in *The Mikado*, acting in plays and so on—the crazier they were. They all knew Norma was voting against me, and they knew the reason why, but there wasn't anything they could do about it. Except to keep on voting over and over again, which they did. But there was always one blackball."

"Really black?" asked Margaret, her eyes enormous.

"Blacker than ink," said Julia. "And the night before Pledge Day they had the formal dinner without me, and I was walking the streets.

"But it seems that alumnae are very important in a sorority. They put up the money for houses and things. And one of the alumnae, who had seen me in *The Mikado*, was determined I was going to be an Epsilon Iota. That night, while I was walking the streets and weeping, she was gathering up a lot of other alumnae and after the banquet they all descended on the Chapter House and said, 'We want Julia Ray! We want Julia Ray!'" Julia chanted as at a football game.

"They called for a ballot and there was still one vote against me. They kept right on voting all night long and poor Norma couldn't hold out. At last, when it was almost morning, everyone was voting yes. So they sent my invitation over by messenger— they had had it all ready, lying on the table. It reached me at the dormitory yesterday morning and I went to the Epsilon Iota house and was pledged right along with the rest."

"Well for Pete's sake!" said Mr. Ray.

"That doesn't sound very . . . idealistic," Betsy remarked. "It isn't a bit the way I imagined sisterhoods were."

"How did you find out all this?" Mrs. Ray asked.

"Oh, I stayed at the house last night," Julia replied. "I slept with Patty and she told me the whole story. Of course, I promised not to tell. So don't you."

"And you don't mind joining now?" asked Betsy.

"Why, no. Everyone except Norma wanted me all along. Even Norma seemed to want me today. She cried when she kissed me good-by. And they sent me these flowers to make up for all I've gone through."

"They ought to have sent some flowers to your mother, too," Mr. Ray observed.

"And to me!" cried Betsy. "And to Margaret! And for that matter to Anna. She has a hot water bottle in your bed."

"A hot water bottle? For heaven's sake, why?" They all began to laugh but it was half crying. They got up and went out to the surrey, Julia with her arm around her mother. They piled in and drove to High Street.

Julia rushed into the house and kissed and hugged Anna and put her bouquet in the ice box and started flinging things about. She sat down at the piano and began to play a new tune.

"I brought you all the *Stubborn Cinderella* music, Bettina."

Mr. Ray didn't go back to the shoe store, and it was like a holiday.

In the evening Tony and Cab and Dennie and Tacy and Katie and Tib came in, and there was more music, and peanut fudge and excitement. Everyone examined Julia's pledge pin and she talked constantly about Epsilon Iota—the house, the girls, plans for the spring formal dance and whether or not she would take Pat.

"I don't think I will," she confided to Betsy, "on account of Norma. After all, she's my sister in Epsilon Iota now."

Usually when young people were rampaging through the house, Mr. and Mrs. Ray went to bed, although Mrs. Ray never went to sleep until the girls came up. Tonight, however, they stayed in the parlor, and when everyone went home about eleven o'clock, Julia and Betsy joined them.

Mr. Ray sat in his big chair, his legs crossed, smoking a cigar. Mrs. Ray, very bright-eyed, sat in her slender rocker. Julia flung herself down on the couch but Betsy stood in the doorway, sensing that her father and mother were now going to make their stupendous announcement.

"Julia," said Mr. Ray, "I want to have a talk with you."

His tone was so serious that Julia sat upright.

"What is it, Papa?"

"It's a talk I might postpone," he went on, "except

for one reason. I suppose there's some expense involved in this Epsilon Iota?"

"Yes, there's an initiation fee. A hundred dollars or so. Are you worried about the money, Papa?"

"Not if you're going back to the University next year. But if you aren't, you may have to make a choice."

"But, of course, I'm going back. I thought that was all settled. I was planning to stay at the U even if the Epsilon Iotas didn't bid me."

"I know," said Mr. Ray. "But your mother and I have been doing a lot of talking. We've made some plans we want to talk over with you. I thought of going into this last week when you were feeling so badly, but it seemed like giving you some help you hadn't asked for and didn't need. It seemed best to let you go through Rush Week on your own steam."

"Which I did," said Julia proudly.

"I was the one who couldn't quite stand it," said Mrs. Ray. "That's why we telephoned you Thursday night. I'm glad now we couldn't get you."

"You know why I didn't call back," said Julia. "I was feeling too badly to talk. The next morning I found out what was in the wind, but I wanted to be sure before I called you, and after that I wanted to surprise you with my pin." She patted it fondly. Then her expression grew serious. "What do you want to talk about, Papa? If you've got any worries I don't need to join Epsilon Iota right now."

Everyone was smiling, but Mr. Ray grew sober. "Julia," he said, "how would you like to go to Germany next year and study with Fraulein von Blatz?"

Julia stared at him. Betsy saw the color drain out of her face.

"I thought," said Julia, "that was out of the question. I thought you felt strongly about my putting that off."

"I did," said Mr. Ray. "But I've come to see that your singing is all you really care for. And Fraulein von Blatz is not only an excellent teacher, Mrs. Poppy says; she's a very fine woman and will have a big class of young Americans living near her in Berlin. It sounds safe enough and your mother and I have to let you go some day. We want you to go now if it's best for you, and I believe it is."

Now Julia was silent, deeply and intensely silent. The parlor quivered with her silence.

"The reason I brought it up now," said Mr. Ray, "is that it has some bearing on your joining Epsilon Iota. Germany would be, Mrs. Poppy tells me, quite an expensive business. You don't just study singing when you go abroad to study singing. You study acting, too, and languages and a lot of other things. I can swing it, but I won't have any money to spare. I wouldn't want you to go to the expense of joining a sorority—"

Julia interrupted. Yet she didn't actually interrupt for she seemed not to have heard the last few things he had said. She got up, still pale, and crossed the room. She put her arms around her father and tears began running down her cheeks.

"But you don't want me to be an opera singer!" she said.

"I never said I didn't."

"You'd rather I just got married. That's why you wanted me to go to the University first."

"I don't want you to be an opera singer unless you're darn' well sure you want to be," said Mr. Ray. "It's a hard life. But your mother has seen all winter that your heart was only in your singing. That's why you went off your nut about the sorority thing. Perhaps you know best about what you ought to do. I'm willing to send you to Germany next year, if you want to go."

Julia finished crying with her head on her father's shoulder, and then she went to her mother and cried, and to Betsy and cried some more, hugging and swinging her around.

"You'll never be sorry!" she said, turning a joyful face to her father. "You'll never be sorry!"

"Julia," said Mrs. Ray. "You haven't answered Papa's question about Epsilon Iota. I'm afraid you're disappointed not to join after being pledged and all. But you'll have to make a choice."

"What choice?" asked Julia. "There isn't any choice. The girls are swell; it was nice of them to ask me. But I don't know what choice you mean."

"Then you're going next fall," began Mrs. Ray, but Mr. Ray interrupted.

"Here's something I haven't told your mother. There's a good chance to send you in June. The Rev. Mr. Lewis is taking a party over for European travel. They will visit London, Rome and Paris and wind up in Germany. He can leave you there when he brings the rest home. How does that sound to you all?"

Julia began to cry again but she dashed the tears away as though she couldn't be bothered with them.

"In June! Papa! I must be dreaming. Oh, dear, I must hurry and give back Pat's fraternity pin."

"But you're not wearing it!" Betsy cried. "Are you crazy? There's nothing but your Epsilon Iota pledge pin on your shirt waist."

"I'm wearing his pin on my corset cover," Julia said. "It's more romantic that way. Oh, dear, dear, dear! I'm so happy!"

"Well, I'll go put the coffee pot on," said Mr. Ray, moving toward the kitchen.

"Is it too late to 'phone Mrs. Poppy? I wonder what roles I'll be singing? She'll start me on Mozart, probably," said Julia, pacing back and forth across the parlor, a smile on her tear-wet face.

20

"Sic Transit Gloria . . ."

BETSY DID SOME THINKING about sororities during spring vacation. They weren't at all what she had thought them to be. Julia's experience made them seem shallow, and the ease with which Julia had abandoned the idea of joining one had been an eye-opener, too.

Sisterhoods! That, thought Betsy, was the bunk. You couldn't make sisterhoods with rules and elections. If they meant anything, they had to grow naturally. She thought how she and Tacy had started to be friends when they were five years old. They had added Tib, Alice and Winona; then Carney and Irma. That had been almost a real sisterhood and it could have gone on forever without hurting anybody's feelings. They might have added Hazel Smith this year.

Or perhaps, Betsy thought, she and Hazel might have had a friendship independent of the Crowd. After all, you couldn't go through life rolling your friendships into one gigantic snowball. You wanted different kinds of friendships, with different kinds of people. She might like someone awfully well whom Tacy wouldn't care for at all. You ought not to go through life, even a small section of life like high school or college, with your friendships fenced in by snobbish artificial barriers.

"It would be like living in a pasture when you could have the whole world to roam in," Betsy thought. "I don't believe sororities would appeal very long to anyone with much sense of adventure."

She wondered whether Julia still had her lofty ideas about sororities and tried to question her. But it was hard to bring Julia back to the subject. She had only a short vacation, yet she had plunged into the study of

German. A singer had to know German, of course, especially if she was going to Berlin.

"Why the dickens didn't I take it up long ago? Here we are living in a town that's half German and we study only Latin. We don't see what a wonderful chance we have to learn a living language. One of your best friends is German, Bettina. If you were studying it, you could practise on her and her parents." And that was all Betsy could get out of Julia, who was on her way to take a lesson in German from the Lutheran minister's wife.

School began again and walking back and forth along High Street, where brownish green buds were swelling on the maples and the bushes around the houses were wearing pale green veils, Betsy continued to try to straighten out the matter of sororities. She had prided herself this year on being a "popular" girl. But she had never been less popular. Unpopularity had lost her a junior-senior banquet chairmanship; it had lost her the Essay Contest. If this went on she wouldn't even have a class or Zetamathian office next year. Yet the school and the school societies, she realized now, were more important to her than Okto Delta.

Of course, the "popularity" with boys had been nice but she wouldn't need to lose that if they gave up Okto Delta. In fact, the boy situation might even be improved by the collapse of the two fraternal organizations.

"Do you know," Winona said, one evening in late April when the Okto Deltas were gathered to celebrate Betsy's seventeenth birthday, "when we talked the boys into getting up that fraternity we should have made them put into their vows that they wouldn't take out any girls but us."

Everyone laughed and someone asked why.

"Because they're straying, that's why. They've almost all got crushes on freshmen girls. Do you feel perfectly sure of Dave?" she asked, looking fixedly at Betsy.

"I haven't seen him for a week," said Betsy.

"Do you know what Squirrelly said to me the other day? 'You Okto Deltas wouldn't mind, would you, if we boys brought some other girls to the parties?'"

"He didn't!"

"The nerve of him!"

"I got so mad I gave him his Omega Delta pin back, and it wouldn't surprise me to see some little freshman wearing it."

"Well, if they can take out other girls, we can go with other boys," said Irma in her soft voice.

"Hm . . . m . . . m! Easier said than done! Girls have to wait to be asked."

"Besides, we've cut ourselves off from several of

the best boys in the class. Look at Stan Moore and Joe Willard! They're certainly the leading juniors and not even in our Crowd. And we've lost Tony."

There was a sharp, rather significant silence.

"Tony is suspended again," Alice said.

"What happened?"

"I hate to say it, but I believe he came to school when he'd been drinking. He goes into the saloons sometimes with that fast gang he runs with."

"He's going around with a perfectly awful girl."

Betsy felt as though a hand had closed over her heart. She was silent through a regretful chorus of remarks that it was a shame, that Tony was an old peach and that something ought to be done about him. When the party ended she walked down the hill with the girls who were singing in parts

"You are my rose of Mexico. . . ."

Walking back alone through the April night, which held the sweetness of spring in spite of the cold, she seemed to hear Tony singing as he had sung so often beside the Ray piano. She remembered his indulgent, teasing fondness with the Crowd.

Tony had needed the Crowd. He had grown up too soon; he had been exposed to too many things too young, and it had made him a little bitter. On the other hand it had given him the experience, the sense of proportion which had enabled him to see the truth about fraternities. The others would have done well to have followed his lead in rejecting them.

But boys and girls who are old for their age need to be with people who are younger and sillier than they are. The Crowd, the normal happy high school Crowd, had been good for Tony. He had needed them, and they had let him down.

"I let him down," Betsy thought. "It was me especially, because Tony likes me. You might almost say he loves me, in a sort of way. I don't know how I'm going to do it, but I'm going to get Tony back. I'll have to manage to break up the fraternity and sorority first, though."

As it happened Betsy didn't need to take the initiative in that direction. In the Social Room next day Carney drew her aside.

"Miss Bangeter," she said, "has asked me to come to her office after school. I can't imagine what it's about. But I know it isn't anything pleasant."

"I'll go with you," Betsy offered, "wait outside the door and carry away your remains."

She waited, and Carney came out of Miss Bangeter's room looking flushed and embarrassed.

"It was about Okto Delta," she said. "She wishes we would break it up. She thinks Greek letter organizations are bad enough in college but in high school they're out of the question."

"What about the boys?" Betsy asked.

"They formed Omega Delta just to keep up with us. And she thinks it won't last long. It's the Okto Deltas she's worried about. I hope you won't mind, Betsy, but I promised her I'd urge you girls to end it."

"Heck!" said Betsy. "I'm willing. And I think everyone else is. It's been so much fun that I'd like to see it go before it's spoiled."

"So would I," said Carney.

"We'll just get together and agree to break it up."

"Sic transit Gloria," said Carney, which Betsy thought was most impressive. Carney went on earnestly, "I'd kind of like to square things with the school before I graduate. I think I'll give a party and invite the kids in our Crowd along with a lot of others—Stan, Hazel, Joe, and Phyllis Brandish. What do you say?"

"I think it's a good idea," said Betsy.

So Okto Delta, which had been born on a golden autumn hillside, disappeared with the last of the winter's frost. It melted away and was no more, and the pins were lost, or dropped into jewel cases and forgotten, or given away to boys who forgot to return them. Okto Delta went out with the school year.

The school year speeded up, as it always did in May. The members of the Domestic Science class entertained their mothers at a luncheon: cream of corn soup, croutons, croquettes, baked potato on the half shell, biscuits, salad, ice cream with toasted marshmallows, cakes and coffee.

The juniors were working furiously getting ready for the banquet. Betsy had told Hazel her idea about turning the school into a park.

"Why, that would be wonderful!" Hazel cried.

"Maybe you can think of something better," Betsy said, trying to be modest.

"No, I can't, nor of anything half so good."

Betsy's idea of a park was being carried out under Hazel's efficient direction.

The Inter-Society track meet was held and the cup went to the Philos. Since they had already secured the debating cup, much hung on the Essay Contest. Joe and Stan wrote their essays in mid-May. Betsy, herself, had no doubt as to the outcome. The Philomathians would win all three cups and it was her fault.

"I could have won the Essay Contest this year. Well, I'll win it next year or I'll know the reason why. There won't be any Okto Delta to keep me from getting the chance."

Folly was pretty well erased from their lives, but the consequences of folly were still with them.

21

The Consequences of Folly

"I DON'T KNOW WHY," said Betsy, "but I just didn't take all Gaston's talk about herbariums very seriously."

"Neither did I," said Tacy.

"Neither did I," said Tib. "But I don't see why we didn't. The very first day of school he gave us instructions about them, and he's mentioned them regularly ever since."

"We bought the paper covers and the glue and things ages ago."

"But then we forgot all about them."

"And now he wants them turned in tomorrow and he says they will count for one fourth of our year's marks! It's awful!" said Betsy, summarizing. "It's a perfectly awful situation!"

They were walking home from school in a mood of acute depression. A spell of warm rain had been followed by heat. The girls had changed that noon into thin, elbow-sleeved dresses. It was suddenly almost summer.

The rest of the Crowd had gone riding in Carney's auto, but Betsy, Tacy and Tib had not been able to go. They had come face to face at last with the matter of herbariums.

"'A herbarium,'" said Betsy, "'is a collection of dried and pressed specimens of plants, usually mounted or otherwise prepared for permanent preservation and systematically arranged in paper covers placed in boxes or cases.'"

"You know the definition all right," said Tib. "But you can't turn in a definition tomorrow."

"How many flowers did he say we had to have?"

"Fifty."

"We might as well tell him we haven't made them and all flunk the course," said practical Tib. "At least we'll be together when we repeat it next year."

"But I can't bear to flunk such an easy course. It's a disgrace!" groaned Tacy.

"Besides that," said Betsy. "I have to get some physics in sometime if I'm going to college."

Their footsteps echoed in a gloomy silence.

Then Betsy stopped. "See here!" she cried. "We're not going to give in. It's just four o'clock now and we have until nine tomorrow to make those herbariums. That's seventeen hours."

"Only nine," said Tib. "We're supposed to spend eight of them sleeping."

"*Supposed* to spend! *Supposed* to spend!" Betsy was scornful. "There's no law about going to bed the night you have to make a herbarium for botany. You both know as well as I do that the Big Hill is simply covered with flowers. We could find fifty different kinds between now and nine o'clock tomorrow."

"But, Betsy," said Tib. "We don't have to just pick them. We have to dry them and press them and paste them up and label them."

"All the harder," said Betsy triumphantly.

"All the harder! It's so hard it's impossible."

"No, it isn't. We'll have to stay at your house all night. We'll go up on the hill right now and pick until it gets dark, and then we'll go to your house and press the things we've found and paste them up.

We can label all night long."

Tacy's eyes began to shine. "Let's try. It would be fun."

"All right," said Tib. "I'm willing if you are. You can come, I think, but we can't let Papa and Mamma know we're awake all night."

They stopped in at the Ray house to telephone. Mrs. Muller didn't object to guests.

"Don't save supper for us," Tib said. "We want to get some flowers for our herbariums so we'll be out on the hill quite late. We'll fix ourselves something to eat when we come in. Don't worry if it's after dark."

Mrs. Ray said that Betsy might stay with Tib to "finish" her herbarium. They walked to Hill Street for Mrs. Kelly's permission, which they also secured. Filling their pockets with cookies and cheese—cheese, Betsy informed them, was very appropriate for such an expedition, being highly nourishing—they went up to the Big Hill.

It was the most enchanting moment of the spring. The heat had brought out little light green leaves on all the trees. Wild plum trees were in bloom, white and fragrant. They were full of bees and the grasses were full of flowers.

The girls picked industriously. They had all provided themselves with boxes and at first these seemed to fill with remarkable speed. They found clover and dandelions, and strawberry blossoms and buttercups, and wild geranium and lupine, and columbine and false Solomon's-seal.

"It's not going to be hard to find fifty different kinds at this rate," said Betsy. "Let's sit down and eat some of that nourishing cheese."

Tacy agreed but Tib warned, "We mustn't rest but a moment. It's getting late." The sun was, indeed, sinking toward the roof of Tacy's house.

They jumped up again presently. Like bird dogs on a scent they scurried in zigzag lines up the hill, picking as they went. Now they didn't seem to find many flowers they had not already found. There were purple violets.

"What about the dog-tooth kind?"

"There are plenty on top of the hill," Tacy said. They reached the top and started searching underneath the trees. They found the dog-tooth violets and spring beauties and wake-robins.

"Are the bloodroots all gone?"

"We might find just three. Here are some Dutchman's-breeches. One for each of us."

They found some ancient hepaticas, too.

Crossing the top of the hill, they dipped into the shadowy ravine. They found jacks-in-the-pulpit. They scrambled down to the stream where iris ought to be in bloom. It was. But twilight had caught up with them now. It was very dark in the ravine.

"How many have you got?" asked Tib.

"I've lost count," said Betsy.

"I have twenty-four, I think," said Tacy.

"I have thirty-two," said Tib. "And it's too dark to hunt any longer. We couldn't see anything now but a sunflower or something so big it would come up and hit us in the face."

"We'd better go home," said Betsy. "We'll get these pressed and pasted up and labeled. Then we'll set an alarm and be up and out with the sunrise. That's the best we can do."

"Maybe," suggested Tacy, "we could sneak in a few garden flowers? There are pansies around our house, and some bleeding hearts, and peonies. Lilacs, too."

"We'll certainly use them. If Gaston doesn't like it, it's just too bad," said Betsy.

Walking down the hill they finished the cookies and cheese. It was growing cool. Birds were calling to each other from tree to tree, and the west was full of gold-edged clouds.

They stopped at the Kellys' for Tacy's "dream robe," though she knew she'd have no need for it tonight. They proceeded to the Mullers', and to Tib's relief her father and mother were going out.

"Get yourselves plenty to eat now," Mrs. Muller

cautioned them. "Matilda left something for you."

"How does it happen you have to work so late. Eh?" Mr. Muller asked. "Couldn't you have collected these flowers earlier?"

"Not the spring flowers," said Tib. She tried to be vague about the whole thing. "We have to turn these herbariums in tomorrow, so we'll be pretty busy this evening."

"Well, get to bed by ten," said Mrs. Muller departing.

By ten! By ten their work was barely started. Flowers didn't dry, they discovered, simply by lying inside the dictionary for half an hour.

"We'll have to dry them in the oven," Tib decided They went down to the kitchen and lit the oven and put their flowers in.

Tib's brothers, Frederick and Hobbie, took a friendly interest. Fred lighted a lantern and went out to the vacant lot behind the house. He brought back quite a handful of weeds. Encouraged by their praise, he took the lantern and went out again—with Hobbie this time—and brought back another handful.

"This work has to be systematized," said Betsy. "We can't all sit here waiting for the flowers to bake. I'll take charge of that, and Tib can start pasting up the ones that are dried, and Tacy can start looking them up in the botany books."

"*Liebchen,*" said Tib. "We can't trust you to sit by

the fire while the flowers bake. You'd get to thinking about something else and let them all burn."

"I'll watch them," Freddie offered.

"That would be good," said Tib. "Freddie is very reliable."

So Fred and Hobbie sat by the oven watching the flowers bake and bringing them upstairs when they reached the proper state of dryness. Tacy and Tib, more deft with their fingers than Betsy, pasted rapidly while Betsy tried to identify the various specimens by consulting the botany books.

Everything was going beautifully when the Mullers' returning carriage was heard outside. The oven was hastily extinguished along with the kitchen light, and the flowers were hustled upstairs. Fred and Hobbie dashed to their room and into bed with their clothes on. The girls turned out their light, too, and when Mr. and Mrs. Muller came upstairs Tib called, "Good night. You don't need to bother to wake us. I've taken the alarm clock."

"It seems to me you could have done some of this work earlier in the season," Mr. Muller grumbled, but the girls pretended not to hear him. When the house was dark and quiet, they cautiously lighted the gas.

Finding the flowers had been hard and drying them even harder, but labeling them proved to be hardest of all. It was easy enough to track down violets and

Dutchman's-breeches, columbine and wild geranium. But some of the weeds Fred and Hobbie had brought in from the vacant lot defied classification. Midnight passed, and one o'clock and two o'clock. They were still working.

"I'm going to get some sleep," said Tib, "and I advise you to do the same. I've set the alarm for five."

So they all lay down on Tib's bed, pulling a comforter over their tired bodies.

It seemed to Betsy that she had hardly closed her eyes before the alarm clock was shrilling. Tib shut it off quickly and they tiptoed into the bathroom to splash their faces before combing their hair. There was no time for puffs today.

"I'd like a cup of coffee," Betsy said, but there wasn't time even for that. They paused in the kitchen to light the oven; they would have to dry whatever flowers they found before Matilda came down to get breakfast. Putting on their jackets, they stole out of doors.

Color was streaking the sky and birds were competing in mad chorus, but the girls were too sleepy to observe the beauty of the dawn. They reached the vacant lot and Tib stooped to begin picking, but then she uttered a disgusted exclamation.

"*Drei Dummkopfen!* That's what we are."

"What's the matter?"

"Flowers don't open until the sun comes up!"

Betsy and Tacy dropped to their knees and they saw that the humble herbage was indeed a soggy indistinguishable mass. There might or might not be blossoms later on these wet and tightly coiled grasses.

"Fine botany students we are!" cried Tacy and went off into laughter which made the robins, thrashers, meadow larks and warblers redouble their efforts at vocal supremacy.

"We might as well have had our coffee," burbled Betsy. "We have to sit here until the sun comes up."

"No," said Tib. "We'll grab handfuls just like Fred and Hobbie did last night. We can see later whether any flowers appear."

"It will add to the suspense," said Tacy, wiping laughter from her eyes, and they all began to pick. They picked until Tib said, "We simply must have fifty kinds now."

They tiptoed into the kitchen and put their scurvy specimens into the oven. Tib made coffee while they baked. Taking weeds and coffee up to Tib's room, they started pasting and labeling again.

"We can't possibly identify all these," said Tib.

"Some of them," said Tacy, "will have to remain forever anonymous."

"I know," said Betsy. "We'll make a point of the fact that we can't identify them. 'Mr. Gaston,' we will say, 'What are these rare and interesting specimens?

We can't find them in any of our learned tomes.'"

They were all feeling silly but as the sun climbed higher and the need to complete their work grew urgent they fell silent and even grim.

Mrs. Muller knocked at the door. "Are you awake?"

"Oh, yes. We've been down and had our breakfast. Tell Matilda not to be surprised if the oven is hot."

At eight o'clock they stumbled out of the house, rumpled, pale, with lines beneath their eyes and herbariums under their arms.

"I think," said Tib, as they walked down Hill Street, "that this was an idiotic thing to do."

Betsy and Tacy grunted.

"Why, I realized last night that I would have enjoyed making a herbarium. I like to do that sort of thing. I could have made a good one."

"So could I," admitted Tacy.

"Well, I couldn't," said Betsy. "But I should have been interested, at least. I'm crazy enough about flowers."

"As a matter of fact," said Tib, "we've had a pretty foolish year. You and I especially, Betsy. It's been fun, and I guess it's been worth it but I wouldn't want another year this foolish."

"Neither would I," said Tacy.

"Me either," said Betsy.

"We're getting a little old for this sort of thing," said Tib, looking severe.

22

The Junior-Senior Banquet

THE JUNIOR-SENIOR BANQUET was drawing near now and Betsy, Tacy and Tib—herbariums and exams disposed of—were working hard on the decorating committee.

It usually met at the Ray house.

"You can just as well meet here. It's so convenient

to school," Betsy had said, and now, as a matter of course, Hazel Smith came in with Tacy and Tib almost every day.

Tib was only an ex-officio member of the committee, but her small artistic fingers made her invaluable.

"My right-hand woman!" Hazel declared.

The four went downtown to buy favors for the fish pond, tissue paper, cardboard for signs. They returned to the Rays' to make fudge or poach eggs, according to their moods and appetites.

Cab and Dennie declared themselves ex-officio members also. Cab covered himself with glory with a NO FLIRTING ALLOWED sign for Lovers' Lane. Margaret wrapped packages happily for the fish pond. One night Hazel, Tacy and Tib stayed all night, spreading from Betsy's into Julia's room, frantically talking Junior-Senior Banquet. It was almost, but not quite, like making herbariums.

Even in the midst of this excitement, Betsy could not forget about Tony. There was a sore place in her heart because of him. He wasn't in school. He had not come to the Rays' for several weeks, and the night before the banquet she telephoned him.

"Can't you come to lunch Sunday night?"

"Sorry. I've got a date."

"What do you mean, having a date on Sunday night? Papa's feelings are hurt."

"I'll bet," Tony replied. There was a brief silence. Then he said, "Maybe your father wouldn't even want me to come? Has he heard about the mess I'm in?"

"My father," Betsy replied, "says you're the only boy who comes to the house who really appreciates his sandwiches. He's clamoring for you, Tony."

"Really?" Tony sounded pleased.

"You show up!" Betsy said. "That's an order. And by the way"—she tried hard to be casual—"don't you want me to save a dance for you at the banquet?"

"I'm not going," Tony said.

"Tony Markham! Not coming to your own Junior-Senior Banquet? You must be crazy."

"You know I've been suspended."

"Suspended isn't expelled. You'll probably be suspended more than once before you graduate. How many dances shall I save?"

"Do you dance with a barb?"

"Evidently," said Betsy, "you haven't been keeping up with school affairs. There aren't any Greek letter organizations at Deep Valley High any more. They're ended. They're *kaput*."

There was another silence, longer this time.

"Is that straight?" Tony asked.

"Of course it is. We all got tired of the things, and besides Miss Bangeter called us down. You aren't the only one who gets called down, you know. We were fools ever to start them, Tony. They lost us all the good committee appointments this spring. They lost me the chance to try out for the Essay Contest. You were the only one in the Crowd with any sense, when you turned thumbs down."

Tony replied quickly this time. His big deep laugh rolled out over the 'phone.

"Sure you can save me some dances," he said. "Two of them. Both waltzes, please. Say, Betsy! You haven't forgotten how to waltz?"

"You'll see," Betsy replied.

Junior-Senior Banquet day dawned hot. It was, by some freak of Minnesota weather, ninety in the shade, but the juniors were too conscious of their responsibilities even to know that it was hot. Wearing their oldest clothes, sleeves rolled up for action, they moved into the high school in a body.

Down in the Domestic Science room aprons were being donned, ovens were being lighted, egg beaters were whirling.

Stan, in overalls, went about chanting his speech, the "Farewell to the Seniors" he had to deliver that night.

Lloyd had brought his auto, and he and Tib and Hazel drove to the woods for boughs of blooming trees. Betsy and Tacy, putting up signs, pounded until their fingers were blue. They dragged settees, pushed tables, ran upstairs and down.

Rain began, and the palms which were to make Lovers' Lane had not arrived. Hazel stared at Betsy and Tacy in misery, and Dave, who was making the fish pond—pants rolled up and hair on end—offered to go out and chop down some trees. But the palms came after all.

And so at last did six o'clock. Tantalizing odors were rising from the Domestic Science room. It was time to go home and dress.

The decorating committee paused for a final proud look. The park was a bower of flowery green. A swing rocked in one shady corner. Lovers' Lane led cool and inviting up the stairs.

Betsy put her arm around Hazel. "It looks beautiful," she said.

"It was a wonderful idea of yours, Betsy."

"You were the big executive who carried it out."

Stan joined them and Betsy lifted a dirty but radiant face.

"It's going to make history, Stan. The banquet given by the class of 1910 will never be forgotten."

"You've worked hard," said Stan. "All your Crowd has."

Betsy knew that this was an apology.

"Save a dance for me," he said.

"I will," she promised.

At home she bathed and dressed hurriedly. Her mother asked whether Dave had, by any chance, signified his intention of calling for her and Betsy said he hadn't.

"I think he will though," she added.

Strangely enough, she didn't care very much. It would not seem tragic if she went to the banquet alone or with a bunch of girls. She was thinking about the park. How Carney and the other seniors would rave about it!

"We did a grand job!" she exclaimed to her family.

Dave appeared at eight o'clock, immaculate, every hair in place.

"You look a little different than you did an hour ago," said Betsy, smiling.

Appraising Betsy in the old rose dress he actually answered.

"So do you," he said.

The tables in the Domestic Science room gleamed with borrowed linen and silver. Irma, Alice and Winona, in ruffled aprons, served. The program committee, headed by Joe Willard, had provided little booklets which he had had printed at the *Deep Valley Sun*. They included the menu, the list of speeches, and the dance program.

Thanks to Joe, perhaps, the menu had a highly intellectual flavor.

*"Now good digestion wait on appetite and
health on both."*—SHAKESPEARE
Fruit Cocktail

"Can one desire too much of a good thing?"—CERVANTES
Roast Lamb and Mashed Potatoes
Mint Jelly
Peas in Timbale Cases
Olives
Rolls
Nuts

"My appetite comes to me while eating."—MONTAIGNE
Tomato and Asparagus Salad
Cheese and Crackers

"Then farewell heat and welcome frost."—SHAKESPEARE
Ice Cream
Cakes
Coffee
Candy

After the dinner there were toasts. Miss Bangeter
spoke on "The Event," and told of past Junior-Senior
Banquets. Stan, transformed as Dave was and completely poised, toasted the seniors. He did better, the
juniors thought, than the senior girl who returned
the toast.

The company repaired to the park to swing and fish in the pond and flirt along Lovers' Lane. Programs for the dance were filled out—Betsy's was completed in no time—and Mamie Dodd began to play the piano in the upper hall, which had been kept clear for dancing.

Betsy came out of the girls' cloak room to which she had repaired to freshen her hair and put powder on her face. She was very happy. She knew she would be tired tomorrow, but the park had been worth it. It had been a glorious success.

Besides, Tony had come and claimed his two waltzes. He had not come for the dinner and she had been worried, but he had arrived for the dancing, looking exceptionally well pressed and well groomed. Miss Bangeter had crossed the room to speak to him.

Waiting for Dave, who had taken the first dance, Betsy saw Joe Willard break away from a group across the room and come toward her. He had never asked her for a dance. In fact, she didn't think he had ever danced with any girl in school except Phyllis. He and Phyllis had always dropped into high school parties too late to fill out programs. As a result they had always danced just with each other and had usually left early. Tonight they had been present when the programs were filled out. There was no reason, Betsy thought, why he should not have asked her for a dance. But he hadn't.

However, he was coming toward her purposefully now.

He looked happy. All the juniors were happy tonight. His pompadour looked very high and light above his dark blue suit.

"May I have a dance, Miss Ray?"

"Why did you have to be so slow? My program is all full," said Betsy and waited fearfully remembering how sensitive Joe had always been. But evidently he had lost that chip he used to carry on his shoulder. Going with Phyllis had made him . . . suave, she thought.

"That was dumb of Willard!" he answered cheerfully.

This was reassuring but nevertheless Betsy was determined not to let him go.

In her freshman year he had asked to walk home with her from a party and she had had to turn him down. After a long time he had asked to walk home with her from the library one evening. Again she had had to turn him down.

"This would be three times and out," she thought. "I have to break this jinx."

She smiled. "I'm going to give you a dance," she said. "Some of these people who took two can just give one up."

"Good!" said Joe. "That's the spirit I like to see.

Who shall we steal from?" He took her program and studied it. "Markham has the best disposition."

"But I like him the best!" protested Betsy. "Tony is a great favorite of mine."

"Who shall it be then?"

"Lloyd. He only took two because Tib was mad at him, and I think she's relenting. When he comes to get me we'll just say there's been a mix-up."

"Mix-up Willard," said Joe, writing down his name. The stolen dance was the eleventh one, the next to the last. His program, except for the eleventh dance, bore only a sprawling perpendicular "Phyllis."

Carney had just come out of the girls' cloak room.

"Did I hear you scratch a dance for Joe Willard?" she asked. "Do you remember telling me that he didn't mean anything to you but the Essay Contest?"

Betsy flushed and smiled.

"What's up?" asked Winona, joining them.

"Joe Willard just asked Betsy for a dance."

"Really? Phyllis won't like this!" Winona took a look at Betsy's program. "Bet a nickel she'll make him go home before we reach number eleven."

The evening sped along from waltz to two-step, from schottische to barn dance.

"I must admit you can still waltz. It's all because I took you in hand when you were young," said Tony.

Betsy had glanced at his program. He was dancing with Tacy, Irma, Carney. She felt with thankfulness that she had taken the first step toward rescuing Tony, although he was not yet out of danger.

At the end of the second waltz she said, "See you for Sunday night lunch?"

"I hope your father has plenty of onions in the house," Tony replied.

His black eyes were teasing, but she knew that he would come.

"I hear," Hazel remarked to Betsy, "that Joe Willard has asked you for a dance."

"What's this about Joe Willard asking you to dance?" Tacy inquired.

"Has Joe Willard really asked you for a dance?" questioned Tib.

"Heavens!" said Betsy. "News spreads fast around this high school."

"I even heard that you scratched a dance to give him one," said Tib.

"Maybe the *Deep Valley Sun* would like a story about it," Betsy replied.

She realized presently that the great news must have reached Phyllis. Phyllis and Joe were standing at the cloak room door engaged in what was plainly an altercation. Betsy couldn't hear what they were saying but from their expressions, the growing tenseness of the conversation, she felt she could interpret it.

Phyllis had said that she wanted to go home; Joe had objected.

"Why, we always go home early," Betsy could imagine Phyllis saying.

Joe would be casual. "Oh, let's wait a little while!"

"I'd like to go now if you don't mind."

"Well, look, Phyllis. I have a date. And she scratched another fellow's dance to give me one."

"Really? Well, you may do as you like. *I'm* going home."

Betsy didn't hear this conversation but she must have imagined it with some degree of exactness, for Phyllis went into the cloak room and came out with her pale green opera cape, and Joe held it for her and they went down the stairs.

In five minutes the news had spread around the hall. Joe Willard had asked Betsy Ray for a dance. She had scratched off a name to give him one and then Phyllis wouldn't let him stay for it.

"I'm afraid Phyllis is boss," Carney whispered regretfully.

"I think he'll come back," Betsy said.

The tenth dance ended and there followed the brief intermission during which boys took leave of their old partners and sought new ones. Betsy waited for Joe. He did not come.

Mamie Dodd started to play the piano. It was a new song Betsy liked.

"The girl I'll call my sweetheart,
Must look like you. . . ."

Couples moved out to the floor, circled. Still Joe didn't come.

Betsy stood alone. She would stand there only a moment. She knew the proper thing to do if you were stranded without a partner, although she had seldom found herself in that undesirable predicament. She started to move toward the cloak room but first her eyes circled the hall and she saw Joe almost running up the stairs.

His mouth smiled but his eyes were stormy and rebellious. He looked as though he had come from a battle. Betsy knew that he had taken Phyllis to her automobile but had refused to go home before the eleventh dance.

Betsy smiled. Joe put his arm around her and they moved out onto the dance floor. He danced well, not smoothly like Dave, nor with Tony's rhythmic skill but with zest and in perfect time. He whirled her as she had never been whirled before.

She was glad to be whirled. It was a triumph to be dancing with Joe Willard. Yet it wasn't just triumph which filled her.

"Does it mean anything?" she wondered. "For next year, of course."

Joe would not, she felt sure, desert Phyllis now, even though they had had a disagreement. He was a fundamentally loyal person. He had been unwilling to humiliate Betsy by leaving her without a partner, and he would certainly not humiliate Phyllis, with whom he had had such a good time all year, by deserting her at the beginning of a gay Commencement week—when she was a senior, too. He would see her through.

But maybe, just the same, he didn't care about her any more. Maybe he never had.

"I wonder, what about next year," thought Betsy, whirling in Joe Willard's arms.

23

Tar

"PERHAPS IT WASN'T such a good idea to rouse the Philos' fighting spirit by putting up that pennant last fall," Carney said.

A group of Zet girls sat together on the alcove bookcase in the high school auditorium. This was gay with Zetamathian blue and Philomathian orange. It was the evening assembly at which the Essay Cup would be awarded.

Always a great occasion, opening Commencement week, this year it held unusual importance. The Philomathians had already won in debating and athletics. If they won the Essay Cup tonight they would have the almost unprecedented honor of holding all three cups.

Betsy found it exciting to be sitting with the others. In her freshman and sophomore years she had been a contestant, and so had sat in regal aloofness on the platform. Down in the teeming, turbulent, rumor-filled auditorium, suspense enveloped her and hemmed her in. It was terrible to think that the Philos might win tonight, but Betsy agreed with Carney that there was danger.

"Joe Willard," she declared, "will win over Stan."

She was a good prophet. The freshman points went to the Philos. The sophomore points went to the Philos. Then, before a screaming, cheering crowd, Joe Willard for the third year in succession was announced to have won his class points. He stood up to take the applause, his yellow hair shining, his face shining, too, with pleasure.

No matter where the senior points went, the Philos had won now, and they almost went mad with joy.

> *"Philo, Philo, Philo*
> *Philomathian. . . . Wow!"*

> *"Poor old Zet. Poor old Zet!"*

And, of course;

> *"What's the matter with Willard?*
> *He's all right."*

Betsy felt mixed emotions. As a Zetamathian she was crushed. This year, she felt sure, she could have been the deciding factor in winning the Essay Contest. The third orange bow, which Miss Bangeter was tying now, reproached and mocked her. On the other hand, liking Joe as she did, she couldn't help rejoicing in his moment of splendid triumph.

The next morning report cards were given out. Tacy and Tib called for Betsy. They met Cab and Dennie on High Street, and just as she had done the previous fall, Tacy cried out suddenly, "What's that crowd doing in front of the high school? Is it on fire?"

"Gosh!" said Cab. "It would be wasteful to have it burn down now when examinations are over."

Something remarkable was going on, for the crowd pushed from the school lawn out into the street. Everyone was looking up at the roof, and Cab and Dennie began to run.

"Were you up on that roof again last night?" Tib cried.

"Heck, no! and neither was Dave!"

But it developed shortly that not Cab nor Dennie nor Dave could possibly have been suspected of this skulduggery. Giant letters were painted on the high school roof. But the paint was orange. The letters spelled out PHILOMATHIAN.

"How could anyone have painted on that steep roof?"

"They must have had a ladder."

"See that strip of black paint underneath."

But it wasn't black paint, they discovered when they reached the school house.

"It's tar. It was put on so no Zetamathian boy could reach the letters and paint them out. Dave Hunt shinnied up to the cupola, all the way to the roof, but then he discovered the tar. He almost got stuck in it."

"He must be mad," Betsy cried.

"Not so mad as Miss Bangeter."

Miss Bangeter, the students discovered when a furiously clanging gong had brought them into the high school, was really angry. She did not even announce an opening song. Tall and terrible, her black eyes flashing beneath the high twist of black hair, she came to the front of the platform.

"Last fall a Zetamathian pennant was put up on the roof," she said. "The perpetrator was reprimanded and it was explained to the whole school that it was dangerous to attempt to climb the high school roof. But last night, as you have all seen, this rule was disobeyed. Will all the Philomathian boys in the school please rise?"

There was a clatter as more than a hundred boys rose to their feet.

"Will you form a line and march past me?"

They formed a line and marched. Carney did not play a tune. The procession wasn't exhilarating and gay. It was awkward, anxious, slow; and it soon became slower.

"It isn't likely," Miss Bangeter said, when the line reached the platform, "that the boys who spread that tar on the roof could have done it without getting some on their own feet. Will each boy stop as he passes my desk and show me the bottom of his shoes?"

The long line filed past her. As each boy passed he stopped and lifted his feet. Now and then Miss Bangeter asked one to step out of line. The others returned to their seats. At the end there were three boys standing beside her. They were Squirrelly, Tony, and Joe.

Squirrelly looked innocent as he always did. Tony's

eyes were laughing. Joe Willard's lips were compressed.

"I take it," said Miss Bangeter, "that you three boys painted the letters on the roof?"

"I did," said Squirrelly.

"I did," said Tony, in his deep voice.

"I didn't," said Joe, and after a wave of surprise which rolled over the assembly room had subsided he said with a broad grin, "I spread the tar."

Miss Bangeter's lips twitched.

"You three may come to my office after school," she said.

Punishment, every one knew, would be severe and it was. The three boys were suspended, but that was a formality, since school was already over. They were obliged, however, to pay for having the letters and the tar removed and that proved to be expensive. Workmen swarmed up tall ladders with buckets and brooms but it was a long time before the orange Philomathian and the black band of tar were erased from the Deep Valley High School roof. In fact, the tar never quite came off.

Report cards were an anti-climax, although Betsy was pleased to find that most of her grades had improved. Miss Fowler raised her to 95; Miss Clarke, grieving about the Essay Contest, perhaps, gave her 93; Miss Erickson, forgiving the "old pill" incident, conceded her 90.

Mr. Gaston awarded a grim 75 to Betsy, to Tacy and to Tib.

"Never, never in my whole life," said Mr. Gaston, (he was twenty-four), "never in my whole career as a teacher," (he had taught for three years), "have I seen such herbariums! Not a fall flower included!"

But he felt a little guilty, perhaps because he could not identify all the specimens they had presented. At any rate, for whatever reason, he passed them.

The chorus was practising in the Opera House for Commencement.

> *"I heard the trailing garments of the night,*
> *Sweep through her marble halls!*
> *I saw her sable skirts all fringed with light. . . ."*

Betsy loved that song, and it wove itself through the events of the torrid June week when Julia, back from the U, was getting ready to sail away to Europe and Carney was getting ready to graduate. Carney's hard work had not been for nothing. She had been accepted for Vassar.

"We . . . are . . . the class of oh-nine," sang Carney, Al, Squirrelly and the rest of the seniors on Class Day to the now familiar tune of "Old, Old is Honeymoon Trail." Then Commencement was upon them.

The Opera House was crowded with proud relatives

and friends, and the graduates sat on the platform with the chorus behind them.

"I heard the trailing garments of the night," sang Betsy and Tacy. There were speeches; Carney made one of them. And the seniors crossed the stage one by one, received their diplomas while loyal hands applauded.

Phyllis in a white lace dress carried a big bouquet of roses. It came from Joe, Betsy felt sure, but she did not see Joe in the audience. Phil came right behind his sister looking sheepishly pleased, not sulky at all.

Carney came, her dimple showing, and she, too, carried roses.

"Do you know who sent Carney her bouquet?"

"Al Larson, I suppose."

"No. It was Larry Humphreys. He's been out in California three years now, but he hasn't forgotten her."

Carney received a large number of presents but none of them, she assured Betsy, was more cherished than the jabot which Betsy finished and delivered, wrapped in tissue paper and ribbon, along with a silver spoon.

"It's very nice," said Carney smoothing the tortured looking object. "I'm going to take it to Vassar with me."

"Will you wear it?"

"I promised to. Didn't I? But just once! Then I'll hang it up as a souvenir."

After the graduating exercises Mr. and Mrs. Sibley gave a party for Carney. It was the one Carney had suggested the day she and Betsy agreed to break up Okto Delta. The Crowd was invited along with many other friends—Hazel and Stan and the Brandishes and Joe.

It was a beautiful party. There was punch in a big crystal bowl. There were little frosted cakes. Young and old moved happily through the front and back parlor and the library of the Sibleys' spacious house. Betsy kept looking for Joe Willard. But he wasn't there.

"He's left for the summer," Carney explained when Betsy asked her at last. "He's going to the harvest fields again."

Betsy wished she had seen him before he left.

"Cab isn't here either," Irma remarked.

"No," answered Carney, looking serious. "He telephoned early this evening. His father has gone to the hospital."

24
Growing Up

CAB'S FATHER DIED. He had been ill for some time, and Mrs. Ray had been sending cakes, pies and hot casserole dishes over to the Edwards family, who lived less than a block away. First he was ill at home and then he was removed to the hospital. One day in mid-June Dennie came into the Ray house to say,

"Mr. Edwards died last night. I was down at the hospital with Cab."

Dennie looked as though he hadn't slept. His curly hair was more than ordinarily rumpled and his eyes were swelled. He didn't have the jaunty carefree look which usually characterized both him and Cab.

The Rays grew suddenly sober, as people in a happy home do when death strikes in another happy home. Betsy didn't know Cab's father very well. She knew he was stern but also just and kind, and that Cab's mother was a gentle, somewhat helpless woman, and that there were several younger children.

The Crowd sent flowers and many of them went to the funeral. Betsy went with her father and mother. The Edwards' house seemed odd and unfamiliar, with folding chairs set out in the parlor, the air heavy with the scent of flowers. Betsy caught a glimpse of Cab in a dark, well-pressed suit, looking pale but composed and manly. He kept close hold of the arm of his mother, whose face was hidden under a thick black veil. The little sisters sat with some of the older relatives. Betsy saw Cab turn and look at them once or twice, especially when the littlest sister cried.

Two days later, when Betsy was baking a Domestic Science plum cake, he came in at the kitchen door. He seemed almost like his usual self and remarked, sniffing, that something smelled good.

"And I produced it!" Betsy said. "Anna is busy washing and ironing for Julia. She leaves the last of the week, you know."

"How soon will it be done?" asked Cab.

"In time to give you a piece."

She couldn't bring herself to mention his father but when they went into the parlor her own father, coming in for dinner, referred to his loss and Cab seemed glad to talk.

"My mother's been wonderful," he said.

"I just stopped in at your house," Mr. Ray replied. "She said the same thing about you."

Cab flushed. "There's been a lot to attend to," he said. "Not just the funeral. My uncle and aunt helped us to make arrangements for that. But Dad's store. . . . Somebody has to pitch in and take his place, and it looks as though it would be me."

"You mean this summer?" Betsy asked.

"Not just this summer." He addressed Mr. Ray. "You know old Mr. Loring has been Dad's clerk for years. He can take charge, but the business wouldn't justify hiring another clerk. I've worked there vacations. I'd fit in pretty well and at the same time I'd learn the business so that I could take over from Mr. Loring some day."

"You won't . . . go back to school?" Betsy could hardly take it in.

"Nope. Will you buy your furniture from me, Betsy?"

"But, Cab, you were going to be an engineer!"

"Mamma can't run the business. She has to take care of the kids."

"But . . . could you . . . can you. . . ."

"Heck!" said Cab. "I'm seventeen."

After dinner Betsy went up to her bedroom. She had cried at Cab's father's funeral. She didn't feel like crying now, but she had a heavy sick feeling.

"Cab isn't going to graduate. He wanted to, just as much as I do. He had all kinds of class spirit. But he's not even going back.

"He's taking over his father's store. And he's no older than I am. I wonder if I could do that if my father died—stop school, pitch in and help my mother."

She looked at herself closely in the mirror.

"I'm seventeen, but I've certainly not been acting it. How silly and kiddish we've all been this year! Well, it's all for over for Cab. He's grown up."

She sat down, knotting her hands tightly together, trying to think.

Cab was one of her best friends. Yesterday he had been as sheltered and carefree as she was. Now he had joined the ranks of those who, like Joe and Mamie Dodd, had no fathers to look after them.

"Just one thing happened. Something that could happen to anyone in a minute. His father dying has made all the difference."

It seemed strange and a little wonderful that Cab had been able to grow up so suddenly, that he had been able to produce when he needed it the strength to take care of his mother and little sisters.

"I don't suppose he knew he had it in him. I hope I have it in me. I hope I could pull out strength and courage like that if I found I needed to."

She got up and began to walk around again.

"Oh, I'm sorry, sorry that Cab is leaving school!"

"Betsy," called her mother. "Don't forget you have a music lesson." As Betsy came down the stairs Mrs. Ray said anxiously, "You look pale. Are you sure you feel able to go? I'll call Miss Cobb."

"Listen to that!" Betsy thought to herself. "My mother and father are always looking after me. I've got to start standing on my own two feet. I've got to start growing up, too."

"No, thanks," she said cheerfully. "I feel fine. I haven't practised a bit this week but I don't think Miss Cobb will expect it. She knows we're in a dither getting Julia off."

"She's busy with the same sort of thing, only less happy," Mrs. Ray said. "She's getting Leonard ready to go to Colorado. He hasn't been getting any better . . . he's been getting worse. So she's sending him out to the mountains."

"Will he get well, do you think, Mamma?"

"I hope so," Mrs. Ray said doubtfully. "But I'm glad young Bobby is so husky."

After her lesson Betsy went into the little back parlor to say good-by to Leonard. He looked even thinner than usual and his cheeks were like crimson tissue paper. But he laughed and joked, saying good-by to Betsy.

"Don't learn too much piano while I'm gone," he said. "I want you to be coming for lessons when I get home again."

"I'm practically a Paderewski this minute," Betsy answered. "I can play the 'Soul Kiss' music. But I intend to keep on studying just because I like your Auntie."

"I'm not surprised," said Leonard. "I like her myself."

He smiled at Miss Cobb, whose answering smile was as calm and cheerful as though he were going to St. John to play football instead of to the Colorado mountains to die.

"I hope he'll prove it by writing some letters," she said. "And not just the 'having-a-fine-time-hope-you-are-too' kind of letters. That's the sort he usually writes."

Betsy tried to imitate Miss Cobb's serene matter-of-factness.

"Will you write to me, too? If you do, and if what your aunt says is true, you'll get the best of the bargain. I write simply gigantic letters to Julia and to Herbert Humphreys out in California."

Leonard's face brightened. "I could use some long epistles like that while I'm in Colorado."

"See that you answer them," Betsy replied.

Leonard's brother Bobby passed her on the steps. He was rushing into the house, rosy and disheveled. Betsy knew why her mother was glad that Bobby was so husky. Miss Cobb would have one out of the four children she had raised.

"That's one promise I'm going to keep," Betsy muttered in an undertone, walking away. "I'm going to write to Leonard every week as long as he lives."

She walked up the hill toward her own home slowly, for the weather was still warm. The air smelled of roses in bloom in every dooryard. There were snow balls in bloom, too, white and luscious, and orioles were singing and whistling in the maples. Betsy kept thinking about Leonard and Cab.

When she reached home she found a postal card lying on the music room table. It lay face up and she saw the picture of the Main Street of a small north Texas town.

She turned it over and found that it was addressed to herself. It came from Joe Willard. He had written, "Did anyone ever tell you that you're a good dancer? Joe."

She stood for some time with the card in her hand before she went upstairs.

Her mother and Julia were busy with the trunk in Julia's room. They called "Hello" and she responded but she didn't join them. She went to her own room.

She put the card first in the handkerchief box where she always put notes from boys she was in love with, but after a few minutes she took it out. It didn't seem to belong there.

She stuck it into the mirror where she sometimes put dance programs and invitations and other gay things. She left it there a while but it didn't seem right there either.

She wandered over to Uncle Keith's trunk, her beloved desk. Above it hung a picture of a long-legged white bird which Herbert had sent her. She kept it above the trunk because it reminded her of Babcock's Bay out at Murmuring Lake.

Still holding the postal card from Joe, she stared at the bird reflectively.

All those resolutions she had made on Babcock's Bay! How they had been smashed to smithereens! She wondered whether life consisted of making resolutions and breaking them, of climbing up and slipping down.

"I believe that's it," she thought. "And the bright side of it is that you never slip down to quite the point you started climbing from. You always gain a little. This year I've gained my music lessons, and all the things Miss Fowler taught me about writing, and a postal card from Joe." That seemed funny to her and she laughed, but she grew serious again.

She thought about those lists she had made in her programs for self-improvement. She hadn't followed them out by any means, but they had revealed her ideals.

At first they had been mostly about brushing hair and teeth. Then she had reached out for charm: green bows, foreign phrases, perfumes, a bath every day. Last summer's resolves to be thoughtful at home and to excel at school, had shown a sort of groping after maturity.

"And this year," she thought. "I haven't even started a list. I've just realized definitely that there were things I wanted to do. . . ."

She was going to write to Leonard, to reach out for people like Hazel Smith, to get Tony away from that wild gang and keep him safe in the Crowd.

"Gosh!" she thought. "I must be growing up."

It came to her that there was more to growing up than drinking coffee at Heinz's.

The whole Crowd, she decided, was growing up. Carney had begun when she worked so hard on those entrance exams for Vassar. Tony had begun when he took his stand against fraternities, and even when he had that fling at wildness which Betsy hoped to end. Tacy had begun in her absorption in music and Tib, when she had seen so clearly how silly they had been about herbariums.

Cab, of course, had grown up more than any of them.

But all of them were growing up, Betsy thought intensely. They would never be quite so silly again. The foolish crazy things they had done this year they would do less and less frequently until they didn't do them at all.

"We're growing up," Betsy said aloud. She wasn't even sure she liked it. But it happened, and then it was irrevocable. There was nothing you could do about it except to try to see that you grew up into the kind of human being you wanted to be.

"I'd like to be a fine one," Betsy thought quickly and urgently.

Anna came up to Julia's bedroom with an armful of freshly pressed clothes for the trunk. Betsy could hear Julia's voice and Margaret's and her mother's. A second trunk stood open in Mrs. Ray's room, for the Ray family was going to the lake as soon as Julia sailed away. Betsy could almost smell the water lilies on Babcock's Bay. She opened the trunk and got out her novel.

"I'm going to finish this, although it's terrible. And I'm going to start another, better one; or maybe I'll do a short story first and send it to the *Delineator*. It's time I started selling my stories. Here! Here! Here!" she thought, laughing. "I'm making a list."

But perhaps people who liked to write always made lists! Just for the fun of it.

She heard the front door downstairs open and Tacy and Tib called, "Yoo hoo!"

"Yoo hoo! Come on up," called Betsy.

She put Joe Willard's postal card into Uncle Keith's trunk.

Betsy and Joe

To Delos

Contents

All's well that ends well.

—Wм. Sнакеspeare

1

A Courier with Letters

AT THE TOP OF Agency Hill, Betsy Ray turned Old Mag off the road into the shade of an elm.

The old mare always climbed the hill at a snail's pace. But once on the summit, out on the high undulating plain that led to Murmuring Lake, she usually, of her own accord, broke into a trot. Today she continued to walk, turning her head—ears enclosed rakishly by the lacy betasseled fly net—to Betsy in the surrey as though to ask whether speed was really necessary. Betsy guided her into the deep patch of shade.

"I know it's hot, old girl," she said, using her father's affectionate address. "And that was a long hill. Let's rest."

Old Mag flapped her tail, shook off flies languidly, and stopped.

Betsy turned in her seat and looked down the road up which she had come—a long dusty road, fringed with butterfly weed and purple vetch. It bisected residential streets which ran in parallel rows all the way down to the river. Beyond this silver streak hills climbed again, giving the town of Deep Valley its name.

Betsy's eye could pick up many landmarks—the red brick turret of the high school she would enter as a senior that fall, and near it, at the corner of High Street and Plum, the roof of her own home, a green, frame, vine-covered house where boys and girls loved to gather after school. Far to the south rose Hill Street, where she had lived as a child with red-haired Tacy Kelly and yellow-haired Tib Muller for playmates. Betsy, Tacy, and Tib had picnicked and explored over every rise of those distant, wooded slopes.

Looking down to Front Street, she found her father's shoe store, and between Front and the river, the shining rails which, less than a month ago, had carried her older sister Julia away to Boston and the S. S. *Romanic* and a summer of travel in Europe. This was to be followed by a winter of study in Berlin. Julia planned to be an opera singer.

Since Julia's departure, Betsy had been visiting Tacy and Tib. Her mother and her younger sister Margaret were settled at Murmuring Lake Inn, to which Mr. Ray drove out every night from the store. Betsy had stayed in town because Carney Sibley, a member of the Crowd, was entertaining a house guest whose visit had brought on an unexpected summer crop of parties.

Deep Valley was quiet now, almost as quiet as it looked, simmering in the heat between its hills. The Crowd was dispersing to lake cottages, and the farms of relatives, and vacations in the nearby Twin Cities of Minneapolis and St. Paul. Tib was going to Milwaukee.

A group of the boys had left that day on a canoe trip. They were paddling down the river to the Mississippi and a brief way along that celebrated stream. Joe Willard had left early in June to work in the harvest fields.

"There's hardly a soul left in town but Tony," Betsy thought. Cab, too, of course. His father had died recently and Cab was helping in the family furniture store. Tony had taken a job at the Creamery.

Betsy was glad she hadn't been forced to spend the hot day at the shoe store waiting for her father.

"You take Old Mag and go along," Mr. Ray had said with characteristic thoughtfulness. "I'll pick up a ride tonight. You might as well get out in time for a swim."

Betsy was pleased to be taking the solitary drive. She was a friendly, fun-loving girl with high spirits, touched off like firecrackers under a match by the company of others. Yet as she grew older, she liked increasingly to be alone.

She wanted to be a writer, and she had already discovered that poems and stories came most readily from the deep well of solitude. Moreover, she had discovered that at seventeen one was growing up so fast that one needed time to think, to correlate all the perplexing changes and try to understand them.

Betsy was very conscious of being on the threshold of the adult world; although, unlike her sister Julia, she did not long to enter it. Betsy had clung to every phase of childhood as it passed. She always wanted to keep life from going forward too fast.

Her friend, Tacy, was the same. They both had gallant adventurous plans for their lives out in what Julia called the Great World. But they were well content to linger in high school. Like Julia, Tacy was musical, an inheritance perhaps from her father, who played a worn, beloved violin whenever time allowed. Tacy sang in a tender soprano voice.

"You grow older in spite of yourself," Betsy thought resentfully, her gaze returning to the red brick turret. She would be graduating from high school next June, in the Class of 1910. Feeling suddenly that she didn't want to be seventeen, she pulled off her gloves and took off her large flower-laden hat.

"I wish I were a freshman again!" she exclaimed.

Bareheaded, her hair blowing, she looked younger, but she did not look like the Betsy Ray who had entered high school four years before. At thirteen, grown suddenly tall and thin, she had been plainly in the awkward age. Now she enjoyed being tall and slender. She loved high heels that made her even taller, large droopy hats, lacy clothes, perfumes, bracelets, and polished fingernails.

She curled her dark hair every night and wore it parted and pomped on the sides. Her skin was pink and white, very quick to flush. She had warm hazel eyes and a bright ready smile which was one of the things her friends liked most about her. Betsy thought it regrettable, for her teeth were parted in front, giving her an ingenuous expression. She preferred to look enigmatic.

Old Mag lurched forward as a sign that she was

ready to go on, and Betsy turned her back to the road. This was wide enough for two teams to pass and ran through fertile farm land. Corn as high as a man's waist rose beside the road, and fields of rye almost ready for the harvest. Meadows were full of tiger lilies, daisies, Queen Anne's lace—and well-fed cows.

Although distant figures could be seen in the fields, the landscape seemed empty. The houses, small and neat beside their big barns, seemed to be asleep. There wasn't a sound except the cooing of mourning doves and Old Mag's hoofs thudding steadily now.

Suddenly Betsy heard another horse coming behind her almost at a gallop. A great cloud of dust arose and poured into the surrey so that she coughed and choked. The other rig did not pass. It drew to a stop beside her.

"Listen my child and you shall hear, of the midday ride of Paul Revere—the second." The drawling voice was theatrically deep. Betsy looked, startled, into black laughing eyes.

"Tony Markham!" Betsy halted Old Mag beside his lathered animal. "Whatever are you doing here and why are you racing a horse on such a hot day? My father would certainly give you a lecture."

"Your father sent me, smarty!"

"My father sent you! Well, I'm sure he didn't

expect you to drive like that."

"Oh, I've only done it since the top of the hill. We crawled up that so slowly, it's a wonder I ever caught you."

"But why did you want to catch me? Papa sent you, you said . . ."

"Yes. Important dispatches!" Tony reached into the pocket of his shirt and produced three letters. Leaning across to the surrey, he handed them to her.

Betsy caught the flash of unfamiliar stamps.

"Letters from Julia!" she cried.

"Yep. Two." Tony looked very well pleased. He took off his hat and ran lazy fingers through his bushy black hair, which was curlier even than usual in the heat. "Your father thought your mother might as well have them . . . not have to wait until tonight."

"Isn't Papa an angel!"

"That's right!" Tony answered. "Praise your father! What about me, galloping up Agency Hill in this heat?"

"Oh, you!" Betsy answered. "How did he happen to find you anyway?"

"I dropped into the shoe store, looking for you. Thought you might go to the Majestic with me. I have two or three hours off in the afternoon, you know. I might as well be with you as with anyone else."

"Well, thanks!" Betsy answered.

"Maybe even a little better," Tony said magnanimously. He spoke in a teasing brotherly tone. He was, in fact, almost like a brother to the Ray girls.

Betsy was very fond of him. With his crest of hair, his black eyes which were bold, laughing, and sleepy all at once, his drawling voice, his lazy movements, Tony was nothing if not lovable. But she worried about him, too. She didn't always like the company he kept. He went with an older, wild crowd, and she had resolved some weeks before to get him back into the high school crowd. She thought he would be safer there, not tempted to leave school before he graduated.

Remembering her design, she smiled at him.

"I'm sorry I couldn't have gone," she said. "Why don't you ever come out to the lake? It's terribly nice out there. Come some Sunday."

"I go up to Minneapolis if the League team is playing at home. I've gone nuts on baseball."

"You go to Minneapolis? But how can you afford it . . . to go that often, I mean?"

"Oh, I don't pay. I hop a freight. I've made friends with a couple of brakemen," Tony explained grandly. "Poker-playing pals of mine."

Betsy didn't like the sound of that.

"Well, you don't go *every* Sunday," she replied.

"The first Sunday you don't go, come out to the lake. Do you hear?"

"Yes, ma'am," said Tony, "I hear and I heed. Well, I must get this nag back to the guy your dad borrowed it from."

"You walk him every step of the way," Betsy scolded. "Papa won't like it if he looks the least bit hot."

"Yes, ma'am," said Tony again. He turned his horse around, picked up the whip as though about to brandish it, then acted alarmed and put it back in the socket with a virtuous look. Betsy laughed.

"Good-by," she called. "We'll be looking for you."

Holding the reins loosely as Old Mag started to trot, Betsy studied the letters. They were postmarked from the Azores Islands, of whose existence she had been unaware until Julia's trip was planned. Julia had said in the letter she sent back by the pilot boat that the Azores would be her first stop.

Her father, Betsy noticed, hadn't opened the letters. "He must have been dying to, but he knew Mamma would like the fun of it," she thought.

The third letter was addressed to her. She looked at it casually, for the importance of any ordinary letter was dwarfed by the arrival of mail from Julia. This wasn't, however, an ordinary letter. The handwriting on the envelope made her catch her breath.

"It is! It's from Joe! Why is he writing to me, do you suppose?" Betsy asked the empty air.

She clucked to Old Mag to hurry, for she didn't want to open the letter quite yet. She felt churned up by the sight of it. Betsy liked Joe Willard a great deal, and she had for a long time, with very little encouragement.

He was a stalwart, light-haired boy with blue eyes and a strong, tanned face. He was in Betsy's English class, where they had long been rivals. For three consecutive years he had won the Essay Contest for which Betsy herself had competed twice. He was an orphan and earned his own living. Last winter he had worked after school and on weekends for the *Deep Valley Sun.*

He had gone around then with a girl named Phyllis Brandish. He had never asked to come to see Betsy and had danced with her only once. Then, out of a clear sky last June, after leaving for the harvest fields, he had sent her a postcard!

Betsy's most loved possession was an old theatrical trunk which had once belonged to her Uncle Keith, an actor, and now served her for a desk. She had put Joe Willard's postcard in that trunk. When the family moved to the lake, the trunk, of course, could not go. But a few selected manuscripts, notebooks, and pencils, an eraser, and a dictionary had gone in a stout box marked "My Desk." The card had been included.

It had come from Texas. The letter, Betsy noticed, studying the postmark, came from North Dakota. She knew that Joe was working his way north with the harvest. But harvest wouldn't have come to North Dakota yet. It hadn't even reached southern Minnesota.

"What the dickens is he doing in North Dakota?" she puzzled.

Old Mag slowed down for a farm house known to Deep Valley folk as the Half Way House because it lay at a point half way to Murmuring Lake. Outside the gate was a watering trough full of fresh water. The farmer who lived there had had so many people stop and ask to water their horses that he had put out the public watering trough to save time. His wife, Betsy had heard, preferred the old, sociable, time-wasting stop in the farm yard.

Betsy climbed out and unfastened Old Mag's checkrein. The trough was set in the shade of a big tree and Old Mag drank long and gratefully. Slowly Betsy ran a finger under the flap of the envelope.

Joe's letter was typewritten, and the printed heading said *The Courier News, Wells County's Finest Weekly, Wells, North Dakota.* He plunged immediately into a surprising piece of news.

Last summer, he said, harvesting near Wells, he had

made friends with the editor of this paper, and his wife. Mr. and Mrs. Roberts were swell folks. He had written to them once or twice over the winter. They knew he was working on the *Sun*.

Mr. Roberts had been taken sick and sent to a hospital, and he had written to Joe. The letter had been forwarded by Mr. Root, the editor of the *Sun*, to Oklahoma, where Joe was harvesting. Mr. Roberts had asked Joe to come and help Mrs. Roberts. Under her supervision, Joe wrote with pride, he was practically running the paper.

He was living with the Robertses.

"I have a big square room with a view into a silver maple. The leaves whisper like a bunch of high school girls, but fortunately I'm not here very much. I'm down at the paper all day long. I like this job, Betsy. I even like the smell of the presses. I can learn a lot about newspaper work this summer.

"I've heard from Mr. Root. I can't do half as well as he expects me to, but I'm going to do my darndest. If you answer, as a well-bred young lady is sure to do (and besides I know you go wild at the sight of a pencil), address me here. Sincerely, Joe."

Betsy didn't hurry Old Mag away from the watering trough. She read Joe's letter twice and then put it with Julia's beside her on the seat. She looked at the windmill turning lazily above the Half Way House with shining eyes which didn't see it at all.

Joe Willard had written to her. He wanted to correspond. And what wonderful news he had to tell!

She was glad she had put sachet bags into her stationery and that she had received for her birthday a sealing wax set, colored sticks of wax and a seal with her initial on it. Scents and sealing wax were la de da, of course, but Julia had told her long ago that even with a boy of your own sort, which Joe certainly was, a little la de da didn't hurt.

"I'll write to him tonight," thought Betsy. She slapped the reins and Old Mag, refreshed by her drink and the rest, went forward briskly toward Murmuring Lake.

2

More Letters

JULIA'S LETTERS WERE READ until they were worn
thin. Mrs. Ray read them first to herself and then
asked Betsy to read them aloud to her and Margaret.
She read them to herself again at intervals throughout the day, and after supper Betsy read them aloud
to her father. After half an hour he wished to hear
them again, so Betsy read them again, and over and

over on succeeding evenings.

Mr. Ray usually took Margaret on his knee to listen. He was a tall, stout, very erect man with satiny black hair, hazel eyes, and a big nose. He listened with a proud fond smile. Mrs. Ray, red-haired, slim, and alert, listened in a rocker close by. The lamp threw their shadows on the unplastered wall, and frustrated moths banged unheeded on the screened door of the cottage. It was one of half a dozen cottages, each with two small rooms and a narrow porch, that surrounded the rambling, white-painted old Inn.

Both letters had been written on board the *Romanic*, en route to Naples. They were long letters. Julia remarked that people said she spent most of her time writing; but she wanted her family to take the trip right along with her. And if ever one person took four others through Europe by means of pen and paper, it was Julia that summer.

The Rays lived a double life. They rested and ate, fished and bathed at Murmuring Lake in Minnesota. But they also took the Rev. Mr. Lewis' "personally conducted tour."

Although landbound, they felt the lazy charm of shipboard life, sitting in deck chairs watching the ever-changing water. The steward prepared salt baths for them. They had breakfast at nine, broth at eleven, luncheon at half past one, tea on deck at four, and dinner at seven.

They went to church in the salon and heard the Church of England clergyman pray for King Edward and Queen Alexandra. They heard Julia, in her little black silk dress, sing at the Ship's Concert. They ate at the Captain's dinner and danced at the Grand Ball.

At the Azores they felt the intoxication of a first encounter with a tropical island—purple bougainvillea climbing over everything; narrow streets with tiny plaster houses painted white, blue, yellow, and pink; whining beggars, clamoring vendors, women wrapped in shawls.

They went on through Italy, Switzerland, up the River Rhine, into Holland, Belgium, France, and England.

Julia enjoyed everything five times as much as the average traveler, she said. "I think of each one of you and look at everything just five times as hard."

Bettina (Julia's name for Betsy) must learn languages at once. "Every cultured person should know at least French."

She was buying presents for them madly. The Rev. Mr. Lewis had promised to bring a box home in the fall when Julia went on to Berlin and her study with Fraulein von Blatz.

"Oh, I'm so happy! I can't believe it is I, Julia Ray,

who is traveling in Europe, having all her cherished dreams fulfilled."

Letters, more than anything else, characterized this summer vacation for Betsy. The Ray cottage was set out on a point with a view across the lake to Pleasant Park, where Mrs. Ray had lived as a girl. Sitting on the porch of the cottage or down on the sandy isolated Point, Betsy wrote to Julia. She wrote to Tacy and to Tib; to Leonard, the sick nephew of Miss Cobb, her music teacher. She wrote to Joe Willard.

Betsy had answered Joe's first letter with praise and encouragement. His reply came, brimming with elation. A land-swindle trial had been going on in Wells County when he arrived in June. It had started out quietly; a crook, Joe said, had been indicted. But the case had developed national ramifications when the crook was discovered to have been aided by a senator. Court was continued in session.

Joe had seen the importance of the case and had started filing the story every day for the Minneapolis *Tribune*. The stories were published, and he was paid space rates. On the day he wrote Betsy, the *Tribune* editor had telephoned, long distance.

"Ordinarily," this august personage had said, "with a story which has ballooned like this one, we would send a correspondent to Wells. But we like your stories. You may handle the case for us."

Joe had accepted with some misgivings. He had not concealed his age, but neither had he mentioned it.

"I'd just as soon they didn't find out how young I am," he wrote. "So I wish you'd keep the assignment a secret. I haven't told anyone what I am doing except you and Mr. Root."

When Betsy received that letter, she went down to the boathouse, took out a boat, and rowed to Babcock's Bay. She liked this quiet backwater, where trees grew close to the shore, making golden-green aisles when the sun shone. She read Joe's letter a second time and a third, then held it between her hands and looked off across the quiet, gleaming water.

"I haven't told anyone except you and Mr. Root." He had picked her for a confidante!

She took out her paper and a pencil and wrote an answer, reading through what she had written, correcting and interlining as she did with her stories. When she returned to the cottage, she copied it all on scented paper and sealed it with green sealing wax.

Joe's typewritten letters and Betsy's scented, green-sealed replies went back and forth regularly after that.

Betsy took to reading the Minneapolis *Tribune*. She looked for Joe's stories and one day she noticed with excitement that the story was signed at the top, "Joseph Willard."

"Isn't it a terrific honor," she wrote to Joe, "having

your name signed to a story in a newspaper?"

A few nights later, her father looked up from his reading.

"I wonder whether this Joseph Willard who writes for the *Tribune* is any relation to the Willard boy who works on the *Deep Valley Sun?*"

"Yes, he is," Betsy replied.

"Uncle, or something?"

"Something," Betsy murmured noncommittally. She felt guilty but she stood by her promise. "Joe has mentioned that case to me. We correspond, you know."

"You certainly do," Mrs. Ray remarked. "You're keeping the mails busy. I don't remember his ever coming to the house, though."

"He never has," Betsy replied. "But he will!" she thought, and smiled to herself.

She clipped all the Joseph Willard articles and kept them in the box with her own stories.

Betsy found time for stories in spite of the time she gave to letter writing. And that summer she started in earnest trying to sell to the magazines. When she finished a story she copied it neatly and sent it away with return postage enclosed to *The Ladies' Home Journal* or *The Delineator, The Youth's Companion* or *St. Nicholas.* As regularly as she sent them out, they were returned.

But Betsy was stubborn. If a story came back in the morning from one magazine, it went out in the afternoon to another. She kept a record in a little notebook of how much postage each manuscript required, when it went out, and when it came back. She was not at all sensitive about her campaign and the family took a lively interest in it.

"Uncle Sam ought to manufacture round-trip postage stamps," Mr. Ray chuckled. "They would certainly be a convenience to Betsy."

"My stories will start selling some day. You'll see."

"Of course they will," Mrs. Ray put in, with her usual monumental confidence in her daughters. "The magazines are full of stories not half so good as Betsy's."

"I like them just as well as the stories in my fairy books," said Margaret.

Margaret, eleven years old now, was up to Betsy's shoulder, and as straight as her father. She was immaculately neat, very quiet and self-contained. She wore her braids crossed in back with big taffeta bows behind her ears. Her serious freckled face was illumined by star-like eyes.

She and Betsy liked to take books down on the Point. The steep bank hid the Inn from their view. Little white-edged waves lapped at their feet, small stilt-legged birds ran along the sand, and reeds at the water's edge made a forest for a Thumbelina.

Margaret read from her fairy books and Betsy read *Les Miserables*. She had begun Victor Hugo's tome in a zest for self-improvement, having heard it called the greatest novel in the world, but she soon became deeply engrossed.

She was following Jean Valjean's adventures one Sunday afternoon, with Margaret deep in the *Blue Fairy Book* beside her, when she heard a rustling on the bank and looked up to see Tony descending.

He had come several times since the day he gave Betsy the letters and she was pleased to be succeeding in her enterprise. It was fun, too, to have a cavalier. There weren't many young people at the Inn this season. She jumped up to greet him and Margaret followed, her face wreathed in smiles.

"Something for you, Margaret," he said carelessly, thrusting a box of candy into her hands. He always gave Margaret the candy he brought. Tony's visits seemed to be to the entire family, although he was Betsy's classmate.

They went up to the cottage to dress for a swim. Betsy and Margaret put on blue serge bathing suits, trimmed with white braid around collars, sleeves, and skirts, long black stockings, laced bathing shoes, bandanas on their heads.

"Very skippy," Tony said.

In the water he romped with Margaret, who was paddling about on water wings. Betsy swam with a joyfully vigorous breast stroke. Then she found a sun hole and floated, staring up at faraway swirls of cloud.

Tony was playing croquet with the family when Betsy emerged from the cottage, dressed for supper. She had put on a filmy pink dress and wore flowers in her hair. Tony leaned on his mallet, his dark eyes teasing.

"Look at Betsy! I swear she's gunning for me. It's no use, girl. I'm hooked. Margaret's got me."

He stayed for supper, of course, and although the Inn had provided a gigantic Sunday dinner, supper was also an abundant affair, with cold ham and chicken, potato salad, green corn on the cob, baking powder biscuits, and plum cake heaped with whipped cream.

Mr. Ray and Tony talked baseball. Mr. Ray enjoyed Tony's accounts of the Minneapolis League baseball games.

"But I don't like your transportation, Tony," he said. "You might lose a leg some day, hopping a freight."

"Oh, they slow down for me!"

"What do you do with your time up there in the cities after the game is over?"

"I hang around with Jake and Harry. They're my brakemen pals."

"Aren't they a lot older than you are?"

"Sure. Ten years or so, but I like to hear them talk. They're full of the darndest yarns."

Betsy was listening intently. She could tell her father was troubled. Tony turned and tweaked her nose.

"What makes you listen so good?" he asked in affectionate derision. "You don't understand about baseball or railroading, either."

After supper, Tony asked Betsy to go rowing. They went down to the boathouse and Old Pete gave them a boat. Tony took off his coat and folded it over the seat, fitted the oars into the oarlocks, and rowed to the middle of the lake.

The water was as smooth as glass. Now and then an insect skimmed along the surface, making a crack in the mirror. Tony rowed lazily, while the sun sank out of sight and diaphanous clouds all over the sky turned pink.

He crossed the oars, looked up and around him.

"Nice. Isn't it?" he said.

Tony never talked much. He teased, joked, and clowned, but he seldom talked about anything important to him. Betsy thought sometimes how little she knew of Tony's life. Other boys talked about school and sports, their larks and scrapes, their girls, books they were reading. A few of them talked about ideas that stirred them. Tony was either fooling or he was silent.

He could listen, though. Betsy talked more about herself with Tony than with any boy she knew. He understood what her writing meant to her. He had shown the same sensitive insight into Julia's music.

Tony loved to sing himself and had a fine deep voice. Basso profundo, Julia called it. Julia had been quite excited for a time by Tony's gift as a singer. But he had no ambition to sing professionally or to do anything else except enjoy life as it passed.

Betsy told him now about the story she was working on. It concerned a New York debutante.

"Sort of a Robert W. Chambers story," she explained.

"But you don't know anything about New York debutantes, Betsy."

"That doesn't matter. I make it up."

He started rowing again and they found themselves near Pleasant Park. The old house was surrounded by tall trees that almost hid it from view. The lawn was enclosed on three sides by a white picket fence. On the fourth side, the land sloped to the water, and there were a boathouse and docks.

"Just think!" Betsy said. "That's where Mamma

grew up. A farmer lives there now."

"Your grandfather is in California, isn't he?"

"Yes. He's Mamma's stepfather. Hers and Uncle Keith's. She was married in that house."

"Well," Tony said. "It was some marriage! I don't know another family that gets along as yours does, Betsy. Honest to gosh, I've always been sort of glad I got acquainted with you Rays!"

And then, having been betrayed into what he considered sentimentality, he changed the subject.

"Let's sing," he said.

They sang while the stars came out and the color of the sky deepened to a rich dark blue. The first sprinkle of stars was followed by armies of them.

They sang everything they knew, beginning with old songs like "Annie Laurie" and "Swanee River"; going on to "What's the Use of Dreaming," Mr. Ray's favorite, and "My Wild Irish Rose," which the beloved Chauncey Olcott had brought to Deep Valley every autumn since Betsy could remember. They sang the songs associated with each high school year.

> *"Dreaming, dreaming,*
> *Of you, sweetheart, I am dreaming. . . ."*

That had been the hit of their freshman year. From the sophomore year they sang:

*"Come away with me, Lucille,
In my merry Oldsmobile...."*

They sang last year's "Howdy Cy, Morning Cy," and finished in style with the duet from "The Red Mill":

*"Not that you are fair, dear,
Not that you are true...."*

They had sung it many times beside the piano at the Ray house. Their timing was perfect, and their voices blended warmly. Someone sitting in darkness on the distant point applauded.

"Say," Tony exclaimed. "We're pretty good. Broadway doesn't know what it's missing!"

"Yes," Betsy agreed, "you and I make a good team."

Tony didn't answer, and her words lingered in the air as words do sometimes, taking on undue significance by reason of the fact that they are left suspended. He picked up the oars and started rowing toward the lights of the Inn, gleaming through the trees.

The next afternoon, when Betsy and her mother were rocking and mending on the porch of the little cottage, Mrs. Ray said suddenly, "Betsy! I think Tony is getting a little . . . well . . . sweet on you."

"Heavens, no!" said Betsy, startled. "Tony is just like a brother."

"He used to be," said Mrs. Ray. "But . . . I have intuitions sometimes where my children are concerned. I think Tony's feeling toward you is changing. I don't like it."

"Why don't you like it?" asked Betsy. "Why wouldn't you like it, if it were true, I mean? Lots of boys have had crushes on me and you never minded."

Mrs. Ray answered slowly, "We're all so fond of Tony."

"Of course!" cried Betsy. "Papa likes him better than any boy that comes to the house. In fact, we all do. So what's wrong?" Her mother didn't reply and Betsy added, "I suppose you don't like those freight-hopping trips to Minneapolis? I don't myself. Maybe I can talk him out of them."

"How do you feel about Tony, Betsy?" asked Mrs. Ray. "You aren't . . . serious . . . are you?"

"Heavens, no!" said Betsy again, and felt suddenly very old. Her mother's tone was the searching one Betsy had heard her use with Julia. It seemed strange to think that she was old enough so that her mother worried about one of her crushes being serious.

"I haven't a crush on Tony or on anyone else," she said, but she felt herself blushing and jumped up hurriedly, pretending to have lost her thimble. She had thought suddenly about Joe Willard's letters, how she looked forward to them, how hard she worked over her answers. She hoped that her mother would not extend her questioning to Joe.

Happily, perhaps deliberately, she didn't.

"Betsy," said Mrs. Ray briskly, when her daughter had shaken her skirts and sat down. "What do you think of the new, long-sleeved tucked waists? Would you like one to go with your suit?"

"Yes," answered Betsy, "I think I would."

3
Back from the Lake

BETSY ALWAYS LOVED the late summer return from
Murmuring Lake to the house on the corner of High
Street and Plum. Mr. Ray had always mowed the
lawn. He had clipped the hydrangeas and bridal
wreath and set the sprinkler going. Anna, the hired
girl, had usually come back a few days earlier, so the
house was aired and clean. But it never looked like

home until Mrs. Ray had scattered books and magazines about, and the girls had cut flowers for the vases.

This year there was no Julia to run to the piano, but Betsy unlocked it and dashed off a few scales just to let the neighbors know that the Rays were back.

The piano had photographs of Julia at all ages ranged along the top. It stood in a light, square hall which Julia had grandly named the music room. To the right, a golden oak staircase curved upward. To the left, an archway led into the parlor, a warm, friendly room, with crisp lace curtains, sofa pillows, pictures and books, a green-shaded lamp, and a brass bowl holding a palm.

The dining room was just behind. It was papered in a dark, fruity pattern above a well-filled plate rail. A gold-fringed lamp hung by a chain over the center of the table. There was a fireplace in one corner, a gong in another, and a fine display of cut glass and hand-painted china on the sideboard. A swinging door led to the pantry and Anna's kitchen.

Anna had already started baking cookies, wearing a broad, pleased smile. Margaret was smiling, too, as she wandered through the house with Washington, the cat, in her arms.

Washington and his companion, Lincoln, the Spitz dog, had spent the summer on Anna's brother's farm.

Abe Lincoln had been excited by the return. He had run around barking sharply, jumping upon forbidden chairs. Washington had relaxed on his favorite pillow with a supercilious air. But he had started purring when Margaret picked him up.

Betsy began joyfully to telephone. It was fun getting back to the Crowd. Carney, who had been graduated from high school in June, was busy getting ready for Vassar.

"Mother and I are going up to the Cities to buy my clothes," she said.

"What joy! When?"

"Tomorrow. So let's go riding tonight. We'll pick up the bunch."

Tacy suggested an afternoon picnic.

"All right. I'll bring my Kodak. And I'll stop by for Tib."

"I'll 'phone her you're coming so that she can have a lunch packed."

"Do. The Mullers are such good providers. What's the state of the Kelly larder?"

"Oh," said Tacy, "fair. I'll put some cocoa in the pail." They had a special, battered, smoke-blackened pail in which they always made cocoa on their picnics.

Walking toward Hill Street, Betsy thought how long she and Tacy had been having picnics.

"It's thirteen years now since we met each other at

my fifth birthday party. And we started picnicking the very first summer."

There was nothing like a picnic! she reflected. If you were happy, it made you happier. If you were unhappy, it blew your troubles away.

Passing Lincoln Park, she arrived at Tib's chocolate-colored house. When she and Tacy were children, they had thought this a mansion, and its ornate style had indeed been the height of elegance. It had a wide porch, a tower, numerous bay windows, and a pane of ruby glass over the front door.

Tib had seemed like a story-book princess, and she seemed so still, Betsy thought, when Tib came running over the green lawn. She was slender and swaying, above ankle-length skirts which fluttered as she ran. Her clothes were fragile, lace-trimmed, and beribboned. Her blond hair, bleached by the sun to a straw tint, was dressed in little puffs which were held in place by a wide band tied around her head. This band was the very newest fashion.

"*Liebchen!* I'm so glad you're back!" She hugged Betsy warmly. "I've been making such a lunch! Deviled eggs, *Kartoffel Salat, Leber Wurst.* . . ."

"You're the most deceptive character," Betsy interrupted. "You look as though you lived on butterfly wings and you talk about *Leber Wurst.*"

They went inside, where Betsy greeted Mrs. Muller

and Tib's brothers, Fred and Hobbie. Mrs. Muller was blond and stocky; Fred was blond and slender; Hobbie, blond and dimpled. Betsy went into the kitchen to speak to Matilda, the hired girl.

Tib brought out a bulging basket. Betsy picked up her own basket and the Kodak, and they started for Hill Street.

Tacy, smiling radiantly, met them in the vacant lot. She looked tall, approaching. She was, in fact, taller than Betsy. Her auburn hair was wound about her head in coronet braids, not so fashionable as pompadours or puffs, but very well suited to Tacy. She had large blue eyes which could brim with laughter one minute, and the next be wistful or shy. Real Irish eyes, Mrs. Ray often said.

"Tacy," said Betsy. "Do you know that you're getting awfully pretty?"

"I was thinking that, too," cried Tib. "Why, an artist would like to paint your picture the way you look right now!"

"I'll snap it after we get up on the hill," said Betsy.

"*Be Gorrah!*" cried Tacy. "It's a *foine* picture they'll be taking of the Colleen from Hill Street."

Tacy affected an Irish brogue when she felt especially silly. She and Betsy loved to act silly, and Tib laughed at all their jokes, which made her a gratifying third.

The Kelly house at the end of Hill Street had seemed big to Betsy once because it was so much bigger than the yellow cottage across the street in which she had grown up. But looking at it now, low and rambling, its white paint fading under the reddening vines, Betsy realized that it was somewhat small for the big family it had to house.

She had always loved the merry crowded house. Warmth and comfort enveloped her whenever she entered the door. All the Kellys loved her; they petted and teased her as though she were still a little girl.

Today only Mrs. Kelly was at home. A large, gentle woman with a tender mouth like Tacy's, she sat with her mountain of darning in the window of the dining room. This big bow window was the heart of the house. Here Mr. Kelly sat in the evening with his newspaper, here on Sunday he played his violin. Here Betsy and Tacy used to cut out paper dolls, looking up at the overhanging hills.

The Kelly house had few of the so-called modern improvements. It was lighted by lamps, there was a pump in the dooryard. But the views from the windows would have graced a castle.

"Mrs. Kelly," Betsy said, when she had kissed her, "I never realized when I was little that your house had such lovely views."

"I've heard Papa say that he bought the house for

the views," Mrs. Kelly replied.

"Well, I'm certainly glad he bought it," said Tacy. "What if we hadn't moved to Hill Street? What if we still lived in Mazomanie, Wisconsin? Why, Betsy, we might not even know each other!"

"*I* lived in Wisconsin," Tib observed. "You might have known me, anyway."

"And I suppose you wouldn't have missed me at all!" cried Betsy. "Listen to them, Mrs. Kelly! Heartless creatures! Practically plotting to get rid of me."

Mrs. Kelly laughed indulgently.

Tacy brought out the pail and Tib said it was too hot for cocoa, but Betsy and Tacy shouted her down.

"No respect for tradition."

"We always have cocoa."

Laughing and wrangling, they started up the steep road behind Betsy's old house, the road which had once seemed the longest, most adventuresome in the world. There had been just one white house on the Big Hill in those days. Now there were several modern cottages. Change had not yet touched The Secret Lane, however. This ran along the summit, a twin row of thickly leaved beech trees.

Beyond it, they came out suddenly on a wide, bright view. The hilltop overlooked a valley so capacious that it seemed empty, although it held scattered farms and a huddle of small houses known as Little

Syria. In the distance, the river wandered.

"Of all the places we used to play when we were children, I love this the most," Betsy said.

They stretched out on the hillside, a slanting coppery sea of goldenrod. A vireo far above them sang continuously and monotonously, like a dull woman talking.

Betsy, Tacy, and Tib began to talk. They talked about their summers—Milwaukee, Mazomanie, and Murmuring Lake. They talked about being seniors. They talked about boys. At least, Betsy and Tib talked about boys. Boys didn't interest Tacy.

However, she volunteered the information that a famous athlete named Ralph Maddox was coming to high school this fall. She had heard her brothers say so. He was coming from St. John, where he had been the star of the football team.

"I hope we can get him for the Zets," she said.

"You want him for the Zets? I'll make a note of it. Just leave it to me," said Tib, patting her yellow hair.

Betsy told them she had been corresponding with Joe Willard.

"How did that happen?" asked Tib.

"How did it happen? He wrote to me, of course. You don't think I'd write to him first, do you?"

"Do you think you'll be going with him this year?"

"No idea," said Betsy. She had announced last year

that she was going to do just that, and then he had gone with Phyllis Brandish! She wasn't going to tempt fate again.

"There's a Joseph Willard who writes for the Minneapolis *Tribune*," Tacy remarked.

"May be related. Do you think so, Betsy?"

"Um hum," answered Betsy, feeling uncomfortable. She wasn't accustomed to keeping secrets from Tacy and Tib. She jumped up. "Let's get some pictures. Maybe we ought to start the fire first. Background for your portrait, Tacy."

They gathered dry wood and made a fire which poured smoky fragrance into the air. While Tacy adjusted the pail, Tib spread a red cloth and set out the contents of the baskets.

Betsy focused her camera. "Get set now!"

Tacy jumped up and put one hand behind her head, the other on her hip.

"No! No!" cried Betsy. "You're not Carmen. You're the Irish Colleen. Remember?"

"Be jabbers, that's right!" said Tacy, and put both hands on her waist, arms akimbo.

Tib pushed her down. Tacy's long red braids came loose. Around her face little tendrils of hair curled like vines. She looked up at Betsy, her eyes full of laughter, the skirts of her sailor suit cascading about her. Betsy snapped.

"Tacy Kelly at her silliest!" she said.

She snapped Tib on a rock, holding out her skirts. Tacy snapped Betsy tilting the jug of lemonade. Tib snapped Betsy and Tacy feeding each other sandwiches.

When the film was used up, they collapsed in laughter.

"Gosh, how silly!"

"Does us good. We're getting too darned serious."

"We're getting too darned old. Gee, seniors this fall!"

"Let's eat. We have to get back early, you know. Carney's taking us riding."

Carney, informed by telephone of Betsy's whereabouts, picked her up at the Kellys'. Tacy and Tib piled into the Sibley auto, too, and they went in search of the rest of the Crowd . . . the feminine portion of it. This group continued the same in character—lively, exuberant, loyal—although its personnel changed from year to year.

Carney, this fall, was going out of it. The Crowd would miss Carney, with her twinkling eyes. Her side lawn was a gathering place; her automobile dedicated to the Crowd.

Hazel Smith was just coming into the group. She was a plain, freckle-faced girl, mirthful and breezy.

Alice Morrison was tall, with rosy cheeks and thick blond hair. She was quiet, but no one in the Crowd enjoyed fun more wholeheartedly than Alice.

Winona Root was tall, dark, and debonaire. She had magic in her fingers at the piano.

Irma Biscay was rounded and alluring. She was a sweet-tempered, merry girl, but the attraction she held for the opposite sex kept her from being very popular with girls. She had not yet returned from her vacation, and the Crowd, cruising along the shadowy streets, discussed the source of this attraction. Betsy, whose hair was straight, laid it to her curly hair. Tib, who was tiny, felt sure it was her lovely figure.

"It's her form," Tib asserted vehemently. "Her form is like that Miss Anna Held's who takes the milk baths."

Alice suggested that Irma's success might spring from the fact that Mrs. Biscay was such a good cook. But Betsy scoffed at that.

"Look at Anna! The boys come to our cookie jar as though they owned it. Yet I don't slay everyone. Irma makes me think of the Lorelei. You know, Tib, in that German song. Let one of our beaus see much of Irma and . . . good-by! He's gone, just as though he had been dashed against a rock."

Tib started to sing.

"Ich weiss nicht was sol es bedeuten. . . ." And the rest joined in, making up English words. The Crowd loved to sing, rolling through the night in Carney's auto. Winona started "I Wonder Who's Kissing Her

Now" and they were singing this with enthusiasm when the auto broke down. (They seldom took a ride anywhere without the auto breaking down.) Fortunately they were near the Rays', and the girls pushed the machine to Betsy's door, singing at the tops of their voices.

They found an indignant group on the porch. Tony was there, sprawled in the hammock, and Dennis Farisy, who looked like a cherub but was not at all cherubic, and Cab Edwards, who had once been Dennie's inseparable companion . . . but Cab seemed older and more mature since he had started work at the family furniture store.

"What do you mean, not being around tonight?" he shouted now, indignantly.

"We were just going home, and it would have served you right," yelled Dennie.

"We wouldn't have stayed five minutes more," drawled Tony, swinging luxuriously.

Winona ran up the steps and dumped him out of the hammock. They started tusseling. Everybody went inside and Winona sat down at the piano. They made fudge. They stood around the piano and sang. They rolled up the rugs and danced.

"All out by ten o'clock," Mrs. Ray called down the stairs.

The Ray family was really back from the lake.

4
The Rays' Telephone Rings

IRMA CAME BACK, as bafflingly attractive as ever. Tom, who had been vacationing in the East, returned to get ready for Cox Military. Dave, Stan, and Lloyd, who had gone down the Mississippi in canoes, reappeared, tanned and full of stories. And at the Majestic Motion Picture Theater, at Heinz's Ice Cream Parlor, and the other haunts of the young, Betsy looked around for Joe. His letters had stopped coming as abruptly as they had started, and the series of stories in the Tribune had ended, too. Probably, she thought, he was out at Butternut Center with his uncle and aunt. She wondered why he didn't call her up.

All the talk was of being seniors.

"It's going to seem queer to be seniors," the girls agreed, looking ahead to that day, not far off now, when they would pass through the wide, arched doorway of the high school wearing their new dignity.

"Poor me! I'll be a freshie again," Carney mourned.

She and her mother had returned from Minneapolis, where they had stayed at a hotel and had bought clothes in the city stores. The girls flocked to her house to hear all about it, Betsy accompanied by Margaret, whom she was taking to Miss Cobb's house for her first piano lesson.

"What did you buy?"

"Oh, a tweed suit with a brown velvet collar and a brown velvet tricorn Gage hat."

"Any new party dresses?"

"I have," announced Carney grandly, "a store-bought party dress! It's pale pink silk with elbow sleeves and a square neck. It's a dear. Come on! I'll show it to you."

There was a rush for the stairs.

Ascending, they heard the hum of a sewing machine.

"Miss Mix is making my school dresses and under-wear. I wish you could see the underwear! It's made of sheeting!" Carney giggled. "Mother wants it strong so it can stand a college laundry. That's what it is to have a New Englander for a parent."

"Good thing it isn't your trousseau," said Tib, who liked lingerie as delicate as cobwebs, lace-trimmed and strung with ribbon.

They piled into Carney's room, where the store-bought party dress was reverently inspected. The suit was displayed, too, and Winona tried on the brown Gage hat, setting it at a ridiculous angle and parading up and down. Margaret struggled to keep her smiles from turning into undignified chuckles when Winona, pretending to be Carney, snatched Larry Humphreys' photograph from the bureau and pressed it madly to her middy blouse.

Betsy jumped up and spoke in a bass voice, obviously representing a Vassar dignitary.

"No, Miss Sibley," she said. "Do not bring that Howard Chandler Christie profile inside the sacred portals of Vassar."

"I always turn it to the wall when I'm studying, your honor," squeaked Winona.

"It makes no difference. Vassar is a girls' college. Leave men behind, all ye who enter here!"

Carney made a dash for Winona and succeeded in

wresting the picture away.

"You're just too silly!" she cried.

"Silly, am I?" said Winona. "Just for that I'll go home and wash my hair." That broke up the party.

"Margaret and I are going to Miss Cobb's," said Betsy.

"I'll walk down with you," Carney volunteered. "I'm going that way, matching ribbons. Heavens, I never thought that going away to college involved so much matching of ribbons!"

Carney, Betsy, and Margaret started down Broad Street under the high trees.

"It's funny to be teased about a boy you haven't even seen for three years," Carney remarked.

Larry and Herbert Humphreys had moved from Deep Valley three years before. Herbert and Betsy were great friends. But there was no romantic feeling between them such as had always existed between Larry and Carney. Carney had never liked any other boy so well.

"Have you heard from him lately?" asked Betsy.

"We still write every week." Carney had a dimple in one cheek which flickered mischievously now. "He wishes he was going to West Point."

"Ah ha!" said Betsy. "Across the river from Vassar."

"But," said Carney, "he's going to Stanford, all the

way across the continent and bursting with girls."

Her smile vanished and she turned to Betsy, frowning.

"I want to see Larry," she said firmly. "I have to find out whether I still like him. Maybe he's changed. I feel as though I couldn't ever . . . get married to anyone else until I know."

"Have you told him that?" asked Betsy.

"No, I haven't. But I should think he'd feel the same way . . . about seeing me, I mean."

"I'd like to be a mouse under a chair when you two meet," said Betsy.

They reached the long flight of wooden steps which led to Miss Cobb's cottage and Carney turned to Margaret, whose eyes were shining with excitement at the prospect of beginning music lessons.

"Good luck!" Carney said. "I'll bet you begin with middle C."

Carney had studied with Miss Cobb, of course. Most of Deep Valley's boys and girls began their piano study with Miss Cobb, a large stately woman with light hair combed smoothly down on either side of a calm, kindly face. There had been a girl and three boys in the little cottage once, children of Miss Cobb's sister who had died. Miss Cobb had broken her own engagement to marry and had taken the whole brood to raise. The two oldest had passed away with their mother's complaint. Leonard was ill with it now, out in the Colorado mountains. Only Bobby, the sturdy pink-cheeked youngest of the lot, lived on with his aunt.

Betsy was glad to be back in the little low-ceiled parlor with the upright piano and the grand piano and the scent of geraniums. Miss Cobb told her that Leonard had enjoyed her letters.

"I've enjoyed his letters, too, Miss Cobb," Betsy replied. She had learned from Leonard's letters—she had learned about courage.

He was not, Betsy suspected, getting any better. But there weren't any complaints about the pain or the discomfort or the boredom. He told instead about the funny things that happened around the sanatorium.

He was interested in music. His letters were full of comments on phonograph records, musicians, and musical compositions. There wasn't a word about not being able to develop his own talent, about how sad it was to be young and full of plans and have a curtain drop across your future like the curtain of a theater . . . only that, Betsy thought, always came at the end of something and Leonard's life had just begun.

A shadow crossed Miss Cobb's face, but it was like the shadow of a cloud passing over a mountain. Smiling, she turned to Margaret. She whirled the piano stool until it was the proper height and Margaret sat down, her back very straight. Miss Cobb struck a note and said, as she had said in previous years to Julia and Betsy, "This is middle C."

Betsy liked that. She always liked things to go on as they had gone before.

She was glad on Sunday to be back in the choir of St. John's Episcopal Church. Tib, Winona, and Irma were all in the choir and there was hushed gossip and laughter in the robing room as they put on their long black robes and the black four-cornered hats. Reverence descended as they formed into a double line, and glory burst, as always, when they marched down the aisle singing.

There was a substitute preacher, for the Rev. Mr. Lewis had not yet returned. He was on his way home. Julia had left the party in London.

"I left London," she wrote, "with Big Ben chiming in my ears. You know that famous clock; it plays a hymn tune at the striking of the hours:

> "*Oh, Lord our God,*
> *Be thou our guide,*
> *That by thy help,*
> *No foot may slide.*"

That's the prayer I'm taking with me to my wonderful experience in Berlin."

"I know the tune those chimes sing," said Betsy. "They have it in chime clocks. I never knew the words before, though."

"They're called Westminster chime clocks. We ought to get one," Mrs. Ray said.

The next letter came from Berlin.

"The moment I arrived," Julia wrote, "was the most ecstatically happy moment of my life. Oh, oh, oh, I'm going to work so hard! Fraulein says I'm too nervous and exuberant. I must calm down, get strength, and then do things."

She added that Fraulein wished her to stay on a few days before going into a pension.

"I'm glad. Her house is so interesting . . . musicians, critics, and artists coming and going. I have only one worry—my trunk hasn't come! So far, I haven't had to dress up, and it's fortunate, for I'm still wearing the suit I wore when I arrived. I wash out my waist every night."

"For heaven's sake!" said Mrs. Ray, when she read that. "What's the matter with the Germans that they can't do a simple thing like deliver a trunk?"

"Probably Julia was so excited that she sent it to Kalamazoo," said Mr. Ray.

"Never mind!" Betsy consoled her mother. "Julia looks pretty in anything." But Mrs. Ray worried about Julia meeting the Great World in a travel-stained suit.

"All the pretty clothes there are in that trunk!" she mourned.

The next night, when the Rays were at supper, the telephone rang. Anna said that a gentleman wished to speak to Mr. Ray. He returned to the table, smiling.

"It's the Rev. Mr. Lewis," he said. "He reached town this afternoon and wants to come right up."

There was an outcry of delight.

The family rushed through peach cobbler—Mrs. Ray left hers untouched upon the plate—and was waiting in the parlor when the Rev. Mr. Lewis arrived.

"You may not have holly around, but it's certainly Christmas for this family," he announced, putting a large box on the table. He wiped his face. "That daughter of yours! When she wasn't writing letters to you folks, she was buying presents."

"For you to carry home!" put in Mr. Ray.

"Glad to do it," said the Rev. Mr. Lewis, grinning. "Glad to do anything for Julia."

"Before we look at a single present," Mrs. Ray said, "we want to hear about her. Exactly how was she when you left her?"

"Exhausted but blissful," he replied. "That puts it in a nutshell. She didn't miss a church or an art museum or an historical monument. She asked so many questions that I was hard put to find answers. She wants to learn, that girl does."

"Did she drive you crazy," Mr. Ray asked, "being late for everything?"

"Frankly, yes." The Rev. Mr. Lewis grinned again. "She caught every boat and train just as it was pulling out. But she was so sweet, so helpful, taking care of people who were seasick, rubbing heads, mending clothes, doing the ladies' hair new ways. . . . She found me the one thing Mrs. Lewis had asked me to bring back, a little mosaic chest, from Rome. Everybody in the party loved her, including me."

The whole house was suddenly lonesome for Julia. Mrs. Ray wiped her eyes.

Mr. Ray spoke briskly. "Well, now that we've heard all about her, how about opening the box?"

It was indeed like Christmas when Julia's box was opened. Most of the presents were already familiar, for Julia had described them in her letters. She had bought Betsy's Class Day dress in Lucerne, which was famous, she said, for embroidered dresses. It was pale blue batiste, heavy with embroidery. Betsy got a blue plume, too, from Paris, for the dress hat she would have in the spring, and white gloves from Paris, and exquisite blue and gold Venetian beads.

While Betsy exulted over these, Mr. and Mrs. Ray, Margaret, and Anna were unwrapping and exclaiming. The Rev. Mr. Lewis was almost as happy as they were.

"Am I Santa Claus or am I not?" he wanted to know.

The night before school began, when Mr. Ray came home, he called Betsy down to the parlor. He had a pleased look on his face.

"See this picture?" he said, handing her a folded copy of the Minneapolis *Tribune*. "Isn't this the Willard boy who goes to Deep Valley High School? The one you've been getting letters from all summer?"

Betsy took the paper, and Joe's eyes looked out at her under their heavy brows. His lower lip was outthrust as usual, giving his face a look of good-humored defiance.

The story beneath the picture said that this was the Joseph Willard who had written such a fine account of the North Dakota land-swindle trial. It made much of the fact that he was only seventeen.

"I saw Mr. Root on the street tonight," Mr. Ray said. "You never saw anyone so pleased. He kept saying, 'That Joe Willard is going to be a top newspaper man, and I taught him all he knows.'"

"Mr. Root is an awfully good friend of Joe's," Betsy replied. She was bursting with pride.

After supper, when Anna was doing the dishes and Mr. and Mrs. Ray and Margaret were reading in the parlor, Betsy sat down at the piano. She played a few jubilant scales, then opened her book of Beethoven sonatinas. She was pounding through the first one when the doorbell rang.

"I'll answer it," she called, jumping up. She opened the front door and there on the porch stood Joe Willard, hot and rumpled but smiling, his hair looking the color of silver above his tanned face.

"Why, Joe!" cried Betsy.

"I came right from the train."

"I've just been reading about you. Papa brought home the paper."

"Of course, the picture doesn't do me justice."

He smiled at Betsy and Betsy smiled at him. A full minute passed before she remembered to ask him in.

"Papa and Mamma will be so glad to meet you," she said quickly then. "Papa has been reading your stories all summer."

As she led him into the parlor, Betsy felt very conscious of the fact that this was the first time he had been in her home. The other boys in her class had swung in the hammock and sat on the front steps. They had sung around the piano in the music room and sprawled all over the parlor and sat in front of the dining room fireplace eating her father's sandwiches. They had danced to the two tunes, one a waltz and one a two-step, Mrs. Ray knew how to play on the piano, and had raided Anna's kitchen time and again. But Joe Willard, the most important boy of all, had never been inside her house before.

He was following her now with the swing in his walk more pronounced than usual, as though he were stirring up courage. When she stopped at the archway, he drew himself erect and his smile was a little fixed. Betsy was amazed, and flattered, too, that the great Joe Willard should be nervous at meeting her parents. She smiled reassuringly.

"Mamma," she said, "Papa, it seems ridiculous that you don't know Joe Willard, but I don't believe you do."

Mrs. Ray stood up. She gave him the gay smile all the young people loved.

"I don't know whether I'll let him come in or not," she said. "He's the boy who always wins the Essay Contest away from my Betsy."

"Oh, let him come in, Jule," Mr. Ray returned. "He's quite a fellow, his picture in the paper and all."

And then Mr. and Mrs. Ray were shaking his hand and Margaret was greeting him, too. She looked grave and appraising, as she always did with her older sisters' visitors. None of them ever quite measured up to Tony, in Margaret's opinion.

Old Mag was hitched out in front, for Mr. Ray had planned to take the family riding that night. Mr. and Mrs. Ray and Margaret left without Betsy, and Betsy and Joe sat down on the porch steps. Betsy hoped that casual visitors like Cab, Dennie, or Tony would have sense enough not to come in when they saw them sitting there.

The twilight was crisp, filled with the smell of burning leaves. The sky above the German Catholic College on the hill was tinted by the afterglow.

Betsy asked Joe about the *Tribune* story, and he explained that the city editor had asked him for a photograph, and when Joe sent it he had found out that Joe was only seventeen. Then he had written another letter which Joe now pulled out of his pocket and showed to Betsy.

"You did a fine job. Privately, you never would have had the chance if I had known how young you were. But you wrote like a veteran. There's a place for you on the Minneapolis *Tribune* when you finish high school and come up to the U."

"Joe, that's wonderful!" cried Betsy. "You're going to the U?"

"I'm going to start there," answered Joe. "Say, you told me you thought *Les Miserables* was the greatest novel ever written. I think *Vanity Fair* is the greatest. Let's fight."

Betsy accepted the change of subject. Joe would be slow to let her or anyone else look through the door of the room where he kept the problems he had met in the past, his plans for the future. Joe Willard wasn't easy to get acquainted with. But Betsy felt a sweet, strong certainty that she would succeed in time.

They sat on the porch and talked while stars appeared above the college and a pearly glow announced that the moon would join them soon. No one else came, or if they came they went away. Betsy and Joe watched the moon rise.

"How do you like being a senior?"

"I like it."

"I have an idea that this year is going to be perfectly wonderful."

"I have the same idea," Joe Willard said, looking at the moon.

5
The Last First-Day of School

As BETSY WOUND HER hair on Magic Wavers, preparing for her last first-day of high school, the importance of that event was dwarfed in her mind by Joe's call. In a way it was dwarfed, in another way it was glorified. The fact that Joe had sought her out, that they were obviously going to go together, put a crowning touch to her joy in being a senior.

She wound her clock briskly and set the alarm

for six. She wanted to get into the bathroom early next morning, to have time to prink. She and Tib had planned exactly what they would wear for the great day. Betsy had decided on her pink chambray dress with a wide pink band around her hair.

She slipped a kimono over her nightgown and threw a pillow to the floor beside Uncle Keith's trunk.

"I guess I'll read over my old diaries, and start the new one tonight," she said aloud.

She got out the three fat notebooks which held the story of her first three years in high school, and the fourth one with its tantalizing empty pages. As she read, the quality and mood of each year returned like a tune.

Her freshman year, and her joy in finding a crowd, her discovery about her writing, and her yearning for Tony.

"I've never been so much in love with anyone as I was with Tony when I was fourteen."

Her sophomore year, and her trip to Milwaukee to visit Tib, the attempt to be Dramatic and Mysterious in order to captivate Phil Brandish, Phyllis' twin.

"After I got him, I didn't want him."

And last year, her junior year, when she had been all wound up in sororities, and going with Dave Hunt.

"That was funny. We were really just friends. Not a bit of a crush."

Through all three years, Joe Willard had stood in

the background, a figure of mystery and challenge, and now in her senior year they were going to go together. How completely and utterly satisfactory!

Betsy dipped her pen in ink.

"Three years ago this fall," she wrote, "I began my first diary and my four years of high school loomed ahead so bigly that the start of my senior-year diary seemed but a vague possibility. Yet here I am starting it!

"How different I feel! One begins one's freshman year wild with anticipation, eager for the days to pass, radiantly happy! But one begins one's senior year with a sense of looking back, a longing to enjoy each minute to the full, a little touch of sadness."

She didn't feel at all sad but she thought that sounded good.

"I would like to stop the clock right here and take a little breathing spell. As Mary Ware said, 'It's so nice to be as old as seventeen, and yet as young as seventeen.' But time goes on, on, on. . . ."

She meant to develop that but she couldn't think just how. Besides, she was getting hungry. She always got hungry when she stayed up late. She opened the door of her room into a dark sleeping house, and crept softly down the stairs.

Out in the kitchen, she lit the gas light and foraged. Finding milk, cold sausages, and part of a chocolate cake, she tiptoed with them back up to her room.

How handsome Joe had looked! How thrilling that he had come to see her on his first night home! When her lunch was eaten, she turned out the gas, opened her window wide, and crept into bed.

The next thing she knew the alarm clock was shrilling and she jumped to her feet, remembering drowsily that if she wanted a leisurely time in the bathroom, it behooved her to get there. After her father started shaving, she wouldn't have a chance. And if she got in just ahead of him, he was sure to rap on the door, saying, "Hurry, Betsy! Remember, I must shave."

She was amply early, and when the breakfast gong sounded she emerged from her room looking as she had planned to look, in the pink chambray dress which was made in princesse style, long and close-fitting, trimmed with white rickrack braid. The wide pink band was tied around her Magically Waved hair; her fingernails were buffed to a pink shine.

Margaret joined her in the hall. It was hard to know whether Margaret, too, had been up early prinking, for she was always so fastidiously neat. She wore a new white middy blouse with a red tie, and the red bows which tied her braids behind each ear were gigantic. She carried a pile of last year's books under her arm.

The tempting smell of muffins filled the air. Anna always made muffins for the first day of school. A plateful of the fragrant, tender pyramids was already on the table, and she brought another shortly, for Tacy and Tib dropped in to call for Betsy. The two girls were full of excitement about Joe Willard's picture in the paper.

"He's back. He dropped in last night," Betsy said, offhandedly.

"He dropped in?" cried Tib. "Betsy Ray! Tell us about it."

"What is there to tell?"

"Do you like him as well as you thought you would?"

"I like him as well as I always did. I've known him for three years."

"She's just being irritating," Tacy said. "You tell us what happened, Mrs. Ray."

"I don't know," answered Mrs. Ray. "We tactfully retreated, didn't we, Margaret?"

Margaret nodded, beaming.

"There's a poem I learned in school," said Mr. Ray. He threw back his head and began a sing-song chant:

> "New hope may bloom,
> And days may come,
> Of milder, calmer beam,

But there's nothing half so sweet in life,
As love's young dream,
Oh, there's nothing half so sweet in life,
As love's young dream."

"Papa!" protested Betsy, blushing. But she wasn't annoyed. "We just had a nice sensible time."

"On the porch in the moonlight," put in Mr. Ray.

"He's so handsome," said Mrs. Ray, "I could have a crush on him myself if I didn't have such a crush on my husband."

"He's not so nice as Tony," said Margaret, in a distant tone.

"Oh, but Tony's different, Margaret," Tacy replied. "There's no fun teasing Betsy about Tony. He hasn't a crush on her."

"And she hasn't a crush on him," Tib added. "You'll understand when you're older."

"Perhaps," said Betsy, "we'd better go to school."

They called out to Anna that the muffins were marvelous and descended the porch, arm in arm, into High Street. The vine over the porch was turning red; and in spite of the summerlike green of the trees, the petunias, zinnias, and nasturtiums still blooming in the borders, Betsy felt the impact of the coming season, the melancholy of September.

For the first time, she missed Cab.

"It'll seem funny not to have Cab walking to school with us," she said, and tried to imagine what it would be like to be giving up school in your senior year. She wondered how Cab was feeling about it, down at the furniture store.

"We'll miss Carney, too," said Tacy.

"She's coming to visit today," Tib announced. "She's going to classes with us."

The school-bound parade surged along High Street: freshmen looked frightened and eager; sophomores, proud; juniors, complacent. Betsy wondered whether she and Tacy and Tib betrayed their consciousness of being seniors as they chatted loftily, well aware of admiring eyes.

They went through the big doors, climbed the stairs past their old friend Mercury, so lightly poised that Betsy never quite believed he was made of stone, and paused in the upper hall. Here was the case which held the silver trophy cups for which the school societies, Philomathian and Zetamathian, competed annually—in athletics, in debating, and in essay writing. The Essay Cup made Betsy think of Joe.

"How will we feel competing against each other this year . . . when we're going together," she wondered.

He didn't appear in the Social Room. He seldom came there. Having a job in addition to his school work, he usually reached school with the last gong and hurried away at the end of each session.

Ralph Maddox appeared, however. The new senior athlete from St. John caused a sensation.

"He's beautiful!" cried Winona.

"He's ravishing!" cried Hazel Smith.

"He's absolutely pulchritudinous!" cried Betsy—all this in hushed voices, of course.

"Hmm," said Tib. "I don't mind getting *him* for the Zets."

Tall, broad-shouldered, with dark washboard curls rising above a classic profile, he looked kin to Mercury out in the hall. He moved a little self-consciously through the buzzing room. Of course, thought Betsy, if you were that handsome you couldn't help but know it.

Carney joined the girls just as the gong rang and accompanied them into the Assembly Room.

"Gosh, I feel superior," she said, "watching the rest of you start the same old grind!"

As usual, Betsy, Tacy, and Tib headed for back seats and found three together. Miss Bangeter announced the opening hymn. Boys and girls stood and sang with a will. They sat, with much banging of seats and scraping of feet, and Miss Bangeter read from the Bible.

She read from the Bible every morning and it was

one of the things, Betsy realized, she would remember from high school. She liked the magnificent prose as it rolled from the lips of the principal, who was magnificent herself, in a dark, austere way.

"I'm sorry for high schools that haven't Miss Bangeter for principal," Betsy thought.

Miss Bangeter read this morning from the thirteenth chapter of First Corinthians.

"'Though I speak with the tongues of men and of angels, and have not charity, I am become as sounding brass, or a tinkling cymbal.'"

Betsy was listening dreamily when the familiar words flashed out with sudden meaning.

"'When I was a child,'" read Miss Bangeter, "'I spake as a child, I understood as a child, I thought as a child: but when I became a man, I put away childish things.'"

Betsy looked across the aisle at Tacy and saw that Tacy was looking at her. She reached for a tablet and a pencil and thought she would write the words down, but she stopped, for she knew she would remember them. They were so apt, so significant, at the beginning of the senior year.

"I put away childish things." You didn't want to, perhaps; but you did. She would have to, and so would Tacy and Tib and all of them.

Betsy felt a wave of that sadness she had not felt at

all last night when she told her diary she felt it. But it was soon dispelled. They went the round of their classes, Carney making derisive remarks.

Spurred by Julia's constant references to the need of modern languages out in the Great World, Betsy had registered for German. Her father had been pleased.

"We have so many Germans in Deep Valley, all over the county, in fact. Lots of them who come into the store can hardly speak English. It's a language you can really use, Betsy."

"That's right," Betsy said. "Why, Tib's father and mother often speak to each other in German. I can talk it with them. And I can talk it with Tib. And I can go to hear sermons at the German churches."

"Besides," said Mrs. Ray, "you can speak it with Julia when she comes home."

"And I can teach it to Margaret. *Nicht wahr,* Margaret?"

"Say *Ja,* Button," Mr. Ray advised.

"*Ja, ja,*" said Margaret, full of laughter.

These fine plans filled Betsy's mind now as she left Tacy, Tib, and Carney and went alone into the first-year German class. Her classmates were mostly awestruck freshmen. Her teacher was the blond Miss Erickson, who had tried to teach her Latin.

Tacy and Tib joined her for physics under Mr.

Gaston. They knew this subject would be hard and had dodged it in their frivolous junior year.

They could relax in the civics class, next on the schedule. Miss Clarke, who had taught them Ancient History, Modern History, and United States History, was a girlish, indulgent teacher.

Last of all came Miss Bangeter's Shakespeare class.

Miss Bangeter didn't teach many subjects. But her senior Shakespeare class was famous. She loved Shakespeare; she had specialized in his works in college. Her class read some of the comedies and tragedies aloud, parts being assigned to the various students.

Betsy had looked forward to it ever since Julia had taken it two years before, and she welcomed it also for another reason. Joe would be there. Even when they hadn't been friends, held apart by that curious hostility which, for a time, had stood between them, they had always enjoyed being together in English class.

He came into the classroom now with that swinging walk which was so much a part of him, and looked around at once for Betsy, who was also looking for him. They smiled at each other.

As soon as class was dismissed, he came over to her.

"I have to get down to the *Sun*," he said. "But not

until I settle something important. When am I going to see you again?"

Betsy thought quickly. Winona was entertaining the girls Friday night for Carney. Saturday night she was going to the Majestic with Tony.

"Why don't you come up Sunday night?" she asked. "Come to lunch. That's what we call Sunday night supper at our house. I don't know why, but we do."

"Seeing as how it's lunch and not supper, I'd love to come," answered Joe. He smiled at Tacy, Tib, and Carney and went out of the room.

The three girls looked at each other.

"Well!" said Tacy.

"About time!" said Tib.

"Hurray!" cried Carney. "I'm glad it happened before I went to Vassar. Betsy's going to go with Joe Willard, *at last!*"

"Don't be silly!" Betsy answered, blushing as pink as the pink chambray dress.

6

The Senior Class President

THE PARTY FOR CARNEY was a noteworthy affair. Of course, her impending departure was noteworthy. She was going so far—half way across the continent—and she was the first Deep Valley girl to go east to college. And she would leave a yawning gap in the Crowd. No more on warm September days would they sprawl on the Sibley lawn. No more on moonlight nights would they go rattling about the country, singing, in the Sibley auto. The girls brought letters to be read on the train and small gifts for the trip. Winona presented a corsage of carnations which Carney popped into the ice box so that she could wear it on the morrow.

They played five hundred. Five hundred was almost as much the rage as bands around the hair. There were dishes of candy kisses on each table, there were prizes, and superlative refreshments—crab meat salad, home baked rolls, cocoa, an enormous sunshine cake. The boys raided and were invited in, which made the party perfect.

It was well that the Crowd got its innings on Friday night, for at the train next morning they were far outnumbered by Sibleys. Carney's own family was reasonably small, but there were Sibleys all over the county. The station swarmed with grandparents, uncles, aunts, and cousins, so that the Crowd got only a glimpse of Carney in the tweed suit and the brown velvet tricorn, with the big bouquet of carnations. Her eyes were shining behind her glasses. The dimple stood out in her round pink cheek.

"Write to us!" the Crowd called when she came out on the observation platform.

"I will, I will."

The whistle blew, the bell began to ring, and the

great oily black wheels started turning. Carney waved with vigor but her lips were set as though it were an effort to keep calm and matter-of-fact.

"I wonder whether college will change Carney," Betsy said, when the train was gone.

"Maybe she'll come back with an eastern accent."

"Carney never 'put on' in her life."

"Some people do, though, when they're in the East only a little while."

"Well, Carney will come back with her same old Deep Valley accent," Winona said positively, and everyone agreed.

Betsy and Tony discussed her departure that night, eating pineapple sundaes at Heinz's after the picture. Tom had already left for Cox, and Al and Squirrelly would soon be leaving for the U.

"You and I will be going off to college next year, I suppose," Betsy said.

"Heck! I probably won't even graduate."

"What do you mean? Of course you'll graduate!" Betsy was indignantly emphatic. "Probably," she added, "you'll go to the U at Minneapolis."

"Well, I'm going up to Minneapolis all right . . . tomorrow," he said wickedly. "The team is playing at home."

"How are you going?"

"In my private car."

"Tony," said Betsy, "you ought not to do that."

"Why not?"

"Papa told you. You might lose a leg. Besides, those railroad men are all too old for you."

"They suit me fine."

"I wish you wouldn't do it," Betsy said.

Tony looked at her across the metal table, his laughing black eyes growing suddenly somber.

"Do you really wish I wouldn't?" he asked.

"I certainly do."

"I might stop it," he said enigmatically.

"I wish you would," Betsy replied. "I worry about those trips, Tony. I like it so much better when you just hang around with the Crowd."

"And with you?" Tony asked. His tone was low. Betsy was hardly sure she had understood what he said. Although Tony was so bold and breezy, he was intensely reticent. He was not given to personal remarks, or at least not with her. And if he had really said what she thought he had said, he wouldn't like having said it when he found out about Joe. She decided to pretend she hadn't heard.

"If you don't go to Minneapolis," she replied, "we'll expect you for Sunday night lunch."

He did not appear on Sunday night, but Joe came early, his blue suit neatly pressed this time, his pompadour burnished by much brushing. He and Mrs.

Ray started talking about books. It seemed to Betsy that he had read everything, beginning with *The Iliad* and *The Odyssey*. But Mr. Ray had never even heard of *The Iliad* and *The Odyssey*. He liked people instead of books. He was wary of intellectuals and Betsy could see that he acted a little guarded with Joe. Joe also seemed a little guarded with him.

Shifting from books, Mrs. Ray told him the news of Julia, whom Joe had known slightly. She showed him Julia's pictures and chatted on about the difficulties with her trunk.

"If I remember Julia," Joe said gallantly, "she doesn't need to worry if that trunk never comes."

He got on famously with Mrs. Ray, but Betsy felt a little fearful when he pushed his way deliberately through the swinging door to the kitchen where her father was making sandwiches.

Mr. Ray always made the sandwiches for Sunday night lunch. They were a family institution. He sat down to make them, looking dignified and benevolent, as he went about his invariable rites—buttering bread, arranging slices of cold meat, cheese, or onions, seasoning them expertly while the coffee he had earlier set to boil exuded its inviting fragrance. He liked to have lookers-on but Betsy wondered what under the sun he and Joe would find to talk about.

As she chattered with Cab at the fireplace, she

kept an ear turned to the kitchen. Certainly a hum of conversation was issuing therefrom. At last she found courage to saunter out, and she found Joe watching the sandwich-making intently, but not half so intently as he was listening to Mr. Ray's story about an old Syrian couple who had come into the store to buy shoes.

When Joe was helping Betsy arrange the cups and saucers on the dining room table, he said, "I always thought it was just people who want to write, like me, who enjoyed analyzing people. But your father is a far better student of human nature than I'll ever be. He likes people better."

Betsy was delighted and even more delighted later when her father remarked, "That Joe's a nice boy, a fine boy, and he certainly does like my stories."

A letter came from Julia the next day, and to Mrs. Ray's dismay, she was still without her trunk. Moreover, she had needed it badly for an event which she dramatically described.

Fraulein von Blatz had taken her to a reception given by the Kaiser . . . no less . . . for an American who was coming to Berlin in a balloon. His name was Wright.

"I asked Fraulein whether it was perfectly all right for me to go as I was. She said, 'Of course, of course,' in that vague way of hers. She doesn't care a thing about clothes and wears a suit and a man's old hat wherever she goes. It doesn't matter, for she's a celebrity, but I'm not—yet.

"We drove clear out to the end of the city to a magnificent estate. Our host was a pompous old officer. He couldn't speak any English and you know my German! But I smiled my most elegant smile.

"Over the garden wall was the field where the Emperor was to greet the balloonist. There were hundreds of troops at attention. The garden was swarming with grand ladies, to some of whom Fraulein introduced me before she disappeared. They wore jewels and trailing dresses and plumed hats and white kid gloves. I didn't even have gloves.

"I began to be conscious of my rags and tatters. In fact, I was fussed. For how could I rise above clothes—as I pride myself on being able to do—when my vocabulary was limited to 'Ach, ja, sehr schoen'? Bettina, you learn languages!

"I fumed and cussed until my sense of humor came to the rescue. Then I began to play with a little girl Margaret's age. (They give such cute curtseys when they are introduced.) She and her sisters, about fourteen and eighteen, were with their governess. Their mother, the Countess von Hetternich, was at the Royal Palace in the Empress' party.

"The youngsters laughed at my German and I tried to help their English. We had lots of fun. The balloonist broke his propeller or something about fifty miles away, so we all had cakes and coffee and went home."

Mr. Ray was interested in the balloonist, but Mrs. Ray could think of nothing but Julia's predicament.

"She must have been embarrassed or she wouldn't have told us about it. Ordinarily Julia never thinks about clothes."

"She thought it was a joke," said Betsy. "And so do I. Imagine her, after all the trouble you took with her clothes, going to the Kaiser's reception without gloves!"

"Tell your mother that Julia's entrée into Berlin society wasn't half so much of a fiasco as Mr. Wright's," said Joe, when Betsy told him about it at school.

School activities were getting under way. Philomathians and Zetamathians were approaching the day when newcomers would be asked to choose societies. Last year on this occasion, Dave Hunt had put the Zetamathian banner on the cupola, thereby goading the rival society, the following spring, into painting Philomathian on the roof.

Miss Bangeter gave advance warnings that there would be no more such goings-on.

"The boys who went up there last year were suspended; if anyone tries it again, he will be expelled."

That settled that, and with roof climbing out of the question, excitement centered on the rushing being given Ralph Maddox.

He was sure to be a Philo, gossip said. He had Philomathian cousins.

"Why, they got him to come to Deep Valley," Winona explained.

"He's practically a Philo now," said Joe. "Boy, boy, this cinches the athletics cup!"

Betsy and Tacy hurried off to Tib. "You promised to get him for the Zets, remember?"

"I remember, I remember," said Tib.

Watching her chance in the Social Room, she gazed up at him naively. "I just have to tell you. We're so thrilled about your coming to Deep Valley. You know, our big football star, Al Larson, graduated. We just needed another football star."

After that wherever you saw the tall, dark, handsome Maddox, you saw Tib, small, blond, and enchanting, smiling up at him.

"Is he practically a Philo now?" asked Betsy.

"Sure," said Joe. "Blood is thicker than water."

"I'll bet you a box of candy Tib gets him for the Zets."

The next day Tib, standing on tiptoe, pinned a blue ribbon into Maddox's lapel, and Joe brought a big box of candy to the Social Room.

Busy as he was, Joe was mingling more with the high school crowd this year. Betsy was glad, for he had always been something of an outsider. Working after school, he had been unable to take part in athletics, and until last year he had not had the money for social life.

He had always found time for the Essay Contest, of course, and last year, as a reporter for the *Sun*, he had attended football and basketball games. He had headed the program committee for the Junior-Senior Banquet and had helped to paint that fateful Philomathian on the roof.

These things had drawn him into the current of school life, and it was good for him, Betsy thought, to ride that giddy current. His experiences had matured him, just as different, less sober, experiences had matured Tony. Like Tony, Joe needed a crowd, needed fun, needed to go with a girl who thought high school affairs were important.

When class elections came along, he arranged with Mr. Root to be late getting down to the paper.

"I'm really interested," he confided to Betsy. "I'd really like to know who's going to steer us through this year of glory. It will be Stan, I suppose?"

Stan Moore had been president through the sophomore and junior years.

"He would be a good one," Betsy answered. "But some kids think that the offices ought to be passed around."

"You've been secretary for two years, haven't you?"

"Yes. And I wouldn't accept it again. Last year I thought I wanted it awfully, but now I can see that it wouldn't be fair. And I'm going to be plenty busy."

They walked together into the Assembly Room and Betsy took her place on the platform with last year's officers. Stan took charge. Hazel started the election ball to rolling by nominating him.

Stan jumped up. "Thanks very much," he said, "but I've had this office twice and I think it's time someone else had it."

Dennie rose. "I want to nominate an outstanding boy and a swell athlete, Dave Hunt." There was a burst of applause. A voice in the rear of the room cried, "I second the nomination."

Alice stood up. "I think," she said, "that we might have a girl president for a change. I have a girl in mind who would be just the one. She's a leading senior and the best girl debater in the state. Hazel Smith." There was another burst of applause even louder than the first, and again a prompt seconding voice.

"We have two nominations," Stan said. "Dave Hunt and Hazel Smith. Does anyone else have anything to say?"

To the surprise of the class, Tony pulled himself lazily to his feet. He had always taken even less interest than Joe in school affairs. He didn't make a speech now, but he stood, for long seconds, in silent scrutiny of all the class. It came to Betsy that he was challenging them. He was, she realized, about to make a nomination which, in his opinion, would test them, and his gaze as much as said that he doubted how well they would come off. That bold, scornful gaze circled the room for a last time, then he drawled in his deep voice, "I nominate Joe Willard," and sank back into his seat.

There was no applause whatever. When Betsy realized that, it was too late to start any. A confused silence had fallen on the room, broken only by Tacy's, "I second that nomination."

Joe Willard! He wasn't an athlete. He had never held a class office. No one had ever thought of him in such a connection.

Yet, Betsy thought defensively, he had always been a credit to the school. Among grown-ups in Deep Valley, he was, without doubt, the school's outstanding student. Men and women knew Joe Willard; they admired him and said he would make his mark. And in school, when you came to think of it, who had been a bigger help to his fellow students? He had written of school events in the *Sun* as no one ever had written of them before. And although he hadn't had time for athletics, his three-time victory in the Essay Contest had been, she assured herself doggedly, as good as winning touchdowns any day.

But, she wondered, was there time for Joe's achievements to impress themselves on the minds of the boys and girls waiting dumbfoundedly to vote? If they had time, she knew that his chance would be good. If time was lacking, she feared that, like sheep, they would ignore Hazel Smith because she was a girl and vote unthinkingly for "an outstanding boy and a swell athlete, Dave Hunt."

Betsy couldn't, she told herself desperately, bear to have Dave win, even though she liked him. Dave already had so much. Joe must win! He must! She looked toward him and saw proudly that he was taking the issue in stride. He looked poised and cool. But she knew that he must have been surprised by Tony's breath-taking nomination, and cut by the silence in which it was received.

Someone moved that the nominations be closed. Ballots were distributed, written, and collected. Excitement played like lightning over the room when Stan stood up to announce the results. He was grinning widely.

"The new class president . . ." he said, and paused. "The new class president," he repeated, speaking slowly, "is Joe Willard."

The applause, which had been lacking before, broke out wildly then. Joe looked flustered, although he was still in command of himself. In response to the cries which rose above the clapping hands, he got to his feet, smiled, and nodded.

Then, in a quick, boyish, heart-warming gesture of gratitude and pleasure, he flung both arms above his head and waved his hands. The applause changed as though at a signal from handclaps to yells, the shrill sweet treble of the girls, a deep chorus of "Yee-ah, Joe!" from the boys.

Betsy's heart swelled. Joe, who had never had time for school politics, who had never had a home to entertain in or parents to entertain for him, who had always held proudly aloof from social life because he was poor. Joe had received the greatest honor his class had to offer. She was grateful to Tony for having thought of it. The idea had never once entered her own head.

After the meeting ended, she sought out Tony.

"That was wonderful, Tony. I don't know why we've never thought of Joe before for a class office," she said.

"I think, myself, it was smart," Tony answered, looking pleased with himself. "He's got more sense than most of these small-timers. He's been around."

That, Betsy thought, was the explanation of why Tony had nominated Joe. He was pleased to see a fellow outsider take command. He had known that Joe only needed to be presented, to be recognized as a leader.

Tony didn't know, she felt sure, that she had any special feeling for Joe. He hadn't done it for her sake, which made it all the nicer.

"It was wonderful," she repeated, smiling at him warmly, and crossed the room to congratulate Joe.

7

The Rift within the Lute

IF ANYTHING HAD BEEN needed to make the start of
the senior year happy, Joe's new honor supplied it for
Betsy. She was gloriously happy. She had never, she
thought, been so happy in her life.

Joe started class business rolling by appointing a
committee on class pins and caps. Oddly enough,
Betsy Ray was on the committee. As president, Joe

was ex-officio member of all committees, and so he joined the group which went down to Alquist's Clothing Store looking for caps. After much hilarious trying on, the committee decided to recommend skull caps made up in the class colors of violet and gray. The committee then renewed its strength at Heinz's, with ice cream swimming in syrups, topped by whipped cream, nuts, and cherries.

The next day, Joe called a class meeting and the committee reported. The skull caps were approved, so the committee, and president, went back to Alquist's and ordered them, with more nourishment at Heinz's.

Still later they were obliged to go down to collect the caps, not neglecting Heinz's, of course. The caps were distributed, causing quite a flurry around school. Cameras snapped as seniors posed, singly and in groups.

"Dearest Chuck," Tacy said to Tib, "you're a sensation in that cap."

"Maddox will adore it, Sweet My Coz," said Betsy.

"By my troth thou sayest true," said Tib, placing the cap at an even jauntier angle.

All the seniors were talking in that vein, for Miss Bangeter's Shakespeare class had started to read *As You Like It.*

They wore the skull caps to the first football game,

the battle with Red Feather, and Maddox, bulking large in his fame and shoulder pads, did indeed cast appreciative glances. The girls went in a crowd, for most of the boys they knew were on the team, except Joe, who, of course, was covering the game for the *Sun*.

Joe didn't have much time for girls at football games. Bareheaded, enveloped in an ancient sweater, pencil in one hand, copy paper in the other, he jogged up and down the sidelines.

The girls did plenty of yelling, but all of it was in vain. In spite of Maddox, Deep Valley went down to ignominious defeat.

The team was weak this year. It did, indeed, miss Al. Dave Hunt was a fine player, but although tall he was very thin, and his long legs helped more at basketball than at football. Maddox had been good in practice, and early in the game he made one flashy touchdown. But he didn't do it again, and he didn't seem able to keep the Red Feather team from piling up a twenty-to-six score.

The home-going crowd was optimistic, however.

"Oh, Maddox just didn't get going!"

"That touchdown showed what he can do."

"Didn't he look gorgeous running down the field?"

"We just have to have a good season," said Betsy, "in our senior year."

She was an incorrigible senior. About everything

she did, she kept thinking whether or not she would do it again.

There was something so familiar about September—golden fields clean-swept by harvest, sumac reddening along country roads, birds in great sociable flocks ready to fly south. The Crowd amused itself in the now time honored ways—going riding, going serenading, going on wiener roasts and beefsteak fries. Betsy kept thinking how different everything would be next year.

A pattern was breaking, never to be re-established. Part of it had already broken. Chauncey Olcott didn't come to Deep Valley this year.

His visit had been a regular autumn event as long as Betsy could remember. The Ray family had always gone in a body to hear him. This year an interloper named Fiske O'Hara came, in a play called *The Wearing of the Green*. Like the Olcott plays, it was an Irish romance full of ballads, which young O'Hara sang as Chauncey Olcott used to sing them.

The loyal Rays boycotted *The Wearing of the Green*. Anna would not go with her Charley. And although those fickle people who attended said that the newcomer was very handsome, with a sweet tenor voice, the Rays would have none of him.

"Don't bring those songs up to the house!" Betsy said to Tony.

"The copycat!" muttered Anna, rolling out cookies

as though she had Fiske O'Hara under the rolling pin.

The pattern was broken, too, because Julia was so far away, and in such strange surroundings.

A brief note had followed her letter about the Kaiser's reception.

"Darlings: Fraulein just came in from the 'phone, to tell me the biggest joke! I made a hit yesterday after all. One of the girls I met, the oldest of those three Von Hetternich sisters, wants to perfect her English, and her mother telephoned Fraulein to ask if I would come and stay with them awhile. Fraulein said it would not only give me a chance to learn German; it would enable me to get to know one of the first families in Berlin. Did you ever hear of such luck? P. S. My trunk has come."

The next letter told about the Von Hetternichs' home.

"You could get lost wandering through it. There are drawing rooms, libraries, separate rooms for every meal, and every member of the family has a suite. I have a huge bedroom and share a little study with Else, the daughter of eighteen. I have a bathroom all my own, and a maid draws my bath every morning. Imagine that, Bettina!"

Julia described the three daughters, Else, Emma, and Eugenia. A brother, Else's twin, had left for boarding school. It was like living in a novel, she said.

To the Rays it was like a serial story. They could hardly wait from installment to installment, as Julia wrote of being petted and showered with presents, sent in a car to her lessons, to the theater, and opera.

The Rays were excited, but none of them was surprised when Julia wrote that the Von Hetternichs wished her to stay on as long as she lived in Berlin. The Countess wrote the formal invitation to Mrs. Ray. Else wrote a letter to Betsy which Julia enclosed in one of hers.

"Please, Bettina, when you reply, be careful to write plainly. English script is hard for her to read. And for heaven's sake, don't shock the dear prim soul! She never sees a man unless chaperoned to death and listens to my accounts of dances with awe."

Betsy and Tacy were enthralled by Julia's adventures, but Tib was unmoved.

"I don't envy that Else," she said. "Living in a palace, being chaperoned to death, isn't half so much fun as going to high school."

Betsy thought she was right as the first senior party began to be talked of. Joe called a class meeting to discuss it. It would be a dance, of course. He appointed a committee to work out details, then gave Dave the chair and went off to the *Sun*.

Tony walked home with Betsy. The weather was

cool, with a spatter of rain in the air. They were glad to find a fire in the grate, and bringing in handfuls of cookies from the kitchen, they settled themselves on the hearth.

Tony had stretched out in a chair and Betsy was pulling a cushion as near to the fire as flying sparks permitted, when he said casually, "This dance they're planning . . . I'll drag you to it if you want to be dragged."

Betsy felt a cold streak sinking through her body. Her disappointment was so intense that it almost brought tears to her eyes. She knew Joe would ask her to the party. In fact, she knew he took it for granted that he was going to take her. And it would be such joy to go with him! She would be proud, too, to show the school that they were going together.

But if she turned Tony down, he probably wouldn't go at all. He would hunt up some of those wild friends of whom her father disapproved. Besides, Tony had asked her first, and the rule required that she accept him.

She jumped up and started poking the fire.

"Why, that would be grand, Tony," she said, her tone as casual as his had been. Tony was keen where people's feelings were concerned. She would have to be careful.

Fortunately, Margaret came in just then from her

piano lesson. She told Tony gravely that she had learned to play "Little Birdie Is Dead." Tony asked her to play it for him, and she complied, which showed how much she liked him. Margaret detested performing.

Unlike Betsy, Margaret showed talent for the piano, and she was a better student in school than either of her sisters had been. But she had none of the ambition which burned in their breasts.

People were always saying to Margaret, "Well, Julia sings and Betsy writes. Now what is little Margaret going to do?"

Margaret would smile politely, for she was very polite, but privately she stormed to Betsy with flashing eyes, "I'm not going to do anything. I want to just live. Can't people just live?"

"Of course," Betsy soothed her. But she could never understand.

Tony understood. He understood Betsy's ambition and Margaret's lack of it. Tony was such a darling, Betsy thought, watching his sleepily benignant look as Margaret played. She was glad she hadn't hurt his feelings, but she passed the rest of the afternoon with a sickish feeling inside.

Joe was both sensitive and proud. Once he had asked to take her home from a party, and again, to walk home from the library with her. On both occasions she had had to turn him down and for months afterwards he had made no gesture toward her. Now they were so close, so happy together. She didn't think he would act like that, and yet . . . she didn't know.

About supper time Joe called up. His voice sounded cheerful.

"I've got an assignment tonight. Bell ringers. Down at the Presbyterian Church. Don't you think you could go, even though it's a school night? Bell ringers are highly educational."

Betsy ran to ask her father and to her surprise he assented.

"I'm glad to have you hear some bell ringers, Betsy. There aren't very many of them any more. They're going out of style, like minstrel shows."

This was astounding luck. Betsy would have been overjoyed except for that dread hanging over her.

They had a very good time. After the entertainment they went to Heinz's, and they talked hard and fast over their cocoa and on the cold walk home. They never seemed to tire of talking. In fact, they never seemed to tire of each other.

Betsy knew he enjoyed her, and she admired him beyond words. He had the beginning of a genuine culture based on his prodigious reading. He had read, she thought, everything. Not only older writers like Dickens, Thackeray, Balzac, Hawthorne, and

Washington Irving, but the stimulating newcomers: Jack London, Frank Norris, O. Henry. Tonight he was telling her about O. Henry's stories; his enthusiasm swept her along like the wind.

It wasn't until they reached her home and the fire that Joe brought up the senior dance. They had hung up their wraps and both were on cushions close to the dying embers. Joe had wanted to put on another log, but Betsy reminded him that the morrow was a school day.

"You can only stay until that last stick breaks in two, which it's just preparing to do."

"Then," he replied, "we must do some talking about the class party. By the way, Miss Ray, I'd like to have the honor of conducting you."

Betsy felt herself flush. She swallowed and tried to keep her tone light.

"By the way, you're too late. Somebody asked me this afternoon."

"What!" Joe started up sharply. "Who is it?"

"Tony."

"Well, of all the nerve!" He sounded really angry, but then he said, "That Markham!" and his tone was milder, almost admiring. "Darn the guy!"

He was silent, frowning thoughtfully into the flickering fire. Then he turned and looked at her with teasing bright eyes.

"All right," he said sternly. "Tony got ahead of me. And there's nothing I can do about it, except go to the dance stag. But after this, Miss Ray, you're going to go to all of the dances with me. This is a blanket invitation. I'll ask you separately, for each party, too, but remember, if someone gets ahead of me while I'm out earning my living, you have already been asked." .

Betsy laughed, but tremulously. "Why, Joe!"

He seemed pleased with himself. "Tony hasn't made any such proposition, has he?"

"No, but . . ."

"Then what's wrong with it? I have to protect myself, since I'm working every night and most of the weekends. Tony didn't think to make such an invitation or he'd have made it. Willard is smart, that's all. Well, what are you waiting for? You're going to accept, aren't you?"

Betsy was laughing, but she was so perilously close to tears that she stopped. She couldn't possibly agree to this plan, but how could she best explain the impossibility of it?

She looked away from him into the fire.

"I can't do it, Joe," she said. "It isn't that I wouldn't like to. Please listen awfully hard and try to understand."

She paused again, for loyalty to Tony would keep

her from telling the real reason. She couldn't mention her fears for him.

"Tony," she said slowly, "is sort of a brother to us. He comes to our house as though it were his own. And we've been going to parties together off and on for years. I just couldn't freeze him out . . . of everything . . . like that."

She stopped but Joe was silent.

"You know, don't you, Joe," she said honestly, "that I'd rather go with you than anybody? I like Tony . . . too well to hurt him . . . but in a different way from the way I like you."

As Joe still didn't reply, she added, "Take back that blanket invitation. You ask somebody else to the dance and we'll go to plenty of parties this winter if you'll just ask me quickly."

Joe looked at her and slowly his clouded gaze cleared.

"All right," he said, and laughed. "I'll play the field. I'll invite some other girl for this party and still another for the next one, unless you'll go with me yourself to the next one. Would it be fair to ask just one ahead?"

"Perfectly fair," Betsy said.

"All right," Joe repeated. "It's a date."

The slender graying stick broke in the center, sending up a shower of sparks. Again Betsy and Joe felt that accord between them. It would take more than a misunderstanding about Tony, Betsy realized, to break it up.

She felt happy again, but when she thought of going to the senior dance with Tony and of Joe taking some other girl, she didn't feel quite so happy as she had felt before.

She remembered a poem from Junior English about the little rift within the lute.

8

Two Model Young Men

THE DANCE, HOWEVER, was wonderful. Even if she had gone with Joe, Betsy thought, it could hardly have been nicer. The great Maddox invited Tib, to the dismay of Lloyd and Dennie, her last year's cavaliers. Cab, attending by special request of the Class of 1910, invited Tacy to go with him.

Joe, after all, went stag.

"Don't think I'm breaking my promise," he said to

Betsy. "I'm just so darn busy that it doesn't seem worth while asking someone I don't give a . . . Never mind! Never mind! I'll always ask someone else when you go with someone else if you'll let me off this time."

Gladly, Betsy let him off.

It was a wonderful party. Tib and Tacy came to dress at the Ray house, lugging satchels, for they planned to sleep that night in Julia's bed. They laced one another's corsets, tied the fashionable bands around one another's heads. Tib, of course, made Betsy's puffs.

In their pastel-tinted dresses, cut princesse, flaring at the ankles to reveal colored stockings, they looked as modish, Mrs. Ray said, as girls in a fashion magazine.

"You look as pretty as posies," Mr. Ray declared.

"You look puny," cried Anna, coming into the parlor where they were revolving for family inspection. Puny was Anna's word for handsome. She turned to Mrs. Ray. "Don't it make your heart ache, lovey, to think how they're growing up? They'll be leaving us soon."

"Oh, we'll have Margaret," said Mr. Ray. "She'll be starting off to dances."

Margaret was watching with sparkling eyes. She had sat in Betsy's room, quiet as the cat in her arms, all the while they were dressing. She liked it that Betsy was going with Tony, and when Tony came in, his curly black crest brushed to a glitter, a new necktie, an immaculate shirt, his suit pressed to knife-edge sharpness, Margaret smiled delightedly.

Betsy was pleased and a little touched by Tony's splendor.

"He's proud to be going out with me," she thought. "It's very good for him."

The resplendent Maddox arrived with Cab. Tib's light little laugh sounded continuously as the boys helped the girls into their coats and slung the ties of slipper bags over their arms. Tib had not lost her heart. She had a very cool, dependable heart. But she was elated to be escorted by the sensation of the football season. She slipped her hand possessively into his arm and tripped proudly beside him through the pungent autumn evening.

At Schiller Hall, they climbed three flights of stairs, and the girls hung their wraps in the dressing room, changed into slippers, powdered their noses, and went out into the ballroom. Mamie Dodd, who played the piano, tantalized them with chords and snatches of music while programs were being filled. Then she swung zestfully into "I Wonder Who's Kissing Her Now" and couples whirled out over the shining floor.

Waiting for Tony to find her, Betsy watched Tib and Maddox. His dark curls and tall figure, Tib's delicate blondness, made an arresting contrast. Many people were watching them, including the chaperones.

"Aren't they sweet!" Betsy heard Miss Clarke exclaim to Mr. Stewart, who coached the football team and was familiarly known as Stewie.

"Handsome is as handsome does," said Stewie.

"He ought not to play football," Miss Clarke replied indignantly. "Think of that classic nose being broken!"

"He took pretty good care of that classic nose at the Red Feather game," Stewie replied.

Betsy was surprised by that remark. Hadn't Maddox made the only touchdown against Red Feather? But she forgot it as Tony came up. She had always loved dancing with Tony. He was not only light and rhythmic, but gaily inventive.

"You could dance on the stage," Betsy told him as they wove new patterns of movement to match the lilting tune.

Betsy saw Joe watching them and smiled a little anxiously. He smiled reassuringly back.

Joe had approached her as soon as she entered and asked for two dances, all it was proper to ask from another boy's girl. Except for those dances, a waltz and a two-step, he was scrupulously careful to leave her and Tony alone.

Through the whole evening, he didn't dance more than once with anyone but Betsy. He didn't stay with one girl a minute longer than he stayed with any other girl, and he ate supper with Miss Bangeter, Miss Clarke, and Stewie, seeming to enjoy their august company. In fact, he was a model, a perfect example of how the young man turned down by his girl ought to behave . . . if he wanted her to have a wonderful time.

Tony had somehow got wind of the fact that Joe had asked Betsy to the party. He was beginning to be aware of Joe's feeling for Betsy, but he had no inkling of Betsy's feeling for Joe. He took the matter lightly, being well accustomed to rivals at the Ray house. He liked Joe and beckoned him good-naturedly to their circle at supper, but Joe couldn't be won away from the faculty.

Tacy and Tib praised both boys' attitudes as they talked the party over in Betsy's room. Betsy was winding her hair on Magic Wavers and Tib was rubbing cream into her satiny face while Tacy watched benevolently, doing nothing to make herself more beautiful. Her thick auburn braids hung over her shoulders down the blue-striped flannel nightgown.

"Joe and Tony were absolutely noble. That's what they were," said Tib.

"They were perfect Galahads," said Tacy.

"I have a good effect on people. Me and the

Blessed Damozel," said Betsy, fastening the last Waver and beginning on the cream. She applied it with strokes suggested in the women's magazines, upward and outward, smoothing out wrinkles which had not yet appeared, and giving brisk pats with the back of her hand underneath her chin.

"What are you doing that for?" Tacy wanted to know.

"It takes off double chins."

"But you haven't got a double chin. You're as thin as a rail."

"Well, I don't want to get one," said Betsy, and continued to slap vigorously.

"She wouldn't have two boys quarreling about her if she had a double chin," said Tib, beating a tattoo on her own flawless underjaw.

"They didn't quarrel. They were models. That's what we were saying," said Tacy. "I heard lots of compliments about you and Ralph Maddox, too, Tib."

"So did I," said Betsy. "Everyone was watching you."

"We did look nice," Tib acknowledged. "He's certainly handsome. But I'm more interested in his football."

Maddox's honors in that sphere didn't pile up so rapidly as Tib would have wished. Football games dotted the calendar, but Deep Valley just couldn't seem to win. The team was admittedly weak, and at first nobody blamed Maddox. But soon disappointment in him began to find expression.

He played right half. He was a magnificent broken field runner and in every game made at least one spectacular touchdown. He was beautiful cutting trickily down field, dodging this tackle, stiff-arming that. But the tricky runs never added up to enough first downs to beat the enemy, and the spectacular touchdowns never added up to enough points to win the game.

And then suddenly, all in a day, the school was talking about the amazing fact that Maddox never got banged up. Dave's nose was knocked south-by-west, Stan lost a tooth, and Dennie always had one black eye when he hadn't two. But Maddox came out of every battle his handsome, perfect self.

Perhaps Stewie had started the talk with that remark which others besides Betsy had overheard. "He took pretty good care of that classic nose at the Red Feather game."

Stewie had followed this up with another cryptic comment to Maddox himself one afternoon during football practice.

"The great mystery, Maddox," he had said, "is that a marvelous runner like you ever is tackled." Maddox had colored in gratification, but he colored deeper with some other emotion when Stewie said, "Mystery is right! Because you have a genius for ending every run out of bounds."

He had said in almost so many words that Maddox shied away from the bruising body contacts which the other men in the backfield accepted with a grin, sometimes twisted with pain, but a grin nevertheless.

Betsy talked the scandal over with Joe.

"Don't make any mistake," Joe cautioned her. "Maddox isn't yellow. But he just plain doesn't want to spoil that classic phiz. So he doesn't like to hit that line. He doesn't like to block. And he doesn't like to tackle. Above all, of course, he doesn't like to be tackled. My guess is that at St. John his team didn't have much competition and he could win with tricky, fast running and never risk his beauty."

"We simply can't go on losing games like this."

"No, we can't." Joe's eyes darkened, and Betsy knew he longed to be on the team. Over the autumn she had realized more and more plainly what it had meant to him not to play football.

Since he couldn't play, he was throwing his heart into his newspaper stories. If rhetoric had been able to win, Deep Valley would have had a championship team. But none of Joe's fighting descriptions stirred Maddox. As October progressed, Deep Valley continued to lose.

When the maples rose like flames along High Street and the hills were russet and gold, the Rays drove out to Murmuring Lake. They went every year at this season to celebrate Mr. and Mrs. Ray's wedding anniversary. It was a little hard to make the familiar excursion with Julia so far away. But they went, and when they had started they enjoyed it heartily.

Betsy told Joe all about it that evening after their return. They were making fudge, or rather, Joe was making it. He scorned Betsy's cooking and fancied his own, so he took charge of the bubbling pan while Betsy watched from the kitchen table.

Joe smiled as he stirred.

"You go every year? Your father and mother must be glad they got married."

"They certainly are," Betsy said. "They always show us where they got engaged. Papa was camping with some other young men on the lake shore and he came up to the house to borrow a cup of salt. Mamma says he didn't need the salt at all. Papa says they needed it desperately. Anyhow, they sat down under an oak tree in the moonlight and got engaged. They always show us the tree."

"Did he get the salt?"

"He went off and forgot it."

"What else do they show you?" asked Joe.

"They show us the bay window where they were

married," Betsy answered dreamily. "It looks down a long avenue of evergreens to the big front gate. Mamma's room was just above it and she says that on her wedding day she sat in an upper window and looked down that avenue, waiting for Papa to come. She was wearing a tea gown, she says. At last she saw a pair of dappled gray horses and a surrey with Papa driving. He had hired a livery rig, a very stylish one."

"He wasn't so rich as your mother's stepfather," Joe suggested, "if he had to hire a livery rig."

"He certainly wasn't," Betsy replied. "He came from an Iowa farm, one of eleven children, and his mother died when he was a boy. She asked him to look out for his sisters and he did.

"He came up to Deep Valley to work and sent money home so his sisters could go to school. Papa wanted to be a lawyer. He would have made a good one, too, but he couldn't afford to go to college himself."

Joe listened thoughtfully, still stirring.

"By and by, though," Betsy said, "his sisters all got educated, and he started his shoe store, and he met this red-haired Julia Warrington, and they fell in love and got married."

"Did your grandfather object?" Joe asked.

Betsy laughed out loud. "Heavens, no!" she said. "How could anyone object to Papa? Grandpa Newton knew that character is more important than money."

"Character's all we've ever had in our family," Joe replied.

It occurred to Betsy that there was a similarity between her father and Joe Willard. Both of them had been forced to be independent when they were very young, and it had given them strength beyond their youth. Both of them, without money, had made themselves persons of quality. Bob Ray had married Julia Warrington. And any girl in school would have been proud to go with Joe Willard. The rich and fashionable Phyllis Brandish had considered him a catch.

"Tell me about your father and mother, Joe," Betsy said.

But again she found herself facing the stone wall of his reticence. He smiled off her request.

"I've read about families like yours," he remarked. "I've learned about all sorts of people from books. Did I ever tell you about the time I resolved to read every book in the library?"

"No. Do," Betsy replied.

She knew that during the years he had been going to high school he had rented a room from a widow in the north end of town. Mrs. Blair had been kind to him, but his real home had been the library. Miss Sparrow, the librarian, was one of his closest friends. He had learned about the world, he had molded his ideals, he had even acquired his manners from the dozens and hundreds of books, books without number, he had read day in and day out, week in and week out, in the Deep Valley Library.

"I was about fourteen," he said, dropping a spoonful of fudge into cold water. "I started with the A's, progressed to the B's, and read straight along the shelves. I bogged down about the time I reached the M's."

"Mrs. Muhlbach was too much for you," Betsy joked.

"Not a bit of it. I liked the old girl. It was George Barr McCutcheon who stopped me."

The fudge had formed a ball in the cold water, so Joe poured it into a pan which Betsy had already buttered. They left it on the back porch and went into the dining room and sat down before the fire.

"While we're waiting for that fudge to harden," said Joe, "tell me some more about your family." He liked to hear about the traditions, the holidays, the family jokes, and the simple everyday doings of the Rays.

There were evenings by the fire with Joe and evenings by the piano with Tony. It wasn't bad, Betsy decided, having two boys crazy about you. She wondered why the idea had distressed her so much at first.

Beverly of Graustark came to the Opera House

and Joe took her to see it. Tony asked her, too, but he was philosophical about it when she said she was already engaged.

"That Willard and his passes!" he said. "Oh, well! I'll sit in the peanut gallery and throw shells at the two of you."

The Red Mill came and this time Tony got ahead of Joe. Betsy was almost glad he had. The music wove a tender, glowing tapestry of all the happy hours she and Tony had shared. They had sung these songs together around the Ray piano and out on Murmuring Lake.

> "*Not that you are fair, dear,*
> *Not that you are true,*
> *Not your golden hair, dear,*
> *Not your eyes of blue. . . .*"

Tony leaned toward her to whisper, "I don't think they can come up to us. What do you think, Ray of Sunshine?" That was the nickname he had given her when they were freshmen.

"They can't come up to *you*," Betsy replied.

She meant it. When the Governor sang, "Every day is ladies' day with me," he didn't make it half so dashing as Tony had always made it. Even the two comedians, although she laughed at them until she wept, were no funnier than Tony could be when he tried.

The mill wheel, turning awesomely, carried the Burgomeister's daughter to her lover.

Betsy and Tony had a wonderful time and they sang the duet with nostalgic fervor all the way up the Plum Street hill.

> *"When you ask the reason,*
> *Words are all too few. . . ."*

No, it wasn't half bad, having two beaus.

9

"Tonight Will Never Come Again"

MADDOX DID not improve.

Deep Valley played Wells, it played Faribault, it played Blue Earth, and the scores didn't get better. They got worse. The seniors were desperate.

"We simply have to win a few games," said Betsy, as a subdued Crowd marched toward Lloyd's automobile after the Blue Earth game. "Just think! This is the last year we'll be coming out to this old field."

"We've been coming for four long years!" Tacy sighed.

"And Betsy still doesn't know a touchdown from a field goal," said Tib, at which Betsy began to chase her, and their gray and violet skull caps fell off.

The Crowd gathered at the Rays' after the Blue Earth game, Dave, Stan, and Dennie bruised and battered, Maddox unimpaired. Joe dropped in late, followed by Cab, who took as much interest in the team as though he were still in school. They drank cocoa and talked football, but no one any longer tried to think up loyal excuses for the defeat. Everyone knew that as soon as Maddox took himself off, the storm of gossip would break. And it did.

"What's the matter with Maddox, anyway?"

"I thought he was supposed to be such a miracle man."

"He's afraid of getting his hair mussed, if you ask me," said Dennie.

Tib said nothing, but she was frowning. Perhaps, thought Betsy, she was getting a little soured on manly beauty unaccompanied by manly achievements. Or perhaps she really liked him and was worried.

At school the pep meetings no longer rang with cries of, "What's the matter with Maddox? He's all right!" He still made most of the touchdowns, but he didn't, all agreed, "pitch in and fight." Someone even hazarded that he had come over from St. John just to injure the Deep Valley team. It was a plot.

"Do you believe that?" Betsy asked Joe.

"Of course not," Joe replied. "He wants Deep Valley to win, but his school spirit isn't strong enough to make him risk that profile."

Joe was depressed. Even his vigorous pen was running out of hopeful excuses and bright prospects for the Deep Valley eleven.

Fortunately, there were school activities other than football, and Betsy was persistently urging Joe to enter them. "The president of the senior class," she said, "should really go out for debating . . . he ought to sing in the chorus . . . he ought to write a paper for rhetoricals. . . ."

"Look," Joe would interrupt, "I'm earning my living. Remember?"

But because school was important to Betsy it became more and more important to Joe. Busy as he was, he found time not only for school activities but also for the aimless, carefree loafing of normal high school students.

On Halloween, he telephoned Betsy in high spirits. "Say, I hear that the juniors are having a dance. Strictly for juniors. Seniors are urged to keep out."

"If you mean what I think you mean," said Betsy, "Tib and Dennie have the same idea."

"All right," answered Joe, "we'll make it a quartet. I'll be up about nine."

It was raining then, but with evening it cleared. Mr. Ray had made Margaret a jack-o'-lantern, and they started out, her eyes shining in a delicious ecstasy of boldness and fear.

Jack-o'-lanterns began to pop up in windows. The doorbell began to ring, but when it was answered the threshold was empty. By the time Tib and Dennie, Betsy and Joe left the house, the dark wet world was filled with the muffled laughter, the rattling and tapping and running feet of Halloween.

The four trouped downtown, and standing outside Schiller Hall, looked up at the lighted windows. They could hear a faint sound of music.

"Here goes!" said Joe, squaring his shoulders with extravagant valor.

As they tiptoed up the stairs, the music became clearer. Mamie was playing a wistful waltz.

> *"Tonight will never come again,*
> *To you . . . and me. . . ."*

They reached the fourth floor and peeked into the lighted ballroom. Jack-o'-lanterns, black cats, and orange streamers made a festive picture. The junior girls looked pretty in their long floating party dresses. Betsy and Tib were wearing tams and coats.

Mamie's music sang on.

> *"Tonight will never come again,*
> *To you ... and me...."*

The two couples danced boldly into the ballroom. Before they had half circled the room the storm broke. Mamie stopped playing, and jumped up from the piano stool, laughing, to watch. Every junior boy in the room had made a rush for Joe and Dennie, who were heading for the door sheltering the senior girls.

Biff! Boom! Bang! Presently the music began again, but only juniors were dancing now. Down at the foot of the stairs in the moonlight, the discomfited seniors were disentangling themselves, trying to make out what had happened and whose foot was whose. As they limped toward Heinz's, they heard Mamie playing.

> *"Tonight will never come again,*
> *To you ... and me...."*

"Let us hope not!" groaned Tib.

At Heinz's they had the sort of fun that Betsy had

grown up with but which was still unfamiliar to Joe. Heinz's had invented an enormous sundae, The Imperial, which cost fifty cents. The two couples ordered one Imperial with four spoons and raced to see who would consume the biggest share.

"I win!" cried Tib, spooning the last cherry.

"What do you mean, you win?" asked Joe, beating off Dennie to scrape the dish.

"What ho, minion! Another!" shouted Dennie. "At least I've got a quarter. Have you, Joe?"

The waiter brought another, calling out good-naturedly, "Take it easy, kids! Take it easy!"

The four walked up the long hill to the Ray house. The Halloween excitement was subsiding now. There were reminders only in the soap marks on doors and windows and the noise of a distant party.

In spite of the Imperials, they went straight to Anna's kitchen and found half a cake. They sat on the kitchen table to eat it, talking and fooling. After Tib and Dennie left, Joe stayed on. Mrs. Ray had to cough several times at the top of the stairs before he went home.

Rain now had taken down the last of the withered leaves. Except for a few oaks, the trees showed bare against the sky. Slowly the world grew browner, the weather colder and more wintry.

Snow started falling. A filmy white blanket on the

ground startled the eye with its half-forgotten, half-familiar beauty.

"It always makes me feel queer to smell the first heat in the registers and see the first snow," Betsy said.

Mr. Ray put on the storm windows. Children got out sleds and everyone got out overshoes. Duck hunters were undeterred by snow, and Deep Valley kitchens were filled with savory odors. Betsy began to hint for invitations to dinner at the Mullers'. No one could bake wild duck as Matilda could, stuffed with apples and served with dumplings and gravy.

Football players slipped and slid on a snowy field, and Deep Valley lost to Faribault. This was the last home game, and it had been preceded by elaborate goings on. There was a big rooters' meeting, and the school marched to the field in a body with the band at the head of the procession. But all to no avail! The score was forty to nothing.

There was only one game left now, the St. John game. It would be a slaughter, everyone agreed. St. John had an undefeated team. Moreover, it was Maddox's old home town.

"We're lucky if he doesn't throw the game," said Lloyd when the Crowd was gathered in the Social Room and neither Tib nor Maddox happened to be present.

"Certainly it's the last team he can be expected to fight," Tony replied.

"He doesn't know the meaning of the word fight," said Dennie. "All he knows is how to comb those curly locks."

"Somebody ought to wake him up," said Stan. "He'd be darned good if he'd only get going."

"All he cares about is combing his hair," repeated Dennie, and suddenly his eyes brightened. He ran his hands through his own curly thatch and dimples flashed out in his cheeks. He looked maliciously cherubic.

"Hey, listen to this!" he said. The four boys fell into a whispered confab.

"What are you kids talking about?" Winona asked.

"Never mind," they replied, walking away.

"Where are you going?"

"To find Stewie. Say, you can come along if you like."

"Can all of us come?" asked Betsy.

"No," said Dennie. "Just Winona. She can be Florence Nightingale." The boys guffawed with laughter, and hooking arms with Winona, they hurried away.

Betsy, Tacy, Irma, and Alice looked at one another. "What can they be up to?" Alice asked.

On the day before the St. John game, Miss Bangeter called another pep rally. The students filed in dejectedly, sure that no matter how loudly they sang and cheered, Deep Valley would lose again. The team sat on the platform looking uncomfortable, with Maddox, as ravishingly handsome as ever, in the center of the front row. Stewie kept running his finger around the inside of his collar.

Miss Bangeter made a speech. The St. John game, she said, was the last one of the season, and the school must remain loyal to the end. Whether or not the team would win wasn't half so important as how the school would support them. She hoped that a large delegation of students would go to St. John for the game.

It was a fine speech, a noble speech. Miss Bangeter made everyone want to support the team. But she didn't convince anyone that the team could possibly win.

Stewie, too, failed, although he perspired and grew red in the face and talked long and hard. Various boys and girls made stump speeches. They praised the team, making everyone squirm, including the heroes themselves.

Joe didn't get up, although Betsy urged and poked him. He just sat and looked blue. But at last Miss Bangeter beckoned him to the platform.

"The president of the senior class," she said, "must always have a word."

Joe stood up and grinned. "I remember one time when the president of the senior class didn't have a word, and that was at the junior dance," he said.

This was uproariously received, and Joe's speech was snappy. But it didn't inspire the audience with confidence. The gloom in the Assembly Room could have been cut with a knife.

"Gangway!"

"Clear the track ahead!"

"Is there a doctor in the house?"

A jumble of cries caused all heads to turn. Everyone started up in excitement as four shouting boys came down the middle aisle carrying a stretcher on which reposed a recumbent form in football uniform.

"It's a dummy."

"He's wearing a St. John sweater."

"It must be a skit. Thank heaven!" Betsy remarked. "This deadly meeting!" Then she grasped Tacy's arm. "Why, there's Winona."

Winona was, indeed, swinging along behind the stretcher, looking taller, thinner, more debonaire even than usual in a nurse's uniform. A chic white cap was perched on her black hair. Her eyes glittered with fun.

She raced to keep alongside the patient, fanning him, applying sticking plaster, and dousing him from a big bottle marked ARNICA. The Assembly Room roared.

"Is there a doctor in the house?" Dennie kept shouting as he and his companion stretcher bearers rushed up the steps at the left of the platform. Up the right-hand steps strolled a figure in a long white coat. He wore wire spectacles and brandished a carving knife.

"Dr. Carver at your service," he said in Tony's deep voice. "And who is the patient, lad?"

Dennie put down his corner of the stretcher and shook sweat from his brow with his forefinger, bringing another laugh.

"A player from the St. John team, doc. I fear he's at death's door."

"Tell me what happened, lad, before I start to carve him up," said Tony, flashing the knife.

"Yes, doc. Yes, doc." Dennie could not quite hold back a grin.

"This poor John Doe here was carrying the ball," he said. "He was slamming down field for a touchdown with ten of the Deep Valley eleven on his heels. The score was tied. A score meant a St. John victory. The crowd on the sidelines was going crazy.

"This poor John Doe has slammed to within ten yards of the goal line. But who bars his way? It is Deep Valley's safety man! It is our famous, our invincible, our fearless hell-for-leather hero! It is Maddox!" Dennie roared the name like a sideshow barker. The audience applauded half-heartedly. Maddox shifted in his seat, and a line of puzzlement marred his perfect brow.

"Maddox, it is!" Dennie went on after a brief pause to fill his lungs. "And John Doe halts. He pales. He trembles. He freezes. He is duck soup. All the Deep Valley rooters know he is and yell in relief. Maddox is going to save the game. But . . ."

And with that "But" Dennie paused while the puzzlement deepened on Maddox's brow and spread to the upturned faces of the pep rally. "But what is this? Maddox ain't making the tackle. He has John Doe cold, but he is giving John time to warm up. Instead of tackling, he speaks!"

Dennie's mobile face, his staring eyes, his wide-open mouth all registered consternation.

"He speaks!" Dennie repeated. "And what is this he is saying? No!" Dennie's voice rose to a hoarse shout. "No! No! It cannot be. But . . ." And now Dennie's stricken eyes swept his audience. "But it is. He is saying . . . ! Yes, he really is saying . . ."

Again a pause. But now the consternation faded from Dennie's face. He smiled sweetly. His hand rockered over his head to suggest curls. Then he spoke, in a stage whisper that swept the auditorium, "'PARDON ME, SIR, BUT MAY I BORROW YOUR COMB?'"

For one instant the school sat stunned. Then it

went wild. It shrieked with laughter. It shouted, clapped, and pounded with unholy glee. The team laughed, too, unwillingly, but a deep flush crept into Maddox's face. He looked around with a bewildered expression and forced himself to smile.

"How mean!" Betsy whispered indignantly to Tacy.

"He had it coming," said Hazel Smith, wiping her eyes.

"I think it was terrible," said Tacy. She and Betsy were not only suffering for Maddox but also for Tib, and as soon as the meeting broke up they rushed to find her.

But Tib was rushing away.

"Where are you going?"

"To catch Ralph. He's got to get out and play at that St. John game. He'll never live this down if he doesn't." There were round red circles on Tib's cheeks. "I'm going to talk to him," she declared. "I'm going to say, 'If you don't win this game, my fine curly-headed friend, I won't go with you any more! Not ever again.'"

"But he can't possibly win it," said Betsy. "St. John has an undefeated team."

"He has to," said Tib, and started running again.

10

The St. John Game

Miss Bangeter's request for a loyal attendance at the St. John game was heeded far beyond her expectations. The depot platform, next morning, was crowded with boys and girls. It was a cold day with a driving north wind. The seniors had abandoned their gray and violet caps. Boys wore heavy woolen caps with ear muffs. Girls wore stocking caps, or tams, or hats tied down with automobile veils. All wore neck scarfs, galoshes, woolen mittens, heavy winter coats.

Maroon and gold rosettes, or maroon and gold bows with long flying ends, graced every coat. There were dozens of Deep Valley banners, a few horns. But in spite of these brave trappings, hopes were low. The team huddled about Stewie, down at the end of the platform. Joe, as a *Sun* reporter, stayed with the team. Maddox stood close to the coach, speaking to no one. There were bitter creases on either side of his beautiful, unblemished mouth.

Rooters asked one another how yesterday's joke had affected Maddox. Most people thought it was deserved, but some considered it ill-advised. It might have made him so mad that he would throw the game.

"I doubt that," said Alice mildly.

"It must have taken all the heart out of him, though," Betsy insisted, and Tacy agreed. Tib didn't speak. She still looked grim.

On the train, spirits lifted a little. The car was warm; no one minded smoke or cinders. Rooters ate Cracker Jack and drank at the water cooler. Lolling in the red plush seats, they practised cheers. Someone had brought a banjo and Winona started a song. Only the team remained gloomy, still huddled around Stewie at one end of the car. Maddox's mouth was still enclosed by bitter parentheses, and he kept his gaze fixed on the window.

Betsy, too, looked out of the window as the train sped along beside the river. Muskrats had built houses at the water's edge. Willows touched the pale landscape with yellow.

She stole these glances guiltily, aware that she should be thinking only of the game. She knew that her interest in football would always be pretended, not real and burning, like Joe's or Winona's. She wanted to win, and she liked the excitement, but she liked the flying landscape more.

St. John was only the second station up the line. Shortly the train was running past small houses and snow-covered gardens. The brakeman looked into the car to bawl, "St. John the next stop!" and with a shriek of brakes, the train jerked to a halt.

As the crowd spilled out of the train, Tacy took Betsy's arm and Tib's. "Just think how often we've planned about traveling together, and now we're doing it!" she said.

Everyone thought it was exciting to be in another town. They walked up and down the Main Street which was so like and yet so unlike Deep Valley's Front Street. There were the same rows of store fronts; banks, big and impressive on the corners; a hotel and the brand new Motion Picture Palace, and a livery stable down the street. The kinds of stores and shops were just the same, but there wasn't a familiar name or face until Winona caught sight of a cousin.

"Poor old St. John! Poor old St. John!" she began to chant.

"You've got your nerve!" he said. "St. John hasn't lost a game this year and your team isn't worth peanuts."

The Crowd roared defiance, "Poor old St. John! Poor old St. John!" The cousin laughed and turned away, and the Crowd went into a bakery and bought cakes and cookies, cream puffs and jelly roll to take out to the field.

This was swept by a biting wind filled with small sharp flakes. The ground was frozen and looked cruel. Betsy saw Joe moving efficiently about, bareheaded, copy paper handy as usual, his windblown face set.

She ran over to him. "How's Maddox?"

"He doesn't talk. I guess it cut him pretty deep."

"Tib lectured him, too."

"Well," said Joe, "he had it coming, but I can't help feeling sorry for the guy."

The St. John players looked very big and confident. The Deep Valley players looked unhappy and cold. While the teams warmed up, the Deep Valley rooters cheered, but the cheering was half-hearted.

Deep Valley kicked off, and the St. John receiver

jockeyed from his own ten to his own forty-five yard line before Dennie brought him down. Deep Valley cheered again, but still half-heartedly.

"Thirty-five yards on the kick-off!" Winona groaned. "The final score will be a million to nothing."

On the next play, St. John drove through tackle, made only a couple of yards. On the next, trying left end, St. John got exactly a foot. Then St. John was stopped in its tracks.

And now, Deep Valley's cheers had a new note—a spontaneous, excited note. Not because, with the fourth down coming up, St. John must kick. Not because St. John, that invincible, that unstoppable eleven, had been held. But because one Deep Valley player had been in on all three plays, had jammed ruggedly into each St. John ball carrier, hauling him up short as much as to say, "Where do you think you're going, Bub?" And that player was Maddox.

"Maddox! Maddox! Maddox! Maddox!" The frenzied repetition lifted into the cold air, rolled across the frozen field, and Maddox waved a hand as though to signal, "Wait till you see what comes next!" Nor did he try to conceal the fact that his lovely underlip, unmarred through all the season, was now as fat as a slab of liver from rude contact with some St. John knee, or hip or shoulder, or maybe even knuckles.

Betsy, quick with a quotation which would have delighted Miss Bangeter, flung exultant arms about Tib, "Richard is himself again!" And Tib, hugging Betsy in return, shrieked "An eye for an eye!" and thought that she, too, was quoting Shakespeare.

Well, if it wasn't an eye for an eye, it was almost exactly Richard, himself, again. Led by a brand new, or perhaps the original, Maddox, as opposed to the one previously on display, Deep Valley did what no other team had been able to do all season. It held St. John's giants, that irresistible force, to one touchdown and a field goal in the first half.

The score, according to the point system used in those days, was 8 to 0.

During the intermission, Deep Valley rooters made the gray sky ring. They talked feverishly, rushed to get information.

"What's happened?" Betsy asked Joe. "What's got into Maddox?"

He beamed into her face, although she felt sure he hardly saw her.

"Plenty!" he cried. "Plenty!"

She couldn't keep him by her side. He would pause for a moment and then he was gone, shouting, cheering, groaning.

Lloyd returned from a visit to the team.

"That lip of Ralph's is bad."

"What's he going to do? Go out of the game?"

"Not a bit of it," he answered, as though the question were absurd. "You couldn't get Maddox out of this game with a corkscrew."

The second half began in an atmosphere of tingling excitement. But in spite of Deep Valley's furious resistance, St. John made another touchdown. They kicked goal and the score stood 14 to 0. Despite furious struggle it was still 14 to 0, with ten minutes of the final half to play.

Oddly enough, Deep Valley wasn't discouraged. It had expected to lose, and it found consolation in the magnificent, unbelievable performance of Maddox. He hadn't stopped St. John. But no one could stop St. John. Defeat was inevitable. Therefore, the sensible course was to find joy in Maddox and let the score go Gallagher.

And Maddox was magnificent! No longer was he protecting his profile. He thought nothing today of his ravishing nose. He did not care a hang for his beautiful mouth, his beguiling eyes. The profile was a smear, part red, part mud. The nose was a blob. His mouth had been banged, swatted, slugged, and probably jumped on until it was less mouth than pucker. His left eye was closed tighter than a drum.

But the right eye of Maddox, the once-again great Maddox, was wide open and full of fire and fight. With the score 14 to 0 and ten minutes to play, it surveyed the battle field with heroic confidence.

St. John had just scored its second touchdown, and Deep Valley was waiting for the kickoff. Close to his own goal line, Maddox balanced lightly, and his voice charged through his fellow players like an electric shock.

"Come on, guys! Three touchdowns in ten minutes. Don't tell me we can't do it!"

St. John kicked and Maddox received. And he ran. He ran like a veteran fox. He sliced left from the fifteen-yard line until he was almost out of bounds but twenty yards forward. Thereafter nobody, not even the watchful Joe, could have told how he went. But everybody knew that in a riot of cheers from Deep Valley and groans from St. John he went this way and that, stiff-arming half a dozen tacklers for a touchdown. A moment later he kicked goal.

Deep Valley called time out. The smear on Maddox's face was more crimson than ever. Somewhere in his eighty-five-yard run Maddox had hit something with his face. Something almost beyond belief had happened to that underlip. Stewie trotted onto the field and Joe ran after him. The crowd watched the conference, saw Dennie swing a fond hand across Maddox's muddy shoulder.

Joe came back for a breathless moment later to report the conversation.

"Better come out, son," Stewie had said.

Maddox had laughed. If there was a touch of histrionics in the laugh he was entitled to it.

"Tape me up," he said. "I'll hold together. But," he added, grinning at Dennie, "don't bother to bring any comb."

That was when Dennie had hugged him.

Dennie kicked off. It was a beautiful kick, high and deep into a corner. A St. John player took it on the four-yard line, ran into destruction, and the ball exploded out of his arms and bobbled sidewise, free and more inviting than a star sapphire.

It was Maddox who had made the tackle, and it was Maddox, scrambling like a frog, who recovered the fumble. It was Maddox who carried the ball on the next play, with head lowered, like a frantic bull, to plough over for a second touchdown. This time he missed the kick and the score stood St. John 14, Deep Valley 11.

Once again he refused to go out of the game when Stewie came trotting onto the field to worry over that lip.

"How much more time have we got?" Maddox asked (and Joe repeated).

"Six minutes."

"I can do it," Maddox said, and although earlier that season the whole team would have resented the first person singular, now everyone conceded his right to it.

"He said it as calmly as he might have said, 'Give me a malted milk,'" Joe reported, and the whole Deep Valley rooting section was sure he would make another touchdown.

But not calmly sure. The Deep Valley rooting section now was made up entirely of maniacs. These banged one another on the head, beat one another on the shoulders, stamped, waved arms and blankets, even tossed overshoes in the air, although any rooter with any sense must have realized that in a little while overshoeless feet would turn to five-toed icicles.

"Maddox! Maddox! Maddox!" The urgent yell—mingled treble and bass—soared up and up.

Deep Valley kicked off again. This time Dennie did less well. A St. John player took the kick behind nice interference on the twenty-yard line and moved to the thirty. And on three plays, the big, bold St. John backfield, aided by the big, bold St. John line, moved twelve yards more. On the next three plays, the same combination made a second first down. On the next three, a third, then a fourth.

Now with the ball on Deep Valley's twenty-two, St. John struck again, off tackle; but this time Deep Valley gave only a yard. Rather, Maddox gave. He was in on the runner like a heavy, tired battering ram. Nor did St. John gain much on the next play or the next; only a yard each time. So it was Deep Valley's ball, on Deep Valley's nineteen-yard line. It was eighty-one yards to go for a touchdown. And once again Maddox asked his same question.

"How much time?"

"Four minutes."

Joe came back with the story.

"I can't run with the ball any more," Maddox said. "Not a long run. My legs are giving out. But look! We'll do it this way. Listen!"

They listened, and agreed, and to the confusion of St. John's followers and the delight of the Deep Valley rooters, hoarse now, but still able to rasp out some sort of roar, they did it Maddox's way.

Maddox smashed six yards through center, his lip crimson, bare of tape because he would not stop to patch it. Stan made three off tackle, because St. John was set to stop not him, but Maddox. Dennie made a first down, loping wide around left end for the same reason. That brought Deep Valley to its own thirty-five-yard line.

Maddox smashed through center, and lost his helmet but would not bother to pick it up. Dave, long, light, and swift, duplicated Dennie's earlier lope. It was first down again on Deep Valley's forty-seven. And so, with Maddox smashing just often enough to make St. John watch him, while Stan, Dennie, or Dave loped the needed distance, Deep Valley got to St. John's forty-yard line, to the twenty-five, and the twelve, and finally the two.

Off on the side line, Betsy and Tacy were screaming, but Tib was standing as stiffly silent as a triumphant little blond school teacher who had succeeded in larruping her class's biggest boy. Joe was watching coolly on the flank, his penciled notes accurate and precise, but his eyes flashing. And all around, Deep Valley rooters even in advance of victory were taunting the sons and daughters of St. John, dejected now even in advance of defeat.

There was a pause, and once more Joe brought back the story.

"You take it over, Ralph," said Stan.

"That's right," said Dave. "You take it, Ralph. We'll open a hole." And the breathless line, gathered around, echoed him. "We'll open a hole."

Maddox looked at them with affection, but his

smeared face, with its incredible lip, set decisively.

"Nope," he said. "I'll open the hole, with some help from the rest of you. Dennie will go for the touchdown."

"No!" cried Dennie. "Say! I've just been going along for the ride."

"You rode me, kid," Maddox said. "But I had it coming and now you're going to get what you wanted."

They couldn't talk him down. That was the way it was. Dennie took the ball, Maddox ran interference, shouldered one tackler out of the way, rammed another full, and, falling, had his nose almost ripped by Dennie's cleats as Dennie's feet flashed through the hole Maddox had made to victory. Dave kicked goal. The final score was Deep Valley 17, St. John 14.

On the St. John side of the field, loyal rooters tried to cheer and didn't do badly. In the Deep Valley section, the cheers were better than good. Everyone was jumping up and down and screaming. Tib wasn't only screaming; she was crying. She kept wiping her eyes and blowing her nose but she didn't seem to know that she was doing it. She kept right on cheering through it all.

Maddox tried to walk off the field but found himself seized by strong, affectionate, and perhaps apologetic hands. Then he was up on the shoulders of Stan and Dave and three or four more. That was the way he went off the field.

The Deep Valley rooters cake-walked off behind him. They cake-walked up Main Street and all who could crowd in had supper in a restaurant which was only slightly less noisy than the football field had been. Winona started a game of drop the handkerchief under an arc light, and they waited for their train at the depot in the midst of bedlam, while chaperoning teachers looked on with sympathetic mirth.

On the return trip, Maddox sat with Tib. His left eye was green, blue, and black, and an enormous bandage covered his lip. Tib's hand was slipped through his arm. She was preening her yellow head.

The other girls hung over him. Even Irma came.

"How did you ever do it?" she asked, her large eyes soft and adoring.

Tib nudged her and clapped her hands lightly.

"Shoo!" she whispered. "Shoo!"

Maddox turned his battered head stiffly to look down at Tib and smile.

11

"Cheer Up"

IT WAS FORTUNATE THAT November was cold, with
snow on the ground and an icy bite in the air, for the
Rays had to create some early Christmas spirit. Julia's
box must be mailed by the first of December. And it
must be crammed with love and fun and the feeling of
home, for Julia was homesick.

In spite of the luxury at the Von Hetternichs', in

spite of her joy at studying in Germany, she was homesick, as she had been at the State University. It was torturing, she said, to be homesick all the time and yet not want to come home.

She definitely didn't want to come home. She was studying the role of Susanna in Mozart's *The Marriage of Figaro*, and loved it. But Deep Valley, the green house on High Street, held her more firmly than she had dreamed they would when she went out into the Great World.

"Oh, dear!" she wrote. "I dread Christmas Day both for you and for me. I'm sorrier for myself, though. You have only me to be lonesome for, but I have each separate one of you to long for and be sorry I was ever bad to."

"As though she was ever bad to any of us!" said Mrs. Ray.

Betsy, feeling weepy, said briskly, "She certainly needs that motto, Margaret."

Margaret was embroidering a motto for Julia. "Cheer Up," it said. Betsy was embroidering one for her father that said, "Don't Worry," in black thread tricked out with red French knots. No one ever worried less than Mr. Ray, and Betsy was very poor at sewing. But all the girls were making mottos, and so Betsy was making one. Whether it would be finished in time for Christmas was problematical. She lost her needle, tangled her thread, pricked her finger, and dripped blood.

"You don't need to bother with French knots. Just keep on pricking your finger," Tacy joked.

Margaret's motto was a model of neatness. Every day when she came in from school, after she had practised her piano lesson and petted the dog and cat, she sat down in her rocker and embroidered.

Mrs. Ray was making Julia a waist, silk, of a violet-blue which matched her eyes. Betsy had bought her a set of collar pins. Anna was stuffing dates and making nougat.

Mr. Ray was sending an extra check. It was what Julia had asked for. She had not realized until she went to Europe how many different kinds of lessons were necessary if you were going to be an opera singer.

By the time the box had gone, Thanksgiving was upon them. This year it was the Slades' turn to entertain. The Rays alternated Thanksgiving dinner with their friends, the Slades.

Betsy liked the arrangement, for Tom was just her age. He always came back from Cox Military full of the latest slang. This year he said, "Curses, Jack Dalton! Give me the child!"

Tom was a large boy, with rough dark hair and thick glasses. In his uniform he was meticulously neat; he had to be. But he didn't like being neat, and in "civvies" he was always rumpled. He liked to read and play the violin.

He was a very old friend. He had sat behind Betsy and Tacy in kindergarten. He liked Tacy.

"Let's go up to the Kellys'," he said off-handedly, after Thanksgiving dinner was over.

The Kelly house was crowded with brothers and sisters home for the holidays. Tom and Betsy were warmly welcomed and offered nuts, chocolates, apples, and spare pieces of pie. But Tacy paid more attention to Betsy than she did to Tom.

"I don't seem to get anywhere with Tacy," Tom burst out, as he and Betsy started home through the gray November dusk.

"Oh, Tacy's like that. She doesn't make a fuss over anybody."

"She makes a fuss over you."

"With boys, I mean. She likes you a lot, Tom."

"Well, she certainly doesn't act it," growled Tom. "Not that it matters! The world is full of girls."

Betsy couldn't permit that. "Not redheaded ones with big Irish eyes," she said.

Tom burst out laughing. "Curses, Jack Dalton!" he said.

The next day Betsy was going to have coffee with Tib, but she went to the Kelly house first. She maneuvered to get Tacy alone and with what she considered great tact brought the conversation around to Tom.

"Dearest Chuck," she said, "if you don't mind a suggestion, you ought to be nicer to Tom."

"Why, Sweet My Coz?" Tacy inquired.

"Well, he's a nice boy. And he likes you. And everybody's going with somebody."

"I don't want to go with anybody."

"You like him, don't you?"

"No more than I do anybody else," said Tacy honestly. "I like Cab and Dennie and Tony and Tom . . . all those boys I know well."

Betsy grew earnest. "You'd better look out. Tom is too desirable a boy to keep running after a girl who treats him like a stick of wood."

"I don't treat him like a stick of wood," said Tacy. "But I certainly don't feel mushy about him."

"He'll start rushing somebody else."

"Let him!"

"But, Tacy, who would take you to the holiday parties?"

"Nobody, probably, and I don't give a hoot," said Tacy serenely.

The puzzle was that this was true. Tacy liked the Crowd, she liked fun, but she just didn't like boys, not in the way the other girls did.

Betsy and Tib talked it over later at coffee. The Mullers had coffee every afternoon. Betsy had acquired the delicious vice in Milwaukee. There were usually cakes—apple cake or coffee cake sprinkled with sugar and cinnamon. At the very least, there were delectable cookies.

Betsy, who had a sweet tooth, dropped in often, and her visits were mirth-filled occasions, for the Mullers, who took a great interest in her study of German, would allow her to speak no English. She must ask for cream, sugar, cakes, say "please" and "thank you," tell her news only in German. Fred and Hobbie, choking down laughter at her mistakes, would point to objects on the table and shout their German names. Matilda came in from the kitchen to join the fun.

But today Betsy and Tib took their coffee upstairs.

Tib was cutting out a dress. She was making some of her own clothes this year.

"I was so fussy that Mamma told me I'd better make them myself, and I told her all right I would," said Tib, running daring scissors through a length of pink silk spread out on the bed.

"Oh, Tib, how smart you are!" Betsy said. "Is that for the Christmas parties? I'm going to have a white wool, trimmed with gold."

"It sounds lovely. I hope there'll be millions of dances. I hear there's going to be one at the Melborn Hotel."

"Really? How marvelous!"

"You'll go with Joe or Tony. I wonder who Tacy will go with?"

"She could just as well go to all the dances with

Tom," Betsy answered, and told about the conversations with Tom and with Tacy.

Tib shook her head. "I hate to say it, but I believe that Tacy is going to be an old maid."

"Oh, Tib!" cried Betsy.

"You don't get married without lifting your finger."

"I know it," said Betsy in an agonized tone. "But she can't be an old maid! She just can't! If all the rest of us get to work, we ought to be able to marry her off. She's so beautiful, with that gorgeous hair and those big blue eyes."

"But she doesn't do anything with them," Tib protested. "I wish I had them for about five minutes."

"You do all right being little and blonde," Betsy said.

"Ralph likes blondes. I'm glad of that," said Tib. She had felt romantic about Ralph Maddox ever since the St. John game. "Lloyd and Dennie are both having fits," she went on, holding a piece of pink silk shoulder to shoulder and looking in the mirror. "I hope Ralph asks me first for that dance at the Hotel . . . if they give it. Who do you want to go with, Betsy? Which one do you like best, Tony or Joe?"

"I've loved Tony for years," said Betsy, lightly.

"You're not answering my question, and you know it."

No one knew which one Betsy liked best, but the rivalry began to attract attention, and the general opinion was that Joe was edging ahead. Word got around school that Betsy and Joe Willard were practically going together.

Miss Clarke, the Zetamathian faculty advisor who had seen Betsy through the Essay Contests, beamed upon them; and Miss O'Rourke, the Philomathian faculty advisor who had sponsored Joe, looked mischievous. Miss Fowler, the little English teacher who had given them both so much encouragement and praise, smiled when she saw them together.

In Miss Bangeter's Shakespeare class they sat side by side at the back of the room. Miss Bangeter, with her dark magnetic eyes and sonorous voice, had almost transformed that roomful of desks and blackboards into the Forest of Arden. Trees with love songs hung and carved upon them seemed to rise between the desks. The sun slanted down through leafy aisles upon gallants and fair ladies, shepherds, shepherdesses, clowns, and courtiers. The Forest of Arden always made Betsy think of the Big Hill.

She underlined a sentence and passed it across to Joe. "Fleet the time carelessly, as they did in the golden world."

"That's what I'd like to do," she whispered.

"That's what we'll do next spring," Joe whispered back, while even Miss Bangeter looked pleased.

12

"Don't Worry"

BURSTING IN TO CALL FOR Betsy one morning in mid-December, Tib and Tacy cried, "Say, what about our Christmas shopping trip?"

This was an annual event, as heavily weighted with tradition as a Christmas pudding with plums. As children they had gone with just ten cents apiece to spend. They had visited every store in town, priced everything from diamonds to gum drops, and bought, each one, a Christmas tree ornament. The last few years, they had been less carefree; they had had real shopping to do. But they had never failed to make the trip, savoring Christmas together all up and down Front Street.

"Of course," said Betsy. "Let's go after school tonight."

There had been repeated falls of snow, and Deep Valley was bedded down in drifts. But bright sun and jingling sleighbells made the cold seem festive. Front Street masqueraded in evergreen and holly. The store windows were full of gifts, and the stores were full of merry harassed crowds and the smell of damp clothing.

The girls bought presents for their parents, for their brothers and sisters, and for other members of the Crowd. Tacy bought beauty pins for Mrs. Poppy, with whom she studied singing. Betsy bought a Deep Valley pennant for Leonard. At last, for old times' sake, they bought the Christmas tree ornaments, each selecting just one after prolonged debate.

As they paid their dimes, they were laughing at themselves, but Betsy admitted silently that she had never ceased to be thrilled by the sight of a Christmas tree ornament, so fragile, so glittery, so full of the promise of Christmas. When they were drinking coffee at Heinz's, she took her silver ball out of its wrappings.

"Just think!" she began—Betsy was always saying

"Just think!" this year. "Just think! This may be our last Christmas shopping trip!"

"What do you mean by that?" asked Tib, startled.

"Well, next year I'll be at the U. You'll be going to Browner College in Milwaukee, probably . . . or maybe on the stage; it wouldn't surprise me . . . and Tacy will be going to the College on the hill, studying Public School Music. We may very well not get downtown together."

"Heavens!" said Tacy. She looked aghast.

"We can't go on doing the same things forever," said Tib. But she looked sober, too.

"Maybe we ought to have more cakes," suggested Betsy, by way of consolation. So they ordered another round of cakes.

They went home laden with bundles, but Betsy had not yet bought her most important gift. She had not even mentioned it to Tacy and Tib. This was for Joe.

He had already bought her present.

"It doesn't amount to much. Just something I thought you might like," he had said with shining carelessness one Sunday night at lunch.

He almost always came for Sunday night lunch now. Tony was often there and the relationship between them had grown a little stiff. Joe was aware that although Betsy's feeling for Tony might be sisterly, Tony's feeling for her was more than brotherly.

And Tony had heard the general rumors about Betsy and Joe.

Tony had the inside track at the Ray house Sunday nights. But Joe was winning a special place, too. Margaret actually permitted him to tease her. He pelted Mrs. Ray with compliments, and when Mr. Ray was making the famous sandwiches, Joe always kept him company. He got Mr. Ray to talk about the shoe store, about his youth, about Deep Valley history. Mr. Ray loved to talk and Joe to listen.

"I think your father is the finest person I ever met in my life," Joe said one night. "He has the finest character and philosophy, he is the happiest. I've been trying to decide what makes him so happy. I believe it's because he never thinks of himself. He is always thinking about doing something for somebody else . . . you, or Margaret, or your mother . . . or Anna, or the shoemaker who works for him, or some poor widow across the slough with a house full of kids."

Mr. Ray, for his part, was highly gratified with his attentive listener. Now when he brought home especially good anecdotes he was eager to share them with the Willard boy. Betsy was occasionally almost annoyed by this. She and Joe didn't have much time together. Sometimes when they were sitting by the fire, happily alone for once, Mr. Ray would join them, sit down, and begin to talk.

"A remarkable fellow came into the store today. Name of Kerr. And guess what he did. I'm always selling the other fellow a bill of goods. But this fellow Kerr sold me. I didn't want to put in a line of knitwear. Never thought of doing it. Perfectly content with shoes. But, by golly, I did!"

Joe was delighted. "How did he manage it?" he asked.

"He was so darned positive," Mr. Ray replied. "He knows exactly what he wants and what you ought to want, whether you do or not."

At this point, Mrs. Ray, to whom Betsy had been lifting eyebrows in appeal, called Mr. Ray away. She asked him to fix a squeaking door.

"Shucks!" said Mr. Ray. "That door has been squeaking for weeks. Why do I have to fix it right now when I want to talk to Joe?"

There could certainly be no doubt about Mr. Ray's liking for Joe, and even Anna, although she adored Tony, allowed that Joe was "puny."

"There was a boy something like that who used to call on the McCloskey girl," she remarked to Betsy. The McCloskeys were a legendary family for whom Anna had worked in a legendary past. When Anna quoted the McCloskeys, it was important.

She quoted them, as Christmas drew near, about cookies. They had always made three kinds, she said, and so she was making three kinds now.

The December issue of the *Ladies' Home Journal* had an impressive page entitled "Twenty Christmas Cookies from One Batter." Betsy showed it to Anna, who sniffed.

"*Ja*, and I'll bet they all taste alike. Mrs. McCloskey's recipes are good enough for me."

Mrs. Ray was rapturously shopping. Betsy was worrying darkly over her "Don't Worry" motto. Margaret was working on something—it looked like a blotter—which she whisked out of sight whenever Betsy came near.

Mr. Ray brought home holly wreaths, which were put up in the windows. He brought home mistletoe, and candy canes. A Christmas tree waited on the chill back porch, sending out whiff of aromatic fragrance whenever the door was opened.

Mr. Ray called the girls aside. "You could never guess what my present for Jule is, not if you tried a hundred years."

"What is it, Papa?" Betsy urged.

"Never mind. You'll find out."

Margaret protested. "You never kept Mamma's present a secret from us before."

Mr. Ray only chuckled.

Margaret, who sang in the seventh-grade chorus, was practising Christmas carols.

"It came upon the midnight clear. . . ."

Betsy and Tacy were practising for the high school Christmas program.

> *"The first Noel, the angel did say,*
> *Was to certain poor shepherds,*
> *In fields as they lay. . . ."*

Betsy was busy with choir practise, too. And there seemed to be a sound of carols in the air even when she wasn't in chorus or choir. She thought sometimes that in spite of the void caused by Julia's absence, this was going to be a wonderful Christmas.

It was getting difficult, though, to divide her time between Joe and Tony. Balancing their claims, she felt sometimes like an acrobat on a tight rope. She consoled herself by thinking of Tony. He wasn't any longer stealing rides on freight cars. He wasn't going with that wild crowd. And soon, certainly, he would get a crush on some other girl.

But Tony, she admitted reluctantly, hadn't had very many crushes during the years she had known him. Moreover, in an offhand nonchalant way, he was letting her know that he liked her . . . too much.

Walking downtown with Joe after school, she asked where he was spending Christmas

"Butternut Center," he replied. "My uncle and

aunt sort of like to have me around."

"Do you suppose you'll get in town during the day?"

"Does your father make turkey sandwiches at night?"

"He certainly does." Betsy smiled. "They're the most famous of the year. He puts cold dressing in them."

"When do you get your presents?"

"Christmas morning, in our stockings. We hang them the night before and then after we've decorated the tree and sung carols, we turn out the lights and fill them. It's lots of fun."

"You Rays know how to do things," Joe answered. "Well," he added, "the last day of school is Christmas Eve. I'll give you your present then and you can put it into your own stocking."

They parted at the usual corner and Joe went on to the *Sun*, but Betsy didn't go to the library. She went to Front Street, and she came nearer to duplicating the traditional Christmas shopping trip than she and Tacy and Tib had done. She traversed Front Street from end to end, looking into every store.

It was proper for a boy to give a girl only books, flowers, or candy. It would be proper for Betsy to give Joe nothing more. A box of home made candy might be the best thing, but she did want to give him something he could keep. She ended at Cook's Book Store, her favorite store in town, and browsing about, she found a small, red, limp-leather edition of Shakespeare. The Avon edition, it was called. She purchased *As You Like It*.

Hurrying to her father's store in order to get a ride home in the sleigh, she passed Alquist's. She remembered that she hadn't bought a present for Tony and went in and bought a red tie. It wouldn't be proper to give a tie to the average boy, but Tony was so much more than just a beau. So much more, and also . . . so much less.

On the evening before the last day of school, the Crowd went to the high school to decorate. They stopped by for Cab and made him go, too. Decorating the school for Christmas was a senior prerogative and a very hilarious occasion.

A few industrious persons really worked, hanging popcorn and cranberry strings and loops of silver paper on a tall evergreen tree set up on the platform. The others drew pictures and scrawled slams on the blackboards, tacked mistletoe in strategic places. Clutching mistletoe, Dennie pursued Winona over the tops of the desks.

Tib ran up to Betsy. "Remember what I told you about a dance at the Melborn Hotel? Well, it's going to be on New Year's Eve. Ralph just asked me."

Betsy had a tightrope walker's shiver. She didn't

want to go to this all-important dance with Tony.

During the rest of the evening she stayed so close to Joe that he asked, "What's the matter? Scared of something?"

"Scared to go home in the dark."

"Gosh!" said Joe. "That's too bad. I have to get down to the roller rink to cover an exhibition of skating. You don't want to come along, do you?"

"I mustn't," said Betsy. "There's too much to do at home."

She thought of bringing up the subject of the dance. After all, she and Joe were almost going together. But Betsy wasn't sure she had the poise. Besides, she didn't want to. It would take away something of the thrill to ask him instead of having him ask her.

She thought she could manage. "If Tony asks me," she planned, "I'll say I'm engaged. It would be just a white lie. Or I'll tell him frankly I'd prefer to go with Joe. He has to know sometime."

Probably, she thought, he wouldn't get the chance to ask her. She had come with Tacy and Tib and would go home with them.

At the time for departure, however, Tony came up.

"I'll walk you home," he said, taking her arm.

"I came over with the girls, Tony, and I think I'd better . . ."

"I think you'd better go home with me," he interrupted, insouciant as ever.

Dennie, Cab, and Lloyd had joined Tacy, Tib, and
Winona. They sauntered along High Street together.
In desperation, when they reached her home, Betsy
asked them all in.

It was the worst thing she could have done. Everyone began to talk about the dance.

"What's this? What's this?" cried Tony. "A dance
on New Year's Eve? Mar-vo-lous!"

He turned to Betsy, and his manner was uncon-
cerned, but not the look in his black eyes.

"How about it, Ray of Sunshine? Will you go with
me?" he asked.

Betsy felt the room listening and panic over-
whelmed her. She couldn't, in this company, say she
was engaged. Julia with her cold confidence could
have done it, but Betsy lacked the poise, and she certainly couldn't be frank. She had to protect Tony.

"Why, thanks," she said. She noticed that some of
the boys were looking at her keenly and tried to act
careless, as though it didn't matter with whom one
went to the New Year's Eve dance.

But it did matter, she felt with foreboding.

Joe was so proud. She had watched him and thought
about him a great deal over the autumn, and she had
never seen him make a frankly friendly overture. She

knew the reason: he felt he had nothing to offer. Other boys and girls had homes to entertain in, parents to give treats. He had nothing. He could never say, "Come on over to my house," and bring a friend in for an apple or a cookie. He didn't want to accept favors he couldn't return. So he never made advances.

Betsy had made the advances. She had been generous with her friendship, with her admiration, with her praise. It was her nature to be that way and it had drawn Joe to her. Some boys might be spurred to greater devotion by a rival, but not Joe.

Betsy went to sleep worrying and she woke up still worrying.

Morning brought a diversion. Before breakfast was over, the doorbell rang, and she found no one less than Carney on the porch, Carney, dimple flickering!

They flew into each other's arms. "Why, you haven't changed at all!"

"Why should I have changed?" asked Carney. Tacy, Tib, and Alice came shouting up the steps. Carney was conveyed with a guard of honor to the high school.

She wasn't the only Old Grad back that day. Al and Pin and Squirrelly were back. Tom was there, quite markedly avoiding Tacy, telling Carney that he would be at West Point next year.

"Maybe," he said, "you'll come over to some dances."

The Christmas exercises went off merrily, with Mr. Gaston a sardonic Santa Claus as usual. There was so much excitement that Betsy wasn't surprised that she didn't encounter Joe. But after the exercises it came to her that he was deliberately avoiding her. He was talking and joking with other groups and didn't even look in her direction.

At last she went over to him with the little package she had brought.

"Merry Christmas!" she said, extending it. "I hope I'm going to see you Christmas night."

"Not a chance," he answered rudely. He didn't take the package and Betsy put it down uncertainly on a desk.

"Why? What's the matter?"

He turned on her fiercely.

"You certainly didn't lose any time in getting Tony to take you to the New Year's Eve dance."

"Why, Joe!" faltered Betsy. "Who told you. . . ." It was, she realized, a stupid answer. It made her sound guilty, as though she had done something wrong. She blushed scarlet.

"The whole school told me," Joe answered hotly. "They've been laying bets, I hear, on which one of us you would go with. I can't take it, and I won't. Either you're my girl or you're not."

Betsy felt sick with misery. "But we've talked that

all over. I thought you understood."

"I understand. I understand that you're not my girl."

"Why, Joe!" But he didn't hear her. He strode off, and the little package she had wrapped with such care in tissue and bright ribbons still lay on the desk. Betsy picked it up, feeling cold inside.

Not ten minutes later, catastrophic news floated across the Assembly Room.

"Joe is taking Irma to the New Year's Eve dance."

"Oh, well!" Tacy was saying. "He couldn't take Betsy. Tony asked her first."

"How under the sun did Irma happen not to have been asked?"

"She was going with Dave. And he has . . . of all things . . . the measles."

Joe was taking Irma. He was mad at her and he was taking Irma. Betsy felt a lump like a clump of burrs in her throat, but she tried to laugh and enter into the fun echoing around the room.

When she was leaving the building, in a group of boys and girls, Joe came up and called her aside. He looked very poised and stiff. He was smiling, and his eyes were bright.

"I want to apologize, Betsy," he said. "Gosh, I made a fool of myself! You have fun New Year's Eve with Tony, and from now on all bets are off."

"All bets are off!" What did he mean by that? Betsy still felt cold inside.

"I'll play the field," said Joe. "I'll really play the field. By the way," he added, reaching into his pocket, "here's something for that Christmas stocking."

Mustering a smile, holding back tears, Betsy took the package and offered her own.

"Merry Christmas," she said. The words were a mockery with Joe looking like that.

Not until she got home and began to unwrap the package did Betsy realize that it was just the same size as the one she had given Joe. Unwrapping it, the lump in her throat got bigger as comprehension grew. It was the same volume, a red, limp-leather, Avon edition of *As You Like It*. Inside he had written "We'll fleet the time carelessly as they did in the golden world."

But Betsy knew he had written that before he knew that she was going to the dance with Tony. She put her face into her hands and began to cry.

13

Christmas without Julia

BETSY DIDN'T ALLOW HERSELF to cry very long.

Downstairs, Margaret was laboriously but fervently pounding out on the piano:

"It came . . . upon the midnight clear. . . ."

Mrs. Ray was laughing. Mr. Ray was demanding tissue paper. The smell of oyster stew was rising from the kitchen.

Betsy got up and went to the window. The gas in her room was not yet lighted, so she could see clearly into the out-of-doors. Snowflakes were whirling against the arc light, and the drifts which covered the lawn had already received a fresh, soft, unblemished blanketing.

It was Christmas Eve, and she was seventeen. Julia was across the ocean, and so there devolved on her the subtle responsibilities of oldest daughter. All the careful planning in the world, the nicest presents, wreaths in the windows, and candy canes in the doorways would not make Christmas Eve a happy time in any house unless the people in that house were happy. If Betsy's eyes were red, no forced gaiety would make the hearts of the others light.

"I couldn't be so mean," Betsy said fiercely. "Please, God, help me to take Julia's place, tonight."

She went into the bathroom to splash cold water on her face, and the music downstairs ended abruptly. Margaret called, "Betsy! Betsy! Come help with the joke presents!" The Rays always wrapped up onions and lumps of coal and other choice articles to put in the stockings along with oranges and candies and small gifts.

"Coming!" Betsy called.

When her cheeks were pink from cold water, she powdered carefully, combed her hair, and put a sprig of holly behind her pompadour. Then she ran down-stairs into the Christmas Eve bustle.

"What do you suppose Papa's getting for Mamma that is such a secret?" Margaret asked, tying a knot firmly over a turnip that was going to Mrs. Ray, "From an Old Beau."

"I can't imagine, except that it's something for the house and sort of for all of us. I wonder what I'm going to get. Nothing big, I'm sure, with Julia having such an expensive year."

Margaret choked, then coughed concealingly.

"That's right," she said with elaborate carelessness. "You couldn't possibly be getting anything big."

"Shall we open Julia's box tonight or in the morning?" Mr. Ray called out.

"I say tonight," said Mrs. Ray. "There's always so much in the morning."

"I say tonight, too," said Betsy. "It will make it seem more as though Julia were here."

"I don't believe in opening anything on Christmas Eve," said Margaret. "But that's a good reason, Betsy. I'll give in."

Anna banged on the gong to summon them to oyster stew. She was wearing a white apron and her hair was curled. The dining room table was set with the company dishes, but the room was littered with tissues and ribbons, and packages, large and small.

After supper was cleared away, Mr. Ray brought in the tree. Cold and a delicious forest smell came with it. It was set up in the dining room, and Betsy and Margaret brought the cardboard boxes of decorations down from the garret.

"Trimming the tree is a messy job," Anna always said. But Betsy, unwrapping the baubles, red, green, blue, and gold, many of which she had bought with Tacy and Tib on their Christmas shopping trips, insisted that it was almost the nicest part of Christmas.

"No," said Margaret. "Coming downstairs Christmas morning in the dark is the nicest." But she, too, loved fastening stars and angels on the fresh, good-smelling branches.

The tree was a beauty.

"We say every year that our Christmas tree is the nicest we ever had, but this one really is," said Betsy, gazing at the tall balsam, which carried its glittering load with proud ease.

When the candles were lighted, she went to the piano. She couldn't play the carols as well as Julia, but she could play them. She was thankful for her piano lessons as the family gathered around her singing, "O, Little Town of Bethlehem," "Hark! The Herald Angels Sing," and the tender "Silent Night."

"Now for the ritual," said Betsy, jumping up. "Silent Night" had made everyone think too hard of Julia.

Margaret recited 'Twas the Night Before Christmas, as usual. But tonight Mrs. Ray read what Betsy usually read, the story of the Cratchits' Christmas dinner, and Betsy read what Julia usually read, the story of the first Christmas, from the book of Luke. She tried to read it as Julia did, gravely and reverently.

"'And there were in the same country shepherds abiding in the field, keeping watch over their flock by night. . . .'"

Outside, the snow was coming down and down and down. She wondered whether it was snowing in Berlin.

After the reading, they opened Julia's box and it did, indeed, seem to bring her nearer. There were gifts for everyone, even Abie and Washington, festively wrapped. Betsy received some popular music by the composer of *The Merry Widow*. It was *"Kind, Du Kannst Tanzen."* She was proud to be able to translate it—"Child, You Can Dance." The presents all looked foreign—gold-embroidered collars, prints of famous pictures, strange little painted boxes.

Before anyone had a chance to start missing Julia again, Betsy proposed filling the stockings. This rite, performed in a dim light, was a sure source of excitement.

"I can't put Jule's present in her stocking until tomorrow, can I, Anna?" Mr. Ray asked.

"In her . . ." Anna began to sway with laughter. "Stars in the sky, Mr. Ray! Sure, we're going to put it in her stocking, if she has a good big one. Ha! Ha! Ha!"

After the stockings were filled, they had cider and Christmas cookies.

Betsy had tried so hard to be like Julia that she had almost forgotten the ache in her heart. Margaret came in to sleep with her and they had fun talking, as they undressed, about Christmases up on Hill Street, across the street from Tacy's, Christmases which now seemed almost like a dream to Margaret.

"I remember that I used to hear the reindeer on that roof," she said.

"So did I," answered Betsy. "And I could hear Santa Claus sliding down the chimney. We didn't have a fireplace, you remember, and the stovepipe leading from the coal stove downstairs ran through our bedroom. It was only about as big as my two hands. But I could imagine Santa Claus sort of thinning out as he slid down and getting round and fat again as soon as he landed on the back parlor floor."

Margaret laughed as she snuggled into Betsy's bed. "I wonder what Julia's doing."

"She'll have a wonderful Christmas with the Von Hetternichs," said Betsy. "It will be like my Christmas in Milwaukee." And she told Margaret stories about that fabulous holiday until Margaret grew sleepy.

After Margaret had fallen asleep, Betsy's thoughts went back to Joe. The Christmas Eve proceedings had cheered her up so much that she began to believe things couldn't be so bad as she had feared. Perhaps, when he opened her gift, he would be affected just as she had been by the fact that they had both bought *As You Like It*. Perhaps he would telephone tomorrow. Perhaps he would even come for turkey sandwiches.

She woke to the sound of her father shaking down the furnace. She had wakened before Margaret, which was a miracle on Christmas morning. Last night's optimism was still with her, and she jumped up and ran to the window.

"Merry Christmas," she whispered into the ghostly world and turned to pounce on Margaret, shouting "Merry Christmas!"

Heat began to come up through the register. The smell of coffee rose. Betsy and Margaret were dressing hurriedly when Mrs. Ray came in.

"Papa says we have to stay here till he calls us."

"Why? What's it all about?"

"I can't imagine," said Mrs. Ray. "I usually catch on, but I have no idea what this secret is. Bob, are you ready?" she called.

"You hold your horses," Mr. Ray replied.

"We're coming!" she threatened.

"You stay there till you're invited down."

There was a hammering. There was a wrenching sound. There was a thud, and another, and Anna's giggle, and a long pause in which Mrs. Ray, Betsy, and Margaret clutched hands. Then Mr. Ray shouted, "Now!"

As they took the first step down the stairs, chimes sounded, wonderfully sweet. Betsy recognized the song. It was the one played every hour by the chimes of Big Ben in London, the one of which Julia had written.

> *"Oh, Lord our God,*
> *Be thou our guide,*
> *That by thy help,*
> *No foot may slide."*

Just as she and her mother and Margaret reached the landing, they heard a deep-toned resonant striking.

"One," they counted, "two, three, four, five, six, seven, eight, nine, ten, eleven, twelve."

"Bob Ray!" cried Mrs. Ray, running down the stairs. "It's a chime clock!"

Mr. Ray was laughing so that his stomach shook.

"Where is it?" asked Betsy, looking around.

"And why did it strike twelve?" asked Margaret. "It isn't twelve o'clock."

"He set it at twelve, to make it exciting," cried Anna. "Stars in the sky! The trouble we took getting that thing unpacked."

The tall grandfather clock stood against a wall of the music room, looking as benevolent and yet as dignified as Mr. Ray himself. The girls danced about it while Mrs. Ray hugged her husband.

"I've wanted a chime clock for ages. Ever since Julia was in London. How did you know?" she cried.

After this magnificent gift, which was really for everyone, of course, Betsy didn't expect very much for herself. She didn't mind. What made Christmas morning so glorious wasn't actually the presents, but the mystery, the thrusting of one's hand into a crammed stocking, the unwrapping of mysterious-looking parcels under the tree.

This began now beside a crackling fire, while Mr. Ray urged everyone to help themselves to coffee, sausages, and toast set out on the dining room table.

It was exciting not only to unwrap your own gifts but to watch others unwrap what you had planned for them. Margaret's eyes sparkled while Betsy exclaimed over the homemade blotter. Betsy waited eagerly as her father examined the "Don't Worry" motto. Anna had pressed it and Betsy had pasted it on cardboard and framed it. The glass hid the deficiencies in her embroidery.

"That's mighty nice, Betsy. I'm glad you're learning to sew. It expresses my sentiments exactly, too."

Margaret had a doll, of course. A beautiful, jointed, bisque doll, with blond curls, a pink dress, openwork stockings, and patent leather slippers.

"How awful it will be, Bob, the first Christmas Margaret doesn't want a doll!"

"I'll always want a doll," Margaret promised, looking sober.

"Either she will or our grandchildren will," said Mr. Ray. "We'll be having grandchildren around in a few years, don't forget."

There was one big box left to be opened. Mr. Ray brought it to Betsy.

"It's almost like the box I got my furs in last year, but I can't be getting furs again. It's probably a joke," she thought.

Mrs. Ray was beaming. Anna leaned forward with delighted eyes. Margaret hugged her father's arm to restrain excited giggles.

Betsy untied the ribbons, pulled off the tissues, lifted the box cover.

"An opera cape!" she squealed. Jumping up, she shook it out. It was pale blue broadcloth lined with white satin, trimmed with silk braid and gold and blue buttons.

"Papa! Mamma! It's a perfect dream!"

"It's time you had an opera cape, now you're a senior," Mr. Ray said.

"It just matches that blue dress Julia sent you," Margaret cried.

"You'll look tony in it, lovey," Anna exclaimed.

Mrs. Ray was talking excitedly. "You would have to have one in the spring anyway. So Papa and I thought you might as well have it now. The New Year's Eve dance is going to be so elegant this year, down at the Melborn Hotel."

Betsy's heart sank. What fun would an opera cape be when Joe was going with Irma? But maybe, she thought hopefully, they would have made up by then? Probably he would telephone today. Certainly he would. She put the opera cape on over her morning dress and paraded up and down.

The day was quite like other Christmas days. Julia was so much on their lips that she seemed to be actually there.

Tony went to church with Betsy. Soft mountains of snow covered the lawns and shrubs. Soft clumps of it lay on the evergreens; soft strips showed white along black boughs. Mr. Ray had already shoveled his walk, but many householders had slept later, so Betsy and Tony had to take to the road.

In the small crowded church, smelling of evergreens and radiant with candles, Betsy sang with all her heart:

> *"O come, all ye faithful,*
> *Joyful and triumphant. . . ."*

She actually felt joyful and triumphant.

Dinner followed with four kinds of dessert—caramel ice cream, mince pie, fruit cake, and plum pudding. The afternoon was filled with grown-up naps and company, Christmas books and games, and the chiming of the clock.

It made one conscious of the passing of time, that clock.

"Oh, Lord our God," and then in no time at all, "Oh, Lord our God, Be thou our guide"; and in what couldn't possibly have been fifteen minutes more, "Oh, Lord our God, Be thou our guide, That by thy help . . ." After that there was nothing to do but wait for the completed verse.

At first Betsy loved it, but that was because she was still happy. She was still sure Joe would telephone. As the afternoon wore away, twilight dulling the snow until it was gray, her hopes dwindled.

The telephone rang, and it was Carney saying that she was involved with family doings and would not be up for supper. It rang again, and it was Anna's Charlie. It rang again, and it was Cab.

Inexorably the clock pulled the afternoon into evening. The Christmas tree was lighted. Mr. Ray was out in the kitchen making sandwiches. Winona was at the piano and Tony was urging Betsy to come and sing.

Joe hadn't come. He wasn't coming. He was still mad at her, Betsy thought, with that swelling back in her throat.

> "Oh, Lord our God,
> Be thou our guide,
> That by thy help,
> No foot may slide."

sang the chime clock and struck eight . . . and nine . . . and ten.

14
The New Year's Eve Dance

THE NEW CHIME CLOCK tolled off the days of the holiday week. As usual in Deep Valley, there was a parade of parties. On the day after Christmas came the church Christmas tree. That was followed by the Crowd Christmas tree. Hazel acted as Santa Claus and made a very funny one. The presents caused laughter, too, for everyone received at least one boudoir cap. The coquettish little mobcaps, trimmed with lace, flowers, or bows of ribbon, were the rage.

"Ye Gods! When do I wear the thing?" asked Tacy, adjusting the delicate confection she had received from Tib.

"For breakfast, silly!"

"But I have to have my hair combed for breakfast," grumbled Alice.

"So do I," said Carney. "Neat as a pin."

"These will be fine for covering up my Magic Wavers," said Betsy, putting the two caps she had received on her head together.

She was acting nonsensical. She acted nonsensical all that week, wilder and more absurd as party followed party. Joe didn't come to any of them; he stayed at Butternut Center. But the chime clock kept reminding Betsy that the New Year's Eve dance was approaching.

There were several parties for Carney—evening parties with the boys, and afternoon parties where she told the girls all about Vassar. To one of these Betsy brought her Christmas letter from Herbert. She called Carney aside and gleefully pointed out a paragraph.

"What kind of a dame has Carney turned out to be? Larry is still mooning about her."

Carney looked serious.

"Well, how *have* I turned out?" she asked, fixing her forthright gaze on Betsy.

Betsy looked at her, pink-cheeked, bright-eyed, in a snowy shirtwaist, a well pressed skirt, and polished shoes. She no longer wore the hair ribbon she had clung to until her graduation from high school. Like the other girls, she now wore a band around her hair with a big bow on the side. But she still had her fresh, woodsy, honest look.

"You haven't changed," said Betsy.

"Are you going to tell Herbert that?"

"Don't you want me to?"

"I suppose so," said Carney. "But maybe Larry has changed awfully. Maybe he's sophisticated now."

Betsy threw up her hands. "I should think you'd go crazy with that Mystery in your life," she said. "Is Larry going to like you or isn't he? Are you or aren't you going to like Larry?"

Carney chuckled.

The Crowd of girls repeated last year's progressive dinner. As before, each course was served in a different home. But this year small programs showed with whom one took the dark icy walk from house to house.

Betsy went with Carney to Irma's for grapefruit with brandied cherries in it. The table was in red.

She walked with Alice over to Hazel's for bouillon

with place cards and favors.

She walked with Katie to her own house for the fish course. Her table was in pink.

She walked with Hazel to Carney's for the meat course. It was, however, chicken, and there was cranberry ice.

She walked with Tacy to Tib's for delectable salad.

With Tib she took the long walk up Hill Street to the Kellys'. They loitered, having an important matter to discuss. Tom had asked Carney to the New Year's Eve dance. Who, then, was going to take Tacy?

They arrived late and half frozen for the Kellys' hot mince pies. Betsy clowned with Winona. She laughed and quipped in the giddiest spirits, for she dreaded the walk to Alice's. Irma was her partner for that.

But Irma didn't mention Joe or the dance. Slipping her arm sociably through Betsy's, as they started down the frozen path, she suggested that they sing. She had a sweet soprano voice, and Betsy sang alto. They sang Christmas carols all the way to Alice's house, throwing the music at the cold bright stars. Betsy felt ashamed, and squeezed Irma's arm when they parted. Alice served after-dinner coffee and her decorations were in the holiday colors.

They went last to Winona's. Betsy walked down with Winona. She wrote in her diary:

"That Winona is a scream. She had fixed up their

dining room to look like a beer garden. And we drank grape juice and smoked cubebs. They're just for asthma, of course, but the boys who were looking in the windows thought they were real cigarettes. We gave 'Florabelle.'"

Betsy had composed "Florabelle" or "She Loved But Left Him" during the holidays. It was supposed to be a takeoff on a melodrama but it was definitely influenced by Shakespeare. The frenzied lovers lapsed frequently into atrocious blank verse. There were grave diggers and a balcony scene.

The shades were closely drawn, for Betsy and Winona had borrowed Winona's father's wardrobe. Winona and Tib were the lovers; Betsy, the villain. The audience, on pillows on the floor, collapsed in laughter.

At the end, there were cries of "Author! Author!" Betsy took her bows, flame-cheeked and mirthful, her thumbs in Winona's father's suspenders, which were holding up Winona's father's trousers.

But when she reached home, the chime clock was striking twelve. And from twelve to one and one to two it wrapped the quarter hours and half hours and hours into neat packages and stowed them away. Betsy stuffed her fingers into her ears. Hot tears dripped into her pillow.

She tried to see the quarrel from Joe's point of

view. That was simple. He was proud. He thought he had been made ridiculous and he was determined not to compete with Tony any longer. But she was proud, too. If he hadn't gotten mad and asked Irma so quickly, she would have tried to explain. But now it was too late. There was nothing she could do.

At last the chime clock brought the New Year's Eve dance.

Tacy wasn't going. She had been given a second chance; Cab had asked her. But she had decided that she would prefer going to her uncle's with the family.

"Her *uncle's*!" said Tib, throwing complete incomprehension into her voice.

"I can't make her out," said Betsy.

"She's sure to be an old maid unless we take steps."

Tib had come as usual to dress for the party with Betsy—and to do Betsy's multiplicity of puffs. The pompadour was rolled over a big sausagelike mat and each puff was rolled over a small one.

"The rat and all the little mice, Tony calls them," said Betsy, acting lighthearted.

The new white wool dress was a dream. Below the tucked, form-fitting bodice, the skirt fell into pleats. It was trimmed with gold and she wore a gold band, of course, around her hair.

Tib's self-made pink silk was a triumph. She wore

pink shoes and stockings and a wide pink band around her head.

"You both look lovely," said Mrs. Ray, dashing in, in her taffeta petticoat. She, too, was dressing for the ball.

Margaret, who was going to stay up for the first time to see the old year out, with Anna, making fudge, leaned over the rail as Betsy and Tib went lightly, proudly down the stairs.

Ralph and Tony waited, pressed and immaculate. Tony held the pale blue opera cape.

"Pretty skippy!" he said admiringly, putting it around Betsy's shoulders.

Betsy didn't like the new opera cape. She felt as though it were a hoo-doo.

The boys had engaged a hack. This unheard-of gesture was a tribute to the elegance of the Melborn Hotel. Betsy felt unbelievably worldly as the hack, on its winter runners, slid along the snowy streets and halted at the illuminated entrance to the Melborn.

They went through the swinging door into the lobby. It smelled of cigars and the fat red leather chairs. They crossed the room and ascended the grand staircase which rose at the far end.

The ballroom was two stories high and over-looked the river. Here Deep Valley gave its most fashionable parties. Mamie Dodd didn't play for this dance. Lamm's Orchestra, behind a screen of potted palms, was tuning up provocatively. The ballroom was decorated with poinsettia and holly. There were red shades on the chandeliers.

"Supper is going to be served in the Ladies' Ordinary," Carney told Betsy and Tib. She looked very pretty in the store-bought party dress, and Tom looked distinguished in his uniform.

The high school crowd seemed stimulated by this entrance into the world of fashion. All the girls looked pretty and the boys were kindled to unusual politeness, gallantry, and wit.

Betsy was excited, almost joyful, in spite of that doom in her breast, but her spirits died like a quenched fire at her first glimpse of Joe. She and Tony were dancing the opening waltz, "I Wonder Who's Kissing Her Now." She was happily floating in his arms—no one could waltz like Tony, no one!—when she saw a light pompadour and stalwart shoulders. Joe's lower lip was outthrust in a look Betsy knew. He was gazing at Irma, whose irresistible face, framed in natural (not Magically Waved) curls, was lifted to his.

"If he isn't crazy about her now, he soon will be," Betsy thought, and suddenly felt completely wretched. But she didn't show it. She smiled glowingly at Tony.

Joe didn't ask Betsy for a dance. The program ran on through "Howdy Cy" and "Ciri Biri Bin" and "Tonight Will Never Come Again." Betsy grew gayer and gayer, but none of her vivacity came from within. Inside, she ached. She ached all over, as you do when you have the grippe.

Laughing and flushed, she barn-danced, waltzed, and two-stepped. She chattered with the other girls about the marvelous party. She rushed up to her mother to exclaim. Tony went with her, to ask Mrs. Ray for a dance. He nodded his head negligently at Betsy.

"That daughter of yours! She's like a balloon on a string."

"Not a balloon! Oh, Tony! No! I only weigh a hundred pounds."

Mrs. Ray smiled at them. Loving parties, she was as happy as Betsy seemed to be. She whirled off with Tony, while Betsy, more sedately, circled with her father, who danced, as he did everything else, with benevolent dignity.

When the New Year came in, the orchestra played *Auld Lang Syne*. Everyone joined hands in a giant circle which revolved, singing:

> *"Should auld acquaintance be forgot*
> *And never brought to mind. . . ."*

Tony's dark eyes were bright with joy. He looked at Betsy as they swung hands and sang. Then the circle broke and people threw confetti and blew horns. Everyone called, "Happy New Year!" "Happy 1910!"

Nineteen-ten! That was the year they would graduate in, the year they had been looking forward to so long. How could it possibly start off so badly, so horribly! In the crowded, clamorous room, filled with laughing voices and the bright rain of confetti, Betsy felt forlorn.

She looked around and found Joe across the room. He was looking at her. But as soon as their glances crossed, he looked away.

And presently she saw him dancing with Irma to "Yip-i-addy-i-ay!"

15
Tacy's Eighteenth Birthday

WHEN BETSY WOKE UP on New Year's morning, she lay in bed looking at the window as it slowly changed from black to gray. She was more seriously unhappy than she had ever been in her life, but she was filled with a new determination.

She wanted to deal with her unhappiness in a manner worthy of her years.

"Like an adult," she said out loud.

She remembered that day last spring when she had found out that Cab was going to leave school and take over his father's business. She had realized then that she, too, was growing up.

She had been slow doing it, she reflected. One reason was that Tacy and Tib both loved her so much. They thought she was just about perfect, which had always made it easy for her to believe herself that she was pretty nice. You don't grow up, she reasoned now, until you begin to evaluate yourself, to recognize your good traits and acknowledge that you have a few faults.

"To begin with," she thought, "I'm too much of a baby."

That came partly from having an older sister. Julia had always taken the brunt of things.

"We used to expect Julia to be perfect," Betsy had often heard her mother say regretfully, speaking of the early years.

Julia had taught her father and mother not to expect perfection from a child. And she had done other kinds of pioneering. She had persuaded her parents that when you reach a certain age you are old enough to do certain things. She had thrashed out such matters as where one was allowed to go, how late one could stay out, the subject of boys.

And in school, as Betsy went from grade to grade and up into high school, she had always had a ready-made place, because she was Julia Ray's sister.

To be sure, Betsy acknowledged, in justice to herself, she had to make good. The teachers had soon discovered that she had none of Julia's talents. She had had to carve out a place for herself with her own abilities. But she had always been given a chance. And meanwhile Julia had sheltered and protected her.

"It's a wonder I braced up for Christmas Eve," Betsy thought. "I'm glad I did."

She knew she had helped the family, and as a matter of fact, she had been happy. That, she realized, was because she had stopped thinking about herself.

"I've heard all my life that that's the way it works. Papa is always thinking about other people and he's always happy. I've got to stop thinking about myself so much—about how I look, how I'm impressing someone, whether I'm popular or not. I've got to start thinking about other people, all the people I meet."

At the moment she didn't want to meet anybody, not even her mother, who would want to talk over the party. She wished she could stay in bed. In the past when she had had blows of one sort or another she had sometimes pretended to be sick. The family had always fallen in with these deceptions, and she had been able to take her time in gathering her forces for recovery.

"Well," she thought, "I won't do that today. I'll go down to the Y and serve punch the way I'm supposed to."

With this resolution, she jumped out of bed. The room was frigid, but it suited her mood. She shut the slot in the storm window with a bang and scratched a little hole in the frost to look out at the world. It was cold, snowy, and desolate. So much the better!

It seemed a little ironic that her companion today was to be Irma. She and Irma had been invited days before to preside behind the punch bowls at the Y.M.C.A. New Year Reception.

"But nothing that has happened to me is Irma's fault," thought Betsy, pulling on her clothes. "She didn't try to get Joe to ask her. He asked her because she's the belle of the school. I might as well start right now being fair to Irma. All of us girls, except Tacy, have had it in for her just because she's so popular with boys."

Smiling a little fixedly, but smiling, she went through the holiday breakfast, the holiday dinner. She dressed in her white wool dress again and went to the reception. The Y.M.C.A. was having an open house for men and women, boys and girls. Tea was served in the parlors, fruit punch in the big gymnasium.

She answered Irma's smile resolutely, and it was diverting to be serving punch to the boys and girls who flocked about their table. In a quiet moment, she and

Irma served some to themselves.

"Wasn't it a wonderful party last night?" Irma asked, sipping.

"Beautiful," said Betsy.

"It was lucky for me," said Irma, "that Tony asked you ahead of Joe. I don't know what I'd have done, Betsy, when Dave got those terrible measles, if Joe hadn't happened to be free."

That was a gallant remark, and Betsy matched it.

"Half the boys in school would have broken their dates to take you, Irma. You know that," she said.

A new wave of guests surged up to the table. Betsy was as busy as Irma; she wasn't envious or jealous. But listening to Irma's sweet laugh, observing her confiding manner, her fascinating way of gazing starry-eyed into people's faces, Betsy felt a pressure about her heart. Joe was free to go with Irma if he cared to. All bets were off, he had said.

She waited with dread for him to appear at the reception, but he didn't come. She didn't see him until the following Monday when school reopened. By that time, Carney had gone back to Vassar; Tom had returned to Cox; Al, Pin, and Squirrelly, to the U. The Rays' Christmas tree had been cast out into the snowy world. Wreaths had been burned and presents put away.

This ended the holidays, and Betsy returned to

school wearing a clean, starched shirt waist and even more stiffly starched resolves.

More snow had fallen. The thermometer had sunk to ten degrees below zero and with regrettable bravado was still descending. Tib, who loved the winter sports, was exultant, but Betsy and Tacy were glum.

"'Blow, blow, thou winter wind,'" Tacy murmured, as, rigid with extra wraps and underpinnings, they hurried through tunnel-like channels in the drifts.

"'Freeze, freeze, thou bitter sky,'" Betsy chanted in return. She might well have added:

> *"Thy sting is not so sharp,*
> *As friend remembered not. . . ."*

For Joe plainly had forgotten the warmth and sweetness of their old companionship. They didn't speak to each other now except for casual hellos in the hall. He stared at a book when she recited in Miss Bangeter's English class. They had changed seats at the new term and didn't sit together any more.

But at least he didn't seem to have fallen a victim to Irma's charms. It appeared that he intended to do what he had told Betsy he would do—play the field.

January brought its usual diversions—sleighing parties, skating parties, debates, and basketball games.

Joe went to everything, and he always took a girl. But it was seldom the same girl twice, although he lavished each one with flattering attentions.

By the time examinations put a stop to such activities, the high school had almost forgotten that the names of Betsy and Joe had ever been linked. It began to think of Joe as a single man again, to wonder when and with whom he was going to settle down.

Mr. Ray inquired for him several times. He wanted to tell Joe when Mr. Kerr came back to town and persuaded him to make a display of knit goods in the window.

"That Kerr! Joe ought to hear how he wangled me this time."

But Mrs. Ray told her husband privately to stop asking for Joe. Betsy knew she had, for Mr. Ray avoided the subject with clumsy finesse. He began to joke about Tony, something he had never done before—the Rays had long since taken Tony for granted.

Tony was happy these days. He was really working at school. And although his manner was always scornfully reckless, he was behaving very well indeed.

"He's trying to live up to me," Betsy thought, with a little twinge of guilt.

He still didn't act lover-like. He wasn't mushy. But he had come quite rigidly to claim the prerogatives of a "steady beau." He called for her at choir practice, took her to all the school activities, and never failed to come for Sunday night lunch.

Betsy tried to make the best of it. Her trait of dogged stubbornness stood her in good stead now. She was surprised at how much it helped unhappiness not to give in to it.

"Last year at this time I'd have been just wallowing in misery," she thought.

She did grow a little thin and tense, and her father kept heaping her plate and saying that she ought to get more sleep. But she protested that she would be all right as soon as exams were over.

As usual, she was cramming for mid-term exams. She and Tib brought their physics notebooks up to date together, and Tib tried to explain the subject, which was easy for her but an occult mystery to Betsy. She helped Betsy in German, too, and Betsy tried to help her and Tacy in English.

No one worried about Civics.

"What would we do without Miss Clarke?" Tacy asked one day. "Each graduating class ought to give her a medal."

They joked and toiled and burned the midnight gas, and examinations were all successfully disposed of in time to celebrate Tacy's eighteenth birthday.

Of the three girls, Tacy got to be eighteen first. She

always had the honor of ushering in each new age. Betsy and Tib were invited to her house for supper, and they walked up to Hill Street gladly in spite of the sub-zero weather.

Winter seemed closer at the Kellys' house. From the bay window, one looked out at the hills submerged in snow with regiments of bare, black trees. When the curtains were drawn, the glowing windows of the Kellys' coal stove expressed winter's cheer as a register never could.

The big family gathered for supper in the dining room, but Betsy, Tacy, and Tib ate alone at a table set up in the parlor. Over creamed chicken, fruit salad, and hot rolls, they talked about past birthdays. The fifth birthday when Betsy had met Tacy. The tenth one when all three had been so eager to get two numbers in their age.

"You had told us, Betsy," said Tib, "that we were going to be grown up when we got two numbers in our age. It was the beginning of growing up, you said."

Tacy laughed. "I got to be ten first, of course. I didn't look any different or feel any different. But I knew why that was. You and Tib weren't ten yet."

"Then *I* got to be ten," Tib continued. "And I didn't look any different or feel any different. But, of course, I didn't expect to until Betsy got to be ten, too, and her birthday didn't come until April."

"Well," Betsy said. "I was right. Wasn't I? After I got to be ten, things did start happening. We all fell in love with the King of Spain."

In the midst of their laughter, Katie came into the room and blew out the lamp. Everyone knew what that meant. She went back to the kitchen and returned bearing a birthday cake covered with eighteen flickering candles. Betsy and Tib started to sing:

> "*Happy birthday to you,*
> *Happy birthday to you,*
> *Happy birthday, dear Tacy. . . .*"

Tacy made a wish and blew out her candles. She blew them all out in one puff.

"Now," said Tacy, pounding her chest grandly, "I'm officially eighteen years old."

"You're of age," said Betsy.

"You're old enough to get married," said Tib.

Tacy looked alarmed. "Oh, no," she said. "I'm eighteen, but it doesn't count yet. It doesn't count until you and Betsy are eighteen. Remember?"

But Tacy was wrong. She was definitely eighteen.

16
Mr. Kerr

"THAT KERR!" SAID MR. RAY, chuckling. "What do you suppose he's made me do now?"

The family, and Tacy, who had come to supper, looked up expectantly. For months they had been hearing anecdotes about Mr. Kerr, the super salesman. He had talked Mr. Ray into putting a line of knit goods into the shoe store. "Although I didn't want it," Mr. Ray always said, "any more than a cat wants nine tails." He had achieved the virtual miracle of getting his knit goods into the shoe store's display window.

"What has he done now?" Betsy asked.

"Now, by George, he's wangled an invitation to come here for Sunday night lunch. He's coming next Sunday if that's all right with you, my dear," Mr. Ray ended, addressing his wife.

"Of course," said Mrs. Ray. "I'm dying to meet him. Is he married?"

"No. A bachelor."

"How old is he? I ought to find him a girl."

"Oh, twenty-seven or twenty-eight."

Betsy groaned. "Heavens! How ancient! Why do your interesting friends all have to be gray-beards, Papa?"

Tacy looked up innocently. "Why," she said, "I don't think twenty-seven is so old."

Everybody laughed and Tacy blushed, as only she could blush, to the roots of her auburn hair.

"All right, honey," Mrs. Ray said. "You can look after Mr. Kerr."

"I'm not even coming for Sunday night lunch this week," Tacy said hastily.

"Oh, yes, you are!" answered Betsy. "Don't you remember? We're invited to Mrs. Poppy's that afternoon, you and Tib and Tony and Dennie and I. She has some plan she wants to talk over. Then we're all coming back here for lunch."

On Sunday, Tib had a cold, but the others went down to the Melborn Hotel, and Mrs. Poppy's plan proved to be engrossing. Her brother, who was an actor, was coming to visit her and put on a home-talent play. Mrs. Poppy wanted Tacy and Tony both to sing solos, and Tib to do a dance. The prospect was so exciting that it drove gray-beards of twenty-seven completely out of mind.

When they neared the Ray house, a stream of music told them that Winona had arrived. The quartet burst in and found that Cab and Lloyd were there, too. Then they saw Mr. Kerr, who was sitting in the parlor with Mr. and Mrs. Ray, somewhat removed by age, as well as by the archway, from the noisy music-room group.

Mr. Kerr was a fine-looking young man, very well groomed. He was moderately tall, with broad shoulders and a frank open face, lively blue eyes, fresh color, strong white teeth. He looked very good-humored, but something in the set of his jaw showed the determination Mr. Ray had described. He looked predominately likable.

He and Mr. Ray had been talking business, Mrs. Ray said.

"We'll never get any sandwiches made at this rate," she remarked briskly. "Tacy, Mr. Kerr is your responsibility now."

Tacy blushed again as only Tacy could. Mr. Kerr surveyed her with his bright appraising eyes.

"And is Tacy my responsibility?"

"She certainly is."

"I agree, if Tacy does," he said.

Mr. Ray went out to make the sandwiches, and Tony strolled negligently after him. Tony, although he acted so lazy, knew how to be useful, mixing an egg with the coffee, filling the pot with cold water, and setting it to boil. Betsy put Anna's cocoanut cake on the dining room table, along with pickles and olives, cream and sugar, cups and saucers. Winona was playing the piano and the Crowd was singing, when they weren't joking, teasing, scuffling, and yelling. Mr. Kerr took everything in with a lively, observant twinkle.

Mr. Ray spoke in an undertone to Tony and Betsy.

"You're seeing," he said, "a smart young man in action. That Kerr is in command of a difficult situation. He doesn't hold himself aloof from those kids, but he doesn't mix too much either. He mixes just enough to make everyone at ease, but not enough to lose his dignity."

Betsy watched and saw that what her father had said was true. Mr. Kerr was completely poised with the pretty girls, the clamoring boys. He didn't make himself one of them. They all called him Mr. Kerr. But he wasn't a wet blanket.

"Smart," Mr. Ray said, as he applied a different sort of skill to buttering bread, slicing ham, adding mustard, salt, and pepper, and cutting the double sandwiches in two halves, slantwise, until a large platter was heaped.

Betsy noticed something else as the evening progressed. Mr. Kerr had been told to take charge of Tacy, and he was certainly doing it. Tacy was habitually shy, and sometimes in a crowd she went off by herself. Tonight, Mr. Kerr followed. Tacy was plied with sandwiches. Her coffee cup was never allowed to be empty. She had the choicest piece of cocoanut cake.

Tacy and Mr. Kerr ate supper together and he talked all the time. He was, Betsy observed, a great talker. Tacy didn't act shy. She was listening attentively, and now and then she laughed or asked a question.

"It's because he's so old," Betsy thought. "She feels as though she were with her own father."

When everyone was carrying out the dishes after supper, Betsy went up to Tacy.

"Do you like him?" she asked.

"Who? Harry? Yes, he's very nice."

Harry! Betsy could hardly believe her ears. Harry!

Then Mr. Kerr *didn't* seem to Tacy like her father.

After a while, when the music gave way to general conversation, Mr. Kerr brought up the subject of cameras.

"Anybody interested in photography?" he asked. "I just bought a new Eastman."

Lloyd had received an Eastman for Christmas, and he and Mr. Kerr plunged into a technical discussion. Betsy said she used a square box Brownie.

"I'm so dumb I can't take pictures with any other kind."

"Why, you take good pictures, Betsy," Tacy said.

Mr. Kerr turned away from Lloyd abruptly.

"I'll *bet* you take mighty good ones," he said, smiling persuasively at Betsy. "Won't you show me some?"

Betsy brought out her bulging Kodak book, filled with pictures of the Rays, of the Crowd, of winter and summer excursions.

"Someone will have to explain this to me," Mr. Kerr said, and presently he and Tacy were sitting on the couch while she told him who was who, laughing as she turned the pages.

"Betsy says this is me at my silliest," Betsy heard her remark, and remembered the picnic up on the Big Hill when she had snapped Tacy acting like an Irish Colleen.

Mr. Kerr and Tacy looked at the Kodak book until the doorbell rang. One of Tacy's brothers had come to call for her.

That was the signal for everyone to go. There was a scramble for wraps and overshoes, a burst of good-nights, shouted plans to meet in school.

Mr. Kerr waited, leafing through the Kodak book until all the young people had gone. Then he closed the book and said he, too, must leave, and Mr. Ray gave him his overcoat. The young man shook hands heartily with Mrs. Ray and Betsy and said to Mr. Ray, "Would you show me which direction I start off in?"

When Mr. Ray accompanied him to the porch, Mrs. Ray turned to Betsy.

"What a delightful young man!"

"Isn't he!" said Betsy. She looked puzzled. "And wasn't he nice to Tacy?"

"They got along beautifully," Mrs. Ray replied. "I was pleased because Tacy is usually so shy."

"She wasn't shy with him," Betsy said. She couldn't quite make it out.

Mr. Ray returned from the porch. He closed the door behind him slowly, and came into the parlor with a strange look on his face. He sat down, rubbing his hands over his forehead, and then put them firmly on his knees.

"Well, I don't know what to think! That Kerr just

said the most amazing thing."

"What was it?" Mrs. Ray and Betsy cried together.

"First, Betsy, he apologized to you for having stolen one of your Kodak pictures. He said you're going to get a box of chocolates in return."

Betsy ran to her Kodak book and riffled the pages quickly. She knew which snapshot would be missing.

"The Colleen from Hill Street!" she breathed.

That was, indeed, gone. Tacy, laughing, her braids loose, her hair blown into curls, was no longer in Betsy's Kodak book.

Mrs. Ray and Betsy stared at each other. Her mother, Betsy thought, looked actually pale.

"But that isn't all," Mr. Ray went on. "In fact, it's only the beginning. Do you know what else he said?"

"Tell us, for heaven's sake!"

"He said," answered Mr. Ray, "that Tacy was the girl he was going to marry. He said he didn't care how long he would have to wait. She was the girl he was going to marry." After a pause in which no one seemed even to breathe, Mr. Ray added, "Tacy had better watch out. If Harry Kerr can talk me into putting in a line of knit goods, he can talk her into marrying him."

"Well!" said Mrs. Ray, color coming back into her cheeks, and her eyes beginning to sparkle. "I never heard the like."

Betsy was stunned. She was dazed and confounded. Marriage was something infinitely remote. It had never occurred to her that it could touch her circle yet. And to touch, of all people, Tacy!

She could hardly wait to tell Tacy, who would be thrilled. Or would she? You never could tell about Tacy. But she would think it was ridiculous, of course. She would laugh long and heartily and remind Betsy of how they were going to see Paris and New York and London and the Taj Mahal by moonlight.

Somehow, Betsy was anxious to hear that laughter. It was thrilling, but it was painful, too, to have Mr. Kerr in love with Tacy. She went up to bed still dazed, and early the next morning telephoned Tacy that she would walk to meet her.

"And see that you're alone! Don't be with Alice, or Tib, or anyone!"

Betsy hurried through breakfast and hurried into her winter coat, tam, and furs. She ran out of the house, in the direction opposite the school house, down the hill to the corner where a watering trough, now frozen and rimmed with icicles, marked the junction with Cemetery Road.

When she saw Tacy coming, she ran to meet her.

"Stand still! This can't be told walking."

She repeated dramatically what her father had said

when he came in from the porch the night before.

"He said he was going to marry you! TO MARRY YOU!" Betsy repeated.

Of course, Tacy blushed. Betsy had expected that, but she hadn't expected Tacy's eyes to light with such a mischievous glimmer. Betsy had expected her to be flabbergasted, dumbfounded, but she didn't seem very surprised.

When she spoke, it was in the Irish brogue she affected when she felt especially merry.

"Well, and sure now, did he?" she said, hooking her arm into Betsy's. The next moment she asked Betsy about a physics formula. Then she brought up the subject of the home-talent play.

Betsy's head was spinning. It felt actually light. Childhood seemed to be receding like a rapidly moving railway train.

"And Tib and I thought she was going to be an old maid . . . if we didn't help her!" Betsy marveled.

17

Up and Down Broadway

THERE WAS NO DENYING that Mr. Kerr's astounding announcement and Tacy's calm reaction to it made Betsy feel blue. She was proud of Tacy's conquest; she was stirred by it. But it made her feel lonely, too.

It was strange to be excluded from something which concerned Tacy. She and Tacy had always shared everything. Tacy had shared Betsy's love affairs.

She had rejoiced with her when things went well and grieved when they went badly. Betsy would gladly have rejoiced with Tacy now, but Tacy didn't need her. She wasn't half so excited about Mr. Kerr as everyone else was. She liked him, she said; and her aura of serene radiance showed that she did. But she had no confidences to impart.

It was fortunate for Betsy that the new home-talent play came along just then. Not only did she feel blue, but school had reached its February dullness. Winter had reached its February dreariness. She needed the tinsel world of make-believe.

All Deep Valley needed it. Tired of snow and more snow, of deceptively fair days followed by rain that turned to snow and sometimes blizzards, of shoveling walks and shoveling coal, Deep Valley yielded itself joyously to *Up and Down Broadway.*

That was the name of Mr. Maxwell's production.

"I'm calling it *Up and Down Broadway* because I'm going to take a cast of amateurs and whip up a revue fit for Broadway," he told Betsy. Broadway was Mr. Maxwell's Paradise; he talked about it all the time.

He almost overflowed Mrs. Poppy's doll-like apartment, for he was fat, like his sister. Like his sister, too, he was a figure of elegance. Blond, with side whiskers, he wore a plaid vest, a satin tie with a diamond stickpin in it, a long coat, and striped trousers.

He wanted Betsy to choose a chorus from among the high school girls. *Up and Down Broadway* wasn't just a high school affair. It was a Deep Valley affair, a benefit for the Elks Lodge. Attractive young matrons, business men with a flair for theatricals, the town's child wonders were all taking part. Most of the singers were from Mrs. Poppy's class.

"*How* I wish Julia were here!" she kept interjecting now.

Choosing the chorus, Mr. Maxwell explained to Betsy earnestly, was important.

"On Broadway," he said, fixing her with a gleaming eye, "the chorus is more important than the principals. You have to have cute snappy broilers, Georgie Cohan always says. Can you find me thirty cute, snappy girls in Deep Valley High School, Miss Ray? They must be able to sing and dance, of course."

"Certainly," said Betsy. She felt that the honor of Deep Valley was at stake.

Fortunately, the high school had plenty of pulchritude. The girls in the Crowd were secured first; then the junior, sophomore, and freshman classes were searched for talent. When the thirty assembled, glowing and smiling, on the bare dusty stage of the Opera House, Mr. Maxwell surveyed them with satisfaction and said that they would be a credit to Broadway.

His pleasure in them was short-lived. His good humor, they were to find, was spasmodic. When coats were doffed and the girls began singing timidly, dancing self-consciously in response to his suggestions, Mr. Maxwell changed completely. His rosy face grew purple. He shrieked and pounded the piano. He told them they were nitwits and dunces, clodhoppers, gawky as a bunch of milkmaids. He made Irma cry. Some of the girls told Betsy that they wouldn't be in *Up and Down Broadway*, after all.

But while they were huffily putting on their wraps, Mr. Maxwell changed again. He moved about jovially, making jokes, beaming. He told them that they mustn't mind him. That was the way Broadway producers always yelled at the broilers. He said they were so cute that he wished Flo Ziegfeld could see them.

After a while, the girls grew accustomed to his rapid changes of mood. It was nervous work, though, singing and dancing to please Mr. Maxwell.

Usually, after they had rehearsed, the broilers sat on boxes or folding chairs around the stage to watch the principals perform . . . especially those from the high school.

Tib's Dutch Girl number was good from the start. She could not sing, but she could talk a song with airy coquetry, and her dancing was light, feathery, and bewitching. Mr. Maxwell wasn't cross with her long, for she was always able to do exactly what she was told. He would stand at the edge of the stage to watch her practise and say to Mrs. Poppy, "That girl has talent. Broadway needs that girl."

When Tacy first heard Mr. Maxwell rave and rant, she withdrew hastily from her scheduled solo. But Mr. Maxwell and Mrs. Poppy pleaded with her to reconsider, and she did. After that, Mr. Maxwell was gentle with Tacy.

> *"I'm awfully lonesome tonight,*
> *Somehow there's nothing just right,*
> *Honey, you know why. . . ."*

She was to sing that all alone on the stage, looking at an artificial moon.

Dennie was to be a ballet dancer. Tony was singing an old Joe Howard success:

> *"What's the use of dreaming,*
> *Dreams of rosy hue,*
> *What's the use of dreaming, dreaming,*
> *Dreams that never could come true. . . ."*

He had sung it for years at the Ray piano; it was a favorite song of Mr. Ray's, and Mrs. Poppy had transposed the music to suit Tony's deep bass voice. Betsy liked to hear him rehearse it, but Tony almost drove Mr. Maxwell to distraction. Mr. Maxwell liked him, of course. Everyone liked Tony. But he was late at rehearsals. He didn't learn his lines. He was always clowning.

At the back of the stage among dusty piles of scenery, Tony would take off Lillian Russell, or he would borrow spectacles to imitate the church choir tenor, whose solo was one of the classical highlights of the show. When there was music, he and Betsy waltzed in the wings. Sometimes they wandered through the empty Opera House, which always reminded Betsy of Uncle Keith.

When she came there to plays, it seemed elegant beyond description—the glittering crystal chandelier, seats upholstered in red velvet, boxes hung with red velvet draperies tied back with golden cords. Now it was dark and chilly and the curtain (which showed a sedan chair and ladies in hoop skirts) was half way up, revealing the barnlike stage. But Betsy was still enchanted by it.

"I even like the smell," she said to Tony, sniffing.

"I feel at home here myself," he replied thoughtfully, gazing around.

Rehearsals were glamorous. They made many new matches—and revived some old ones. Take Dennie and Tib! Maddox was the star of the basketball team now, but such was the influence of Thespis that Dennie was crowding Maddox out of Tib's life.

All the girls were thinking that perhaps they should go on the stage, that their talents were better suited to Broadway than to Deep Valley High School.

Of course, everyone was getting behind in school, and Betsy was dimly worried because she wanted to make the Honor Roll. She knew that she ought to be practising, too, "A Night in Venice" for Miss Cobb's recital. And Joe grew stiffer and stiffer in the classroom, and she heard that he had bought two tickets for the show. But none of this seemed as real as it would after *Up and Down Broadway* was over. What was real now was the big, bare Opera House filled with staccato excitement.

The dress rehearsal was terrible. Mr. Maxwell shouted at the top of his voice. The girls wept and the boys stormed, but nobody could possibly have been persuaded to leave.

On the day of the performance, it snowed, as heavily, as persistently, as though there hadn't been a flake all winter. But nobody minded. The house had been sold out for weeks, from the first row in the parquet all the way to the rafters.

After Betsy was dressed for the opening number in her glow worm costume, she visited Tacy and Tib in their dressing room. Tib was cool and poised, arranging her yellow curls under a winged cap. Tacy was so pale that the paint on her cheeks looked grotesque, and her hands were as cold as ice.

Betsy kissed her on the top of her head.

"Cheer up!" she said. "It will all be the same a hundred years from now."

But Tacy was too wretched to joke. She was stiff with wretchedness.

On the stairs which lead up to the stage, Betsy met Tony. He was wearing a plain dark suit, but his face was painted, and charcoal made his black eyes look even wickeder than usual.

"Come on!" he said, catching her hand. "Let's take a look at the audience."

Sets were being run into place on the stage, and they made their way cautiously to the curtain, found two peep holes, and looked out.

The audience was streaming in. Betsy saw her father and mother and Margaret. Where the dress circle met the parquet, in the very center of the house, were two wide, well-padded seats. These had been built especially for the excessively stout Mr. and Mrs. Poppy, who were seated in them now, Mr. Poppy in a dress suit, Mrs. Poppy in a low-cut gown, with plumes in her yellow hair.

Joe was coming in with a girl Betsy didn't know.

She was very, very pretty. They talked all the way down the aisle, and she kept turning around to smile into his face while he was helping her off with her coat and laying it over the chair.

Betsy felt that pressure about her heart. She turned and smiled meaningfully into Tony's black-rimmed eyes. This was unfair to Tony, and she knew it, but she didn't seem to care.

"Take a look at Margaret," she said. "She looks so serious. I know she's praying for you."

"You praying for me, too, Ray of Sunshine?"

"You don't need anybody's prayers. You're wonderful."

"Say that again."

But the orchestra was tuning up now, and Mr. Maxwell, suave and smiling in a dress suit, called everyone out on the stage. He told them he knew the performance was going to be fine, because it was good luck to have a dress rehearsal go badly.

"On Broadway we're scared to death if the dress rehearsal goes well. I've known Belasco to call off a performance just because the dress rehearsal clicked."

Betsy thought this sounded a little excessive, but she had to admit that in spite of last night's mistakes and wearisome confusion, *Up and Down Broadway* went off to perfection.

The high school chorus opened the show:

"Shine, little glow worm, glimmer,
Shine, little glow worm, glimmer...."

The stage was dark at first, and the girls carried phosphorescent wands. Then the lights went on, and the girls in their black and orange costumes were themselves the glow worms. The audience stamped and whistled. It seemed that Deep Valley thought broilers important, just as Broadway did.

The leading lights of the town did their numbers, and the high school celebrities did theirs. Dennie, with his cherubic face, made a fetching ballet dancer. He wore a short-skirted tulle dress, a feather head-dress, ropes of pearls, earrings, and long white gloves with bracelets and rings outside. A big spangly ornament on one black-stockinged leg almost brought the house down.

Tacy came out on the stage like a sleep-walker. Her dress was of old blue Liberty silk, covered with gauze of changing coppery colors. Mr. Maxwell had wanted her to wear a picture hat, but Tacy had unexpectedly objected. People didn't go out singing to the moon in picture hats, she said. She hadn't even dressed her hair in the fashionable puffs, but wore her familiar coronet braids. And although she looked beautiful, she looked just like Tacy when the curtain rose and the spotlight found her gazing at a tinsel moon.

"I'm awfully lonesome tonight,
Somehow there's nothing just right,
Honey, you know why. . . ."

The house was very quiet listening to Tacy's harp-like voice. At the end there was a burst of applause, and after Tacy reached the wings where Betsy and Tib were listening tensely, there was another burst so loud that she had to go back. She was slow returning this time.

"What can it be?" asked Betsy, peeking.

"Flowers, probably," said Tib.

Every girl performer received a bouquet. Their families sent them if no one else did. But Tacy came into the wings with a bouquet no father would have sent. It was the biggest bouquet anyone had received that evening. Her arms could hardly hold the dozens of long-stemmed yellow roses.

Betsy and Tib spoke together, the same words, "Mr. Kerr?"

Tacy nodded happily. "He came all the way from St. Paul just to see the show."

The most professional number on the program was undoubtedly the Dutch Girl's song and dance. The quaint costume with its many petticoats emphasized Tib's tiny waist, and she didn't forget one of the winning smiles or dainty gestures Mr. Maxwell had taught her. The chorus came out and danced behind her for many, many encores, and she had flowers galore.

Yet Tib wasn't the hit of the show. To everyone's surprise, especially Mr. Maxwell's, that honor went to Tony.

When the music for his song began, he strolled carelessly out on the stage and straddled a chair. He got out his pipe and filled it, tamping down the tobacco as thoughtfully as though he were sitting in the Rays' parlor, with all the time in the world. The orchestra kept on playing. Then, holding the pipe in his hand, his arms folded on top of the chair, he began to sing:

> *"What's the use of dreaming,*
> *Dreams of rosy hue,*
> *What's the use of dreaming, dreaming,*
> *Dreams that never could come true. . . ."*

His lazy charm, his rich deep voice won the audience completely. He was called before the curtain again and again. He sauntered out, at ease and smiling, saluted nonchalantly, retreated. He couldn't sing an encore, for he had none prepared. At last Mr. Maxwell signified to the orchestra that Tony could repeat the chorus, and he did.

"You are worth a million,
There is not a doubt,

.. ..

.. ..

Then your pipe goes out."

Betsy and Tony, Dennie and Tib went to the Moorish Cafe after the show. Betsy and Tib kept a little of their make-up on their cheeks and felt like actresses. Joe and the pretty girl were there, but Betsy ignored them. She flirted gaily with Tony.

She started a game which had just reached popularity, writing down dashes which, properly decoded, spelled out words and messages.

Her "---- ----- ---- -- --- ----?" was translated at last: "What color eyes do you like?"

Tony pulled his curly thatch and wrote, "---- ---- --- ---- -- - ----." "They have the name of a girl."

"Hazel!" Tib shrieked, and Betsy wrote (in code, of course), "I like curly hair."

Tony's eyes sought hers with laughing boldness. He set down dashes firmly. "I like unnaturally curly hair."

Dennie seized the pencil then, and Tib peeped over his shoulder. Their table resounded with mirth.

Tib came to stay all night at the Rays'.

"You were darling," Betsy told her as they undressed. "You really ought to go on the stage, Tib."

"Maybe I will," Tib said. "But there are lots of things I like to do. I like to draw, I like to cook, I like to keep house. . . ."

"If I were making up a plot," said Betsy, "I'd have Mr. Maxwell getting back to New York and telegraphing for you to come and go into the Follies."

"You can make up all the plots you like," said Tib, matter-of-factly. "But I'm going to go through high school and graduate along with you and Tacy."

"Betsy," she added after a moment. "You're getting to like Tony pretty well, aren't you?"

"What makes you think so?" Betsy asked.

"You acted that way tonight. Joe didn't like it, either. I could tell, the way he stuck his lip out."

"That . . . go-to-the-deuce . . . look, you mean," said Betsy flippantly.

But she didn't answer Tib's question.

18

"Toil and Trouble"

BETSY SAT AT THE PIANO, practising Nevins' "A Night in Venice," which she was going to play at Miss Cobb's recital. She played badly, for she felt cross. She had been feeling cross for some time, although she tried not to show it . . . ever since *Up and Down Broadway*, in fact.

She had been having difficulties with Tony. Encouraged by her coquetry that night, he had changed.

All winter, in spite of the fact that he had been going with no one but her, he had not acted lover-like.

"He was never spoony," she thought. "And not because he doesn't like me, either!"

He liked her—too much. She had known for some time that he did. She had seen it in his touchingly good behavior, his mock-serious gallantries, the adoring look his black eyes held sometimes. But he had tried not to show it. He would have kept on trying—because he thought she didn't share his feeling—if she hadn't given him false hopes.

She had brought it all on herself. Just because she had seen Joe with that girl at the show! And after all, he hadn't taken her out again. She was just a girl who had been visiting in town. Of no consequence at all! Betsy brought her hands down bitterly on the keys.

In the Crowd, she had been snappish. She had quarreled violently with Winona and Irma—Betsy, who never quarreled! They didn't speak for three days until Irma apologized for something she hadn't even done. She had quarreled with Cab about whether he had broken some casual date. It was something that really shouldn't have mattered a fig.

"I don't know what ails me," Betsy thought. "Of course," she added defensively, "I'm working pretty hard."

She was. Everything that had been pushed away and put aside while *Up and Down Broadway* was in preparation now had to be faced. In Miss Bangeter's Shakespeare class they had finished the comedies, *As You Like It* and *The Merchant of Venice*, and were deep in the grim tragedies of *Hamlet* and *Macbeth*.

> *"Bubble, bubble,*
> *Toil and trouble. . . ."*

Toil and trouble expressed exactly what she was going through, Betsy decided. In physics she was facing an examination on "Light."

"Why does anyone have to do anything about light except enjoy it?" she demanded, running a scale.

In German, she was struggling with adjectives. It seemed so unreasonable of the Germans to change their adjectives, for gender, number, case.

"Why can't they just say *klein* for 'small'? Why does it have to be *kleiner, kleines, kleine*, and goodness knows what else! If one adjective is good enough for English, it ought to be for German," stormed Betsy, banging.

The Honor Roll would be announced soon. And Betsy wanted to be on it. She wanted to be on the program commencement night, to give an oration as Carney had done.

"I should have thought about that earlier in the year, or last year, or the year before that, or the year before that," she told herself, making a discord.

She wasn't properly prepared even for Miss Cobb's recital, although Miss Cobb had been planning it happily for months. Well, Betsy thought, she would stick to her practising for an hour this morning if it killed her.

But she wasn't too sorry when the telephone rang.

It was Alice, who was also to play at Miss Cobb's recital.

"Betsy! Have you heard? Miss Cobb has left for Colorado. Leonard died last night."

"Leonard . . . died?"

She could hardly take it in.

Then Leonard had lost his fight! He would never compose that music which had been running in his head. He would never hear the operas, the great orchestras he had longed to hear.

"There won't be any recital, of course," Alice said.

After she shut down the telephone, Betsy stared at it through a blur of tears. She was sorry she hadn't written Leonard that long funny letter about *Up and Down Broadway* which had been rolling around in her head. She would never write it now, and he would never read it. It would have made him laugh.

She thought about Miss Cobb. Dear, brave Miss Cobb! This was the third child to die, of the four she had taken to raise. And she had been so cheerful all winter, although the news from Leonard had been bad.

Betsy dashed the tears out of her eyes and went upstairs to her mother's bedroom, where Mrs. Ray and Miss Mix were busy with the Easter sewing.

"Oh, I'm so sorry!" Mrs. Ray said, when Betsy had told her the news. "It's a very good thing she has Bobby."

Bobby, the one remaining nephew, was a youthful, masculine counterpart of his sturdy aunt. The family enemy wouldn't get him, at least.

"Let's ask Bobby up to supper while his aunt is gone," said Mrs. Ray. "Ask Margaret to telephone him."

Betsy went reluctantly to tell the news to Margaret. Margaret had taken Miss Cobb into the small circle of her affections along with Washington and Lincoln, Mrs. Wheat and Tony. And Margaret had deep feelings, although she could never express them. She could never find an outlet for her emotions in small ejaculations of pity or sympathy as other people did.

She said nothing at all now, just stared with dark, troubled eyes. When Betsy asked her to telephone Bobby, she marched away, her back very straight. But she went into the coat closet and stayed there a while before she telephoned.

Betsy closed "A Night in Venice" and put it away. She never wanted to hear it again.

But she did. Bobby came to supper. And after a few days Miss Cobb returned from Colorado with Leonard. Half the high school went to the funeral, and Miss Cobb's pupils sent a big wreath. Then lessons began again. Miss Cobb looked pale, but she was as calmly cheerful as ever. She didn't mention the recital, though. There was no recital that year.

Sadness weighed Betsy down for several days, although there was good news at school. When the civics class was leaving the classroom, Miss Clarke beckoned to her.

"Will you drop in to see me after school?" she whispered.

That meant, Betsy knew, that she had been chosen for the Essay Contest. She ought to be glad, but she didn't feel anything. She just felt tired out.

In English class, she did what she rarely did these days, glanced across the room at Joe. He was leafing through *Macbeth*, but just as she looked at him he looked at her. He didn't smile. He only looked at her and turned back to his book. But Betsy felt sure that he, too, had been asked to write in the Essay Contest. He was thinking what she was thinking: they would be competing again this year!

Entering Miss Clarke's room, she tried to muster a

smile which would match Miss Clarke's kind excitement.

"I've some good news for you, Betsy. The Zetamathians have chosen you again for the Essay Contest. The Philomathians have chosen Joe, of course."

"Of course," said Betsy, smiling.

"And . . . I want you to know . . . there was no dissenting voice about you this year. Miss Bangeter, Miss Fowler, and I all think you are the one to represent the senior Zetamathians."

Betsy tried to look as happy as she knew Miss Clarke expected her to look.

"What is the subject?" she asked with forced eagerness.

"It is 'Conservation of Our Natural Resources.'"

"'Conservation of Our . . . Natural Resources'?" Betsy repeated blankly.

"You know," Miss Clarke said helpfully. "Keeping up our forests and things. You like the out-of-doors, Betsy. I think you can write a good essay on that subject."

Betsy felt dubious, but she tried to act assured.

"I'll get right to work," she said.

As a matter of fact, she put off going to the library. She dreaded meeting Joe at the little table in the stalls where contestants for the Essay Contest worked. She didn't feel up to seeing him across the table, his bent head shutting her out.

More good news followed. The Honor Roll was announced, and she was on it! She would give an oration at Commencement and Tacy would be singing a solo. Tib had the leading role in the class play.

"Oh, bliss! Joy! Rapture!" they cried.

Rejoicing, they went to Mr. Snow's Photographic Studio to sit for their class pictures. Betsy had one taken in her shirt waist, wearing her class pin; another, in her Class Day dress, the pale blue embroidered batiste Julia had sent from Switzerland. They got the proofs, and Betsy saw that in the shirt waist picture she looked just as she really looked. But the Class Day picture was dreamily flattering.

Miss Mix was making her beautiful clothes, because she was a senior. They included a new tan suit with a frilly white waist for Easter. Betsy bought her Easter hat—a big rough straw, turned up at one side, covered with red poppies. It was glamorously becoming.

Easter came early. And as though nature understood, spring came early, too. Long since, there had been pussy willows in the slough and blackbirds, with red patches on their wings, calling in raucous voices. Now the sun had melted the snow to gray slush. Patches of soggy exuberant grass appeared.

On the day before Easter, when Betsy and Margaret were coloring eggs in the kitchen, Mrs. Ray rushed in.

"Mail from Julia!" she called, waving a letter.

Every letter from Julia was an event, but this one brought especially dramatic news. Julia was going to spend Easter at the Von Hetternichs' castle in Poland.

"Only a hundred rooms are open," Julia wrote, underlining the "only."

Mrs. Ray telephoned Mr. Ray, and when he came home Betsy read the letter aloud to him. After they had eaten supper and Margaret, as usual, had made a nest for the Easter bunny out on the lawn, Betsy read the letter again.

Her father looked at her thoughtfully after she had finished.

"Julia doing all this traveling," he said, "puts an idea into my head."

"What is it?" the others wanted to know.

"I think that Betsy ought to do a little traveling—to the farm."

"To the farm?" asked Betsy. She added jokingly, "Why not Chicago or New York?"

"You don't need Chicago or New York," said Mr. Ray. "You're tired out."

"Are you thinking of the Taggarts?" asked Mrs. Ray, mentioning the farmers Betsy had visited the summer before she went into high school.

"No," said Mr. Ray. "I was thinking of the Beidwinkles, German customers of mine. They were in the store today and asked if one of you girls wouldn't like to come out. Why wouldn't Easter vacation be a good time?"

"Oh, not Easter vacation, Papa!" cried Betsy. "There's a party planned for almost every day."

"That's the trouble," said Mr. Ray. "That's just what I'm getting at. You don't need parties. You need a rest. Don't you think so, Jule?"

"Yes," said Mrs. Ray. "I hate to have her miss the parties." (Mrs. Ray loved parties.) "But you do seem tired, Betsy. You have all spring."

Betsy wanted to cry. She wanted to cry if anyone looked at her these days. But she certainly didn't want to go to a lonesome old farm away from all the fun and excitement of Deep Valley. She winked her eyes rapidly.

"I'll go to your Beidwinkles sometime, Papa. I'd love to. But not in Easter vacation. Please!"

"All right," said Mr. Ray, but he looked dissatisfied.

The telephone broke in on the conversation. It was Winona, suggesting that since the night was so warm, with a moon, it would be fun to go out serenading. Betsy agreed, and soon Tony called for her. A group of eight boys and girls wandered down the street in the mild air seeking the houses they would favor with song.

Tacy didn't come. Mr. Kerr was in town, Alice said.

But Irma was there to lead the sopranos, and the Crowd sang with full throated joy "My Wild Irish Rose," "On Moonlight Bay," "Rose of Mexico."

Betsy loved singing, especially in parts. And Tony wasn't acting mushy tonight. He held her arm in comradely fashion, while his deep voice plunged downward in the bass, inventing impudent harmonies. When they walked he was full of tomfoolery, making everyone laugh.

"Wouldn't I be foolish to go to the country and miss fun like this?" Betsy thought.

After an hour, the serenaders broke into smaller groups. Tony and Betsy called good night and started up Plum Street Hill.

"Say," said Tony, "this is a swell night."

"Just like summer," Betsy answered, looking up at the moon.

"Summer!" said Tony, turning her about. "That calls for ice cream!"

"Heinz's?" she asked.

"Heinz's! But let's not eat it there. Let's make them give us a sack and two spoons."

Mr. Heinz, of course, complied. He was used to the vagaries of the young. Betsy and Tony took a quart of ice cream to Lincoln Park, that pie-shaped wedge of land with an elm tree and a fountain on it which stood where Hill Street began. They sat down on the bench and consumed ice cream with relish, making absurd conversation.

When they had finished, they fell silent. Moonlight flooded everything and made a cloudy shadow of the big elm tree. Tony had been cheerfully unromantic all evening. Betsy was astonished, and taken unprepared, when suddenly he put his arm around her and kissed her.

She jumped up.

"Tony Markham! What are you doing?"

Tony got up, too, but only to kiss her again.

"There's nothing so strange about it, is there?" he asked. "We're going together, aren't we?"

"No . . . not exactly."

"We certainly are."

"We certainly aren't!" cried Betsy. "Not if it means acting spoony like this. I hate this."

"You're acting stupid," said Tony, roughly. "If you don't like me . . ."

"I do like you . . . but not in that way."

She started toward home, Tony walking beside her in silence. He was angry. She could tell it by the swift pace of his walk, usually so slow. She wasn't angry with him; she was angry with herself, angry and confused.

They reached her house. By the arc light on the corner she saw the little nest Margaret had put out.

Since their departure, the bunny had visited it. It contained a fluffy hen and a flock of yellow chicks.

Betsy pointed to it, trying to speak naturally.

"Isn't that cute?"

But Tony didn't answer. They paused awkwardly.

"Come in?" she asked.

"No, thanks," he answered. He brought his hand up to his cap in a reluctant concession to manners, walked rapidly away.

When Betsy went in the house, she dropped down on the sofa and started to cry. The house was dark and she didn't want the lights. "Oh, dear! Oh, dear! Oh, dear!" she wept. She felt forlorn and ashamed of herself.

Tony had not meant any disrespect when he kissed her. He respected her; he looked up to her. She knew it. He understood, too, that you didn't let boys kiss you unless you were in love with them. She had let him think she *was* in love . . . or falling.

And he was really in love with her. She knew it as well as though he had told her. He probably would have told her, if she had been different tonight. He might even have said that he wanted them to be engaged. But maybe not. Tony, although so bold, was inarticulate. It would have been hard for him to find words for that. He would have meant it, though.

Still crying, she jumped up and tiptoed down to the

basement. She went to the small room where luggage was kept, brought out her satchel, and tiptoed upstairs. She started throwing piles of clothing into the satchel.

Tomorrow, after Margaret had found her nest, after Easter church and dinner, she was going away. She was going to ask her father to take her to the Beidwinkles' after all.

19
Beidwinkles'

BETSY WOKE EARLY on the morning after Easter, flooded by a sense of peace. She had slept dreamlessly on a puffy feather bed beneath Mrs. Beidwinkle's fresh-smelling sheets, her patchwork quilts and downy comforter, and she lay staring at a framed motto which said "Grüss Gott" in cross stitch, unable for a moment to remember where she was.

The window was a square of gray, but through the slot in the storm sash, she could hear a delicious jumble of bird voices. She recognized the killdeer shouting his own name and the robin going joyously up and down.

She felt happy. It came to her that she had not been happy for a very long time. Now the things which had been making her unhappy . . . the quarrel with Joe, the worry about Tony, the nervous, strained anxiety about school affairs—all these had faded away. She lay in bed smiling.

Presently she jumped up, closed the window, and poured water from the pitcher into the bowl. She gave herself a vigorous cold sponge, despite the fact that the room was chilly. She dressed warmly, putting on a red flannel waist and a plaid skirt. Not bothering with puffs, she braided her hair and turned it up with a ribbon. She realized suddenly that she had forgotten last night to put it up on Magic Wavers. When, she thought, bursting into a laugh, had she ever forgotten that before?

She and her father had arrived late, after supper. She had not even unpacked her suitcase, except for her dresses. She saw them on hangers in the closet, her Peter Thompson suit, the white and gold wool dress. Why on earth had she brought that? she wondered. She must have been crazy when she packed, thinking that parties pursued one everywhere.

Briskly, she laid her underwear and shirt waists in neat piles in the bureau drawers which stuck when she tried to open them, but were immaculately papered inside. She arranged her toilet articles on top of the bureau and set her family photographs around. She laid out her comb and brush and mirror.

There was a little table in one corner which would be perfect for her writing. She brought it up flush to the window, which looked out into a bare box elder tree and across the Beidwinkles' front lawn, a sheet of gray snow in the gray light.

She took the starched white spread off the table, folded it, and put it away. Then she set out her tablets, notebooks, and pencils, her pencil sharpener and her eraser and the ruler she had brought . . . goodness knew why! She added the Bible, her prayer book, and the dictionary. There!

"I'm going to start a story this morning," she decided. "I think it will be about a girl who goes away somewhere, to Newport, maybe. I'll bet it will sell, too," she added. (None of last summer's stories had sold, although she had kept them continuously on the go.)

Last night's impression of the house returned as she literally skipped down the narrow stairs. It was the cleanest house she had ever been in, and it looked very old-fashioned, with rag carpets and crocheted tidies on the chairs.

There was an organ in the parlor, she noticed, peeking into that formidable room. The horsehair chairs sat about in prickly splendor. On a square table there was a gigantic family Bible with a velvet-covered photograph album on the ledge beneath. On a round table were wax flowers under glass, with a stereopticon set on the ledge.

Betsy and her father had sat in the kitchen, which was, she soon found out, the most used and the pleasantest room in the house. It was large, with blue and white curtains, red geraniums in the windows, and a wood-burning cook stove, its nickel trim polished to the gleam of solid silver.

Fire was roaring in the stove this morning, and beside it Mrs. Beidwinkle leaned over a crate which held a flock of chirping yellow chicks. She was a large, big-busted woman with a childlike face. Her graying hair was parted and brushed smoothly down over her ears, in which tiny earrings were set. Graying braids were twisted round and round to make a bun in the back.

Betsy stooped to admire the chicks.

"The sweet little things! May I help you get breakfast?" she asked, feeling rather proud of being down so early.

Mrs. Beidwinkle laughed gleefully. "Breakfast!" she ejaculated. "Mein Mann milked the cows two hours ago. We had breakfast then. I have my wash on the line and was just going to have a little coffee."

"Do you get up so early every day?"

"Earlier in the summertime. But you are to sleep as late as you can. I always have second breakfasts. My second can be your first."

On a red-cloth-covered table Mrs. Beidwinkle set out coffee cake and a plateful of cookies, thickly sliced homemade bread, and a bowl of milk. She poured a cup of coffee for herself and offered one to Betsy, but Betsy didn't want it. It had obviously been reheated and looked as black as ink. The bread and milk, coffee cake, and cookies were delicious.

Betsy enjoyed talking with Mrs. Beidwinkle, who plainly enjoyed talking with her. All her children—four sons and five daughters—were married and gone.

"But Amelia lives near. She is the youngest one."

Mrs. Beidwinkle was full of legends of her children, their illnesses, their love affairs, their triumphs and disappointments, the death of one. When she got up at last, saying that she must bring in her wash, Betsy put on her cravenette and went out to explore.

It was cold. The wind almost blew her off her feet, and the windmill was whirling. Big clouds, some dark, some pearly white, sailed in a gray sky.

She went to the barn, where she made friends with

a sheep dog and saw a litter of kittens. Big, bearded Mr. Beidwinkle, less impressive than he had seemed last night, called out to her from a shed where he was tinkering with a plough. He introduced her to small, grizzled Bill, the hired man.

They weren't so busy as they would be later, Mr. Beidwinkle said. He couldn't start ploughing until the frost was out of the ground. Meanwhile he was repairing and oiling farm machinery; he and Bill were building a new chicken house; he was hauling wood from the wood lot.

Betsy returned to the house, cold and blown, went up to her room, and started her story.

After dinner, which was eaten in the kitchen, she helped with the dishes, then went up to her room, undressed, and took a nap. She slept from two to four, got up and dressed again, put on her cravenette and overshoes, and took another walk.

It was colder than ever; she couldn't face north. But the smell of spring was in the air. A crow flew out of an oak tree, flapping his big wings and croaking, "Caw! Caw! Caw!" She saw the green spears of tulips on the south side of the house.

She ate voraciously at supper, which was like a second dinner, with beer for the men. Mr. Beidwinkle addressed his wife in German and Betsy volunteered the information that she was studying it. They were delighted.

"*Sie sprechen Deutsch, ja?*" Mr. Beidwinkle asked.

"*Ein wenig,*" Betsy replied. "I'd love to try to talk it with you sometimes while I'm here."

Bill began to point out articles on the table, giving their German names. But Betsy had played this game with the Mullers. She cried out the names before he had a chance to utter them and soon everyone was laughing. She was so expert that they had to point to the cupboards, to the stove, to find words she didn't know.

After supper, the Beidwinkles went into the back parlor, where a ruddy-windowed coal stove reminded Betsy of Hill Street. Mr. Beidwinkle and Bill buried themselves in German newspapers, Mrs. Beidwinkle went to work on her embroidery. Betsy started *Little Dorrit*, which she had brought from home, but her thoughts kept going to the organ locked away in the front parlor.

At last she mentioned it hesitantly. "Would you mind if I went in sometimes and played your organ? Not tonight when Mr. Beidwinkle is reading, but tomorrow maybe."

"What?" cried Mr. Beidwinkle. "You play the organ? Mamma! She plays the organ. We can make music."

Mrs. Beidwinkle was as excited as her husband, and Bill, too, eased himself to his feet.

"That organ is never played since our last daughter

married and went away. Ach, we would be happy to hear some music again!"

Mrs. Beidwinkle bustled into the front parlor and lit the lamp. Mr. Beidwinkle and Bill came in and took chairs, and Betsy began to feel stage fright.

"I don't play very well, you know. Not like my sister, Julia. I just thought maybe I could practise . . ."

"You practise, and we listen," Mr. Beidwinkle said. "You are used to an organ? *Ja?*"

"No. But I don't think it's very different from a piano."

Mrs. Beidwinkle unlocked it proudly. She pointed out the eleven stops, the knee swells, the pedals covered with Brussels carpet. Betsy sat down timidly, and tried them out. She started her simple repertoire.

"Can't you sing?" Mr. Beidwinkle demanded.

Betsy was nonplused. Of course she could sing; she had been singing all her life. But she didn't sing for people all alone, as Julia and Tacy did. She just sang.

She discovered now that she could sing if she had to for other people, all alone. Mr. and Mrs. Beidwinkle and Bill were looking so radiantly expectant that she couldn't disappoint them. Finding the proper chords, she sang "Juanita" and "Annie Laurie" and some of the other old songs her father loved. Then she began on the popular songs: "Tonight Will Never Come Again" (at which Mrs. Beidwinkle wiped her eyes), "I Wonder Who's Kissing Her Now," "The Rose of Mexico," "Yip-i-addy-i-ay." Bill liked that one.

At last she began the new song Julia had sent her at Christmas. Just for fun she sang it in German—"*Kind, Du Kannst Tanzen....*"

Mr. Beidwinkle laughed and slapped his knee. "Gollee, gollee," he said over and over.

After that, every evening Betsy sang "Tonight Will Never Come Again" for Mrs. Beidwinkle, who always wiped her eyes, "Yip-i-addy-i-ay" for Bill, and "*Kind, Du Kannst Tanzen*" for Mr. Beidwinkle, who chuckled and said, "Gollee."

Betsy went upstairs and into her little room smiling. It was cold, but she didn't mind. Without lighting the lamp, she sat down by the window and looked out at the ghostly landscape.

She was glad she had studied German. There had been such satisfaction in being able to talk a little with the Beidwinkles. And she was glad that when Julia went away, she had learned to play the piano! She would never play well, she knew. She could never sing like Julia. She didn't even want to; she wanted to write stories. But how pleasant it was to be able to play enough to give pleasure to people!

"I'm going to write Miss Cobb and tell her. She'll be glad to hear."

Her thoughts turned to Leonard. She had thought

about him when she was out walking today. She felt a little better about Leonard out here in the country. It was just being close to nature, she supposed. In the country you felt as you never could in town the return of spring after winter. You felt a sort of pulse in the earth, which proved that nothing dies, that everything comes back in beauty.

Leonard was coming back . . . in some place beautiful enough to pay him for leaving the world. God knew all about his music, too. He would use that music someplace.

"I should have known that in church Easter morning. I'm surprised that I didn't. But I was awfully mixed up."

She was thankful to her father for having sent her out here. The trip had already given her perspective. The problems about Tony didn't seem so difficult now. There would be some way to get back to the old loving friendship.

The days fell into a pattern similar to the pattern of the first day. Betsy had her first breakfast with Mrs. Beidwinkle's second. She took a walk every morning and every afternoon, going farther and farther afield. The weather warmed up, melting the snow, so that there was a terrible mixture of ice, slush, and water underfoot. But there were compensations.

There was the vivid spring sky. There was the

spring taste in the air. There were buds swelling on the trees in the wood lot, and white bloodroots, pink and lavender hepaticas under wet mats of last year's leaves. There were meadow larks rising with a flash of yellow to sing in a rapture that made one catch one's breath.

She finished her first story and began a second one. She finished the second and began a third. She and the Beidwinkles talked in German every night at supper. Mrs. Beidwinkle taught her a poem in German which she recited to uproarious applause. Every evening she went into the parlor and played the organ and sang.

She wasn't homesick. She remembered how homesick she had been at the Taggarts' farm four years ago. That farm had been just as nice; the Taggarts had been just as kind as Mr. and Mrs. Beidwinkle. But she had suffered so much with homesickness that for months the mere memory of it had filled her with desolation. Now she was happy from morning until night.

"You do grow up," she thought.

It was pleasant to talk with her mother, who telephoned sometimes in the evening. And she had letters from Tacy and Tib. But the letters seemed to come from a great distance. She had forgotten the woes which had weighed her down at home.

"Betsy," Mrs. Beidwinkle said on Friday at dinner. "We would like to have a little party before you go home."

"A party?" asked Betsy, startled. The word surprised her. She associated parties with the Crowd and Deep Valley, not this peaceful haven.

She saw that Mr. Beidwinkle and Bill were watching her eagerly. Mrs. Beidwinkle looked as pleased as a child.

"*Ja,*" she said. "We would like to invite Amelia and her husband to come and hear you sing."

"To hear me *sing?*"

"*Ja,*" said Mrs. Beidwinkle. "On Saturday night. We'll have refreshments. It will be a regular party."

Betsy knew then why she had brought the white wool dress!

That evening Mr. Beidwinkle remarked, "Tomorrow's Saturday. Mamma usually goes to town with me on Saturday. Would you like to go along?"

"To town?" asked Betsy, startled.

"To Butternut Center. We buy at Willard's Emporium, there."

Somewhat to the Beidwinkles' mystification, Betsy blushed. Her heart began to pound inside her shirt waist. Willard's Emporium! She might see Joe! She wanted to see him, but she didn't want to seem to be running after him. He knew she knew that he spent his vacations with his uncle and aunt in Butternut Center.

That was where she had seen him first, four years ago, when she was taking the train home after her visit with the Taggarts. It was a very little village, just a depot and a grain elevator, a white church, a sprinkling of houses, and a general store. The store was Willard's Emporium, where she had gone to buy presents for her family.

Joe had waited on her. She had been struck by the way he walked, with a slight challenging swing. She remembered his very light hair brushed back in a pompadour, his blue eyes under thick light brows, his lower lip pushed out as though seeming to dare the world to knock the chip off his shoulder.

He had been reading *The Three Musketeers*, she remembered, but he had put it aside when she said that she was going to buy presents. He had been amused at her statement that no Ray ever came home from a trip without bringing presents for the rest.

No Ray . . . ever came home from a trip . . . without bringing presents! Suddenly Betsy's heart raced faster. Why, she was away on a trip! She would have to buy presents. She simply had to go to Willard's Emporium.

Looking up, her cheeks still flushed, her eyes dancing, she replied, "Of course. I'd love to go. How early do we start?"

20

Butternut Center

IT WAS VERY EARLY, still dark and cold, when Mrs. Beidwinkle knocked at Betsy's door. That morning springtime concert of the birds, to which Betsy had become accustomed during her week at the farm, was more uproarious even than usual. It sounded like a contest, but a contest without rules or regulations. Each bird was trying to sing down every other bird, caroling, warbling, whistling, some humble anonymous performers chirping wildly, while others executed elaborate arias.

Lighting the lamp, she dressed quickly. She put on the plaid skirt and the red blouse, of course, braided her hair, looped it up with the red ribbon. It hadn't been put up in Wavers all week. She had forgotten about Magic Wavers.

Still sleepy, she stumbled downstairs into the kitchen. The coffee, freshly made, was stimulating and delicious. She put on her red tam and cravenette and high buckled overshoes and went out into the barnyard.

The world was still gray, but the east was a river of crimson. It seemed strange to see the windmill whirling against that lurid sky. A team of horses was pawing the ground in front of a wagon full of milk cans. Mrs. Beidwinkle was critically directing the addition of a case full of eggs. The egg money went to Mrs. Beidwinkle; she didn't want any eggs broken.

Mr. Beidwinkle helped Betsy to a box covered with a rug, which was placed just behind the high seat. "I'll bet you never rode to town with milk cans before," he said.

He and Mrs. Beidwinkle climbed into the seat, he clucked to the horses, and they were off.

It hadn't frozen the night before, Mr. Beidwinkle

pointed out. Yesterday's pools and puddles were pools and puddles still. The road was very muddy. Down and up, down and up went the heavy wheels, making a sucking sound, and Betsy would have bounced on her box if she hadn't held fast to the seat in front of her. Slowly the sky paled and light spread over the prairie.

Mile after gray-white mile slipped past: frozen fields which would soon be ready for the sowing; planted groves of trees which would soon be green; orchards which would soon be fragrant bowers of pink and white. Farm houses were flanked with big red barns, granaries, and silos. At last they saw an elevator sticking up over the prairie ahead.

In Butternut Center, Mr. Beidwinkle went first to the depot and unloaded the milk cans. Then he drove down the street to Willard's Emporium, and with Mrs. Beidwinkle watching, unloaded the eggs.

Betsy scrambled down from her box and went into the store. Excitement fluttered inside her as she went, but Joe wasn't there. Probably he hadn't come out this week. Probably he was working at the *Sun*. She realized with a pang of disappointment how much she had counted on seeing him.

Mr. Beidwinkle had disappeared. Mrs. Beidwinkle was now supervising the counting of her eggs by a tall, square-faced man, Joe's Uncle Alvin, probably. Well,

Betsy thought, she must buy the presents whether Joe was there or not, and she started browsing along the overflowing counters.

Willard's Emporium seemed to have everything under the sun for sale. Kitchen stoves, straw hats, clocks, calico, buggy whips. She remembered how Joe had helped her buy cheese for her father, a butter dish for her mother, side combs for Julia, doll dishes for Margaret, a mouth organ for Tacy.

She paused before a case full of china and looked at a little speckled vase. That would be nice for the wild flowers Margaret would soon start bringing home from the hills.

She felt someone looking at her and turned to see Joe.

His blue eyes, under those heavy brows, were boring into her. His lower lip looked defiant, and so did the swinging walk with which he came toward her. She blushed.

"What are you doing here?" Joe asked. His tone was almost rough.

"Don't act as though you were going to put me out," she said. "I'm buying presents to take home to my family."

"Oh." He seemed nonplused.

"The Rays always take presents home when they've been away on a visit."

"Oh."

"It's an old family custom," Betsy said, and smiled.

Joe looked odd. Something in his face seemed to melt. He didn't smile, though.

Betsy kept on talking. "I've picked out this little vase for Mamma. Don't you think it's nice? But what do you suppose Papa would like? Now don't say cheese again!"

Joe smiled. And when he smiled there were the most attractive, warming crinkles in his face. One of them looked almost like a dimple, but you didn't associate dimples with Joe Willard. His eyes began to shine.

"How about tobacco? Pipe tobacco? Willard's Emporium will throw in some pipe cleaners in honor of . . . in honor of . . . well, to be brief, we'll throw in some pipe cleaners."

"That's fine," said Betsy. "Now, Margaret likes things for her room."

"How about a calendar? Here's one full of dogs and cats. This ought to suit her."

"Yes. This will do." Betsy kept her eyes lowered longer than she needed to, the expression in his eyes was so disturbing.

"When you were here before, you bought something for Tacy, too."

"Of course. I want something for Tacy and Tib."

"Lollipops. A pink one and a yellow one."

She looked up to laugh. Joe's face was alight and glowing.

"You staying with the Taggarts?" he asked, coming nearer.

"No. The Beidwinkles." She nodded to Mrs. Beidwinkle, who had disposed of her eggs and was buying groceries now. Her purchases bulked so large on the counter that it looked as though she were going to start a store herself.

"I adore the Beidwinkles," said Betsy.

"I adore Mrs. Beidwinkle myself. What's more, she adores me."

He went swinging toward her, and Betsy followed.

Mrs. Beidwinkle's face did indeed wreathe itself in smiles when Joe spoke. "How do you do, Mrs. Beidwinkle. How are you today?"

"Hello, Joe," she said. "Do you know Betsy?"

"We're classmates," Betsy put in.

"She's terrible in school," Joe said. "How does she behave at your house, Mrs. Beidwinkle?"

Mrs. Beidwinkle frowned at him. "She behaves like a nice little girl. She wipes the dishes and sings for us every night. We wish she stayed with us all the time."

Joe turned to Betsy. "A good report! I never expected it."

"Mrs. Beidwinkle," he said, turning back to her, "won't you let me see Betsy home? There are some places around here I'd like to show her. Maybe my uncle would loan me the phaeton."

Mrs. Beidwinkle beamed. "Why, of course," she said. "I don't mind at all. In fact, I'd just as soon have Betsy out of the way today."

"Aha!" cried Joe. "I knew that report was too good to be true. What does she do? Bite her nails? Track in on your floor?"

Mrs. Beidwinkle pushed him, laughing. "*Dummkopf!* Nothing like that. Betsy knows, or she can guess."

Betsy raced after Joe, while he searched out a youth named Homer. Homer, looking at Betsy curiously, promised to take Joe's place at the store.

They raced back to the square-faced man who had been waiting on Mrs. Beidwinkle. He *was* Uncle Alvin, but he didn't look at all like Joe. Joe introduced Betsy and then nudged her to retreat. He returned to her, smiling.

"Uncle Alvin says I may drive you home."

They raced up some stairs which ran from the street to the second floor. There was a small parlor, as crowded as the store beneath, but with fat chairs and sofas covered with tidies, and embroidered sofa cushions. Betsy met Aunt Ruth, who was spare, sad, and kind. They clattered down the stairs again.

"I have an idea," said Joe.

"What is it?"

"Haven't I heard you say you like picnics?"

"Joe!"

"Then we'll take along some crackers and cheese."

"And olives and cookies . . . Nabisco wafers, maybe, and that kind with marshmallows on top."

"Why, you little glutton! I'll slice some bologna, too. What else shall we take?"

"A bottle of milk," said Betsy. "If you can borrow some cups."

"Of course I can," said Joe, and went clattering back upstairs.

He left Betsy again to hitch up the horse. She went happily around the store until he returned with a stocky cream-colored animal hitched to a buggy with a fringed adjustable top.

"Rocinante," said Joe, helping her in. "Ever read *Don Quixote*? Do you get these literary allusions?"

They put the top down. They wanted the whole width of the sky from end to end, the whole width of the flat prairie landscape.

With their basket and Betsy's presents at their feet, they drove down the single street, which was all of Butternut Center. The muddy road was very muddy, so that the buggy lurched in and out of holes. But Joe and Betsy didn't mind.

They didn't mind anything. They didn't mention Tony or their quarrel. Their happiness overflowed the phaeton and ran like spilled water to the edge of the horizon on both sides.

"Joe," Betsy said, "you don't look like your uncle."

"No. I look like my mother's people. He's my father's brother. My father," Joe went on, "died when I was a baby. He was a lumberman, yanked down trees in the north woods. I've always been strong as a horse, and I guess it's because of him."

"How did your mother look?" asked Betsy.

Joe paused before he answered.

"She was beautiful," he said slowly, at last. "People toss that word around a lot, but my mother really was. She had dark golden hair and blue, blue eyes and the reddest, sweetest lips I ever saw.

"She was a dressmaker . . . after Father died, that is. She worked hard; too hard. I can still hear that sewing machine. I tried to help when I got old enough, but I couldn't do much."

"What did you do?" Betsy asked.

"Sold papers at first." He paused as his thoughts went back. "Once, when I was about nine, I lost my route list. I borrowed a bike from another boy to go back and find it. When I returned the bike and thanked him, I offered to shake hands. I thought, from the books I had read, that that was the proper thing to do. But all the boys hooted. I'll never forget it."

He looked at her suddenly. "I never told that to anyone before."

Betsy didn't answer.

❦ 553 ❦

"Mother was a great one for books, too," Joe continued. "She's the one I get my love of writing from. I found poems and unfinished stories and bits of description among her things after she died."

"How old were you then?"

"I was twelve. Uncle Alvin is the only relative I have on either side. He and Aunt Ruth gave me a home and I helped them in the store until I was fourteen and finished country school. I had to come to Deep Valley then, to high school."

"I'm glad you did," said Betsy.

They drove on and on. No matter how far they drove, there was no variety in the landscape. It was just prairie, poles, and wires! Prairie, poles, and wires! But there were song sparrows trilling on the wires. There was heavenly warmth in the air.

It grew so warm that Betsy took off her cravenette, her tam.

Joe turned and looked at her. His eyes studied the red hair ribbon.

"You look different," he said.

"That's right," Betsy replied.

"Your hair isn't curled. Do you know," he continued, studying her critically, "I like your hair straight."

He liked her hair straight! If he had looked through all the poetry books in the world he couldn't have found a better compliment to pay her.

Joe wanted to know when they ate, and they

stopped Rocinante at a point where a brook, just unfrozen, babbled with frantic joy over brown leaves. He unfastened the horse's checkrein and gave him some oats. He took out their basket and they found a large rock which provided a seat a little above the soggy ground. There they ate their bread and cheese and bologna and olives and cookies, smiling at each other.

"Do you know," Betsy said, "this is the first picnic I've ever been on with you? That seems strange, for picnics are so important and . . ." She blushed.

"Go on," said Joe, "finish it."

Betsy didn't answer.

"Why are picnics so important? I know why I am, of course."

"They just are. There's nothing so nice as eating out of doors. And I've discovered since I've been visiting the Beidwinkles that I like to live in the country. I shouldn't like to be a farmer's wife. I'd be no good at it. But to have a house in the country and write would be nice."

"Very nice," said Joe.

They started riding again, and Betsy realized suddenly that the sun was getting low. She remarked that she liked sunsets almost as well as she liked picnics.

"We'll ride until the sun sets, then. What else do you like?"

"Sunrises. But I don't see very many of them."

"What else?"

"Oh, dancing, and writing stories, and reading. I've been reading *Little Dorrit*. Have you read it?"

"You haven't said the right thing yet."

They stopped Rocinante to watch the sunset. Rows of clouds made a pearly accordion, the creases touched with gold.

Mrs. Beidwinkle met them at the kitchen door.

"Well!" she said. "I thought you were lost, for sure. I was just going to send Bill out looking for you."

"All my fault, Mrs. Beidwinkle," Joe replied.

"I'm sure it was your fault. Betsy, come here!"

Betsy came there and Mrs. Beidwinkle whispered in her ear.

"Maybe," she said, "Joe would like to come to the party?"

Betsy smiled and gave the invitation. Joe accepted.

It was a wonderful party. Betsy had never been to a party quite like it. They had supper first—Joe stayed for supper—and Rocinante had supper in Mr. Beidwinkle's barn. After supper, Betsy washed the dishes, then went upstairs to put on her white wool dress.

Mrs. Beidwinkle wore her Sunday black silk dress with a brooch at the neck. Mr. Beidwinkle wore his Sunday black. Bill put on a paper collar and loaned a tie to Joe.

In the back parlor, a table was spread with a hand-embroidered cloth. Mrs. Beidwinkle set out bottles of beer and soda pop, rye bread with caraway seeds, thin slices of sausage, Dutch cheese, egg salad, and cake, cookies, and a jelly roll she had baked the previous day. She had made ice cream, too, she said, but she wouldn't bring that out until they were ready to eat.

The Beidwinkles' daughter and her husband arrived. Amelia, in a flower-sprigged dress, her husband, red-faced and suspicious, in a high choker collar. Betsy, in the white wool dress, feeling like a visiting countess, sat and talked with them.

They went into the parlor and looked at the photograph album. Betsy showed Joe all the bearded men, the anxious ladies, the stiff boys and girls in the album. They looked through the stereopticon set at views of the Holy Land, Niagara Falls, Europe with Side Trips to Egypt, Algeria, and the Madeira Islands.

At last Mr. Beidwinkle said, "How about some music?"

Betsy wondered for a panicky moment whether she could play the prima donna in front of Joe, but she certainly couldn't refuse. Her singing was the whole reason for the party. So she went to the organ.

She urged Amelia and her husband and Joe to join in, which they presently did. Amelia's husband, it developed, loved to sing. He took off his stiff collar and sang with a will. They sang Betsy's repertoire of songs not once, but twice, three times, while Mr. Beidwinkle and Bill sipped their beer contentedly and listened. At the end Betsy had to sing alone: "Yip-i-addy-i-ay" for Bill, and "Tonight Will Never Come Again" for Mrs. Beidwinkle who wiped her eyes, of course, and "*Kind, Du Kannst Tanzen*" for Mr. Beidwinkle, who laughed and said, "Gollee!"

Then they went to the parlor and had ice cream and cake and cookies and jelly roll and soda pop and rye bread and egg salad and sausage and cheese.

They ate and ate until Amelia and her husband said they must go home and Joe said that he must go, too. The others looked tactfully away while he said good-by.

"Be back for school Monday?"

"Yes. I'm going back tomorrow night. Papa's driving out for me."

"See you in Deep Valley then."

"See you in Deep Valley."

He looked into her eyes very hard, with his blue eyes which looked so bright and happy. He shook hands with her hard. Then he was gone.

21

No Ivy Green

ON MONDAY, MISS RAYMOND, who directed the high school chorus, announced that there would be a rehearsal after school. It was time, she said, to begin work on Commencement music. This made all the seniors look self-conscious.

"Commencement!" Tacy leaned across the aisle to groan.

"It's creeping up on us!"

Betsy welcomed the rehearsal because it would give her a chance to talk to Tony. She had come back from the Beidwinkles' determined to talk with him frankly. He realized now that she didn't care for him in a romantic way, and probably he would soon get over that feeling about her. She wanted to tell him that they must keep on being friends, good friends.

She looked for him while they were waiting for rehearsal to begin, but he was elusive. He took his place with the basses at once, instead of fooling around with the girls, as he usually did. She would see him at the end, Betsy decided, and at last Miss Raymond got the chattering group quiet.

She announced the numbers they would sing for Commencement . . . Schubert's "Hark! Hark! The Lark!" and a musical setting of Dickens' poem about the ivy.

"It has a bass solo in it and, of course, Tony Markham must sing that," said Miss Raymond, smiling. Since *Up and Down Broadway* Tony's reputation as a singer had expanded.

The words of "The Ivy Green" were grim.

> *"Oh, a dainty plant is the ivy green,*
> *That creepeth o'er ruins old!*
> *And right choice foods are his meals, I wean,*
> *In his cell so lone and cold. . . ."*

Betsy and Tacy looked at each other and shivered.

"Why the dickens did Miss Raymond choose that?" Betsy whispered. But when Tony's voice rolled out in the solo she knew why.

> "*Creeping where no life is seen,*
> *A rare old plant is the ivy green.*"

It was perfect for his deep-pitched velvety voice.

At the end of rehearsal, Betsy blocked his way into the cloakroom with a casual joking remark. But Tony was unresponsive. His big, sleepy eyes that had always looked at her so laughingly, so teasingly, were cold. They didn't look like Tony's eyes at all.

He had more poise than Betsy had. She couldn't keep acting flippant in the face of that cold gaze. She blurted out her message without preparation.

"Tony, I want to talk with you. I want to straighten things out between us."

"Nothing needs any straightening out."

"Yes, it does. Will you come up to see me tonight?"

"Sorry. I'm busy."

"Tomorrow night?"

"Tomorrow night I'm even busier."

He left her abruptly. She would have to wait for another chance, she thought, turning away.

But no other chance came. For now Betsy and Joe started going together—in earnest. Things were different from what they had been back in the autumn. Then when they were together they had spent their time mostly talking about books and school. Joe had plainly enjoyed her. He had reveled in the company of a girl whom he liked wholeheartedly and who he knew liked him. But except for gay extravagant compliments, he had never talked personalities.

Now he was crazy about Betsy and didn't care who knew it.

The whole school knew it. The school was electric with it as schools are sometimes with affairs of that sort. The truth was in Betsy's eyes and Joe's, in the way they passed notes, and met after classes, and lingered in the halls. At the library, where they were studying for the Essay Contest, Miss Sparrow regarded them fondly. They strolled back to the Ray house slowly, through the purple spring twilights.

Tony didn't telephone Betsy nor come to see her. He hadn't been at the house since she returned from the Beidwinkles'. Margaret had asked for him at first; now she only looked at Betsy with grave accusing eyes.

Betsy's eighteenth birthday came along. She received a jade ring in a silver setting from her father, engraved calling cards from her mother.

"Miss Betsy Warrington Ray," they said.

Margaret gave her a burned wood hand-mirror. She had made it herself in school.

From Joe came a dozen red roses. Betsy put them in a big vase on the parlor table. She put one in her hair when Tacy and Tib came for supper-with-birthday-cake. She put one in a bud vase beside her bed and sniffed it rapturously before she went to sleep.

At the last Zetamathian Rhetoricals, Betsy and Tacy sang their Cat Duet. They had sung it every year since they were in the fifth grade and the audience now joined in the caterwauls. But Tony didn't laugh. Looking in exasperation at his sullen face, Betsy resolved again to talk with him. She would do it Friday at the senior-faculty picnic.

"And nothing will stop me!" she declared.

Friday proved to be an ideal day for their famous annual picnic. The weather was so tantalizingly warm that even if they had been in school they couldn't have kept their minds on their books. At Page Park, the willows on the river bank were covered with tiny leaves. Birds were singing; the picnic ground was strewn with dandelions; and the seniors were wearing their gray and violet skull caps.

It was strange to be mingling, almost on an equal footing, with the teachers. The seniors paid their respects to Miss Bangeter in pairs, but they were flippant with the others.

Winona flirted openly with Stewie. Betsy tried out her broken German on Miss Erickson. She and Tacy told curly-haired Miss O'Rourke that they had memorized all their geometry propositions without understanding them. She chased them with a switch.

Betsy and Joe went up to Mr. Gaston. "Seen any apple blossoms lately?"

Betsy had quarreled with Mr. Gaston in her sophomore year about the color of apple blossoms. Tib, always daring, even mentioned the herbariums she and Betsy and Tacy had made once under strange conditions.

The seniors had provided overflowing baskets and they ate at the long wooden tables. They swung, they waded in the river and skipped stones. The senior boys challenged the men teachers to a baseball game. Joe pitched; he was good, too, Betsy noticed.

It was a notable senior-faculty picnic. But Betsy didn't speak to Tony for the reason that he wasn't there.

On Saturday he wasn't at the Inter-Society Track Meet. The Zets won. The Philos had already won the athletics cup, so the Essay Contest was of vital importance to both sides now.

Sunday evening Margaret came running upstairs and burst into Betsy's room, her eyes glowing.

"Betsy! Tony's here. He's come for lunch."

"Really?" Betsy swooped down to give Margaret a hug. Running downstairs, she remembered that Joe wasn't coming. He was covering a Christian Endeavor convention which was meeting in Deep Valley. Perhaps Tony had known that Joe wouldn't be there? But as soon as she saw him she knew that it wouldn't have mattered. He was the old Tony.

He had Washington on his shoulder and Abie followed at his heels. He greeted Betsy carelessly, annexed Margaret's hand, and strolled out to the sandwich-making. He himself made the coffee.

"You're sure of a good cup of coffee tonight," he joked with Mrs. Ray.

He was oblivious to the excitement his presence caused when the Crowd started drifting in.

Winona played the piano, and the Crowd sang. Harmonizing voices rolled out the open windows into the soft spring night: "My wild Irish rose. . . ." "I wonder who's kissing her now. . . ."

"What's the use of dreaming. . . ." Tony sang that alone, by request, straddling a chair as he had done in *Up and Down Broadway*.

> *"What's the use of dreaming,*
> *Dreams of rosy hue,*
> *What's the use of dreaming, dreaming,*
> *Dreams that never could come true. . . ."*

It was wonderful to have Tony back, and acting just like himself.

When he out-stayed the others, Betsy began to worry. Maybe that frightening ardor would return when they were alone? But it didn't. They did the dishes. Tony scraped and washed, Betsy wiped, and they talked and joked as usual.

Here was her chance, she thought, to make that speech she had planned. But she hated to break the mood of the evening with a speech. Moreover, it seemed unnecessary with Tony's attitude so matter-of-fact.

They returned to the parlor, and Tony went to the pile of photographs lying on the table, class photographs with the seal of the class in the upper left hand corner. They had been delivered the day before, and the Crowd had been busily exchanging them. Tony had not asked for one of Betsy's, but he looked them over now.

The large beautiful one, taken in the blue Class Day dress. The small Betsyish one, taken in a shirt waist.

"Do I rate one of these?" Tony asked.

"Of course," Betsy replied. "And you're going to give me one of yours."

"Heck!" said Tony. "I didn't sit for one."

"You didn't . . . sit for one! Why, Tony Markham! How can you graduate without a class picture?"

"You'd be surprised."

"Which one do you want?" Betsy asked. "The big one or the little one?"

"The little one."

"The big one is much prettier."

"But it doesn't look like you."

"Oh, thanks," mocked Betsy.

"Sorry," said Tony. "Is it my fault if you're not good-looking?"

It was the old Tony come back, and Betsy felt a weight lift from her heart. But when they said good night she discovered that it wasn't the old Tony after all.

She strolled out on the porch with him, as she had done a thousand times. The stars were low and bright over the German Catholic College. Tony was telling her that he had hopped a freight and gone up to Minneapolis with his brakeman friend on Friday. That was why he hadn't been at the picnic.

"I wish you wouldn't do that, Tony," Betsy said. "I'm like Papa. I worry for fear you'll lose a leg."

"All right," said Tony. "I can almost promise you I won't do it again."

"You can?" Betsy asked, delighted.

"Almost," said Tony. "Well, good-by, Ray of Sunshine." And to Betsy's surprise he kissed her. He didn't ask if he might kiss her. He merely kissed her. She was so startled that she couldn't find a word to say.

No words were necessary, for Tony swung off the porch and went down the walk. He didn't even look back until he reached the arc light. Then he turned and lifted his hand in a rakish salute.

"Good-by," he called again.

Betsy stood on the steps, disturbed and puzzled. Tony usually said "So long!" There had been something strange in the way he said "Good-by." It had been strange, too, that he kissed her.

The next day at school she looked around for him. He wasn't there. At chorus practise Miss Raymond was annoyed.

"Where is Tony Markham? Does anyone know where Tony is? We can't practice 'Ivy Green' without him."

Nobody knew.

The next day he was still not at school. He wasn't there the next day either. On Thursday there was chorus practise again.

Miss Raymond distributed copies of a new song. It was from Wagner's *Tannhäuser*—"Hark! Hear the cannons' thunder pealing."

She asked Tib to collect the copies of "The Ivy Green."

Someone waved a hand. "Why, Miss Raymond? Aren't we going to sing 'The Ivy Green'?"

"No," said Miss Raymond.

"Why not? We have it all learned."

"Tony Markham won't be here."

"Tony won't be here? Why, of course he will be! He's graduating."

Betsy felt color creeping into her neck and face.

"I understand he won't be here," Miss Raymond replied. "I can't give you any details."

After chorus practise, Betsy sought Miss Clarke. Miss Bangeter was the one to ask, of course, but she was too awesome. Miss Clarke could always be approached.

"Miss Clarke, do you know what's happened to Tony Markham? Miss Raymond says he won't be graduating."

"That's true," Miss Clarke answered. She took off her glasses and polished them nervously. "Tony's gone away."

"But where?"

"Nobody knows. He's gone away, that's all."

Betsy looked into her face with entreaty. "But what do they think? Has his mother told Miss Bangeter? Tony's a very, very dear friend of mine. I didn't know he was going away."

Miss Clarke hesitated. She lowered her voice.

"Yes, his mother has talked to Miss Bangeter. But she doesn't know where Tony has gone. He left a note and told her not to worry."

"Could he have graduated? Were his grades all right?"

"I think so."

"I'm so sorry. I'm so sorry," Betsy said.

She thanked Miss Clarke and went out of the room, out of the building, down to the street. Tony was gone, and nobody knew where. Betsy didn't see exactly what she had done that was wrong, but she felt to blame. She had a lump in her throat.

Two things comforted her. Tony had said he wasn't going to be stealing rides on the freight cars any more. That meant, Betsy reasoned, that he had some sort of a job.

And the kiss he had given her! It hadn't seemed angry or accusing or desperate. It had been gentle, it had been loving. But it had definitely, she realized, been good-by.

22

Surprises

IT WAS HARD telling the family about Tony.

Anna cried sadly, "Stars in the sky! We'll never see him again!" Mrs. Ray exclaimed, "Oh, his poor mother!" Mr. Ray said with stout optimism, "He'll be back! Don't worry!" But his face was sober. Margaret got up and went to her room and shut the door.

The other Rays looked at each other.

"You'd better go to her, Betsy," Mrs. Ray said. For Margaret talked more freely to Betsy than to anyone else in the family, although even Betsy didn't understand her very well.

Betsy waited a little while, then followed her upstairs, knocked on the door, and went in.

Margaret was sitting very straight in her little chair. Her eyes were red. Betsy sank to the floor and put her arms around her.

"Margaret! You know, I love Tony, too."

"I thought you *didn't* love him," said Margaret in a choked voice. "I heard Mamma say that just the other day. She said that was the reason he'd stopped coming here."

"But I do love him," Betsy insisted. "You know, Margaret, there are lots of kinds of love in the world. I love him in a different way from the way he loves me, that's all. I feel badly, too, about his going away."

Margaret was silent a moment. Then she put her hand into Betsy's. "Where do you suppose he's gone?"

"I don't know," answered Betsy. "But I know one thing, Margaret. He's not hopping freight trains."

"How do you know that?"

Betsy told her about the promise. Margaret's small tense faced smoothed out a little.

"And I'm like Papa," Betsy continued. "I think we'll hear from him."

"Do you?" asked Margaret.

"Yes, I do. We'll hear. You wait and see."

She tried to believe this and be happy as May came in with all its sweetness. Dooryards smelled entrancingly of lilacs; hillsides smelled of the wild plums in dazzling snowy bloom. Warmth came suddenly. One day the girls were wearing their spring coats; the next, they were in thin dresses.

Betsy had two new gingham dresses. One was blue, the other a gay red plaid. She wore them both with the big straw hat covered with red poppies and had never, Anna said, looked punier.

And one Saturday morning, Joe called for her to go to the high school and write the Essay Contest.

Joe didn't give a hang about the Essay Contest. He had, Betsy realized, a different attitude from hers about high school. It was more the attitude Julia had had. He was looking ahead to his own Great World, to the University, the Minneapolis *Tribune*.

High school was still important to Betsy. The Essay Contest was important. She assumed that Joe would win, but as a loyal Zetamathian she was going to try her hardest.

"I'll do my best, too," Joe said. "But how can I think about 'Conservation of Our Natural Resources' when it's so much more interesting thinking about Betsy?"

The high school was empty except for Miss Clarke and Miss O'Rourke, waiting, of course, in the upper hall.

"All notes and books must be left here," Miss Clarke said, as usual.

Betsy waved her pen and Joe jokingly pushed up his cuffs to show that he had no notes concealed. They went into the algebra classroom where two juniors, two sophomores, and two freshmen were already seated. The bell rang and they started to write.

Joe finished first, but when Betsy came out he was waiting for her.

"I did my best," he said, "for the sake of dear old Philo. But somehow I have a notion my essay isn't much good. It seemed to get all mixed up with Betsy. The color of her hair. The way she blushes. The way she sings when she dances. I just couldn't seem to get going."

"Well, I did," said Betsy. "But I don't believe a word you say. I think I'll have the unutterable chagrin of losing again to Joseph Willard."

With the Essay Contest out of the way, they had to think about Commencement orations. Betsy chose for her subject "The Heroines of Shakespeare," and began to reread Shakespeare's plays.

Joe's subject was "The Bread Basket of the World." He wasn't doing much research. He had done it in harvest fields, he said, from Texas to North Dakota. He was already writing.

Tib was practising for the class play, *A Fatal Message*; Tacy was practising her Commencement solo.

> *"Sylvia, take the lily, daffodil,*
> *Sylvia, take whate'er the garden grows,*
> *But Sylvia only shook her pretty head*
> *As she picked a simple wild red rose. . . ."*

And all of them being members of the chorus were practising madly on "Hark! Hark! The Lark!" and "Hark! Hear the cannons' thunder pealing."

"Lots of Harks!" Tacy remarked.

To make life even more exciting, graduation presents began coming in. They came by every mail and were brought by friends every day. Betsy had received a Prayer Book and Hymnal, a hand-embroidered corset cover, a blue silk party bag, beauty pins, Dutch collars, a little silver pin tray, the U. of M. Gopher.

Everyone was cramming, too, for final examinations, and these at last arrived. The seniors shuddered when they thought how awful it would be if they didn't pass.

"To think of being flunked out *now*!" they cried.

Now Betsy's oration was finished and she was learning it.

"The heroines of Shakespeare are essentially human," she chanted all day long. She asked Joe, "What's your opening line?"

"I let Walt Whitman write it," he answered, grinning. But he didn't say what it was.

Festivities opened, of course, with the junior-senior banquet.

"Remember how hard we worked last year?" Betsy, Tacy, Tib, and Hazel asked each other.

The juniors had been working feverishly for days, and on the big night the high school was turned into a street fair with booths. Frankfurters were made of red tissue paper with fortunes inside. Betsy's said she was going to live on a farm.

Following Joe's lead the year before, the menu was full of literary allusions.

> "... *sit down; at first and last,*
> *the hearty welcome.*"
> —SHAKESPEARE

And the dinner was marvelous, beginning with fruit punch, and ending with demitasse and 1910 mints. In between were prime rib roast of beef, asparagus, fruit salad, and other good things.

There were toasts. Joe, of course, spoke for the seniors. And the toasts were followed by dancing. Betsy wore the pale blue Class Day dress, Tacy wore pale green, and Tib wore lavender.

The next day was Betsy's last day of real school. She said so that night at supper.

"What did you do?" her father asked.

"Oh, finished my physics notebook, practised my oration for Miss O'Rourke, opened presents, and wept."

Mr. Ray got up abruptly and went into the parlor. He had been acting strangely for several days. He had been too cheerful, which usually meant that he was worried about something. He had gone around the house whistling, but with a little line between his brows.

"I believe Papa hates to see you graduate," Mrs. Ray said in a low tone.

"Maybe he's lonesome for Julia," whispered Betsy. "It's an awfully long time since we had a letter."

Mr. Ray suddenly reappeared in the doorway.

"Do you like surprises?" he asked, looking at the group around the table.

For a moment they were too startled to reply.

"You know I don't," Mrs. Ray said at last.

"Neither do I," said Betsy.

"I do sometimes," said Margaret. "But not after I know there is one. Then I can't bear to wait. What is it, Papa?"

The line between his brows melted away.

"Julia," he said, smiling broadly, "is on the bounding billows."

"Julia!" Mrs. Ray stared in stupefaction. Betsy jumped up and began to scream. Margaret was too ladylike for that, but she hugged Betsy.

Anna came running into the dining room. "Stars in the sky! What's going on here?"

"Anna!" gasped Mrs. Ray. "Julia . . . Julia. . . ." Then Mrs. Ray began to cry and Mr. Ray went around the table and hugged her.

"Julia's on the way home," he explained to Anna. "She wrote me at the store, and told me not to tell anyone. But Jule doesn't like surprises."

"Oh, Bob! Bob! Oh, Anna! Anna!" Mrs. Ray wept, and Anna came around the table to help hug her.

"Of course she doesn't like surprises, my poor lovey! We have to clean this house, if Julia's coming. Don't we, Mrs. Ray?" Anna wiped her eyes and blew her nose.

"I know," Mr. Ray said. "That's what Julia was afraid of. You'll even scour the coal scuttle."

"When will she be here?" Betsy asked.

"Might be any day now. I don't know just what boat she's coming on. But I know she's on the way. I wrote and told her to come. She'll be going back, of course. But I thought she ought to be here to see Betsy graduate."

"She'll be here to see me graduate!" cried Betsy. She ran to telephone Tacy, Tib, and Joe. Margaret went to the piano and started practising on her new piece, "Woodland Fancies."

"I want to have it ready for Julia," she explained.

Mrs. Ray and Anna began planning. They were going to wash the curtains and bedspreads, polish the floors, polish the brass and silver.

"We'd better start baking, too."

"That spice cake Julia likes."

"And she always liked that Perfection Salad I used to make for the McCloskeys."

"But, Bob," Mrs. Ray asked suddenly, "how will we know when she's coming, if she's planning to surprise us?"

"She's going to wire me at the store the minute her boat lands," Mr. Ray replied.

Monday was Memorial Day, but the parade was abandoned because of rain. It poured from every corner of the sky. Betsy practised her oration at the Opera House in the morning, and in the afternoon she washed her hair.

The following day was the Assembly at which the Essay Cup would be awarded. The day after that was Class Day. And the day after the day after that was June third, Commencement Day itself. If Betsy's hair was going to be soft and shiny for this great week, it must be washed, rain or no rain.

There was one advantage in the downpour. It made visitors so unlikely that Mrs. Ray and Anna decided to continue their cleaning into the afternoon.

"After all, we don't know how many days we'll have. That wire might come any time."

"I'll bathe Abie," said Margaret, "to get him ready."

Mr. Ray was at home from the store on account of the holiday. He retreated with his cigar to the bedroom. Mrs. Ray, still in a house dress, was polishing silver, Anna was washing windows, Betsy was drying her hair, and Margaret was rinsing Abie when the front doorbell rang.

"The hack's out in front," Anna said.

"Who under the sun could be coming in this rain! You'll have to answer, Bob," Mrs. Ray called, closing the door which led into the kitchen. She didn't close it entirely. She peeked around it. Anna peeked in from the parlor, and Betsy and Margaret peeked down the stairs.

Mr. Ray opened the door, and in walked Julia!

The Rays forgot all about not liking to be surprised. They smothered Julia with kisses. Mr. Ray broke away only to pay Mr. Thumbler and bring her suitcases and trunk into the hall.

Julia had changed.

"You're fat! You're fat as a roll of butter!" Mrs. Ray cried.

"The Von Hetternichs eat all the time. Besides, Fraulein wants me fat. I have to be fat to sing opera," Julia said.

"You look cute," Betsy said. She did.

"Let me see my baby sister," Julia cried.

Margaret stepped proudly forward.

"Why, she's grown tall! Bettina! Stop rubbing your hair and let me look at you."

"Did you know," joked Betsy, "that people were wearing their hair this way? Wet, I mean. It's all the rage in Paris."

"Speaking of Paris," said Julia, "open my trunk! I brought something from Paris for your graduation outfit."

Mr. Ray unlocked the trunk and as Julia hunted through it, flinging things in all directions, they all watched her. She looked very different; and not only because she was plump. She looked foreign. She looked fascinating. She wore earrings!

There were presents for everyone. Paris waists for Mrs. Ray and Betsy. Betsy's was a pleated pink silk. There was a German doll for Margaret, a musical jewel box for Anna, a Meerschaum pipe for Mr. Ray.

Mrs. Ray forgot to change her house dress. Betsy forgot to curl her hair. Abie dried himself, running about and shaking his damp little body.

Julia went from one to another, giving them hugs and kisses.

"Oh, it's so good to be home!" she kept saying. "So good, good, good to be home!"

She went to the piano and started to play.

"How's Tony?" she called suddenly.

Silence fell into the room like a stone into a lake.

"There's bad news about Tony," Betsy began. "That is, we hope it isn't bad. But Tony's gone away."

"Where?" Julia whirled about.

"Nobody knows. He left unexpectedly."

"He'll be back," said Mr. Ray. "You know Tony. He'll show up one of these days."

"Most any day," added Mrs. Ray, with such brightness that Julia sensed a sore subject, and turned back to the piano.

Betsy told her the story that night. It was wonderful to be back in Julia's room, upon which the old gay confusion had descended. Wrapped in her kimono, Betsy sat in the window seat while Julia undressed. Then she changed to the foot of the bed and they talked till long after midnight.

Julia's comment on the situation was clean-cut.

"It's a very good thing he went away. You meant to be kind, but you weren't being kind, really, when you deceived him all year. Now that he's cut loose, he'll find himself, I'm sure. I always knew you liked Joe, Bettina."

But Betsy couldn't go into that, even with Julia.

She asked about the Von Hetternichs.

"They were wonderfully kind, but I got bored with my life there. Rich people's lives are very stuffy. I grew to love the girls, of course, but what made the winter really glorious was my work."

She talked with the old contagious enthusiasm about operas and operatic roles, where and when she would make her debut.

"It can't be for a long time. I've so much to learn. You've no idea how much."

"When are we going to hear you sing?"

"Not until I've had a chance to practise. And I want you all to understand that I'm just a beginner."

The next day the sun came out and the curtains in the Ray house were hung at sparkling windows. The kitchen was fragrant with the smell of spice cake baking. Neighbors dropped in, the Poppys, the Crowd.

A boy from Windmiller's Florist Shop came with a long box for Julia. She looked at the card.

"He's absolutely dippy," she said, throwing it down.

"Who's *he*? Who's *he*?" Betsy and Tib demanded.

"Someone I met on the boat. A New York man."

She didn't even open the box, but the others did, squealing. It held a forest of American Beauty roses.

"And I thought that for once you didn't have a beau," Betsy said jokingly.

"Well," said Julia, "I didn't in Berlin. Not exactly, that is. Of course," she added, "Else had a twin brother but he was just nineteen. And I didn't give him a bit of encouragement."

"Oh, didn't you!" Betsy scoffed.

Julia was still Julia, only more so. That night she played the piano and Betsy stood beside Joe to sing. Everything was wonderful! she thought. Julia had come home to see her graduate. She and Joe were going together. If only she could know that Tony was all right . . . somewhere!

The next day, when Betsy came home from the Opera House where she had been practising her oration, she found Margaret waiting in front of the house.

Margaret was standing as straight as a tulip, and a smile spread across her small freckled face.

"Betsy!" she cried. "I thought you'd never get home. I've had a letter from Tony."

"Margaret!" Betsy pounced upon her.

"He wants to correspond with me," said Margaret, trying not to sound proud.

"Where is he?" Betsy asked eagerly.

"He's in New York. He's an actor, like Uncle Keith."

"An actor!"

"He's on the stage, and he likes show business. He says it's the life."

Betsy sat down on the steps abruptly.

"Margaret," she said, "I don't believe I was ever so happy in my life!"

Margaret sat down beside her, after dusting off a little place to sit on and spreading the skirts of her stiffly starched gingham neatly beneath her.

"I'll read you his letter if you like," she said, drawing it out of her pocket. She did not give it to Betsy, but read it slowly and carefully aloud.

"'Dear Margaret, I wonder whether you would like to correspond with me? I'd certainly like to have some news of you and the rest of the gang.

"'I'm in New York. I'm in a musical show called *Lulu's Husbands*. I'm in the chorus now but Maxie thinks I'll be doing better soon. He thinks I can sing comic bass roles.

"'That Maxie (he's Mrs. Poppy's brother) wasn't fooling when he said he knew Broadway. I wired him from Minneapolis—couldn't do it in Deep Valley for fear of someone tattling. He said he could get me a job here, and he did.

"'Tell Betsy not to worry about my not graduating. A high school diploma doesn't matter in show business. And I like show business. It's the life! I've told my folks, and everything's hunky dory.

"'Betsy will be graduating along about now. See that she uses that curling iron! Give her my love, will you? Give my love to all the Rays. They don't make cakes like Anna's in New York or sandwiches like your father's.

"'I'm depending on you, Margaret, to tell me all the news. Love, Tony.'"

"There's a postscript, too," said Margaret, as Betsy did not speak. "He's sending me a Statue of Liberty to put on my bureau."

23

"After Commencement Day, What?"

JULIA'S FINGERS HAD LOST none of their magic when it came to dressing Betsy's hair. She dressed it in a Psyche knot—all the rage in Paris—for the Assembly Tuesday night at which the Essay Cup would be awarded. Betsy was wearing the pale blue Class Day dress, for she would be sitting on the platform, and she might . . . she just might . . . have to rise and bow as a winner.

Joe was in a fever for fear she wouldn't win.

"I can't stand it, if you don't. I'll cut my throat. Of course, you know, it's not of the slightest importance. . . ."

"Then why," Betsy wanted to know, "would you cut your throat?"

"Oh, well! I know you want to win the darn thing."

"I shan't care at all if I don't. And I don't expect to. After all, I was competing against that Joseph Willard who signs his stories for the Minneapolis *Tribune*."

But she won. Standing on the platform, before a roaring assembly, decorated in orange and turquoise blue, Betsy received her class points. Miss Bangeter smiled when she announced it.

Joe, clapping vociferously, joined in the Zetamathian cry:

"What's the matter with Betsy? She's all right."

He even started to join the chant, "Poor old Philos! Poor old Philos!" but he caught himself in time.

The Zetamathians won the cup, which gave them two out of three. All the Zets were happy about that. And other Philos than Joe were pleased that Betsy had won at last. Winona looked almost as happy as

Tacy and Tib. Miss Fowler was radiant and Miss Clarke wiped her eyes.

The next night, Class Day, was Tib's night of glory. She played the lead in *A Fatal Message* with triumphant success. The play came last on a crowded program. Preceding it, various members of the Class of 1910 delivered the Class Will, the Class Prophecy. Everyone was ribbed and slammed.

Betsy Ray was supposed to will a curling iron to a straight-haired sophomore. Tib willed all the junior boys to the junior girls. It was prophesied that Tacy would demonstrate a henna rinse, that Hazel would become the first woman president.

Cab, who had come to share in the fun, enjoyed it all hugely. He was wearing a new gray tailor-made suit.

"See?" he said to Betsy. "I can have the suit if I can't have the diploma."

He joined the Crowd, which swarmed into the Ray house afterwards for one of Julia's rarebits.

Commencement Day, that never-to-be-forgotten third of June, dawned hot.

"Shades of my ancestors!" Betsy wrote in her journal. "Such a day!"

The telephone kept ringing, for all the girls in the Crowd had to confer. The doorbell kept ringing, too, as presents arrived. There was a telegram of congratulations to Betsy from Julia's man. There were red roses from Joe.

Betsy rehearsed her oration to Miss O'Rourke in the Opera House. She rehearsed it again to Julia, who made some suggestions about putting in expression. Betsy ignored them. She went about muttering, "The heroines of Shakespeare were essentially human. . . ."

Tacy sang "Sylvia" for Julia, who gave her some pointers straight from Berlin. Tacy tried to profit by them but she was getting nervous. Her eyes had a hunted look and she swallowed with difficulty.

Tib alone was completely carefree; she had done her chore the night before.

"Nothing to do now but collect my diploma!" she said airily.

"Get out of our sight!" Betsy and Tacy moaned.

There was an early supper at the Rays', so Betsy could start dressing. This was the first appearance of the graduation dress. It was a fine white voile, trimmed with yards of lace and insertion, ankle-length, with elbow sleeves.

Her mother, Margaret, and Anna watched while Julia dressed Betsy's hair.

"Too bad to spoil it with a hat," Betsy said. But, of course, she had to. A pale blue picture hat with the sweeping pale blue plume Julia had sent from Paris. Her father held her pale blue opera cape and Anna brought out Joe's red roses, which she had been keeping fresh in the ice box.

Anna watched glumly as Betsy revolved.

"What's the matter, Anna? Don't I look all right?"

"Of course, lovey. You look even punier than the McCloskey girl did. But when Margaret graduates, I'm going to marry Charlie."

"Anna! You wouldn't!" cried all the Rays together.

Betsy put on her long white gloves. She was wearing white slippers, also. They didn't go into a party bag tonight, for Betsy, Tacy, and Tib were riding to the Opera House in a hack! Mr. Thumbler called first for Tacy and Tib, and both of them were sitting inside, wearing picture hats and opera capes and carrying flowers, when the vehicle stopped at the Ray residence.

"We're late," said Tib. "But it doesn't matter. Things can't begin without us because you two are both on the program. I have very important friends."

"I wish they would begin without us. I wish they'd *finish* without us," said Tacy through chattering teeth.

"Stop and think!" Betsy said. "We're graduating! Remember, Tacy, how you cried and went home on your first day of school? If I hadn't grabbed you and pulled you back, you might not be graduating now."

"I wish I wasn't," chattered Tacy.

"And if I hadn't come back from Milwaukee, I wouldn't be with you. I'm certainly glad I came," said Tib.

The hack rolled down the hill to Second Street and

around to the back door of the Opera House. The girls were greeted by a burst of fragrance . . . from bouquets and the blossoming boughs with which the stage was decorated.

As they took off their hats and opera capes, Betsy kept muttering, "The heroines of Shakespeare were essentially human. . . ." She wasn't so nervous as Tacy but she didn't feel exactly calm.

The Class of 1910 was brought to order, seated in ascending rows on the stage. Betsy and Tacy, because of being on the program, sat in the front row, and Miss Bangeter placed Tib there, too, right next to Betsy and Tacy. She said it was because Tib was so small.

Tib looked angelic in a white chiffon dress she had made with her own hands. It looked different from the other girls' dresses; Tib's clothes always did. Tacy's dress was organdy, very white and crisp, below her crown of auburn braids, her fear-struck eyes.

Down in the pit the high school orchestra started to play, "Morning, Noon and Night in Vienna." The music made Betsy's heart shake.

"This is a very important occasion. It's momentous," she kept thinking. But she couldn't seem to realize it, and slowly the curtain rose.

The graduates searched for their families seated in the auditorium. Betsy found her father, a pansy in his buttonhole, looking too cheerful; her mother, in a new hat with roses, looking stern; Julia, in earrings, looking fascinating and foreign; and Margaret a picture of dignity. Anna didn't look glum any more. She was wearing her best hat with a bird on it.

Betsy saw the Kelly family, too, and Mr. Kerr; the Muller family; Joe's uncle and aunt.

She rose with the chorus and began to sing:

> *"Hark! Hark! the lark,*
> *At heaven's gate sings*
> *And Phoebus 'gins arise. . . ."*

The joyful music filled the auditorium . . . and her breast.

But her nervousness increased as the program ran on. While Hazel, who preceded her, delivered her oration with the poise of a star debater, Betsy kept saying under her breath, "The heroines of Shakespeare were essentially human. . . ." She couldn't remember what came after that. She hadn't the faintest idea.

When her turn came, she stepped to the front as if in a dream. The lights swam and the faces beyond the footlights blurred.

"The heroines of Shakespeare," she began, "were essentially human. . . ."

And when she had said that much she remembered it all. It came pouring out almost too rapidly. She drew a long breath, bowed quickly, and sat down.

She wished she could give some of her glad relief to Tacy, who now took the center of the stage. Tacy looked desperate. She couldn't retreat. She had to go on, so she did.

And, of course, she sang beautifully.

> *"Sylvia, take the lilly, daffodil,*
>   *Sylvia, take whate'er the garden grows. . . ."*

At the end an usher came hurrying down the aisle. He handed her a corsage of tiny white roses tied with a big bow and dripping with ribbons. She had already received flowers from her father. She went back to her seat, smiling, and Betsy and Tib leaned over.

"Mr. Kerr?" they asked.

Tacy blushed happily and nodded.

Oration followed oration. "For Pearls We Dive," "The Farmer of the Twentieth Century," "Factory Life for Women." Joe came last with "The Bread Basket of the World."

"As Whitman says, 'The earth never tires.'" That was his beginning, and he told vividly of wheat rolling in a golden torrent from threshing machines, of mill wheels turning, of the middle west feeding the world. He spoke clearly and he didn't forget. But Betsy thought he was as near to being nervous as she had ever seen him. He went at a brisk pace back to his seat.

The President of the school board spoke. His topic was, "After Commencement Day, What?"

"An era in your life is ended," he said, and Betsy, Tacy, and Tib regarded each other with bright mischievous eyes. They would have wiped away mock tears if they hadn't been sitting in the very front row. They all felt silly, they were so relieved to have the oration and the solo over.

But the truth of his statement dawned on Betsy presently.

He took his place behind a table piled high with parchment cylinders tied with white ribbons. He called the names of the graduates in turn, and each one crossed the stage to a burst of applause.

"Irma Biscay." She was dewy-eyed and radiant.

"Dennis Farisy." That was Dennie looking cherubic.

"Dave Hunt." He looked sober as a judge.

"Tacy Kelly." "Alice Morrison." "Tib Muller." "Betsy Ray."

For four years they had been in high school together. Some of them had been together since kindergarten. Now they were being blown in all directions, like the silk from an opened milkweed pod.

What would happen to Winona, returning now to her seat looking chastened, to Hazel, accepting her diploma with a frank smile of pleasure and pride? The President of the school board reached the W's and Joe. Then the curtain went down. It was over.

595

The girls didn't walk home together. Tacy went with Mr. Kerr. Tib went with Ralph, and Betsy went with Joe. They strolled slowly through a warm night full of fireflies, smelling of the honeysuckle in bloom over Deep Valley porches.

Joe was leaving the next day for North Dakota. He was going to work again on the Wells *Courier News*.

"Can I see you tomorrow?" he asked.

"Of course."

"What shall we do? Go riding?"

"I'll tell you," said Betsy. "I'll take you up on the Hill. Why, you haven't even seen the Secret Lane."

"Tomorrow then," said Joe, "I see the Secret Lane." And he left her on the porch of the Ray house.

Joe Willard had lived in Deep Valley for four years, but he had never been up on the Big Hill. He didn't even know which hill the Big Hill was.

"Lots of them are big," he said. "Agency Hill. Pigeon Hill. Why isn't one of them the Big Hill?"

"Agency Hill! Pigeon Hill!" Betsy repeated scornfully. "Better not let Tacy hear you talking like that. *This* is the Big Hill!"

They had reached the little yellow cottage where Betsy had lived until she was fourteen years old. Across the street stood Tacy's house. Beyond that on Hill Street there weren't any houses. There was a bench where they sometimes took their supper plates. There were the hills, billowy and green, running one into another so that you couldn't quite tell where one ended and another began.

Waving at the Kellys, they climbed the steep road which rose behind Betsy's old house. Betsy showed him the thornapple tree she and Tacy used to play under. She pointed out the place where wild roses used to grow, and roses were in bloom there that moment! Flat, pink, wild roses, with yellow centers, very fragrant. Betsy picked some and put them in her hair.

At the top she showed him the Eckstrom house. There was a ravine behind it.

"We thought the sun came up out of that ravine," she said.

"Who lives in these other houses?" asked Joe, looking around at the pretty modern cottages now perched on the brow of the hill overlooking Deep Valley.

"We don't know. We ignore those houses. They weren't here when we were little," said Betsy, leading him on.

"This is the Secret Lane," she said, and they went down a path bordered with beech trees, which cast such heavy shadows that the grass was sparse beneath them. No flowers grew there but the chilly waxy Ghost Flowers.

"Our club used to meet here," Betsy told him. "It was the T.C.K.C. Club. You never could guess what that stands for."

Joe wasn't listening too attentively. He looked harder than he listened . . . looked at Betsy. Now he said, "I love the way the color rushes up in your face when you talk."

They came out on the crest of the hill overlooking Little Syria and the slough and Page Park and the river. They sat down in the grass, and Joe picked a strand and started to chew it. Betsy took off the big straw hat covered with poppies and put her arms around her knees.

They looked down the grassy slope, full of yellow bells and daisies, over the valley at the changing shadows cast by the drifting glistening clouds.

Joe began to recite a poem they had learned in junior English.

> "And what is so rare as a day in June?
> Then, if ever, come perfect days;
> Then Heaven tries earth if it be in tune,
> And over it softly her warm ear lays."

Betsy took it up:

> "Whether we look, or whether we listen,
> We hear life murmur, or see it glisten. . . ."

She broke off. "I'm happy!" she announced.

"So am I," said Joe.

There was a pause.

"That was a pretty serious talk last night, that 'After Commencement Day, What?'" Betsy said.

"Did you think so?" Joe asked.

"Yes. The older I get the more mixed up life seems. When you're little, it's all so plain. It's all laid out like a game ready to play. You think you know exactly how it's going to go. But things happen. . . ."

"For instance?"

"Well, there's Carney. She went with Larry the first two years in high school. Now he's gone to California and she can't fall in love with anyone else until she sees him again. And how is she going to manage to do that?"

"Well, she isn't through Vassar yet," said Joe.

"And there's Cab. He thought as much as any of us that he would go through high school, but he didn't, and he never will now. He won't be an engineer at all."

"He will be if he wants to enough," Joe replied.

"And there's Tony! On the stage! I always thought Tib was the one who would go on the stage."

"Maybe she will."

"And Tacy and I were going to go around the world. We were going to go to the top of the Himalayas, and up the Amazon. We were going to live in

Paris and have French maids. We were going to do all sorts of things, and now that Mr. Kerr has appeared! He says he's going to marry Tacy, and you know how he made Papa stock knitwear!"

Joe laughed. "I don't think he's selling Tacy a bill of goods. I think Tacy likes him."

"Yes," Betsy said. "I'm afraid she does."

"What about you?" Joe asked, looking up at her as he lay in the grass.

"Well, I was always sure I was going to be an author. I'm sure of it still. But I ought to begin selling my stories. I've been sending them out for almost a year now, and I don't even get a letter back. Just a printed slip that says they thank me for thinking of them. Do you write stories and send them out?"

"I write them, but I haven't started sending them out. I'm afraid they aren't good enough."

"I'm sure they are," Betsy cried. "I can't imagine you writing anything which wasn't perfectly wonderful."

Joe looked at her. "I think it's perfectly wonderful that you think so," he said slowly. "I never had anybody to have confidence in me until I met you."

"You never needed anybody. You had confidence in yourself."

"But it's a wonderful feeling, Betsy, having you like me."

"I liked you the first time I saw you in Butternut Center," said Betsy quickly, and then she stopped, color rushing up into her face.

"There it goes," said Joe.

"I can't help it. I shouldn't have said that."

"Why not?"

"It sounds . . . bold," said Betsy, at which Joe laughed and sat up abruptly. He kept on looking at her.

"You're coming to the U, aren't you, Betsy?" he asked.

"Yes, I am. A writer needs a lot of education. Besides, I want to learn a way to earn my living. You can't start living on your stories when your stories don't sell."

"I'm glad you're going to be there," Joe said. "Because I am. I'm going to be working at the *Tribune*, you know. I'd like to finish at Harvard, if I can."

"Harvard!" Betsy breathed in admiration.

"But first of all," said Joe, "I'm going to go through the U."

Then he kissed her. Betsy didn't believe in letting boys kiss you. She thought it was silly to be letting first this boy and then that one kiss you, when it didn't mean a thing. But it was wonderful when Joe Willard kissed her. And it did mean a thing.

"Remember what that fellow said last night?"

asked Joe. "'After Commencement Day, What?'"

"Of course," said Betsy. "That's what we've been talking about."

"I've got the answer," Joe said. "After Commencement Day, Betsy." He smiled and looked enormously pleased with himself. "How does that sound?"

Betsy didn't answer.

"It sounds just right to me," Joe said. "It has the right ring. Sort of a permanent ring."

Betsy smiled, and her fingers lay in his, but she spoke firmly.

"Never mind how it sounds," she said. "You've just graduated from high school. You have college ahead of you. You can't go talking about permanent rings."

Joe's expression changed to gravity.

"I know why you say that," he said. "You understand, I think, that I've always had a Plan for my life. In order to carry it out, I had to rule out girls, and I didn't mind. Even last fall, although I liked you a lot, I wouldn't let you come into my Plan.

"But I've been doing a lot of thinking, Betsy. That Plan has been twisted about to let you in. You're in it, now, that's all. I wouldn't like it without you. I wouldn't give a darn for my old Plan if you couldn't be in it."

They looked into each other's eyes and Betsy felt tears in her own.

Joe kissed her again. He took the wild rose, drooping now from the heat, out of her hair, and put it in his wallet and put the wallet in his pocket.

Betsy jumped up. She shook out the skirts of the plaid gingham dress that she had worn because it was Joe's favorite. She picked up the brown straw hat covered with red poppies.

"We must be going," she said. "Your train leaves this afternoon. Remember?"

"I hope you're going to write me lots of letters," said Joe. "The kind you wrote last year, sealed with green sealing wax and smelling sweet."

"Of course I will."

Hand in hand they went back through the Secret Lane, to the steep road that led down to Hill Street.

But there, at the top of the hill, Joe stopped. They paused and looked out over the town—the red turret of the high school, the leafy streets, the rooftops, the river, the shining rails that would take him away.

"After Commencement Day, the World!" Joe said. "With Betsy."

Maud Hart Lovelace and Her World

(Adapted from *The Betsy-Tacy Companion: A Biography of Maud Hart Lovelace* by Sharla Scannell Whalen)

Maud Palmer Hart circa 1906

MAUD HART LOVELACE was born on April 25, 1892, in Mankato, Minnesota. Shortly after Maud's high school graduation in 1910, the Hart family left Mankato and settled in Minneapolis, where Maud attended the University of Minnesota. In 1917 she married Delos W. Lovelace, a newspaper reporter who later became a popular writer of short stories. The Lovelaces' daughter, Merian, was born in 1931.

Maud would tell her daughter bedtime stories about her childhood in Minnesota, and it was these stories that gave her the idea of writing the Betsy-Tacy books. She did not intend to write an entire series when *Betsy-Tacy*, the first book, was published in 1940, but readers asked for more stories. So Maud took Betsy through high school and beyond college to the "great world" and marriage.

The final book in the series, *Betsy's Wedding*, was published in 1955.

The Betsy-Tacy books are based very closely upon Maud's own life. "I could make it all up, but in these Betsy-Tacy stories, I love to work from real incidents," Maud wrote. This is especially true of the four high school books. We know a lot about her life during this period because Maud kept diaries (one for each high school year, just like Betsy) as well as a scrapbook during high school. As she wrote to a cousin in 1964: "In writing the high school books my diaries were extremely helpful. The family life, customs, jokes, traditions are all true and the general pattern of the years is also accurate."

Almost every character in the high school books, even the most minor, can be matched to an actual person living in Mankato in the early years of the twentieth century. (See page 317 for a list of characters and their real-life counterparts.) But there are exceptions. As Maud wrote: "A small and amusing complication is that while some of the characters are absolutely based on one person—for example Tacy, Tib, Cab, Carney—others were merely suggested by some person and some characters are combinations of two real persons." For example, the character Winona Root is based on two people. In *Betsy and Tacy Go Downtown* and *Winona's Pony Cart,* Maud's childhood friend Beulah Hunt was the model for Winona. The Winona Root we encounter in the high school books, however, was based on Maud's high school friend Mary Eleanor Johnson, known as "El."

Another exception is the character Joe Willard, who is based on Maud's husband, Delos Wheeler Lovelace. In real life, Delos did not attend Mankato High School with Maud. He was two years Maud's junior, and the two didn't meet until after high school. But as Maud said, "Delos came into my life much later than Joe Willard came into Betsy's, and yet he is Joe Willard to the life." This is because Maud asked her husband to give her a description of his boyhood. She then gave his history to Joe.

Maud eventually donated her high school scrapbook and many photographs to the Blue Earth County Historical Society in Mankato, where they still reside today. But she destroyed her diaries sometime after she had finished writing the Betsy-Tacy books, in the late 1950s. We can't be sure why, but we do know that, as Maud confessed once in an interview, they "were full of boys, boys, boys." She may not have felt comfortable about bequeathing them to posterity!

Maud Hart Lovelace died on March 11, 1980. But her legacy lives on in the beloved series she created and in her legions of fans, many of whom are members of the Betsy-Tacy Society and the Maud Hart Lovelace Society. For more information, write to:

The Betsy-Tacy Society
P.O. Box 94
Mankato, MN 56002-0094
www.betsy-tacysociety.org

The Maud Hart Lovelace Society
277 Hamline Avenue South
St. Paul, MN 55105
www.maudhartlovelacesociety.com

*Murmuring Lake Inn, where the Rays vacation, is based
on Point Pleasant Inn at Madison Lake, Minnesota.
There is an inn called Point Pleasant on the same site
today, although it's not the same one.*

*Maud's
older sister,
Kathleen, at
the lake.*

About *Betsy Was a Junior*

THE PERIOD from 1908 TO 1909, which corresponds to the account of Betsy Ray's junior year in *Betsy Was a Junior*, was an eventful one in Maud's life. As is the case with all of the Betsy-Tacy books, much that happened to Maud made its way into the story—although at least one major event did not.

Betsy Was a Junior opens at the end of an idyllic summer spent by the Rays at Murmuring Lake. But the summer of 1908 was not quite as idyllic for Maud or her friends. A typhoid epidemic caused by contaminated water struck Mankato in June. The situation was so serious that the head of the public works board was forced to resign and the city engineer was removed from office, accused of dereliction of duty.

Maud's family, vacationing at Madison Lake, was far enough away from Mankato to be relatively safe. But several of Maud's friends and their families were affected: Mildred Oleson (Irma) and her parents, Bick's (Tacy's) father, and Marney's (Carney's) father were struck with the fever. Fortunately, they all survived. But Paul Ford (Dennie) lost his father, and Tom Fox (Tom Slade) lost his mother—a blow to the Harts, who had always been close to the Fox family.

Although the typhoid epidemic is not mentioned in the story, it may have found fictional form in the death of Cab's father and Betsy's new-found maturity at the end of the book.

Like Betsy, it appears that Maud and her crowd had lots of fun during their junior year—perhaps as a reaction to the sobering events of the summer. A happy occurrence at the beginning of the book is Tib's return to Deep Valley. Although it didn't happen in quite the same dramatic fashion, Midge Gerlach, one of Maud's closest friends, did return to Mankato after spending several years in Milwaukee. Midge instantly became one of the Crowd and was often right in the thick of things, as can be seen in many Crowd photographs of that time.

Another important factor in Crowd fun was the Willard family auto. As his fictional counterpart, Mr. Sibley, said he would do in *Heaven to Betsy*, Marney's father, W. D. Willard, purchased an auto at around this time. In an unpublished memoir, he described it as follows: "We bought our first automobile—a two-cylinder Buick, two seater, engine under the floor, right side steering, shift outside, acetylene lamps (which were very uncertain)." It cost Mr. Willard a grand total of $1,178.95.

This is the year that Maud's sister Kathleen left Mankato to attend the University of Minnesota—or

Some of the Crowd in the Willard (Sibley) family's second auto. Midge (Tib) is at the wheel with El (Winona II) at her side. Bick (Tacy) is in the backseat, at the far left.

The Oktw Deltas, from left: Midge (Tib); Mildred (Irma); Bick (Tacy); Maud (Betsy); El (Winona II); Marney (Carney); Ruth (Alice); and Tess (Katie).

the "U," as it is still called by state residents today. Like Julia, she was swept up in the sorority rush—she pledged Gamma Phi Beta in real life, not the fictional Epsilon Iota.

As in the book, sororities also became part of Maud's life. Dazzled by Kathleen's description of sororities, Maud and some of the rest of the Crowd formed Oktw Delta. (Maud used this spelling, but the word appears as "Okto" in the book.) The eight girls who joined were the same as their counterparts in the book. Maud's scrapbook contained many Oktw Delta souvenirs such as placecards from a progressive dinner and a program from a party given by eight of the boys for the sorority.

We can guess that the real-life Oktw Delta did not create such bad feeling in the high school as the fictional one did. Unlike Betsy, Maud *was* named head of the entertainment committee for the Junior-Senior banquet, and the Oktw Delta organization was not disbanded at the end of Maud's junior year. A December 1910 article in the *Mankato Free Press* reads: "The Oktw Delta club gave its annual progressive dinner last evening. . . . On Monday evening, the club gave its annual Christmas tree." Evidently, the club survived for at least another two years.

A new member of the Crowd and Betsy's love interest in the book is the silent Dave Hunt. During her

The sheet music for the "Morning Cy Barn Dance."

This cartoon of Maud was pasted in her high school scrapbook. The labels point to "naturally curly hair," "red dress," and "red socks," and the name on the dance card is "Bob."

junior year, Maud dated a boy named Robert (Bob) W. Hughes, who appears to have been the inspiration for Dave. We don't know for sure if he, too, was the strong, silent type, but it seems quite likely.

Maud also received a curling iron as a joke present at a class assembly. Pasted in her high school scrapbook is a card signed "Class 09," which reads: "Miss Maude Rosemond Palmer Hart Jones Gifford Hodson Wells Hoerr Morehart Ford Hughes Weed & etc.

Collection of Minnesota Valley Regional Library

Maud appears just as pleased about her Christmas furs as Betsy is in the story.

1910 Annual

Betsy's silent beau, Dave Hunt, was based on Bob Hughes.

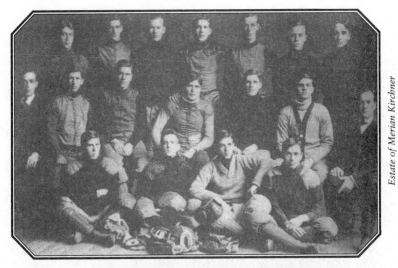

*Crowd members on the 1908 Mankato
High School Football Team pictured here include:
Bob Hughes (Dave Hunt) in the back row,
second from left; Paul Ford (Dennie) in the middle
row, second from right; and Jab Lloyd (Cab)
in the front row, third from left.*

We would like to see you curl that new crop of whiskers now flourishing on your lily-white intellectual brow." Maud appears to have been even more popular with boys than Betsy!

At the end of the book, Betsy reflects on the past year of silliness and resolves to be more grown-up. We don't know if Maud made a similar resolution, but like Betsy, Maud certainly had a rollicking junior year.

About Betsy and Joe

MAUD'S SENIOR YEAR in high school, fictionalized in *Betsy and Joe*, took place from September 1909 to June 1910. It was a time of great change for Maud, just as it is for her alter ego, Betsy, and it began with two of her best friends leaving Mankato.

At the beginning of the book, we learn that Betsy's sister Julia has departed Deep Valley for "the Great World" at last, to spend the summer traveling in Europe before settling down in Berlin to study opera. Readers will not be surprised to learn that Maud's older sister, Kathleen, also took part in a European tour. The June 30, 1909, issue of the *Mankato Free Press* reported: "Miss Kathleen Hart, daughter of Mr. and Mrs. T. W. Hart of this city, left this morning for Boston, Mass., from which city she will sail on Saturday for Europe. She will join a party going to Europe under the guidance of Rev. Willisford of this city. Miss Hart will make a three months' tour of that country [sic] and then go to Berlin, Germany, where she will receive instructions in vocal music for a year."

Reading and re-reading Kathleen's letters was a big part of the Harts' home life during this period, just as

Maud is reading aloud from one of Kathleen's letters while her parents, little sister, Helen, and grandmother listen.

it was for the Rays. And almost every time Betsy quotes passages from Julia's letters in the story, Maud is really quoting from Kathleen's. Kathleen was eventually offered a position at the Hamburg Opera, but, like Julia, she returned to America, having decided to pursue her career at home.

Maud's good friend Marion Willard (Carney) also left Mankato in 1909. But unlike Carney, Marion first spent a year at Carleton College in Northfield, Minnesota, before being admitted to Vassar the following year as a freshman. It was probably simpler for fictional purposes to send Carney to Vassar in the fall of 1909, without the one-year detour to Carleton. Readers can follow Carney's story in *Carney's House Party*, one of the three Deep Valley books, which is set during the summer between her sophomore and junior years at Vassar and tells what happens when Larry Humphreys finally comes back into her life.

In 1909, the Harts pasted a series of photos into a book as a Christmas gift for homesick Kathleen in Berlin. This photo shows Stella Hart weeping as the mailman walks away. The inscription reads, "No mail from Kathleen."

And as in the Betsy-Tacy books, Maud based much of the story on real-life events, down to the smallest detail. While writing the book, Maud wrote to Marion: "I'll send you a copy of *Betsy and Joe* as soon as I can get my hands on one, or a set of galleys. For in that book Carney goes off to college, Vassar, in the clothes you described for me. Since I used them for fall of 1909 . . . you'll have to tell me about some more clothes."

Blue Earth County Historical Society

Maud's friend Marion Willard (Carney) is shown here in her graduation photo.

Estate of Merian Kirchner

Maud is wearing the necklace of Venetian beads from Kathleen in her graduation photo.

❧ 17 ❧

This cartoon of Maud pasted in her high school scrapbook is labeled, "Miss M. R. P. Hart in her senior year, her hair as curly as ever, still the object of devotion of all the H.S. boys."

In spite of these losses, Maud still managed to have a fun senior year. She and Midge Gerlach (Tib) were cast for a part in a show called *Up and Down Broadway*. Maud had a small part, but Midge did a dance number. The newspaper review of the show said Midge was "a bewitching little personage in her part, and her dancing brought forth a round of applause, which was well deserved." However, neither Bick Kenney (Tacy) nor Mike Parker (Tony) took part in the show as their fictional counterparts did. Mike Parker left high school well before the end of the year, but he didn't go off to Broadway like Tony does. We don't know if Mike rivaled someone for Maud's affections during her senior year, though we do know it couldn't have been Delos (Joe), because they had not yet met.

This is the year that Betsy finally beats Joe and wins the essay contest. In reality, Maud's rivals in the essay contests, far from being Delos or any other boy, seem to have been other girls. Maud lost to fellow Crowd member Ruth Williams (Alice Morrison) in her junior year, and to a girl named Alice Alworth in her senior year. We don't know if Maud competed in her freshman or sophomore years because, contrary to the description of the yearly contest in the books, contestants were not selected from each high school class—they tended to be mostly seniors.

Maud graduated from high school on June 3, 1910. Just like Betsy, Maud gave an oration entitled "The Heroines of Shakespeare." Bick Kenney (Tacy) sang a solo. The president of the school board spoke. And the chapter of Maud's school days in Mankato came to a close, leaving her looking forward to "the Great World."

Fictional Characters and Their Real-Life Counterparts

Betsy Ray	Maud Palmer Hart
Julia Ray	Kathleen Albertine Hart
Margaret Ray	Helen Hart
Bob Ray	Thomas Walden Hart
Jule Ray	Stella Palmer Hart
Tacy Kelly	Frances "Bick" Vivian Kenney
Tib Muller	Marjorie "Midge" Gerlach
Bonnie Andrews	Constance "Connie" Davis
Irma Biscay	Florence Mildred Oleson
Phil Brandish	Carl George Hoerr
Mamie Dodd	Mamie Skuse
Cab Edwards	Jabez "Jab" Alvin Lloyd
Dennie Farisy	Paul Gerald Ford
E. Lloyd Harrington	James H. Baker Jr.
Herbert Humphreys	Helmus Weddel Andrews
Larry Humphreys	Robert Burke Andrews
Dave Hunt	Robert William Hughes
Katie Kelly	Theresa "Tess" Catherine Kenney
Harry Kerr	Charles Eugene Kirch
Al Larson	Henry Orlando Lee
Tony Markham	Clarence "Mike" Lindon Parker

Stan Moore	Herman Hayward
Alice Morrison	Ruth Fallie Williams
Pin	Charles Ernest "Pin" Jones
Winona Root I	Beulah Ariel Hunt
Winona Root II	Mary Eleanor Johnson
Carney Sibley	Marion "Marney" Willard
Grandma Slade	Mary Warren Pitcher
Tom Slade	Thomas Warren Fox
Hazel Smith	Harriet Ahlers
Squirrelly	Earl Elmer King
(Aunt) Ruth Willard	Josephine Wheeler Lovelace
Joe Willard	Delos Wheeler Lovelace

THE COMPLETE BETSY-TACY SERIES

THE BETSY-TACY TREASURY
The First Four Betsy-Tacy Books
ISBN 978-0-06-209587-9 (paperback)

THE BETSY-TACY HIGH SCHOOL YEARS AND BEYOND

HEAVEN TO BETSY AND BETSY IN SPITE OF HERSELF
Foreword by Laura Lippman
ISBN 978-0-06-179469-8 (paperback)

BETSY WAS A JUNIOR AND BETSY AND JOE
Foreword by Meg Cabot
ISBN 978-0-06-179472-8 (paperback)

BETSY AND THE GREAT WORLD AND BETSY'S WEDDING
Foreword by Anna Quindlen
ISBN 978-0-06-179513-8 (paperback)

THE DEEP VALLEY BOOKS

EMILY OF DEEP VALLEY
Foreword by Mitali Perkins
ISBN 978-0-06-200330-0 (paperback)

CARNEY'S HOUSE PARTY AND WINONA'S PONY CART
Foreword by Melissa Wiley
ISBN 978-0-06-200329-4 (paperback)